Come Join Our Disease

Sam Byers's writing has appeared in *Granta*, the *New York Times*, ~~Ti...~~ , *Idiopathy*, was sho...ed for the Costa First Novel Prize, longlisted for the Desmond Elliott Prize and the winner of a Betty Trask Award. His second novel, *Perfidious Albion*, was longlisted for the RSL Ondaatje Prize and the Orwell Prize for Political Fiction and shortlisted for the Encore Prize.

Further praise for *Come Join Our Disease*:

'A deeply admirable achievement, a novel that sets out to do something incredibly risky and sees it through, diving deep into the foetid swamp and breaking through to the other side . . . *Come Join Our Disease* is so bold and interest⌐ ⌐ can imagine it becoming a cult classic, but eve⌐ ⌐isses it to the realms of something tr⌐ ⌐tery of tone and attentiveness t⌐ ⌐him as one of the most accom⌐ ⌐. The world he creates is so full⌐ ⌐ you read afterwards feels a bit half-hear⌐ ⌐wenty pages from the end a meditation on human ⌐ ⌐tegration – and the love that can arise from sharing in one another's decay – moved me to tears. It felt piercingly wise and, dare I say it, beautiful.' *Sunday Times*

'The faddish desires and moral certainties of modern life are dealt a hefty blow in this bold, unflinching novel . . . [a] disturbingly exceptional novel.' *Observer*

'A blistering critique of twenty-first century life. By turns unnerving, disgusting and enthralling, the novel exposes the limits of radicalism and the alienation inevitable in a society where even altruism has become a commodity.' *Financial Times*

'A clever novel of ideas sustained by some memorably gross-out bits as well as sharp class politics, it resembles a feminist *Lord of the Flies* for the wellness era.' *Metro*

'Politically astute, endlessly quotable and highly visual . . . [Sam Byers] can write, is one smart cookie, and *Come Join Our Disease* is quite outstanding.' *Irish Times*

'A poignant story of friendship and isolation, of human connections made and lost.' *Guardian*

Further praise for *Perfidious Albion*:

'A mordant, needle-sharp satire.' Jonathan Coe

'The Martin Amis's *Money* of our times.' David Baddiel

---

by the same author

Idiopathy
Perfidious Albion

COME
JOIN OUR
DISEASE

SAM

BYERS

faber

First published in 2021
by Faber & Faber Limited
Bloomsbury House
74–77 Great Russell Street
London WC1B 3DA

This paperback edition first published in 2022

Typeset by Paul Baillie-Lane
Printed and bound in the UK by CPI Group (UK) Ltd, Croydon CR0 4YY

A CIP record for this book
is available from the British Library

ISBN 978-0-571-36009-3

Supported using public funding by
**ARTS COUNCIL
ENGLAND**

MIX
Paper from
responsible sources
FSC® C171272

2 4 6 8 10 9 7 5 3 1

'So we picked you up . . . and set you down before food, and said: Eat, build up your strength so that you can exhaust it again obeying us.'

J. M. Coetzee, *Life and Times of Michael K*

ONE

On the worst nights, it felt as if everything encroached at once. The rain found every gap and inlet, soaking into the earth and rising back up through the strata of flattened cardboard on which we slept. The cold breached all our bundled layers – our damp and matted jumpers, our cast-off coats and scavenged sleeping bags. Often, I awoke to the sound of fights outside, clumsy fingers rooting for hidden valuables, a man's boozy breath in my ear. I slept in my clothes and boots, tucked my scant cash in my sock. People who knew me left me alone. Others I had to hurt a couple of times before they learned.

Dawn was always a relief. The night was over, the trials of the day not yet begun. Whatever had passed in the darkness was forgiven. For a few seconds, as the sun offered its first tentative touch and the sky, on a clear day, lost its blackness and became first bruised and then bloody, those of us that lived on the encampment – that stubborn mess of tents and lean-tos, sheets of tarpaulin and stolen boards propped against poles and trees – were briefly allowed to feel all the things denied to us in the night and through much of the day: faint hope, tentative warmth, a moment of ease.

So to all the other insults and injustices of that day, the violence of the officials' arrival and the destruction of their passing, I must add this: that they caught us, whether deliberately or not, at our freest.

I heard them before I saw them: a low, hive-like hum down the road. I guessed the time at soon after six. It was early March. The morning still carried the residual chill of that year's long winter,

3

but you could feel the promise of spring in the air. When I pushed aside the draped tarpaulin under which I slept and rose stiffly to my feet, I saw that others had already gathered and were staring off down the road, towards the deepening drone of whatever was approaching. For a strange, still moment, it seemed like the most natural and ordinary meeting of people: a small group of neighbours, hands on hips, speculating as to what was afoot. But then the convoy rounded the bend, and in an instant we were alone and scrambling, neighbours no more.

The more military-looking police were at the front: two vans with grilles on the windows bearing black-clad, visored officers. Behind them were ambulances, uniformed cops, and buses for whoever the task force managed to round up. Lastly came the vehicles of non-specific destruction: the JCBs and bulldozers, the skip trucks, an unmarked van filled with contracted workmen in hard hats and hi-vis overalls.

We scattered. People ran for the pieced-together structures that had been their homes and began throwing things into bags, tossing aside tarpaulins and ground sheets, uncovering their secret caches of money, food, drugs. There were children in some of the tents, and they began to scream, which set off the panicked barking of the encampment's dogs. As people shouted to each other, language became an irrelevance. Wherever you were from, a global shorthand was at work: *police, trucks, run*.

I managed my fear by cataloguing my minor advantages. I was fast, I was alone, I had attached significance to only a few small possessions. Humble comforts were a trap. You fought for something that kept you warm, but then it came to mean something to you, evolved into some meagre symbol of achievement, and you clung to it, even as it slowed you down. Around me, as I began to run, too many people were making this mistake – hamstrung by what they carried, stumbling as they dropped unwieldy items under their feet.

By this point I'd gathered my rucksack and the little bundle of valuables at the bottom of my sleeping bag and was moving quickly. The encampment had been pieced together on a patch of waste ground, recently cleared to make way for development. A raised train track and arched bridge provided shelter on one side. Beyond that was a high fence that marked the border with a largely disused industrial estate. This was the direction in which most people were heading. Once over the fence, the empty warehouses and equipment stores, the huddled buildings and maze of units that formed the estate, would offer ample opportunity to scatter and, like droplets of spilled water absorbed into the earth, vanish back into the city.

For a moment, the shouting, the chaos, seemed to diminish. The fence was in our sights. Briefly, I glanced back at the broken-down boxes on which we'd slept, the scattered cans and pots from which we'd eaten. It was, I thought, a perpetual cycle. Detritus, repurposed, became possessions. Now our abandoned belongings were trash once more.

Beyond what remained of the encampment, the convoy was fanning out. One of the police vans swung rightward, heading towards the fence, clearly intending to cut us off. People began to shout again. As those in the middle of the crowd saw the approaching van, they changed their minds about the fence and peeled off, making instead for the other side of the encampment. I tried to tell them: *If we all stay together, they'll never be able to stop us.* But panic had set in. We were disparate, confused, vulnerable.

Just as the first few people reached the fence and began to climb, the police vans stopped and threw open their back doors, releasing a trio of barking Alsatians. There is something primal, something wild, about the human response to an attacking dog. It gets in your blood, is carried to every major organ. As the animals fired themselves into the crowd, our trembling herd-selves took over. We were gazelles on a plain, outrunning death. Those with children, by instinct, swept them up, pressed them to their chests, wrapped their hands around their heads. Ahead of me, someone fell. People leapt over the tangle of limbs, not even stopping to see who it was, perhaps fearful that recognition would give rise to pity, pity in turn to hesitation.

By this time I was being pushed from behind, carried along by the panicked swell. Ahead, I could see policemen pulling people from the fence. Only a few had made it over. I turned, briefly stalled, then made for open ground. Behind me, I heard the urgent percussion of paws. Within a few steps, the dog was on me, clamping its teeth around my ankle, bringing me down, then moving its jaws up to the collar of my coat. I rolled onto my back. Looking down, under my chin, I could see the eyes of the dog looking back at me, surprisingly calm. The dog growled and tightened its hold, its nose now pressed against my throat, its rancid breath hot and damp against my jugular.

Around me, the screams and shouts, the engine noise, the boot-steps and bellowed orders to stand still seemed to fade, until I could hear, instead, my own pulsing blood in my ears, the rhythmic breath of the dog and the beat of its heart against mine. I lay back, softening. The dog placed a paw on my chest, warning me not to struggle. I thought of all the blood in all the veins of all the animals, human and otherwise, on that rough patch of ground, all of us breathing together, in stasis and tension, and felt myself, almost relievedly, give in.

I reached up and laid my hand on the back of the dog's neck. It sharpened its growl, warning me. I patted it gently and it calmed again.

'Alright,' I said to the dog. 'Alright.'

Out of the corner of my eye, I saw black steel-capped boots approaching. A man's voice said, *Stay there*. Because there was nowhere else I could possibly be, I obeyed.

Navigating the system, you become accustomed to the dingy impersonality of certain settings. Across the country, at any given moment – across, I assume, the world – lives are unravelling in rooms of crushing uniformity. Interview rooms. Advice rooms. Holding rooms. Rooms with nothing more than a simple desk, a single strip light, and a burnt-out worker typing notes while you lay out your case. On the wall, always, there is a generic canvas of a flower.

The particular room in which I found myself contained two men. The desk between us was less a working surface than a barrier, stretching from wall to wall and bolted at both ends, meaning I had to enter through a separate door and hallway. It was a neat statement, I thought: the clearest signifier of bureaucracy, repurposed as a blunt communication of division. The men across from me were protected; I was held at bay.

They were not the usual faces of officialdom. They seemed to have attended a recent PowerPoint presentation on the projection of sincerity. They leaned across the table, nodding at everything I said. Both of them had loosened an extra shirt button, as if an open collar was the gateway to an open mind.

'We apologise for the set-up,' said one. 'We don't get to choose the rooms.'

'If we were running the show?' said the other. 'Very different story.'

I said nothing. The tactic in these situations is always to say nothing. There are legal factors, of course, but really it's a matter of principle. I don't engage with authority because I don't tend to recognise it to begin with.

'We see this a lot,' said the first man. 'The whole quiet thing.'

The second man folded his hands on the table, cocked his head to one side and tightened his lips, a pose I imagined gradually evolving through an instructor's subtle corrections of form.

'People have had a lot of bad experiences,' he said. 'It's a barrier.'

I looked between them. It was dawning on me that they were neither policemen nor council workers. They wore no identification or badges. Their clothes were slim-fit, pastel toned, expensive. Man number one was wearing a watch that monitored his unwavering heartbeat.

'Let's maybe introduce ourselves,' said man number one. 'Break the ice a little. I'm Seth.'

'And I'm Ryan,' said man number two.

'Maybe you'd like to introduce yourself now?' said Seth.

I stared at them, saying nothing.

'OK,' said Seth. 'That's fine. Like we said. Lot of bad experiences. Lot of mistrust.'

'And also, we know who you are, anyway,' said Ryan. 'So the introduction would really just have been, as Seth said, an icebreaker.'

The statement was delivered flippantly, but was clearly intended to be unnerving. I remained unmoved. Of course they knew who I was. Their precise role might, at that stage, have been unclear, but they were still, in one way or another, representatives of the authorities. After picking us up, the police had fingerprinted us all at a makeshift processing centre located, ironically, on the same semi-abandoned industrial estate towards which so many of us had tried to flee. After fingerprinting, we'd been divided up according to a system that remained undisclosed to us. After that we'd been photographed, then divided again. Finally, a man in shirtsleeves who, without quite knowing why, I knew immediately was not a policeman, called my name and, after checking me off a list, shepherded me into a private room, where I sat for long enough to lose all sense of time, and from where I was ushered, stiff-legged, exhausted, disoriented, into an unmarked car and driven, via a deliberately circuitous route, through suburban South London to a featureless office complex on the periphery of a peripheral borough, inside which was the room I now occupied, adrift in time, shaky with hunger, more bored than frightened. The announcement I was known meant nothing. Clearly, I was here because I was known, because I had been, in some way not yet revealed to me, selected.

I decided to fix the men with a slight, knowing smile and sustain the expression regardless of what they said or asked me. People in authority find this unsettling. If you're lucky, they start babbling.

'Your name is Maya Devereaux,' said Seth. 'Do you mind if we call you Maya?'

I moved my eyes from Seth to Ryan and back again, still with that faint smile.

'You've been homeless for about a year,' Seth continued.

'Give or take,' said Ryan.

'You'd been at the encampment over a month,' said Seth. 'Which puts you there pretty soon after its inception. Before that you were most likely at whatever encampment preceded this one. You know how it goes: one borough breaks up a hotspot, a week later it magically reforms across town.'

I decided to concentrate on my breathing: keeping it even, keeping it slow. When they stepped outside and talked about my case, I wanted the word they kept circling back to in their minds to be *unfazed*. By this point in my life I didn't even really have to act. I'd sat on this side of numerous similar tables. I'd stared at an incomparable number of thickly painted walls and deeply worn carpets. I could have discoursed at length on the subject of mass-produced airbrushed canvases.

'You're English,' said Seth. 'We know that.'

'Just in case you were planning on using the whole *please, no English* routine,' said Ryan.

'You have no disabilities, no impairments, no history of mental breakdown,' said Seth.

'Or none recorded, anyway,' said Ryan.

'Right,' said Seth. 'Lot of undiagnosed stuff in situations like this. We understand that.'

'Actually,' said Ryan, 'we can help with it.'

'We can help with a lot of things,' said Seth, giving me what he clearly thought was a significant look. 'If you let us.'

They were quiet again. My breath was a count of four in, four out. I had placed one hand on the table in front of me. I began tapping my forefinger lightly against the tabletop every few seconds, like a dripping tap.

Seth smiled. 'You're a tough nut to crack, Maya,' he said.

'You know,' said Ryan, with exaggerated gentleness, 'we have facilities here.'

They let that sink in a moment, searching my face to see if anything registered. Clearly disappointed, Seth clarified.

'A canteen,' he said. 'Showers.'

'Free to use,' said Ryan.

They looked pointedly at my hand, the finger of which was still calmly tapping, as if trying to draw my attention to its condition. I didn't need to look at it. I knew its condition intimately: sharp-nailed, callused, deeply grimed.

'We've got clothes too,' said Seth. 'We already know your measurements, so . . .'

'Good to go,' said Ryan. 'Say the word and it's done.'

Tap . . . Tap . . . Tap.

Finally, they looked at each other. A question, followed by an agreement, passed calmly and silently between them. They were used to this, I saw. There were processes they could follow, stages through which they could move. A quick glance, and the tactics wordlessly changed.

'OK,' said Seth. 'We understand.'

'We're asking a lot of you,' said Ryan.

'We're asking you to trust us based on nothing,' said Seth.

'The year you've had,' said Ryan, 'trust has probably not been something you've been dispensing freely. We get that.'

'I mean, look at the situation here,' said Seth. 'You're woken at dawn, chased by dogs, arrested, fingerprinted, bundled off to some sort of . . . facility.'

'You're going to be wary,' said Ryan. 'You're going to be understandably and perfectly reasonably on guard.'

I stopped tapping, folded my hands, said nothing.

'So,' said Seth. 'How about a bit of background?'

It was beginning to dawn on me that none of the usual routines appeared to be forthcoming. No threats, no thinly veiled disgust, no ostentatious pity. Instead, Seth and Ryan had the air of men about to deploy a brochure, pitch some rare opportunity to invest. I knew the signs because I had done it myself: puked out sales patter, turned glossy literature in the direction of sceptical targets. I couldn't decide what would be more insulting: threats or promises. I felt confidently immune to both, but my patience for platitudes was finite.

'We work for Green,' said Seth.

They let that sit there a moment, accustomed, I sensed, to some sort of reaction.

'You've heard of Green, I assume?' said Ryan.

When I didn't answer, Seth continued.

'Tech solutions, communications, web content, search. Your basic highly disruptive global player.'

'Yadda yadda yadda,' said Ryan. 'You get the picture.'

'We work in a very specific department of Green,' said Seth. 'Giving.'

'Not a department you will necessarily have heard of,' said Ryan.

'Green don't tend to trumpet it, because that would be undignified,' said Seth. 'But they are very much in the business of giving.'

'And we're tasked with targeting that giving,' said Ryan. 'Because untargeted giving isn't really giving, it's just . . . seepage.'

'Hence,' said Seth, 'the opportunity programme.'

He said it with a flourish, spreading his hands palm upwards, somehow including me in whatever the phrase was intended to indicate. There was a long, expectant silence, during which I maintained my static smile and shuttled my eyes from Ryan to Seth and back again.

'People usually get excited at this point,' said Seth.

'Not, like, *crazy* excited,' said Ryan. 'But, you know, tentatively hopeful and intrigued.'

'Actually though,' said Seth, 'your reaction is very promising. Different, but promising.'

'I know what you're thinking,' said Ryan. 'You're thinking: this is just another revamped work programme. This is slog your guts out for less than minimum wage and help the government get their numbers down.'

'You're thinking,' said Seth, 'fuck that.'

'But this,' said Ryan, 'is not that. This,' he said, pausing for emphasis, 'is a *unicorn*.'

The aim, Seth and Ryan said, was to humanise homelessness. Select a candidate, offer a comprehensive second chance, then make that second chance public and build a following. Wealthy corporations giving a percentage of their money away had become the norm; broad-brush philanthropy couldn't cut through the noise. People wanted a singular arc, an outcome attached to a face, a narrative of measurable change with which they could engage. Payoff was an even split: a new life for the candidate, brand boost for the sponsors.

'And before you say anything,' said Seth, pausing proceedings while his grand announcement of my individual-in-question status still hung in the air, resonating with significance, 'we know what you're thinking.'

I still had not, at this point, said anything. I wondered if they really did know what I was thinking, if that was part of the programme.

'You're thinking: why me?' said Seth.

This was not what I was thinking, but I had to admit that the question was interesting, and so I said nothing.

'We did a lot of research into the encampment,' said Ryan.

'Ran a lot of data,' said Seth. 'Got to know you guys pretty well, I must say. You, however, really stood out.' He leaned forward across the table, hands clasped. It seemed to me that by this point he'd settled comfortably into the idea that he would simply monologue until I seemed to understand.

'The . . . I don't want to say *problem*, so I'm going to say *unique challenge*, with a project like this,' he said, 'is empathy. Specifically: individual empathy. Because everyone empathises with the homeless up to a point, right? I mean, people empathise with the *idea* of homelessness. I bet if you did a poll that just said, *Should a wealthy company like Green help the homeless?*, you'd get a pretty overwhelming response in favour of assistance. And, you know, we could do that. We could do the vague, generalised, giving-money-to-charity thing. But we wanted to think a little bigger, or in some ways, a little smaller. We wanted something, or someone, people could really get behind. Someone they could go on a journey with. We wanted the whole thing to be less abstract, more . . .'

'Personal,' said Ryan.

'Right. Personal,' said Seth. 'So we started looking around, doing our research, pulling a few profiles. And what did we find? To be honest: a whole lot of obstacles.'

'Which we totally empathise with,' said Ryan. 'I mean, we understand those obstacles and we sympathise.'

'But we had to be practical,' said Seth. 'Because what we're asking people to do here is *get behind* someone, to believe in them, to follow them on their journey, and to be totally blunt about it, there are some journeys nobody wants to go on.'

'Like, for example, the journey from drug-addicted wreck to still being a drug-addicted wreck,' said Ryan.

'Or from illegal immigrant to deported immigrant,' said Seth.

'Downer,' said Ryan. 'Right?'

'What we found was that quite a lot of the journeys we encountered were pretty much just subtly adjusted versions of that journey,' said Seth. 'Meaning they weren't really journeys at all, they were just . . . dead ends.'

'Because look at this from Green's point of view,' said Ryan. 'It's not just about the starting point, it's about the destination.'

'Right,' said Seth. 'It's both. The individual in question has to be someone the general public can empathise with and feel drawn to *right away* . . .'

'And then *grow closer to* . . .' said Ryan.

'And then ultimately end up in a really good place with,' said Seth.

'And much as we wish we could construct that journey with someone who's really . . . you know . . . on the skids . . .' said Ryan.

'The truth is that it would be difficult,' said Seth. 'And somewhat risky.'

Seth settled back in his chair again, wrapping me in the satisfied, confident gaze of a man who feels he knows precisely what he needs to know.

'And then we found you,' he said. 'And we were like: *hello*. Because you're not really like the others at the encampment, are you, Maya?'

It seemed he'd decided he was going to try to get me to speak again.

'I mean, you must have felt that, when you were there?'

He was more determined this time, more sure of himself.

'There must have been a feeling of . . . difference,' he said.

'Separateness, even,' said Ryan.

I decided to reintroduce the beatific smile. In some ways, it was genuine. They'd mistaken facts for insight. They thought that knowing me and knowing *about* me were the same thing.

'Look at your background,' said Seth. 'You're not an immigrant. You're not, as far as we can tell, a user of hard drugs. You don't have any criminal convictions. And a year ago you were . . .'

'Just like us,' said Ryan.

Seth smiled. 'Or nearly like us, anyway,' he said.

'You had the *potential* to be like us,' said Ryan.

'And where has that potential gone?' said Seth. 'Potential doesn't just vanish.'

Ryan shook his head. 'It's still there,' he said. 'Weaker, maybe. But still there.'

'After all,' said Seth, 'it's only been a year.'

'A *year*,' said Ryan. He looked me up and down, taking in my matted hair and blackened hands. 'Think what's happened in a year.'

'And then,' said Seth, 'think what could happen in *another* year.'

Ryan spread his hands palm upwards, signifying infinite possibilities. 'Good things,' he said, raising one hand higher than the other as if they were a set of scales, 'or bad things.'

'A year like the year you've just had,' said Seth. 'Or a different year. A *better* year.'

'That's kind of where we come in,' said Ryan. 'Because our research suggests very strongly that a personal narrative that becomes public or shared is a narrative that is far more likely to remain on course.'

'It helps the individual in question shape their lives,' said Seth. 'It gives them a sense of meaning and purpose. And meanwhile it helps the people *around* that person *understand* their life, and extract wider meaning from it.'

'So you can see,' said Ryan, 'why the story we choose is so important.'

'Toothless, violent crack addict. Starts off homeless. Briefly enjoys not being homeless. Makes no inroads into the crack habit. Gets homeless again.' Seth waved a hand in the air. 'Like, what's that story saying?'

'Whereas,' said Ryan, his voice softening as he rather transparently tried to engineer what he would no doubt later describe as a *moment*, 'young, attractive professional, peripherally employed in the tech world. Makes a few perfectly understandable mistakes. Gets perfectly understandably depressed. Loses her job. Misses her rent. Winds up homeless. Gets offered a second chance by a benevolent organisation. Cleans up. Goes to work. Gets back on her feet. Maybe meets someone. Maybe gets married, buys a house, has children . . .'

'Now that's a story,' said Seth.

'*Your* story,' said Ryan. 'If you want it to be.'

They both sat back, making a show of being spent, as if they'd given it all they had, and now were forced to rest.

The urge to walk out of there was near-total. They weren't the first to have tried the inspirational approach. They were no different to the men who tried to slip into my tent at night, I thought. Empathy was just another tactic of manipulation. Even if our desires aligned, they had to be shown, out of principle, that what they wanted was of no consequence to me, that I had no interest in helping others by accepting their help.

But then I thought about the last year of my life: the first few nights on the street, when I'd managed to sleep only in the predawn hours, when sheer exhaustion enabled me to close my eyes without immediate and startling fear; the way the cold, that winter, seemed to take up residence beneath my skin, in my bones and organs, so that even when I had the money for a cup of tea or something to eat I would sit huddled against the radiator or heater in the cheapest cafe I could find and still be unable to stop shivering. I thought of voices and hands in the urban dark; moments of terror beneath underpasses and in the darkened corners of car parks; the people I'd had to fight off; the man out of whose arm I tore a chunk of flesh with my teeth. These were people just like me. I either dispatched them or made my way with them for a while, watching them struggle, watching them, in two instances, die: one from hypothermia gone alcoholically unnoticed, the other from an infection left stubbornly untreated. I thought of the shelters and hostels into which, after too many nights outside, I'd begged and harangued my way: rows of teetering bunk beds in a reclaimed warehouse near Pentonville prison; mattresses on the floor of a church. I thought of the grim, despairing rooms in which news of failure was dispensed; the desperate clamour of drop-ins where people pleaded their cases over the din of other people pleading their cases, holding up shattered Samsung phones through which brothers and sisters and far-flung friends tried to translate the money and shelter that were being denied. I remembered the nights at the encampment, sleeping with my rucksack in a lover's embrace, the rain crawling in under my tarpaulin. I looked down at my hands, noticing the way that the dirt was not so much on the skin now as under it, absorbed into cuts and scratches which then healed over. I could, I thought, smell myself, there in that over-lit, over-heated room. I could smell Ryan and Seth too: the detergent they used on their clothes, the halo of cologne in the air around them. *How long?* I thought to myself. *How long can you live this story when you know how it ends?*

They were looking at me, poised, slightly tense. I nodded, opened my mouth to let what scant air there was in that little room trickle down into my throat and wake up my voice.

'OK,' I said. 'I'm listening.'

Two hours later, forms filled, consent given, certain rights predictably waived, I stood, for the first time in perhaps two or three years, in a hotel, naked, my clothes in a pile at my feet, alone and momentarily safe.

I stared at the bed before me. It was the bed of sleep-deprived fantasies: fat white pillows piled three deep, complex layers of sheets and blankets, the linen with that stiff near-shine of industrial laundering. Without going any nearer, I imagined I could feel the cool gloss of those sheets on my skin, the mounting warmth of my cocoon as I lay inside it.

It felt strange to be naked, to not be doing anything about my nakedness. Nights of elemental exposure had acclimatised me to being clothed. Even on the occasions I was able to shower, I kept the time I was undressed to a minimum. Nudity was a vulnerable indulgence, a gamble. Now it seemed a luxury in itself.

I wanted to be as clean and fresh as the bed when I got into it. The feeling of laundered sheets on showered skin, the particular luxury of the sleep that follows, had long been one of my pleasures. Before, in my old life, I'd always scheduled fresh sheets for a Friday night, so I could wash away the residue of the office, drift into a restorative sleep, and wake refreshed. Back then, I was washing away a working week, sleeping off five early starts. What was I washing away now? How much sleep would it take to rebalance a year of unrest?

The shower cubicle was a crystalline lozenge in the corner of the windowless bathroom. I set the water running and listened to its pattering hiss and the whine of the extractor fan as it siphoned off the steam. It wasn't the first shower I'd had in a while, but it was the first in too long to remember that was fully private and scalding hot. My habit had been to shower weekly or fort-nightly, depending. A day centre near London Bridge offered the kind of all-in-a-row showers that reminded me, unpleasantly, of PE lessons at school: the demeaning, shameful ritual of develop-ing bodies thrust into unnecessary proximity that always followed the demeaning, shameful ritual of developing bodies thrust into unnecessary physical competition. At the day centre, shame was not an issue. We were all well past awkwardness. But the lack of privacy still stung. Sometimes, I would seek out a gym that offered free introductory sessions. There, I would walk straight past the sweat and clank of the weight rooms and make for the showers, which at least, in the more upscale establishments, were separated from each other by thin, shoulder-height divides.

On a shelf in the shower was a row of bath products in match-ing bottles of mossy green. One by one, I began dumping their contents into my palm, catching wafts of seaweed, eucalyptus, lime. I didn't even care which substance was supposed to perform which specific task of de-griming. I wanted to cover myself in all of them: shampoo, conditioner, body scrub, moisturising cream. My hair was tangled and knotted, but the slippery fluids swept through it, glossed it with silicone. Though it was less tangled, I did the same with my pubic hair, which was untrimmed and abundant, before working my fingers around my vagina and performing the kind of washing you never feel quite able to do in a communal shower. When I was done, before reaching for the towel and patting myself dry, I stood a moment, the cool but not cold air refreshing against my skin after the sting of the water, watching as the whining extractor fan sucked up everything evaporating from my body and flung it out into the night.

Finally, I stood ready, scrunching my feet into the thickness of the hotel carpet, staring at the bed, feeling in a rush my exhaustion, which, like my blood, seemed to have been brought to the surface of my skin by the shower. I knew exactly how my head would sink into the pillow, I thought, how my shoulder would broach the mattress, how I would pull the covers to my ear and feel, just as I always felt as a child, when my mother had tucked me tightly into bed and rubbed her hand over my hair until I squirmed, that so long as I was covered nothing could harm me. I reached out, pulled back the blankets. Tucked beneath the mattress, they resisted me. I peeled them open from one corner like a sardine can and slid myself inside, packaging myself up. The linen was just as I had imagined, the pillows soft, but the sheets and blankets squeezed me too tightly, as if lashing me to the bed. I kicked at them, pulled them first one way, then the other. Then I got back out of bed and tore them free completely. But now they were tangled, and when once again I got beneath them they were heavy, oppressive. I threw some off, then all of them. But then I was exposed, naked, victim again of that childhood sense of there being no shield, no armour against the things I might imagine in my sleep. Finally, I gave up and left the bed completely. In a corner of the hotel room, wedged against a wall, I made a bed for myself that was tolerable. One pillow, a single blanket, the carpet rough and the floorboards beneath it firm.

As I slept, I dreamed I was in a van full of naked, barking women. When the van stopped, the rear doors were opened, and we poured out, slavering, into an encampment of frightened and fleeing dogs.

Slowly, I eased my way into hotel life. After a couple of nights, I graduated from the floor to the bed. A few days after that, I ceased my routine of creeping down to the breakfast buffet, smuggling cereal and coffee back up to my room and eating in bed with the television blaring. I began to accept that my presence was sanctioned, that I was not some interloper about to be detected and expelled. I started dressing for breakfast, going downstairs with my hair wet and my skin still raw from the shower, sitting at my little corner table like a travelling executive, summoning from the staff another helping of eggs, fresh coffee, pastries. I realised I had become something I had not been allowed to be in some time: just another person, a body in a roomful of bodies, hardly worthy of a second glance.

My stomach was unused to regular and substantial food. I had a bout of constipation, then diarrhoea. I kept telling myself that I should eat as much as possible, that I still didn't know how long this might last or when the chance might come again, but my appetite was still low, subdued through months of sporadic consumption. It was at the stage now where hunger was not always something that registered beyond the day-to-day hum of my body. I had to remind myself to eat, even when it seemed I didn't need to.

Either through boredom or mounting confidence, I became bolder in my explorations of the hotel. I used the spa, the lounge, the bar. Twice, I ordered a massage for myself. Physical contact had been hard to come by. When it did happen, it was furtive, fleeting, muffled by layers of damp and musty clothing. On the massage table, I tried to practise being touched in a way that had my well-being at heart. The masseuse seemed to understand. She was slow and patient, the action of her fingers firm but never invasive.

With nothing to demarcate my days, time became formless and vague. This was hotel time, TV time: endless and slow and gooily soft. I wondered if, amidst all this indulgence, I was really returning to myself, or simply losing myself anew. I'd been sharpened through a year in which only the most pressing necessities merited attention. In the hotel, the guiding edge of my need became blunted. I ate in advance of hunger, stayed warm enough that even imagining a chill became impossible. The result was that I felt myself vanishing. Who would I be when there was nothing left to want?

I kept expecting Ryan and Seth to appear, but for over a week there was no word, only the occasional delivery of clothes or other items they clearly regarded as essential: a laptop, a mobile phone, a backpack. At some point, it seemed clear, this state of rest would end. I was almost beginning to welcome the idea. This was the longest I had remained still in months. The urge to move, to *be*, was overwhelming.

I could, of course, have walked out, returned to the streets. More than once, I stood in the hotel lobby, backpack in hand, ready, or so I thought, to disappear back into the bustle. But what would I be returning to? Amidst the chatter of night shelters, squats, encampments, certain wisdom is common and unchallenged: that chances are few and difficult to grasp. What would be the worse future – seeing this through and finding it flawed, or running away and never knowing what *this* was? And anyway, I would think, turning from the doors and the sunlight, leaving the breeze behind me and retreating to my room where the window couldn't be opened, the streets would always be there. That, in a way, was their beauty. Other plans, other lives, could be attempted and abandoned. If you'd survived them once, the streets would always take you back.

Finally, Ryan and Seth appeared. A message was sent to my room. I found them in the hotel lobby, which doubled as a cafe and workplace for passing freelancers. A long counter ran along the generous window, at which sat a row of young, sharply haircutted, slim-silhouetted men and women tapping away at silver laptops and sipping complicated coffees. It struck me that everyone in the city is unsettled, unaccommodated, hustling. We are all, each in our own way, looking to poach the things we need in order to shape an existence. Food, Wi-Fi, an electrical socket, space, shelter, peace. The only difference is in the order you ascribe to your needs, the money you can spend to have them met.

'Maya.'

Ryan and Seth were seated at a shin-high table around which were arranged four chairs. They both stood when I arrived. Seth held out a hand, which I shook.

'You look . . .' said Seth, then shook his head, as if words wouldn't do.

'Wow,' said Ryan, leaning past Seth to shake my hand.

Seth took pictures on his phone, moving round me, experimenting with angle and light. When he was done he tapped around on his screen, executing a final command with a flourish of his forefinger.

'Sent,' he said.

'Sent where?' I said.

'Instagram,' said Seth. 'We've made you an account.'

'So far it's basically just us being you but we'll give you the login and you can start getting your own content up there,' said Ryan. 'You know: selfies, pictures of what you're eating. That kind of vibe.'

'What I always say to people,' said Seth, 'is don't overthink it. Just make it a habit. Part of your day. That way the content stays fresh.'

'Not that freshness is really going to be an issue here,' said Ryan, 'given your background. It's like, pictures of food and fluffy white pillows are popular whatever. But for you? Pictures of food and

23

fluffy pillows are a whole new thing. They're . . .' He frowned, searching for the word. '*Moving*.'

I sat down in one of those chairs that masquerades as an easy chair but which then, when you sit in it, reveals itself to be far too firm. I held out my hand, gesturing towards Seth's phone. He looked briefly hesitant, then handed it over with exaggerated ease.

I ran my finger up and down the screen, scrolling through posts. The account was called *Maya's Journey*. At the bottom were pictures of the encampment's scattered remains being dumped into skips, cheerfully captioned with things like *Out with the old!* and *Lot of memories here, but the future beckons!* Then there was the shot of me they'd taken when I was first held and processed: padded with warm and waterproof layers, glaring puffy-eyed at the camera. I felt a shiver of recognition, as if I was looking clean through my exterior, into the rawness within. Finally came the shots he'd just taken. Me, buffed and shined and superficially altered.

I handed Seth his phone without comment. They pulled up the two chairs opposite me and did their little performance of getting comfortable – wriggling in, folding their legs in complementary directions.

'So,' said Seth. 'How are you doing?'

I shrugged.

'Fine, I guess,' I said.

'Great,' said Seth. 'Really great. You want to maybe elaborate on that a little, or . . .'

'The hotel's nice,' I said.

Ryan seemed to seize on this – leaning forward and holding up a hand.

'*The hotel's nice*,' he repeated. 'That's very good. That's a real start.'

'Why not snap a pic of your room?' said Seth. 'Say something like, *Having an amazing time here at the Masterson Hotel?*'

'Maybe even tag them,' said Ryan. 'Like, *Hey @mastersonhotel, thanks for the incredible room.*'

'Look at it this way,' said Seth. 'What's the name of your Instagram account?'

It seemed that their strategy for getting me to talk involved prising out the answers to questions that didn't need to be asked.

'*Maya's Journey*,' I said.

'Right,' said Seth. 'So ask yourself: where am I on that journey? Where am I *right now*?'

'And then share it,' said Ryan.

'And in sharing it,' said Seth, reaching a hand into the space in front of him and drawing it slowly to his chest, 'bring people *with* you on that journey.'

I sipped my coffee. It seemed slightly diluted, lacking in body and bite. Already, my tastes and expectations were evolving. Everything had to keep getting better, or it would feel like it was going stale.

'Maybe,' I said, 'you should tell me exactly what it is I'm supposed to be doing.'

They exchanged a look.

'Absolutely,' said Ryan. 'So. The job.'

'As I'm sure you know,' said Seth, 'getting back into employment is basically a nightmare if you've been, or are, of no fixed abode.'

'Just from a basic admin perspective,' said Ryan. 'Putting together some kind of history, gathering your references, trying to explain the gaps in your living arrangements, etcetera etcetera.'

'Even finding some appropriate clothes for the interview,' said Seth.

Ryan nodded.

'So what we've done,' said Seth, 'is we've totally squared that away.'

'When we picked you out of the encampment,' said Ryan, 'that was the shortlisting process.'

'And when we spoke to you afterwards and told you about the programme,' said Seth, 'that was the interview.'

'It wasn't,' said Ryan. 'But what we're saying is that to all intents and purposes it was.'

'There's a lot of interest in what we're trying to do,' said Seth. 'We were in a position of power, so we flipped the script.'

'We said: Hey, you know what? If you want to be on board with this, if you want to be part of Maya's Journey, then you're going to have to send *us* an application,' said Ryan.

'And boy did we get some applications,' said Seth.

Ryan nodded. 'It was application city.'

'But after a robust auditioning process,' said Seth, 'a fairly clear front-runner emerged.'

'Does the name Pict ring any bells?' said Ryan.

I shook my head.

'Pict are major,' said Seth.

'Major major,' said Ryan.

'When we told them about the opportunity we were extending to you,' said Seth, 'they were very excited. They wanted to package an opportunity *within* that opportunity.'

'And take it from us,' said Ryan, 'it's a hell of an opportunity.'

'Remember the unicorn of opportunity?' said Seth. 'Well that unicorn just had a baby.'

'A *baby unicorn*,' said Ryan. 'You know how rare those are?'

'You start on Monday,' said Seth.

'Start what?' I said.

'Think of it like an internship,' said Ryan, 'only with halfway decent pay.'

'And a whole lot of perks,' said Seth.

'Right,' said Ryan. 'One of the real stand-outs of Pict's application was all the stuff they bring to the table that *isn't* work.'

'For example they have I would say the best wellbeing programme of any company in this city,' said Seth.

'You start work with them,' said Ryan, 'and they start work on you.'

'And at the end of it,' said Seth, widening his eyes, 'you're *considerably* improved.'

I had a few more days of idle quasi-freedom in the hotel and then, before I'd really allowed myself to digest what had happened or imagine what was to come, I was commuting to work on my first day, squeezed onto the Overground with however many hundred sweating and reluctant souls heading workwards. I had, I reminded myself, managed this once. Perhaps I could manage it again, even if, before, I had been unable to endure it for very long.

People often describe a moment in which something snapped – a singular, sudden event. I wish that had been my experience, that I'd been able to reach the point I reached more efficiently. Instead, there was simply a slow fade, the gradual winding down of the mechanism that enabled me, day after day, to get out of bed as the sun came up, eat two pieces of toast, shower and dress, walk to the station carrying a cardboard cup of coffee that was exactly like the cardboard cups of coffee carried by all the other people walking to the station, slide unnoticed and unimportant through the stirring city, and arrive at a desk with nothing to look forward to but the moment I would be able to leave that desk and retrace my steps, eat, sleep, and begin again. By the end, I had fantasies of violence, of some terminal confrontational episode on my commute or in the office, but those instincts went unrealised. Instead, I simply stayed up deeper into the night, slept less, rolled into work later and later, completed an ever-dwindling fraction of the tasks allotted to me, until I was quietly, blessedly, let go. That was the exact term my manager had used as he sat in front of me in the smallest, coldest meeting room our building contained, shuffling a printed summary of my shortcomings and transgressions: *You're going to be let go.* I remember marvelling at the irony, the release and relief it implied. All our babble about the importance

27

of work, and this is the euphemism we choose to describe its ending: the same phrase we whisper in the ear of a dying relative; an expression best applied to the return of an animal to the wild.

Of course, one letting go begets another. Once I was let go from work, I began to let go in a far more generalised way. This was also something that was said to me: *You're letting yourself go; don't let yourself go.* I wanted to say, *No, you don't understand, I've* been *let go.* I couldn't tell if I was proud or ashamed, if I'd failed at something that was expected of me or succeeded at something I expected of myself. Either way, the letting go was comprehensive, and as it continued, the people around me began their own process of letting me go in turn. I had the stink of failure on me by then. People were wary of it. They lent me money once, but never twice. By assisting me, they seemed to feel they were encouraging me, validating what they saw as my choices. In return, I let them go too. I remember my father, sadly counting out five-pound notes the last time I saw him, stopping only when I placed my hand on his and said, *Please don't, Dad.* Rent became due, then overdue, then due again. Arrears mounted; patience wore thin. I found myself let go a final time.

Now, here I was, doing it all again. I can't say I was excited. I can't even say I was particularly happy. Instead, I felt only the perceptible easing of my musculature that accompanies the arrival of money where before there was none. Just as when you sleep on the streets you become accustomed to the distinctive and persistent knotting of your body that results from never quite finding respite from the cold, so too when you're poor you learn not to notice the way your shoulders creep always towards your ears, the way your fists are often clenched without conscious effort, the heavy ball of anxiety in the centre of your stomach that becomes indistinguishable from hunger or immediate fear, and the way, at night, you cease dreaming and begin simply counting, tallying the steady bleed-out of your resources.

I looked around at my fellow passengers, all of them selecting one of the two or three permissible poses for the self-respecting commuter: leaning against the carriage partition, holding a rail with one hand while scrolling through emails with the other, or folded neatly into their seat, pulling every external facet of their body inwards lest their limbs should touch those of a stranger. Were they happy? Most of them, I thought, looked exhausted. Their eyes were sunken, dark-rimmed; their skin was pale. Throughout the carriage there was the lingering waft of early morning bodily expression: dehydrated breath and long-incubated farts. Had any of them really planned for this? Was this genuinely what people had imagined for themselves? Or had they simply been discouraged, as all of us are, from imagining anything else?

Outside, a rising mist swaddled the metropolis. It had a Mesozoic air, I thought – buildings looming out of the fog like pre-human beasts. This is how I had always imagined the city as a child: as a community of giants bestriding the landscape. Later, sleeping out under the buildings' gaze, I had still sometimes seen it that way. Now, not for the first time, I would live and work amidst it. Five mornings a week, one season after another, in summer sunlight and hacking winter rain, this would be my reality. I would change, just as I had changed before. If I grew in the wrong direction, the city would correct me. If I could not be corrected, it would let me go.

On the street where I was to work, the food sellers were already setting up their stalls for the lunchtime rush. The air was filled with the complex smell of culinary preparation: freshly chopped onions and peppers, fiery marinades, slow-cooked meat. A whole industry had been built around keeping workers like me fed. In their stalls, under thick tarpaulin and hand-painted signs advertising their wares, the food sellers worked with a smooth efficiency, chopping, washing, mixing. I imagined them rising at ungodly hours, layering up their warmest clothes, then returning again in the late afternoon, exhausted, reeking of stale oil and garlic, their fingers nicked by their knives.

I turned down a narrow side street that was home to a small gallery, a design office, and an old-fashioned London cafe with checked plastic tablecloths that looked strangely embattled and out of place amidst the stalls of fashionable cuisine. The Pict office was at the far end, occupying a corner building. I pushed in through the revolving door and smiled at the woman in reception.

'My name's Maya,' I said. 'I'm supposed to start work here today.'

She didn't quite smile, just lifted her eyebrows and cocked her head. 'So here you are,' she said. 'He's expecting you.'

She picked up her phone and dialled a single number. 'Hi Harrison,' she said. 'She's here.'

Then she replaced the receiver and gestured to a row of comfy chairs.

'Have a seat,' she said. 'Harrison's on his way down.'

Is it possible to dislike someone based solely on their name? I felt as if I resented Harrison before I'd even met him. Since his name was the only thing I knew of him, I had to assume it was the source of my prejudice. Or perhaps it was simply the environment: the receptionist's not-quite-smile, the sense I had in places like this that they kept you waiting deliberately, so as to establish an imbalance of power. Such was my ingrained experience of officialdom: waiting anxiously in drab reception areas while the time of my appointment ticked by, watching as the people before me emerged from their ten-minute time slots, wiping tears out of their eyes and hurling abuse at some weary official.

'Maya.'

In my reverie, I had turned my attention to my hands, which I had rested in my lap. I was rolling my thumbs over each other, admiring the neat paring of my nails, the comparative softness of my skin, remembering the way my hand had looked as I tapped my finger on the table during my interview with Ryan and Seth. Caught unawares, I looked up quickly, slightly guiltily, and found myself meeting the gaze of a man in his early forties wearing selvedge denim and boxfresh

Adidas, doing a kind of squinting smile he'd clearly been told was charismatic.

'Harrison,' he said, stepping forward and shaking my hand as I stood up. 'I'm kind of the man around here but we try not to see it that way.'

He turned and gestured for me to follow, walking quickly up a half-flight of stairs and following a windowless corridor to a keypad-protected door, talking as he went, not looking back as I trailed behind him.

'I'll do the guided tour,' he said. 'But you won't take it in so don't worry. We learn by doing. Here at Pict the aim is to get you doing as quickly as possible. No induction, no trial period, just *go*, use your instinct, your initiative.'

'What exactly do . . .'

'Do we do? Fair question. Common question. No-one ever seems to know what we do. You know why? Because when we do it well, no-one even knows that what we do needs doing.'

He punched numbers into the keypad and opened the door onto an open-plan office filled with people tapping away at terminals.

'This is where the magic happens,' he said.

No-one looked up. Most had headphones on. All were peering intently at their screens. In front of them, each had what appeared to be an oversized trackpad, across which they swept their index and middle fingers, left and right.

'We've set you up over here,' said Harrison, leading me to an empty desk in the middle of the room. 'People are kind of excited, if I'm honest with you, so we've put you where people can see you. You'll be more of an inspiration that way.'

'Inspiration?'

'Change your login after I've gone,' said Harrison, pulling a spare chair up to my terminal and gesturing for me to sit down.

He waved across the plastic desk partition to a woman in her twenties.

'This is Naz,' he said. 'She'll be buddying you. Naz, this is Maya.'

Naz waved with one finger, smiled into the space between us without taking her gaze from her computer screen.

'People don't like to break flow,' said Harrison. 'Don't take it personally. Couple of weeks, you'll be zoning like everyone else.'

He tapped away at my keyboard. The terminal came out of screensave to show some kind of dashboard. There were columns that said things like *Viewed*, *Processed*, and *Removed*. Under each column was a slightly ominous-looking zero.

'Don't worry about your numbers for now,' said Harrison. 'This is about settling in. We get that. Your goals are going to be different.'

He moved to a column labelled *Stream*. When he clicked on it, a spinning buffer icon appeared, followed by a picture of a naked woman strapped to the underside of a horse, semi-penetrated by the probing tip of its enormous member.

'Okey-dokey,' said Harrison brightly. 'You're good to go. So. This is your first image. You swipe it, it gets replaced, you do another one. Simple as that.'

'Swipe it?'

'Left for no, right for yes.'

'But no or yes what?'

'Is this image appropriate? Yes or no?'

'Appropriate for what?'

'We try not to get too granular. We don't get into, like, profound moral discussions or anything. And we don't get sucked into the whole *yeah but is it art* vibe either. None of our clients are porn sites, so no real complexity there. You'll read the guidelines, obviously. But my advice? If in doubt, swipe left. The kind of websites we're working for aren't really in the business of nuance. And yeah, OK, sometimes people kick up a fuss when something gets *censored*, in inverted commas, but not nearly as much as they do when they click on a link expecting a kitten and what they actually end up with is a picture of one man being sick into another man's anus.'

He swiped left on the woman being fucked by a horse. It was replaced by a grainy snapshot of a ten- or twelve-year-old girl, naked, on what looked like a cheap hostel bed.

'That's something you kind of have to get used to,' said Harrison, swiping left and bringing up an image of two men on a beach, both in swimming trunks, their torsos bronzed, their arms around each other's shoulders. 'Aha, a right-swipe.'

He turned to face me.

'Simple, right?' he said.

'Sure,' I said.

'OK, so let's go through health and safety. We take wellbeing very seriously here. *Very* seriously. We kind of have to, given the nature of what we do. So: first thing to say, if at any moment you feel triggered, don't panic, just raise your hand in the air and a team supervisor will make their way over to you. OK? Don't suffer in silence, but don't suffer noisily either because that in itself can trigger others. You'll touch base every couple of weeks with our on-site counsellor, just to make sure you haven't seen anything that's, like, burning a corrosive hole in your soul. Oh, and detoxes are mandatory. We send you away for a few days, you live on vegetable juice, do some yoga, you come back recharged and refreshed and ready to wipe even more shit from the face of the internet. Sound good?'

I had no idea how it sounded. I was struggling to process what was being described.

'Sounds good,' I said.

'First trip's next weekend,' said Harrison. 'Timing's perfect. You'll have seen enough to need a cleanse, but you'll still be fresh enough to be shaped. You'll love it.'

He swiped right on the bare-chested men, stood up, patted my shoulder, and vanished.

I slid into the seat he'd vacated – 'my' seat – and fiddled with the settings to establish the right height and posture. Already, the office environment felt awkward against my skin. The air conditioning was too cold; the seat, which still carried the after-impression of Harrison's body, was too warm. I lowered my screen a little, tilted it, then put it back to how it had been. Then I moved the oversized trackpad around the desk until the positioning of my wrist against its padded base felt halfway natural. I had forgotten the significance of these micro-adjustments, the way office life so quickly shrinks your bodily priorities, until even the slight over-extension of your mouse-finger can seem unbearable.

The image on my screen, which had slid into place the moment Harrison had dispatched the men on the beach, was of a woman with a broken nose and two black eyes. I wanted to ask: *What's the caption?* Conceivably, it could have been part of a police appeal, or a campaign against domestic violence. Equally, though, it could have been posted as a threat. I played it safe and swiped left, bringing up a woman in a porn-pastiche of a school uniform getting fucked by two anonymous male torsos with cartoon abs and skin that had been waxed to a cyborg shine. Again, I swiped left. Next was a little girl on a beach wearing a one-piece swimsuit, laughing as she ran from what was clearly a rapidly advancing wave. A quick swipe right and I found myself looking at an image of an old woman shot in merciless high-definition monochrome. She was naked from the waist up, staring straight at the camera, her expression one of profound and moving calm. I looked at the wrinkled sag of her breasts, the detailed folds of skin around her stomach, and felt confused.

I looked up at Naz.

'What . . .' I said.

'Uh uh,' said Naz, not looking away from her screen. 'Don't get into the query habit. That way lies madness.'

I swiped left, playing it safe. Now I was looking at two men, fully clothed, in a crowded city square, kissing. I swiped right.

I told myself that, physically, if not mentally, I had endured far worse than this. I was warm. I was clothed. I was fed. Soon, I would

34

have money. When I had money, I would have somewhere to live. As jobs went, this was not the worst I could imagine.

I looked at the clock. Four minutes had elapsed.

An hour later my eyes were beginning to burn. When I spotted Harrison striding purposefully towards me, I felt not the reflex tension that ordinarily accompanies the sudden proximity of your new boss, but a deep and desperate relief at the opportunity to sit back in my chair and angle my head away from the computer.

'Maya,' he said. 'How's it going?'

'I think it's going OK?' I said, hating the questioning uplift my voice unconsciously appended to my answer.

'You don't sound very sure,' said Harrison.

'It's going great,' I said.

'Great,' said Harrison, somehow injecting the word with a spontaneity that suggested my previous answer had been struck from the record. 'Quick query though. Your Instagram: what gives?'

I wasn't sure what he was asking. I tried to play for time by telling him what I was fairly sure he already knew.

'Well it's called *Maya's Journey*, and I guess the idea is kind of—'

'Right,' said Harrison. 'Pro-tip, OK? Any time you tell me something, assume I already know about it. Because nine times out of ten I actually do know about it, and on the one time out of ten I don't know about it I probably don't need to know about it. I'm not saying, *Hey Maya, tell me about your Instagram feed which obviously I have already looked at.* I'm saying, *Hey Maya, I just looked at your Instagram feed and I'm not seeing anything about Pict.*'

'Oh. OK. I mean, I—'

'Which is fine, to be clear,' said Harrison, holding up both hands in a placatory gesture. 'Because you've been here, what? An hour? And you've almost certainly had other things on your mind, so . . .'

'I just wasn't sure if—'

'If Pict would welcome the publicity? If Pict, having signed up to be part of your very incredible journey, would want people to know that they're part of your journey?'

'If it was appropriate to—'

'I see what you're saying. You weren't sure what Pict's guidelines were around personal social media accounts and the expression of, like, opinions and interests on those accounts, and whether there would be some kind of . . .' He gestured vaguely.

'Conflict?'

'Conflict. Right. And you know what? You're right. Best to clarify. Because that can get messy. So, to clarify: no. There is no conflict. Does that help?'

'It does, yes.'

'Because, just to clarify further, in your situation things are not quite as clear as they might be for some people. For you, there is not really any distinction between work and personal social media presences because . . .'

'Because of the programme.'

'Because of the programme. Exactly.' He put his hands on his hips and nodded once. 'This was very productive, Maya. Thank you.'

'No problem.'

He strode off again, patting a couple of workers on the shoulder as he went. I looked up at Naz.

'Snap a pic of the logo over the front door on your lunch break,' she said. 'Then put some kind of personal item on your desk tomorrow and snap a pic of that and say something about settling in and making the place your own.'

'Thanks,' I said.

'Pleasure,' said Naz.

The flow of time was glacial, the working day a polar ice cap succumbing over aeons to climatic pressure. Set in uncomfortable juxtaposition

36

with the near-stasis of the office, the timescales of my own body began to feel wild and frenetic. My heartbeat seemed inhumanly fast, my breath crazed and shallow. It occurred to me that I was experiencing butterfly time. A day had opened out to become a lifespan, revealing all the enfolded acres of time within it.

At lunch I bought an enormous falafel wrap from one of the stalls and tried to eat it while walking, burning off the need to be in motion. I snapped a picture of the outside of the office and posted it to Instagram. I snapped a picture of my falafel wrap and posted that too.

Back in the office, image after image of violence and degradation crossed my screen. Humans and animals, men and women, adults and children. Torture was popular, as was rape or the illusion of rape. At some point I must have been given someone's entire cache of atrocity imagery to parse. I saw grainy historical photos of emaciated corpses, presumably Jewish, stacked in mass graves; Rwandan machete killings; napalm strikes in Vietnam; gangland executions in what looked like Mexico. Then there was a whole sequence of gross-out work: people vomiting and shitting, often onto or into each other; people baring their anuses for the camera; bloodletting; scarification; pain rituals. The question of whether to swipe left or right began to take on some deeper, darker meaning, as if the question were no longer what was acceptable in the context of the internet, or Pict's determinedly vague guidelines, or even what was acceptable to *me*, as an observer, parsing this stuff, but simply what was acceptable, full stop, as if I was being asked to decide not on what images could be seen by others, but what actions could be performed in the first place. Was *this* OK? And if so, why not *this*?

At five, everyone shut down their computers and began their personal processes of recovery, massaging their eyes, stretching their fingers, breathing deeply. I wondered what they would do after work, what strategies they had in place for erasing one day and readying themselves for the next. Ordinarily, I would have assumed they drank or rendered themselves comatose with drugs, but Pict seemed to take health seriously. I was already signed up for the detox retreat, and on top of that I'd received three different emails about meditation sessions, early morning pre-work yoga, a running club. I imagined them all listening to mp3s of self-hypnosis on the Tube, returning home to a dinner of raw vegetables, falling asleep to looping whale song and Amazonian bird-call.

My process of recovery was less virtuous. I rode the Overground in the early evening light, watching the city shift into its post-work persona and trying not to imagine that I was now pressed into an enclosed and rapidly moving space with the owners of all the images to which I'd been subjected during the day. Was this perspiring, mouth-breathing, excessively staring man beside me, who had used his grip on the pole between us as an excuse to slide the knuckles of his right hand up and down my ribcage, the very man who had attempted to post a picture of a blow-jobbing tween to the internet not three hours previously? Was that refined-looking, heavily perfumed woman a few feet away, eyeing her fellow travellers with thinly veiled disgust, in fact the owner of an unnecessarily comprehensive image library of dogs being beaten with hosepipes?

By the time I got off at my stop and walked back to my hotel, I was exhausted, slightly sickened. I wanted to be alone in a darkened room, eyes closed, senses down-tuned and muffled. I ate straight away so as not to have to leave my room later. I was, despite my enormous lunch, strangely hungry. The phrase *keep your strength up* kept stealing into my mind like the earworm hook of a half-remembered pop song. Keep my strength up for what? For staring at pictures? Or for the whole apparently endless ordeal – the daily commute, the long sit, the eroding faith in humanity? There were few fellow diners at that early hour – a clearly jet-lagged businessman, a small family of German tourists – but what few there were I tried not to look at. It was so much harder now, I felt, to sustain the veneer of distance and unknowing that makes sharing a city, a society, possible.

Another layer of the world's skin had been peeled back, and now everything was markedly more ghastly. I wondered if I might feel differently had the stream of horror been de-anonymised. Then, at least, the depravity could have been individuated. As it was, it seemed universal: the shared shame and mass brutality of our churning collective unconscious.

Upstairs, showered and swaddled in a hotel robe, I tried to counter the day's imagery with whatever innocuous output I could find on the television – a romcom, a film about an adopted chimpanzee, a documentary about children at play – but all I achieved, as I drifted into sleep, was a confused and strobing slideshow: couples kissing, holding hands on a nocturnal walk; a naked man with half his head caved in; two children building a sandcastle; a young black man lying dead on an American street, his brains splattered across the side of his car.

The next day I did it all again, only this time my pre-work routine was coloured by the knowledge of what was to come. Already envisioning the water torture of images, I sought space in my own mind. As I dressed, I neither turned on the television nor looked at my Instagram feed. At breakfast, I found a table beside the window and tried to use the grey city view to ease my transition from the shapelessness of dream-time to the streamlined flow of waking life. But the sense of distance afforded by the glass seemed sinister, as if the city, and everyone in it, were now just a series of images on a screen.

The feeling of remove remained with me during my train journey. Even when I was in physical contact with my fellow passengers, my body pressed awkwardly against theirs in the intimacy of the commuter crush, I was still acutely aware of life sliding by outside the carriage – a phenomenon I could now no longer experience in the flesh, but merely observe as it passed. By the time I got to the office and sat down at what I already thought of as *my* desk, a new certainty had taken hold: all the things I'd long imagined would help me feel a part of the world again – a job, a roof over my head, a small space carved out for myself in the vastness of human experience – had only made me feel more separate and shut out. Until a month ago, the city had been cruel, but it had always been open, and always around me. Now it seemed as if it was forever someplace else, distant and unreachable, despite the fact that I lived in it.

Already, this early on in whatever this process would turn out to be, I found refreshment in even the slightest novelty, the tiniest crack in the surface of my routine. This morning, it took the form of a message from Ryan and Seth. They'd found me a flat; I was to live there from tonight.

I spent the day visualising my new home. Layering up its details in my mind helped counter the effects of the images I was supposed to process. By mid-afternoon, it became so splendid, so gilded, so utterly divorced from any tangible reality that, not content with mere fantasy, I felt compelled to erect a scaffold of justification around my imaginings. With the level of public scrutiny this experiment was supposed to attract, I thought, the usual poky, gloomy bedsit would never do. The flat, like the project itself, would need to be a flagship, somewhere I could Instagram to my heart's content. Such was the strangeness of knowing that my life was a 'journey'. Now that someone was shaping my story, I imagined I could augur with confidence, make predictions based not on probability or experience, but on my understanding of narrative logic.

The day done, another however-many images approved or erased, I google-mapped the address and followed the throbbing blue dot by bus and then by foot to a one-bedroom flat above a betting shop in E17. The lock was stubborn, poorly fitted. As I opened the door, I was met with conflicting odours: damp, fresh paint, weapons-grade air freshener. Inside, I found a tiny galley kitchen slotted awkwardly into the landing; a poky, windowless bathroom with a mildewed shower cubicle and no bath; a bedroom whose double bed left almost no room around the circumference, and a lounge into which the noise of the street below intruded so acutely that I had to check to make sure the window was closed. The only nod to indulgence was an oversized television, its screen still covered with plastic film.

On the kitchen worktop was a white envelope with my name on it. Inside was a note from Ryan. He said they hoped I liked it and that I felt they'd got the 'balance' right. Naturally, they didn't want to put me anywhere awful, or dangerous, but too much luxury would disrupt the arc. People wanted to see me work my way up, rebuild myself, not stumble into comfort. He used the phrase *humble beginnings*. He also said that they'd advanced me some money against my first pay cheque, and that I should think about buying some person-alised touches for the flat. Keep it vintage, was his suggestion. Stuff that would get likes on Instagram. Inside the envelope containing the note was a debit card and a scrap of paper on which was printed what I assumed was my PIN. When I turned the scrap of paper over, I saw that Ryan had written *Don't forget to burn me!* on the reverse.

I took off my coat and shoes and paced the flat from the back wall to the front. Then I lay down on the bed and stretched out. I had never lived alone. From the day I left home, my life had been a procession of housemates. Some were friends, some were simply presences in places I'd rented. Then I was on the streets, where true solitude is all but impossible. Even in the hotel, I had been able to fool myself into an imagined communality. I went downstairs for breakfast and dinner; at night, I heard muffled voices from other rooms, footsteps and whisp-ered discussions in the hall. Here, I would wake alone, eat a bowl of cereal or a piece of toast standing in that tiny kitchen in the half-dark. In the evenings I would come home to that chilly, unlived-in feel. I would switch on lights, the heating, the television. Then I would kill time, eating and staring at the screen, until I slept.

The week came and went, thickening into familiarity. Then the weekend intruded. I had devoted my attentions to settling in at work, using the flat only as a place to sleep, shower, and eat, like some sort of purely functional recharging dock. Without work to go to, though, the flat became inescapable. I had no option but to find a way of living in it.

I ate my breakfast sitting on the sofa, a bowl of cereal wedged into my crossed legs, a spoon in one hand, my phone in the other. Ryan and Seth had said that a trip to buy things for the flat would be popular on Instagram. I thought that perhaps if I took the time to scroll through my feed then I could gather some ideas.

Ryan and Seth had followed people on my behalf. It was an odd selection: tech types and industry notables, lifestyle bloggers and assorted members of what I could only term the general populace. But despite this supposed diversity of users, taste was surprisingly universal. It was a scavenged aesthetic: people drank out of jars, ate their food off tiles. Their tables and chairs seemed not so much purchased as reclaimed, with rough, deeply grooved and heavily stained surfaces. The apartments in which these objects appeared were all too often white-walled and bare-floored, like museums or galleries designed to best exhibit the carefully grimed junk.

In their clothes, as well, people seemed to be once again, as they had when I was a teenager, courting the forces of decay. Distressed denim had made a return. Chunky jewellery fashioned from repurposed trash was in evidence. And yet, like the white walls and crisp bed linen of the apartments so carefully stocked with key pieces of detritus, this nod to erosion was set always against a glossy contemporary backdrop. Makeup was pristine; bodies were tanned, toned, and scrubbed to a resonant glow. It was a strange, slightly unsettling juxtaposition. Was the purpose of all that scuffed detritus to lend an added aura to the white-washed walls and moisturised skin? Or was all that maintenance, both architectural and bodily, in the service of better highlighting the impeccable, selective eye that had picked out those key decaying details?

One area where perfection and purity still stood unopposed, however, was food. In the average Instagram meal, thrown-together chic made no appearance. Instead, nutrition had been elevated to its own kind of art form. Scrolling through images with my thumb, I passed picture after picture of deep-green smoothies, lattes with hearts and swirls embossed into their dense white milk-foam, neatly layered burgers held together with miniature flags and displayed alongside salads that looked like they'd been assembled one leaf at a time. Breakfast in particular had become a sort of ritualised offering to the Instagram gods. Eggs, usually poached, were everywhere, always with an artful slit in their side, their bright-yellow yolk dribbling out over rustic bread. All the food emphasised health. There was talk of eating clean, eating raw, detoxing. Food was assessed not only by its appearance and taste, but by its supposed properties. This smoothie was great for energy, that breakfast offered emotional sustenance. Accordingly, meals were always photographed with a kind of beatific, filtered glow, as if everyone I followed on Instagram only ever ate breakfast at sunrise and dinner at sundown.

And yet, I thought, finishing my humble bowl of cereal, there was so much of it. Experienced as a stream, my Instagram feed was an exercise in deranged collective gluttony. Everyone into whose life I had just voyeuristically peeked may well have been perfectly healthy alone, but together they were participating in a shared mania, a mass binge.

I looked around at my small lounge, which I had barely used in the few days I'd lived here. It was fine, habitable. I'd seen and lived in far worse. The sofa was a faded, floral affair, faintly stained but basically clean. The carpet was an inoffensive blue-grey, worn and marked in all its most commonly traversed places. Did it really matter what items of furniture and decoration I bought for the flat when I would only be retracing the steps of all its previous tenants anyway? I imagined person after person before me, male and female, navigating the confines of this living space – standing in the

43

kitchen on the darkened, roughened patch of linoleum in front of the toaster; carrying their breakfast or snack along the worn trail that led to the lounge; settling down into the pre-existing divot on the sofa and thumbing the buttons on the TV remote as a globule of jam or butter fell from their toast and landed squarely in the half-erased ghost of an oily stain gone by.

One of the worst aspects of living on the street is that you feel as if all your failures are written on your body: the poor choices, the instances of appalling luck, your habits and shortcomings and diseases. Walking from my flat to the shops, I realised all that was gone. I was simply a woman in jeans and a sweatshirt, fingering folded money in her pocket. For the people who passed me, I would no longer be the subject of conversation, as I always imagined I had been before. *God, I saw this woman today . . .* they'd say to their partners, their housemates, their family, as they unpacked their shopping or unwrapped their takeaway and settled down to food and cups of tea. Perhaps now, instead, I would make those remarks to someone else, about others. Was that progress? The speed of society's forgiveness was both reassuring and troubling. This was a world that had spat me out without hesitation or remorse. Now it accepted me back without interest or apology. In doing so, it caused a new kind of vanishing. I was lost in the throng, making the same journeys as all my fellow city-dwellers, scrolling through pictures of all the same objects as everyone else, wondering if I too could own them.

It was a busy Saturday morning. In front of me, the street market was in full flow. Fruit for a pound a bowl, e-cigs and cheap incense, cushions and knock-off fashion. Behind the stalls were the small, determined businesses: international groceries, second-hand mobile phone shops, fabric merchants. All around me, people were fingering produce of various kinds – hefting mangoes, running a thumb over a bolt of silk, haggling over the price of batteries.

I started by buying fruit and vegetables, toiletries. Several stalls further down I came across a set of cheap patterned throws that I thought might enliven my flat's shabby furniture. I quickly had too much to carry. I was hanging flimsy plastic bags from every finger. A man waved to me from behind a pile of semi-ripened bananas, gesturing at his stock and holding up a battered wooden packing crate. Buy some bananas, he said, and he'd throw in the crate for free. After I took him up on his offer, he helped me pile my purchases into the slatted wooden box, then lifted it up to save me bending down. It was the first time since coming off the streets that I'd taken the weight of anything. I was aware of an early, almost unnoticeable change in my body: I felt stronger, fuller. Before, when I'd been unexpectedly required to engage in physical activity – dragging scavenged flotsam back to the encampment, for example, or being woken, as on that last morning, by the sudden arrival of threat from which I had no choice but to run – I had always been acutely aware of the empty reservoir of energy from which my muscles were trying to draw. I was forever running on fumes, and my body, operating always at the outer limits of its reserves, shook with panic and effort as a result. Now, as I took my crated haul of food and toiletries and woven fabrics from the man on the market stall, I felt the muscles in my arms and back and torso reach deep into the core of myself with their roots, tapping new sources of previously unavailable nourishment. It was a strange moment to feel powerful – stood there in front of a market stall with the shouted prices of fruit and vegetables ringing in my ears. I wished, in a way, that it had occurred at another time – when I was chased down by that dog, for example. But of course, if I had not been weakened and caught then, I would not have been strengthened and stood here now.

As I turned away from the stall, my box of purchases in my arms, a new question nagged at me. Where would I put this strength now that I had it? What was the point of being strong if I was no longer fighting, fleeing, or resisting anything? What would happen to all that energy if, finding no outlet, it turned inward, and fed on itself?

By the time I thought this, though, I was already rubbing up against the limits of my new-found physical ability. It was a fifteen- or twenty-minute journey back to the flat, but in less than half that time I was sweating and shaking. At the corner of the long road that led back to my new home – a road which inclined just enough to make me feel that I should summon more energy before beginning this last leg – I put my box on the ground and leaned against a wall, running the back of my wrist across my sweating brow and taking a few deep breaths while my biceps and thighs momentarily recovered. It was a kind of ego-check, a slightly deflating encounter with reality. I'd had a brief glimpse of how far I'd come; now my body was offering me a long, deep look at how far I still had to go. That previous year was archived deep in my physiological record. It would take more than a few square meals and a few decent nights' sleep to erase it. Probably, I thought, it would never entirely disappear. It would merely scar over, its presence no longer strong enough to affect me, but its traces permanent, visible, rough to the touch.

As I lifted my head back up and opened my eyes, I became aware of a woman crossing the road towards me, her gaze making it clear that I was in her sights. I recognised her immediately – not her features or her clothes, which were the usual palimpsest of found items layered over one another – but her gait. She had a stiff-legged stagger, as if each step were a controlled fall. Her name escaped me, but I had run into her two or three times, as tends to happen in the comparatively small circle of shelters, hostels, and food banks. She had, briefly, been at the encampment, but I had not spoken to her then, and after a short time, like many people there, she had melted back into the world. At least once, though, we had talked – in a communal dining hall filled almost exclusively with homeless men. We'd eaten together, then showered together, speaking only occasionally. She'd told me she expected to be housed any day.

'Hey,' I said as she stepped awkwardly up the kerb on my side of the street. 'Hey, it's . . .'

I couldn't quite explain to myself why I was so pleased to see her. It was, in many ways, awful to see that she was still out here. But hers was the first familiar face I'd seen in a long time; the first person with whom my own experiences, however loosely, aligned.

'I don't want to trouble you,' she said.

'No,' I said. 'It's . . . Don't you . . .'

'But I'm just trying to get a few quid together for a bite to eat, and . . .'

'We . . .'

'I haven't eaten today. I don't like to ask. I'm not asking for much. But if you've got even just a bit of change . . .'

It was clear she had no recollection of me at all. I wondered if it was the context that had confused her, or simply her desperation. In this state, I thought, she might not recognise anyone. All she would be looking for would be the possibility of help.

'You know, I used to be . . .' I said.

'Even if it's just a quid,' she said. 'Anything.'

'Of course,' I said, giving up on reminding her, but feeling as I did so my own sadness at letting the memory go. I felt in my pocket for my money, then remembered with an awful, sickening lurch that I'd dropped my last few bits of change into the hand of the man on the market stall as a thank you for giving me the box. I could have given her a note, of course, but to my deep disappointment I found I didn't want to. I'd had so little for so long, I thought. Now I had to be careful with what was mine.

'I'm so sorry,' I said. 'I gave the last of my change to . . .'

I watched her face fall, knew only too well the feelings behind her expression.

'Sure,' she said, turning away. 'Never mind.'

'Why don't you take some fruit?' I said, gesturing to the food in my box, which was on the pavement at my feet. I reached in and held up one of the throws I'd bought for the flat. 'Or what about this? This could be quite warm. You could . . .'

She looked at the throw, at my sad bunch of bananas, and then at me, at my face, at the pathetic pleading she could no doubt read in my eyes. Her lip curled, and she smiled – a smile not of kindness, but of pity.

'Don't worry about it,' she said flatly, and began walking away, her body rocking from side to side as she moved slowly forward on those stiffened legs.

I watched her go, the emptiness that had followed my over-exertion now opening out into something wider and deeper, leaving me entirely hollow. Here I was, I thought: stronger, healthier, safer, yet unrecognisable to myself and others, lost in the changes to which I'd been subjected.

Standing there, beached by the receding promise of a recognition I'd craved and failed to find, a memory came back to me, arrowing its way through the cavernous space of my solitude. I remembered squeezing myself into a phone booth, wiping rain from my hair and eyes, feeding change into the slot with frozen fingers, and then, at the sound of a familiar voice, pressing the cradle to end the call, and listening instead to the hum of disconnection, the drumbeat of a deluge on the phone booth's roof.

Back at the flat, my instincts conflicted with each other. I wanted to shut myself away; I craved the comfort of food and warmth, television and soft furnishings. At the same time, I knew those things had separated me not only from the woman I'd just met in the street, but from the person I'd been when I met her before. I was glad to be home, and yet I knew it wasn't my home, that nowhere would ever really be my home. But then, I thought, perhaps that was exactly the reason I should enjoy it as much as I could: because it wouldn't last; because one day I would find myself missing it the same way I now missed what had gone before.

I tried to distract myself with nesting. I cleaned the bathroom, polished the mirror, laid out my little bottles of shampoo, conditioner, and body wash from the hotel. There, they had blended perfectly with the aesthetic of the bathroom – the folded towels and sparkling fittings. Here, like any souvenir displaced from its origins, they looked foreign and ill at ease.

I opened out the throws I'd bought at the market and spread one across the bed and the other over the sofa. They were cheap and thin, but they were colourful, and something about the mere fact of colour was pleasing to me. I wished, quite suddenly, that I had bought more things in more lurid colours. The white walls not only of my own flat but of seemingly every flat on Instagram appeared suddenly characterless and oppressive. I wanted to live among fleshy pinks and bloody reds, the veiny blue of Mediterranean skies.

Now that I'd emptied it out, I took my crate to the bathroom and scrubbed it down. Washed and scraped, the cheap wood came up in a pleasing blonde. I positioned it at an artful angle to the corner of my sofa and dressed it with a cup of steaming tea. Then I snapped it from various angles, selected the best, and posted it to Instagram with a caption about the best things costing nothing. I was referring to financial cost, but when I read it back it seemed to mean something else, some deeper, more permanent toll.

I made pasta with cheap pesto and ate it on the sofa staring blankly at the television. One of the side effects of narrativising my experiences so consciously was that I now had no tolerance for the life stories of others, either fictional or real. Instead, I wanted the vague and slow-moving ur-story of the Earth, the deep emptiness of the cosmos, a journey with no arcs or stages or achievements. As I watched a probe orbit Mars, my phone flashed and vibrated repeatedly. In the infinite space-time of social media, my humble market crate was echoing and sparking. People were posting hearts and kisses, prayerful hands and smiling faces. Briefly, I felt the lost warmth of recognition. But between the two objects of my attention, I was confused as to the source: the instantaneous response of Instagram, or the timeless expanse of the galaxy, where a signal could travel for light years and never meet with meaning.

n the week that followed, routine established itself in my life with suffocating speed. Standing on the train, clutching my medium-sized black coffee in recyclable cardboard, or sitting at my desk, pausing in my infinite scroll through images of degradation and numbing violence just long enough to enact the accepted face shapes and passing interactions of office life, I felt the crushing force of habit around me and, as if in panic, kicked against its pressure through a familiar feeling of envy towards those who seemed to traverse their days with ease. Everywhere I looked, people were smoothly engaged in the process of belonging. They smiled at each other, brought in food to share, organised cards for the unwell, the departing, the recently aged. Their emails were aglow with emoji. They said, *Let me help you with that*, in such a way as to be sure that everyone had the opportunity to observe them helping you with that. Their salaried tasks complete, they gathered for post-work drinks in carefully selected, never-too-intimate bars and began, with seamless transition, the unpaid labour of camaraderie and networking. They backslapped, shoulder-rubbed, glad-handed. And I just watched, shut out, a low-budget shopper with her face pressed against the glass of a pricy department store window display.

I knew these sensations, of course – knew them intimately and uncomfortably. At first, I tried to tell myself they were the result of my time away, outside the system. I was adjusting, settling in, learning again how to do this. But I knew this wasn't true. The list of things

I couldn't do and failed to understand and never quite succeeded in faking went far deeper and stretched far further back than just this job, or this year, or this decade, and included far more than the dull choreography of careerist manoeuvring. It was something I felt, and had long felt, in almost every supposedly quotidian social experience: that vital information and training had been denied me, that the keys to what others regarded as personhood had, in my case, been lost. Looking around the office, at the way my colleagues' faces morphed from screen-based attention to interpersonal empathy as if cleanly switching modes, I knew with a certainty that burned in my gut that these were not just people who knew how to enthusiastically impress the boss, or charmingly chat to their colleagues, or make just the right gesture when their desk-buddy was upset or unwell. These were people who knew, at a family gathering, how to reach for a baby and bounce it on their knee, how to effect an easy familiarity and careful respect with their in-laws, how to strike up a conversation in a room full of people, how to dance or how to move on the dancefloor as if not knowing how to dance didn't bother them – how, basically, to *be*.

Each block of working days was tolerable, I found, if at least a single thread of novelty was woven through it. Last week it had been the flat, this week it was my upcoming Easter weekend detox – an event my colleagues spoke of in tones at once enthusiastic and cautionary.

'Oh my God,' said one person, passing my desk and lingering in a three-second window of forced informality. 'You are going to so totally love it. I wish I was going again for the first time.'

'Oh my God,' said another person, who yesterday had spent their three-second window of informality at the desk of a nearby neighbour and so clearly thought it was now my turn. 'Brace yourself.'

'My tip?' said a third person, perhaps aware that several of their colleagues had dallied at my desk and now feeling faintly competitive as a result. 'Carb-load before you go. Otherwise you'll collapse.'

Rather than feeling he had to choose between these differing attitudes, Harrison seemed comfortable embracing them all – a fact that became evident when, as I was preparing to leave the evening before my retreat, he enthusiastically squeezed my shoulder with one hand while slipping me a waiver with the other.

'Just standard,' he said. 'Nothing to worry about. Wow, this is going to be so amazing for you, Maya. I'm genuinely humbled by the small part I have been able to play in offering you this opportunity.'

I scanned the waiver. Its clauses were blunt: illness, permanent injury, death.

My train to BodyTemple left at 6 a.m. I boarded with two minutes to spare, sweating and stressed and weighed down with supplies for the journey – crisps that claimed to have been cooked by hand, pre-packaged wraps of roasted duck in plum sauce, two chocolate muffins the size of an average orange which I knew, even before I found my seat and sat down, that I would eat first, and a beaker of foaming, milky coffee with my name misspelled in marker on the side. The novelty of excess showed no sign of wearing off. I felt as if I was catching up on food the way some people caught up on the news or a particularly compelling TV series. What were the major developments? What were the twists? I needed to try it all, absorb it all. And anyway, my health was temporarily irrelevant. I was about to spend the weekend on some unimaginable regimen. It didn't matter what I ate on the way there. It would all be erased by the end of my stay.

BodyTemple clearly took the *retreat* concept seriously. It was tucked between two villages in a fold of land somewhere in the Peak District. The train would only take me so far. I was to get off at Leeds, I had been told, then get another train, and then, at the end of that journey, I would be met by car and taken as far as the entrance to the driveway, along which I would have to walk as vehicles were not allowed any closer. The invitation letter had warned me to pack light, wear sensible shoes, dress for the possibility of rain. After that, apparently, everything would be taken care of. The letter phrased all this so it seemed more like a philosophy than an itinerary. There was, they seemed to suggest, something symbolic about the extent to which they could and could not support you with your journey. They didn't quite use the expression *begins with a single step*, but it was there, suspended between the lines of their welcome pack.

Outside the grimy windows of the train, London melted into fields. I always forget that the windows of trains are slightly tinted, that they lend the day a misleading pallor. For much of the journey I therefore imagined that the outside world was sympathetically reflecting my inner state: gloomy, reluctant, dimmed to half its full capacity. Within forty minutes I had eaten all of my food. An hour in, I bought more from the refreshments trolley. Twenty minutes after that I had eaten all of those too and couldn't bring myself to buy more. A weird sense of judgement surrounds eating in public. I imagined the gaze of the man who worked the trolley as I bought all the same things again, my fellow passengers looking up briefly from their streaming videos, shaking their heads slightly, then returning to their distractions.

I tried to recall my last extended period of travel, but couldn't pin it down. There had been, at some point, an outing to Manchester with my then-housemates. We'd drunk wine on the train, kept drinking for much of the journey. Three young women, drunk, laughing, growing louder as the journey wore on. We'd drawn the exact same gazes then that I imagined attracting for my eating now. At the hotel, we had all passed out in our rooms. It should have felt disappointing, but somehow it had been exactly the break we needed. Such was the point we were at in our lives: between work and worries and sleeplessness, oblivion was the most restful holiday of all.

The journey was uneventful. I managed to sleep, and when I awoke I was in Leeds. I hustled between platforms, found the next train, tensely counted the stops as it threaded its way through the rolling landscape, and amused myself by trying to spot fellow retreaters. There were giveaways – a bottle of coconut water here, a hand with a fading henna tattoo there – but mostly they were indistinguishable from the serious walkers: sheathed in Gore-Tex walk-wear, fleecy tops and high-tech boots.

At the appointed village, we disembarked, nodded awkwardly to each other in the car park. There were six of us. People seemed uncertain about introductions. They made uncontroversial jokes, discussed the weather, kicked at gravel, and fiddled with the straps of their rucksacks. No-one said, as I wanted to, *What the fuck are we doing here?* Instead, the atmosphere was one of tentatively excited anticipation. These were women who *wanted* to do this, I realised. Not everyone, like me, had been forced to attend as a condition of their employment.

A neon-jacketed middle-aged man in a people carrier turned up and ushered everyone on board. The women were giggly in his presence. He had the air of a man who was used to it. To any question that was asked of him, he offered one of two answers: *All will become clear*, or *I'm just the driver*, the latter delivered in such a way as to suggest that he was not, in fact, just the driver, but that saying he was just the driver was part of some wider approach to life we would never really be able to understand.

As promised, he dropped us at the bottom of the driveway and we made the final approach on foot. I'd expected a period building showily converted, but the edifice that greeted us as we rounded the corner and peered past the trees was clearly purpose-built, all black wood and floor-to-ceiling glass.

'It's for the light,' someone said, gesturing at the enormous windows. 'They take light very seriously here.'

My urge to run is a finely tuned reflex. It can make itself known in the most mundane of moments: a boring conversation with no possibility of interjection, a man who leans or stands too close.

At BodyTemple it was a continual hum in my head, an aching urge that needed minute-by-minute management. It began the moment we stepped inside and were introduced to Chad, the Lycra-clad programme director, who ended every sentence with *OK?* and who bounced lightly from foot to foot while he talked. It built and deepened as he showed us round, handed out timetables scorched onto small balsa-wood boards with boxes of time allocated simply for *Juice*, and led us through spacious, wood-floored, white-walled studios with stacks of fleshy-pink yoga mats in the corners. By the time he showed us the airy, skylighted attic space that would serve as our dormitory, the row of neatly made, white-linened beds, and, finally, the communal showers – a porcelain tunnel studded with chrome nozzles – it was a full-tilt, screaming survival instinct.

'I always say, BodyTemple isn't just about getting to know *your* body,' said Chad, bobbing and weaving through the changing room. 'It's about getting to know *the* body. OK?'

People were exchanging glances, widening their eyes slightly, pre-emptively laughing off the upcoming embarrassment. You could almost hear the tick and whirr of their minds as they calculated: would it be possible to get up and shower before everyone else? Would it be possible to shower *after* everyone else? My calculations were different: would it be possible to leave in the night? Could I walk to the nearest village?

At this point Chad announced that we must be hungry. He led us out of the changing rooms and back downstairs to the dining room: a generously French-doored space with one large table in the middle.

'No cliques,' said Chad proudly. 'No exclusions. OK?'

We found space at the table. Other women, clearly having arrived earlier in the day, joined us. There was awkward small talk.

'I'm Angie,' someone said, giving a little wave.

'Rachel,' said the woman to my left.

These were the kinds of names I now found myself outnumbered by: Rachels and Rebeccas and Angies and Pams. Nothing that was difficult to spell. Nothing that might lead you to comment on its beauty, or ask as to its provenance.

'Ever done anything like this before?' said Angie.

'Not really,' I said.

'Me neither,' said Angie. She tried a smile but I could see the quiver in it. Rachel leaned across the table and patted her hand.

'You're going to love it,' she said. 'Like, I know we've only just met? But I can tell. You're going to love it.' She turned to me. 'You, I can't quite tell if you're going to love it, but you're going to get a lot out of it.'

'Rachel senses things,' said a woman a few seats down. 'I'm Debbie. Hi.'

'I wouldn't say senses,' said Rachel. 'I'd say more like intuits.'

We had the what-do-you-do conversation. My feelings about having something I did were ambivalent. I heard myself being vague about the details of my work, opening up a space of ambiguity in which working for an online image company could sit anywhere along a spectrum of achievement and importance.

Waiters appeared with trays and placed in front of each of us a tumbler full of thick mauve liquid. People picked them up, smelled them. I dipped a finger in mine, then licked it. It was the consistency of Greek yoghurt and tasted vegetal, slightly earthy. When I sipped a little more, I could feel its entire journey down my gullet and into my stomach. *Maya's Journey*, I thought, without quite knowing why, and snapped a shot for my Instagram before downing what remained.

'Someone tell me this is just a starter,' said Angie, wrinkling her nose and glugging.

As it turned out, it was just a starter. Plates of raw greens arrived in front of us. There were enormous leafs of kale, spiralised courgette, avocado scattered with seeds and dressed with an astringent reduction.

'Someone tell me this is another starter,' said Angie.

Juices consumed, we started in on the kale. There was something distinctly bovine about the task. It seemed to require more chewing than had ever been necessary for any other food: minutes of work to break down a single mouthful of fibrous matter. Nobody talked; the task was too consuming. All I could hear was a great collective crunching and smacking and swallowing.

'Mmmm,' someone said.

'*Mmmmm*,' someone else said, more forcefully.

A kind of contest developed. Who could enjoy this food more? Who could best express their virtue by way of expressing their enjoyment? Who, at the end of all that chewing and swallowing, could appear the most satisfied, the most happily fed?

Angie, I noticed, couldn't finish hers. I suspected it was too much chewing. Twice, she had raised a hand to her jaw and winced. She looked round the table and gave that little smile again, the one that seemed to have tears a short distance behind it.

'It's lovely,' she said. 'I'm just not that hungry right now. It's the travel, you know?'

Everyone nodded sympathetically while judging silently. Angie, I could tell, was aware of this judgement. She hung her head and looked at her hands in her lap. I thought about my train journey, when I'd been embarrassed to buy any more food from the buffet trolley. Always this sense of shame, I thought. Always this sense that what you eat and how much of it you get through marks you out in some way.

After eating, we did a digestive meditation, led by Athena, who had introduced herself as Chad's partner without clarifying whether she meant it in the business or sexual sense. Chad didn't seem like the settling-down kind. He seemed like the kind of man who'd erected an ideological exoskeleton around his wandering desires. I wondered, as I always wondered with men like Chad – yoga teachers and spiritual guides and personal trainers – if he got his kicks by fucking his clients. If he did, it didn't seem to be bothering Athena. She was showily, almost pretentiously calm. She smiled at everything, appeared grateful for every transient, fleeting experience, whether positive or negative or indeterminate.

'How is everyone?' she said, sitting cross-legged at the front of the studio wearing loose-fitting white cotton trousers and a tightly tailored white T-shirt.

An awkward series of murmurs formed the collective reply. People nodded, smiled, mumbled *yeah* vaguely.

'Great,' said Athena. 'So we've just eaten, and before that you've all just arrived and are probably feeling, like, *very* un-centred right now, so what we usually do around this time is just some grounding breaths and then a nice meditation, OK?'

Again the murmured chorus of vague assent.

'So,' said Athena. 'Legs crossed, back straight, eyes closed. Gaze behind the eyelids is turned upwards towards your third eye chakra. Hands are folded in your lap or placed on your knees. Take a long, deep breath through the nose and hold it. Then let it all out of the mouth like this, *hhhhaaaaaaaaaaaaaa*. And again. In through the nose . . .'

Breathing became a kind of battle. I would inhale, focus, then realise towards the end of my exhalation that somewhere in that passing moment I had lost myself to thoughts. I tried to tie my attention to Athena's voice. When I succeeded, my mind stopped me. I asked myself why I was doing this, why I was trying, unquestioningly, to do what she asked. I was here, after all, not through choice, but through necessity. I had invested nothing in this experience, would probably take nothing from it. And anyway, neither Athena nor anyone else in the room could tell if I was succeeding or failing. They were all concentrating on their own achievements and distractions. I could do the whole retreat like this, I thought: zoned out, distanced. But why would I need to do that? What would I be protecting myself from? Since I was here, why *not* try, why *not* go into the experience with a mind, if not fully open, then at least cautiously ajar? But then it occurred to me that perhaps even this tentative receptivity was the result not of my own inclinations but of Chad and Athena's ideological tranquillisers, already going to work on my mind. It struck me that this is what happens when you begin to concentrate on what's happening in your head: you stop understanding it. You can no longer tell a true thought from a reflex feeling, or a thought that stems deeply and honestly from your inner being from a thought that has been planted there and encouraged to grow by someone else.

'And now just let the breath be natural,' Athena said. 'Feel it go in. Feel it come out. Don't judge it. There is no good breath, no bad breath. Only breath. Coming and going. Don't hold on to it. Don't seek it out. Let it come and go. Let it breathe you. Let yourself, your whole body, be breathed by the breath you are watching.'

I had barely begun to breathe, and already I was exhausted by what I'd thought. The noise of who I was did not take kindly to my attempts at silencing it. At the slightest suggestion of stillness, my mind, as if drowning, kicked out wildly. It feared not existing, I realised. It had to talk to itself constantly to reassure itself it was there.

'On the next outbreath,' said Athena, 'do not breathe in. Just stop. Let it all out and stop.'

I did. I exhaled as far as I could and stopped. The moment I did so, all thoughts and sound in my mind ceased. I felt suspended in time.

'Notice how you don't need to breathe quite yet,' said Athena. 'Notice how you are calm and quiet.'

We were all silent, literally breathless, still.

'Notice what death feels like,' said Athena. 'Notice that it is not something about which we need to panic. In a moment, when you breathe in, notice how good it feels to be alive, and notice how that thought eclipses all others.'

When, I wondered, was the last time I had been so still, so momentarily free of concern, so unfearful? For a long time, even before I was

60

homeless, fear had kept me going. On the streets and in the encampment, fear had kept me alive. At night, curled in my sleeping bag with everything I valued held close, it was fear that kept me alert even as I drifted into sleep. In the morning, it was fear that woke me. Now, I wondered what it really was that I had been afraid of. Death, it seemed from the slight glimpse of it I had now been afforded, was not all that terrifying. But what I experienced in that held, empty breath, was not, I thought, the same death as the death I had been afraid of in the past. It was *my* death: mine not just because it was happening to me but because I was choosing to make it happen. Death in general was not the problem. My issue was with death as the ultimate negation of choice. That, really, was what I had feared, and it came in many forms: theft, violence, rape, expulsion from society, loneliness, illness, hypothermia, starvation. All the things I'd guarded against were really the same thing: the erasure or circumvention of my will.

And this, I saw now, as I breathed in and felt my own warmth and life returning, was why my thoughts about the retreat were so muddled. I had arrived under duress. I had convinced myself I had no need of what was on offer. I had shut myself off from the possibility of anyone altering what I wanted. But sitting here now, listening to Athena, I realised something that terrified me: I wanted *something*. I didn't know what it was. I doubted I would find it at BodyTemple – I doubted, in many ways, if I would find it at all – but whatever it was, and whether I would ever find it, I knew now that I wanted it. To a person like me, a person who, through a year of having nothing, had self-defensively evolved to want nothing, and who had come to believe that the very sensation or act of wanting anything at all will ultimately undo you, the thought was its own kind of surrender, its own kind of death.

That night we lay in our single beds, lit by the porcelain glow of the moon as it peered through the skylights, arrayed in a panorama of discomfort. The others, I knew, were adjusting to dormitory sleeping. They were excessively aware of each other's presence. They could hear each other breathing, stirring, intimately scratching. These sounds, enhanced by the heightened state of attention we'd all now entered, disturbed them, woke them, but were not as discomfiting as the sounds each of them imagined they might make when their guard was down. Sleeping is an exposed state. The exact nature of this exposure occurs to us only when we sleep in the proximity of someone else. The women around me, I knew, feared the embarrassing emittances of their own unguarded bodies, the snores and farts and infantile gurgles. They feared their nocturnal bodily needs, the shameful tiptoe to the toilet, the sound of their coursing urine or plosive faeces ringing out through the semi-silent dorm. They even feared the things they might say in their dreams, the secrets they were capable of revealing. In the morning, they would rise tentatively, interrogate each other euphemistically. *Did you sleep well?* would mean *Did I wake you? What did I do?*

I knew all this because I had felt it before, myself, and more strongly than any of these women could probably imagine. I remembered my first night in a shelter, sleeping on a sagging army bed in a freezing church, the chill beating up from the stone floor; the reek of damp and dust and unwashed, festering bodies; the sounds of violent coughing from shot lungs; the schizophrenic self-interrogations from darkened corners; a woman saying over and over again, *she does, she does, she does*; another woman laughing at nothing; someone sobbing; someone snarling at everyone else to shut up; a constant, muted clamour of shuffling and creaking and sly, sinister movement; and outside, always, the noise of the city at night: a howling drunk; bantering boys; a girl practising her rapping at 2 a.m., her flow loose and ecstatic and charged with hollow threat, as if she was venting at a city she resented, safe in the knowledge it would ignore her. Even now, over a year later, I could recall every footstep that passed by my bed that night, every unfamiliar voice that whispered, somewhere above my head, *Is she sleeping?* And I remembered too my fear of sleep, the vulnerability of unconsciousness, and my terror of saying in slumber the things I'd suppressed when awake: *You smell, You're mad, Stay away from me*.

Now, in the dormitory, my sleeplessness was for the opposite reason to the women around me. While they grappled with novelty, I felt smothered by the familiar. It should, in many ways, have been traumatic, a disturbing flashback. The experience's uncanniness, however, lay not in its discomfort, but in its unexpected ease. I had missed this, I realised, this sense of others' presence. This was what a night in a room full of women revealed to me: that my life had changed; that I was safe, dry, warm, and alone.

In the morning, as ever when people have slept together for the first time, we couldn't look at each other. We nodded, smiled, then turned our attention away from each other's faces, towards the humdrum detail of the day's beginning: pyjama buttons and hair ties, contact lenses, makeup bags, balled socks. We got in each other's way, apologised, stepped aside. We spoke from behind our hands for fear of our breath. In the bathroom, we lined up at the sinks, swilling and spitting. I had not yet, since the start of the programme, seen a dentist. My long-untended gums bled when I brushed them. I found myself ashamed of the frothy, crimson streak that slid into the plughole, as if it spoke of some personal failing or shortfall. When Angie, at the next sink along, also spat blood into the stream of the flowing tap, we looked at each other and smiled.

I used the toilet, but only to urinate. All of us, I realised, were using the toilet only to urinate. Shitting was too intimate. It would come later, when we knew each other better.

Breakfast was a deep-green juice with an unwashed tang. There was no tea or coffee, just one mug each of hot water with a chunk of lemon floating in it. The juice didn't so much satisfy my hunger as

63

temporarily obscure it, as if a thin veil of modesty had been draped over the form of my need. I wondered how long it would be before someone – probably Angie, who was already, as she sipped her juice, looking tearful and fragile – cracked completely. We were all, I could tell, feeling the early stirrings of fury as the desperate inadequacy of the juice became clear. So strange, I thought, that people wanted to put themselves through the experience of hunger artificially. I was alone among the women, I assumed, in having experienced genuine starvation, meaning its recreational simulation held no thrill.

During breakfast, and in advance of the upcoming yoga class, people made efforts to slip away to the toilet. I took my leave just as my neighbour turned away from me to begin a conversation with someone else. I was suddenly self-conscious about excusing myself. In the toilet cubicle, I perched tensely on the seat, waiting for something to happen. Nothing did. My bowels, hearing the noises of other women in other stalls, shrank in embarrassment.

After what passed for breakfast, we began what passed for pleasure: ninety minutes of yoga with Chad, who arrived in the studio with his legs vacuum-packed in Lycra and his torso completely bare. He was extraordinarily thin yet somehow excessively muscular at the same time. The effect was inhuman, mantis-like.

'How are we all feeling this morning?' he said, bouncing to the front of the room, his shoulder muscles rippling.

There were nods, vague murmurs. Chad smiled.

'First morning's always strange,' he said. 'You're still carrying round all those toxins. You'll feel very different once we start to sweat them out. But before we do that, let's get ourselves in the right headspace with some chanting. OK?'

Chad led the chanting. It was in Sanskrit. He said it meant *I wish everyone happiness* but it could have meant anything. We knelt, eyes closed. Time distended. After a few rounds of chanting it was as if only the chanting existed. We were simply a shared hum, a communal vibration. When I opened my eyes again, the objects and colours around me seemed to float slightly. Chad sprang to his feet in an easy movement and instructed us to 'find' downward dog. I had done yoga before, years ago, and had even, in the encampment, kept up with some simple stretches in an effort to counter the effects of balling myself tight against the cold. I'd never been as clenched as when I was homeless. Even by the time I got to BodyTemple, some muscles still felt as if they hadn't fully relaxed. Now I was putting those muscles through their paces. They seemed, initially, to thank me for it. Quickly, though, they began to hum with pain. By the time we began holding the more advanced poses, rivers of sweat were running from my armpits towards my fingers, from my groin down over my thighs, and, when I was upside down, from my face into my dangling hair.

'Pull that tailbone in,' Chad roared. 'Feel it. Really feel it. Release the head. Let it go. Are you feeling it?'

Over to my left I heard a sound somewhere between a moan and a ragged gasp.

'Don't fight it,' commanded Chad. 'Holding now for ten breaths. OK?'

By the time he said this, I had already taken thirteen frantic breaths. The burn in my arms and legs made it feel as if the muscles themselves were pulling clean away from my skeleton.

'I can't . . .' I gasped, my voice throaty and pinched and depressingly pathetic.

'Know that this is OK,' he said. 'Know that pain is simply heat, building in the body. Don't block it out. Snuggle into it. Feel its warmth. OK?'

The class managed a strangled, collective *nnnnnn*. We'd been reduced to consonants.

'Maya,' said Chad, kneeling close to my upturned head, his sweat-shined forearms flexing as he brought his face level with mine. 'Are you here to change?'

'I . . .'

'I said are you here to *change*, Maya?'

'I'm . . .'

Chad addressed the whole class.

'Don't be scared of change,' he said. 'Don't think that change is simply something we initiate here, now, at BodyTemple. Change is happening all the time, every second. All we're doing here is noting it and accepting it.'

I wanted to say that it wasn't change itself that was the issue, more the rate at which it was expected to occur, but I had no breath.

'It's been, I think, more than ten breaths,' someone managed to gasp.

'Holding for seven . . .' said Chad calmly. 'Eight . . .'

On the other side of the studio, someone collapsed onto their mat with a screeching exhalation and a wet, sweaty slap.

'If you lose it,' said Chad, 'just find it again.'

My limbs were spasming uncontrollably. I stared downwards towards my mat and imagined myself swimming, pushing deeper into all that pressure and agony, leaving behind the reassurance of the ocean's unbroken, sunlit surface.

'OK,' said Chad. '*Slowly* come down. One vertebra at a time.'

I lay flat, panting. My mat was pooled with sweat. It occurred to me that I might have been liquefying completely.

'Well done everybody,' said Chad. 'Great work. Let's move into corpse pose, OK?'

We lay on our backs, palms and feet upwards, eyes closed, pantomiming morbidity. If death were offered, I thought, I would not at that moment have said no.

We staggered to the shower rooms to get clean. Dignity was competitive. By this point our muscles and joints were seizing fast but we all laboured to look loose and aglow.

'That was wonderful,' said Rachel, barely managing to keep the strain out of her voice. 'I feel completely renewed.'

She lowered herself onto a bench and sipped gingerly at a canister of coconut water. I could tell by the way she breathed between mouthfuls that she wanted to gulp it down. Around us, women were peeling off their Lycra, revealing bodies in various conditions of toning. All of us were pulling in our stomachs, trying to stand tall. My vision was still narrowed, my heart hammering away in my chest. I thought about the strength required to undress and felt only a deep and debilitating exhaustion.

'I feel like I could do it all over again,' said Debbie, stretching ostentatiously in the middle of the changing room. 'I just feel so energised.'

I took a sip of water and tried not to be sick. I was beginning to cool, the sweat drying across my face and chest. As the adrenaline began to disperse, the pain began to intensify. Tomorrow, I knew, I would wake to a body that felt like a stranger's: reluctant, disobedient, foreign.

We filed into the showers, conversation dwindling as exhaustion took over. As we lined up in front of the nozzles and turned on the hot water, each of us unscrewed the tops of our personal products, turning the narrow and quickly steamed porcelain corridor into a tunnel of scented vapour. Everyone had their own distinct ritual. People were donning abrasive gloves and buffing their skin to a violent glow. Two women were beating their bodies with wooden paddles designed to stimulate circulation. Others were taking the opportunity to shave their armpits and legs. Such were the methods of maintenance: abrasion, blunt-force trauma, diamond-edged blades.

Beside me, Rachel peered out from under foaming whitecaps of shampoo and ran a single, soap-reddened eye up from my ankles to my chin, stopping short of meeting my gaze.

'You know, I really envy your body,' she said.

'Really?' I said.

She nodded.

'Absolutely,' she said. 'Your body can still *become* something. For me it's just about keeping it as it is.'

*

Showered and freshly sensitised to the air around us, we settled down in the seminar room for a juice class. A man called Vaughan stood at the front behind a table of multicoloured produce and ran his hands over the contours of what he called an extraction device.

'Number one rule of extraction,' he said. 'Keep it rainbow.'

My focus was fading in and out. Any reserves I might have arrived with had by this point been depleted. Reality was starting to feel untrustworthy. The tri-tone *aaaahhhhh* of the air conditioning had become choral, at times orchestral. When Vaughan fired up his extractor it went through my brain like a chainsaw.

'Always ask yourself when you're extracting,' he shouted over the roar, the tendons on his arms pulsing and writhing as he fought to keep the machine stable, 'what do I want to be? What can these ingredients help me become?'

Vaughan's extraction machine, into which he had casually tossed three raw beetroots and a fistful of kale, became a swirling, psychedelic lava lamp.

'Feel the extractor as it extracts,' said Vaughan, running his hands over the lingam of his machine. 'Experience its vibrations.'

It occurred to me that I was feeling its vibrations from two rows back. Beneath me, my chair felt distinctly apparitional. All of my atoms, it seemed, were dispersing. If Vaughan had tossed me an unpeeled beetroot and told me to get on with it, I would have torn into it with my teeth and swallowed whatever I could break off.

When Vaughan snapped off the turbo engine of the extractor I achieved a moment of approximate stability. Then he started pouring his liquid into little paper drinking vessels – the product of his extractor such a vivid, hyperreal purple that I thought I saw it pulsing as it oozed from machine to cup.

'Please tell me those are just tasters before we have, like, a much bigger extraction,' Angie whispered behind me.

'I know what you're thinking,' said Vaughan, who'd probably heard but didn't want to shame anyone. 'That's it? How am I going to sustain myself with just a single shot of this extraction? Well let me tell you, this one mouthful of extraction contains the equivalent nutrients to two square meals, so in many ways it's a total binge.'

I tried to find a way to rest my forehead on my hands without it looking like a posture of despair. I decided there was no way to pull it off and so lolled backwards in my seat. I had reached the point of hunger where the thought of eating becomes paradoxically nauseating.

We filed up to the front and each took a shot.

'Now, don't drink it immediately,' said Vaughan as everyone brought the little cups straight up to their gaping mouths. 'When we consume things too quickly . . . OK, some of you have already consumed yours. That's OK. Definitely nothing to beat yourselves up about. But next time give yourself a few moments. Your body wants to smell what it's going to consume. It wants to prepare itself. Those of you who have not yet consumed: feel the saliva rising. Feel those stomach acids preparing themselves for duty. Let your body know that nutrients are about to arrive. Feel how grateful it is even before you actually allow the liquid into your mouth and feel it drip ever so slowly down your . . .'

Off to my right, Angie had started retching the way a cat does: opening her mouth with a wet *whap whap whap* like someone was striking the back of her throat with a ping pong paddle, moving backwards with each heave as if to reverse away from whatever arose.

'That's OK,' said Vaughan. 'That can happen. Very natural. Don't fight it, Angie, just let it . . . There you go.'

Angie was too empty and weakened to projectile vomit. Instead, with a final damp thwack of her soft palate, she assumed a stiffened, quivering, open-mouthed pose and allowed a thin stream of purple liquid to unfurl itself from her throat like a coloured shoelace.

'All very positive,' said Vaughan. 'All very natural. Sometimes the extraction can draw bodily toxins towards it, which allows the body to expel . . . OK, obviously, sometimes when someone is expelling it can be kind of contagious? So let's just move away from what has been expelled and take a moment to . . .'

A panicked rush away from Angie had left her panting and bent double over the puddle of tie-dyed bile at her feet.

'Was that . . .' she said between heaving breaths. 'I mean . . . Do I get another one, since I lost that one?'

We fell into a rhythm – distinct, reassuring through being predictable, but not easy. We drank juice and pined for caffeine, ate leaves and pined for bread. We twisted ourselves into position and longed for release. Then, released, we sat still and wished we could move. Through it all, more than anything else, I was desperate to shit. My stomach had distended to the point of agony. During yoga, I felt a terrifying pressure in and upon my belly. Several times an hour, my anus alerted me to the presence of imminent, insistent matter. Whenever the opportunity arose, I slipped away, sequestered myself in the toilet cubicle, and awaited a delirious release that never came. Instead, my thighs shaking and a cold sweat beading across my skin, I was greeted by absence in the place of a presence, a fleeing headwind like that announcing an onrushing train at the mouth of a tunnel, and then a discernible clenching, a change of bodily mind, a retreat.

We were, I realised, as we battled the urge to eat, to rest, to break the silence, to shit, moving always against life's grain. Our every instinct, our every unthinking desire, our every unquestioning reflex action, was challenged. I hated it, chafed against it, felt curtailed and controlled in ways to which I was not accustomed, but I also loved it, not because of how it felt or what it achieved, but because of what it implied: that nothing is inarguable, that every facet of life, be it physical, mental, social, or political, can be resisted. On one level, we were being controlled. Our daily routine was dictated. Our bodies were no longer quite our own. What we put in them, what they released, was subject to scrutiny and order. But by abstaining, we were taking the ultimate control. Even our physicality, our biology, no longer held any power over us. If, together, we could exercise this much dominion over the deep and mysterious and hitherto irresistible patterns and schemes of our bodies, what else could we resist? What other forces could we reverse?

Of course, not everyone saw it this way. To some, we were not resisting at all but yielding, synchronising ourselves with what they regarded as the natural processes of life. These were the women who closed their eyes and smiled unexpectedly; who rolled tongue-loads of juice around their mouths and savoured not only the taste but their own reaction to the taste; who rose in the morning smiling and rested and stood at the ends of their beds looking out at the rising sun through the skylight and gave thanks to the world and each other. Others agreed we were resisting, but felt eroded by the effort. Angie was an obvious casualty. Her skin was waxy, her hair lank. Her eyes were always tearful or reddened. She just wanted it to be over, she'd say to anyone who would listen. She wanted it all to be over so that she could go back to her life and her tastes and the things that made her feel safe. I felt for her, comforted her when I could, but I also, in my own way, fed off her misery, and found in it an odd and slightly shameful inspiration. If I had learned anything over the past year of my life, it was that any true resistance, any genuine escape, is met with swift and certain punishment. Angie's isolation, her sorrow, her despair, became a kind of reverse proof. If someone was in agony, something profound was being threatened.

This thought changed the way I approached the retreat. Instead of resisting the discomfort, I stepped into it, embraced it. At each yoga class, I pushed myself a little further, stretched a little deeper, twisted a little tighter. I began to find myself dissatisfied with any-thing that didn't hurt. We were supposed to chant, silently, under

71

our breath, *Let go, let go,* or *I wish everyone happiness, I wish every-one happiness.* Slowly, though, my own mantra emerged. *Feel it,* I snarled at myself as my body spasmed in pain. *Feel it, feel it, feel it.*

Chad and Athena talked frequently about peace. Inner peace. Outer peace. Peace in our lives. Peace in the world. By tapping these natural rhythms, they said, by rebuilding the relationship with our bodies and spirits that had been lost, we would not only find peace but create it, generate it, spread it. By the last day, however, I was moving in a very different direction. I wanted tur-moil, pain, rage. Where others cultivated a soft-eyed smile, a chic and radiant tranquillity, I felt my gaze becoming harder, colder, crueller. Our different directions, I thought, stemmed from our divergent experiences. Others at the retreat had felt too much, and now were getting away from feeling anything at all. I, on the other hand, had spent too long training myself to feel as little as possible. Now that I felt stronger, I craved all the sensations from which I'd previously protected myself, and so I embraced what the others avoided. It was a journey, for me, not away from pain, but into it, away from the fantasy of bliss.

That is not to say, however, that when the time came I wasn't ready to leave. On the contrary, I was itching to get out of there. This itching was literal, physical. The cleanliness of that place, the purity, was abrasive. I felt it on my skin, in my stomach. On the last afternoon we lay in corpse pose, reflecting on what Athena called our journey, on the yogic movement from birth to death and back to birth, and all I could think about was eating and shit-ting and bringing myself off before I fell asleep in my own bed. Except, of course, it wasn't my own bed. Nothing, I thought, as I lay there with my eyes closed and my palms turned upwards, was my own. Even my body, disrupted from its habits and rhythms by the BodyTemple regime so that it could enact more comfortably the tasks and routines of the Pict regime, now belonged to some-one else.

72

*

At the bottom of the driveway, as we waited for the ferryman in his people carrier, we exchanged hugs and email addresses and generally made a show of parting. But at the train station, as we gazed up at departure boards, looking for trains in different directions, the speed with which we returned to ourselves was almost frightening. All that work, I thought, all that *change*, and in just a few pressured seconds while we checked times and platforms, we reset. *I'm this way*, someone said. *I'm that*, said someone else. Everyone had already, prematurely, hugged in the driveway, so now there was nothing left but a simple wave and a little smile. We wouldn't, whatever we claimed, miss each other. Instead, as with so many other loose and temporary groups I had been part of, we would simply disperse, and whatever had resulted from our meeting would be ours to pursue or forget alone.

After the sanitised seclusion of BodyTemple – its incongruous balance of rural isolation and sterile modernity – the experience of being on the train, surrounded by other bodies, breathing stuffy, shared air and feeling against my skin the familiar contact of grimy, foreign surfaces as we sped towards the smog and clatter of the capital, was disorienting yet oddly exhilarating. The train was overbooked; we were packed in tight. Every inch of available space was crammed with bodies. I was lucky in that Pict had booked me a seat. Others, less fortunate, were stood in the aisle, in the area around the toilets, pressed up against doors and windows and rubbish bins. It was a cool day, but people had run for the train, heaved their oversized luggage through the narrow doors and wrestled it onto the racks. Following the exertion, and finding themselves wedged against each other in an overheated train carriage, they began to sweat. Within ten or fifteen minutes of pulling out of the station, the air of the carriage was clogged with the collective reek of sticky skin beneath man-made fabrics. After a weekend surrounded by carefully cleansed and scrubbed bodies in meticulously detoxified surroundings, I felt sensitised and attuned to every rising bodily odour. For others, I imagined that the smell of the train carriage was a single, dense olfactory experience. For me, as I turned my face and guided my nostrils from passenger to passenger, it was more of a sequence, a scale, as if I were able to pick out not simply the combined scent of the massed travellers, but individual armpits, signature sweats, the rank breath of dehydrated mouths hanging open. It was the season for last-ditch coughs and colds. Accompanying the multi-instrumental arrangement of smells was a whole percussion ensemble of hacking, sneezing, throat clearing, wheezing, snorting, and phlegm-swallowing. Everyone was doing their best to isolate themselves, but in such crowded conditions it was impossible, and soon a kind of collective acceptance seemed to set in. We were going to have to breathe each other's expelled germs, inhale each other's festering smells. This was something that could neither be fought nor avoided. Already in a weakened state from their luggage heaving and platform dashing, people seemed to soften into this collective contamination, giving themselves over to it with unusual abandon. My own thoughts, I realised, were probably also the thoughts of others: that there would be no possible way of completing this train journey in these conditions without contracting something, meaning I was effectively already ill, meaning in turn that, in a strange sort of way, I could relax.

I had a window seat at a table of four. The man in front of me, whose knees were pressed against mine beneath the streaked and scarred Formica of the table top, had squeezed himself in without removing his coat. His forehead and face were now glossed with sweat. From a brown paper bag he was clutching in his lap he removed a steaming, meat-filled pasty, which he began to devour so feverishly that it was difficult for him to both breathe and protect his tongue from being burned. He inhaled loudly through his mouth with each bite, then panted out a humid, gamey vapour as he chewed, swallowing only when the food had been both macerated and sufficiently cooled. With each fresh bite and cooling exhalation, he sent another jetstream of beef and onion odours across the table, stirring in my stomach not repulsion, as would have been the case a few days ago, but a hunger so sharp it was almost violent. Suddenly, as that meaty scent mixed with stagnant breath struck my nostrils and zoomed along receptors to my brain, I recalled, in a great and almost overwhelming rush, all the things I hadn't eaten in days, and it was all I could do to restrain myself from leaning across the table and devouring not just the man's pasty but the hand that held it and probably a good deal of the arm to which the hand was attached. Afraid of being seen and judged by a fellow retreater, I had failed to buy snacks at the station. It would still be hours before I was home, before I could eat what I liked and exhale properly and let my stomach muscles relax, and even this would be but a temporary state before I was due back in the office, where I would be expected to hold yet another unnatural pose and paste yet another expression of submission across a face that felt less and less like my own.

I found myself thinking of the journey up, of my daily commute into the office, and of the series of commutes before that, seemingly long ago now, before everything changed and unravelled. During those journeys, I had chafed against my proximity to other people. Every cough, every hot blast of early morning, coffee-soaked breath, every sniff and snuffle, every manly nostril so casually excavated with a probing thumb, every fart-smell and armpit and sweating brow, had seemed a kind of insult, something to be borne, at best, in dignified, eyes-front silence, as if everyone was impure but me, as if everyone else smelled and coughed and perspired while I stood serenely amidst the crush with the scent of potpourri rising from my skin. Now, after the clinical, polished sanitation of the retreat, I revelled in the humanity. I wanted, quite suddenly, for all of us to smell together, eat together, sweat together. It bothered me that we were wearing clothes. Imagine the carriage, I thought, densely packed, overheated, poorly cleaned, and all of us naked inside it, pressed up to each other's skin. The image was not sexual; my lust was unrelated to libido. It was a craving for a different kind of contact, a recognition that all the things that repelled us about each other were all the things we had in common.

My seat carried the faintly greasy perma-warmth of public transport upholstery. I could sense everything it had absorbed: the back sweat, the damp crotches, traces of city rain. Across the surface of the lightly tinted window, I could make out finger marks, palmed streaks where, I assumed, children had erased crude drawings made in the condensation. Even as the scent of the now-obliterated pasty faded, the smell of cheap, unhealthy food was all around me, no doubt deep in the train's fittings and atmosphere. Stale crisps and cooling grease, a hint of vinegar, coffee. And through it all, each time someone activated the sliding door and broke the barrier between spaces, came the waft of the train's toilet, the commingled funk of mass defecation.

I ran my hands over the seat fabric either side of my thighs, feeling its coarse nap, trying to commune with the bodies that had touched it. I let my hands travel further, to the crevices either side of the cushion, those unseen creases storing the shed matter of people's passage. Under my fingers, I felt crumbs, chunks of bready rubble, beads of tissue paper – the ur-secretion of urban life.

I closed my eyes, imagined myself on a train empty of people but rich in the forensic detail of their presence. I saw myself curling round in my seat, bringing my legs up, leaning down until my face was as close to the central crevice as I could get it. At this magnification, the grime took on new life, became its own miniature city-scape. I imagined the magnifications beyond, those that couldn't be made with the human eye, picturing this humble crack into which tumbled the crumbs of civilisation as a bustling bacterial colony, with processions of bugs wending their way between sky-scrapers of discarded litter. Life! I thought. Teeming life! I opened my eyes again, checked the attention of my fellow passengers and, seeing that they were lost to their devices, their food, their slumber, licked the end of my finger and swirled it through this abundant, overlooked space, gathering hairs and crumbs and who knew what against the dampened skin, before lifting the finger to my mouth and sucking on it, feeling the transmission of all it had gathered, the movement of stubbornly indissoluble grains and fibres towards the back of my throat and up into my gums, from where, acting on reflex, my tongue tried to clear them, only to become entangled with a hair. I imagined myself kneeling, my face pressed as deep as I could get it into this fold where so much lived, something oddly thigh-like about the seat cushions as they pressed into my cheeks, inhaling and licking and drinking it all in. I was disgusted. I even retched slightly. But I was alive, more so than ever.

I took a bottle of water from my bag and washed everything down. My stomach, which by this point seemed full to the point of bursting, groaned, heaved, and then settled. I let my head fall back, my eyes close. I listened to the chattering hum of the carriage, the computer games and mobile phones and crackling wrappers and conversations about where people had been, where they were going. I felt the pulse of the rails beneath me. Everything, like the chanting and the subsuming, total pain I'd communed with in Chad's yoga class, was vibrating, throbbing at life's unique frequency. I felt caught up in the echo, absorbed, almost cradled. And then, quite suddenly, I felt exhausted, and I slept.

London came upon my senses like a glorious illness. You know you are there, I've always thought, even before you see anything of the city. It has its own atmospheric signature, its own distinct patina of grime. My lungs, my skin, sensitised by the retreat, welcomed this sense of return. I felt embraced by smog. I wanted to lift my cheeks to the sky and exfoliate in acid rain.

The Tube was incubator-hot. It was late in the day. Commuters carried the tentative solidarity of exhaustion, and again there was that paradox of togetherness. We knew that we shared something, yet looking up to confirm what we had in common was frowned upon. Instead, people lost themselves to their phones, their e-readers, or their inner lives, sitting with hands folded and eyes closed as the train hurled itself through the city's bowels. I looked straight ahead, at the blackness of the window, watching my form distort wildly in the curve of the glass. With a barely perceptible tilt of my chin, I was suddenly enormous, elephantine, my forehead stretched into a sinewy ribbon. Another adjustment, and I was foreshortened: all chin and hair minus a face.

At my stop, I stepped outside and felt again that sense of life around me, only now it seemed less to be teeming and more to be struggling. A homeless man sat with his head bowed and his hands cupped, shivering in a tattered sleeping bag. The owners of late-night off-licences and cafes stood in their doorways smoking, the bags under their eyes and the lines on their faces standing out in heightened contrast under the street light and the neon glow from their signs. Behind me, a woman was screaming into her phone, *You used to be fire, man, you used to be actual flames, and now look.* From the rolled-down window of a waiting car, weed smoke wafted out on a cushion of pillowy sub-bass and a man said something about my arse I couldn't quite catch. Above us, the stars were obscured, the street lights the jaundiced yellow of day-old urine.

Back home, still tingling inside and out from the detox, the deep flexing, the skin scrubbing, and the chill wind that had washed my face as I walked, I felt purged and purified and alone. I had been, in a very literal way, drained. There was little left inside me, and what clung to my skin was a record only of my last few hours:

the train, the walk home. I was used to a more thorough record, a sense of myself through time. Something about all that cleansing, I thought, all that peeling and purging, had reduced and exposed me. I was supposed to feel renewed. In a way, I did. But the rawness was unpleasant, queasy, as if a defensive membrane had been torn.

Few shops were open at that time. I'd had to make do with the all-night Turkish off-licence on the corner of my road. There, I had fallen on all the things I'd been denied. I bought three loaves of crusty, unsliced white bread, all of which, as was always the way with this particular establishment, were coated with fine shelf-dust. As well as carbs and wheat, I craved sugar, snatching up fistfuls of chocolate from the shelves beneath the counter while the old man who ran the shop looked on with a mixture of fascination and disgust. As I paid, I could feel him eyeing my body, as if he expected it to be different. Nothing triggers that special masculine recoil like an over-eating woman. I wanted to tell him I was correcting days of denial, months of scarcity before that. But at the same time I wanted to tell him nothing, to give as little of myself as possible. My focus was on consumption, not expression. I wanted to go home, lie on my rented sofa, and force white bread down my throat until I exploded.

And that was essentially what I did, practically collapsing into my flat, allowing my rucksack and coat and shoes to fall away behind me like shed skin, opening my arms so that my off-licence bounty could tumble onto one end of the sofa, and then sinking heavily into the remaining cushion space, letting my head fall back, closing my eyes, and feeling around for a loaf of bread. I tore off the wrapper, held the loaf up to my face to inhale its yeasty warmth, and then sank my teeth gloriously into its outer edge, feeling the initial resistance of the brittle, ageing outer layer, followed by the doughy, chewy welcome of the centre. I had been hungry before, many times. So many times, in fact, that each had simply bled into the next, until hunger was no longer an episode but a basic unbroken state that shifted in intensity but never truly diminished. I had grown used to it, learned to live around it, until for the most part it joined the background noise of bodily experience filtered out by the conscious brain: the flow of blood through veins, the churning work of the intestines. This, though, the hunger that followed a total purge, was different. My body felt not so much ravenous as enraged, affronted, shocked. Something had been taken from it, it seemed to think, and it would do anything to replace what was lost.

Ordinarily, I would have showered. In the time since I'd started work, I had fallen back into old luxuries and routines, scrubbing the day and the city from my skin when I returned home, steaming the fatigue from my muscles. Now, though, a reversal had taken place. The memory of the train, of the grubby gap between the seats, the slightly greasy feel of the upholstery, the incubated culture of the atmosphere, still clung to me, and I didn't want to be rid of it. If anything, I wanted to thicken it. As I ate my bread, I felt that thin layer of dust, no doubt made up at least partially of exhaust fumes from the street outside the shop, adhere to my fingers. I ran the bread bag over my hands, taking up as much of that fine substance as possible, and then I ran my hands over my face and up through my hair, revelling in the contact with something worldly.

I stayed up late into the night, or early into the morning, feeding myself and staring without engagement at the television. My discomfort with human narrative was still strong; only the Nature Channel seemed tolerable. I ate and watched, ate and watched. Great white sharks knifed into view out of oceanic gloom. A killer whale reared out of the surf and snatched into its mouth a flapping baby seal. In steaming Amazonian jungle, ants flowed over the bark of a tree, enacting their sinister ritual of consciousness. Somewhere above, birds, guided by magnetism, moved south, sleeping on the wing, oceans and earth scrolling beneath them. And I sat in the middle of it all, a human woman on her sofa, gorging on foodstuffs foraged from her own nocturnal habitat. Drifting in and out of sleep, the LCD glow lighting the backs of my eyelids, dream and television merged. I became an alligator in an African river, torpedoing out of the red-brown rapids and closing my jaws around a sipping gazelle. I became a blind earthworm, plucked from the ground by a robin's beak. I ate and was eaten. I inhabited and was parasitically possessed. When I snapped to, crick-necked against the sofa's arm, it was early dawn, and orang-utans were picking fleas from each other's fur. I felt swollen and pained. My belly seemed enormous. I stumbled, over-fed and under-rested, to the toilet, but when I sat on the seat with my head in my hands and waited for movement, nothing happened. My digestive system was still locked up tight.

The rest of the day – a bank holiday – was agony. My body, shocked first by famine and then by flood, refused to relinquish what it had stored, and yet I couldn't stop eating. I staggered to the off-licence and restocked. The old man looked at me as if he could see my body growing before his eyes. My clothes felt unbearably tight and so, back home, I took them off and lay naked on the sofa, eating and observing the natural world, writhing in the painful tension of my own skin. Would it be possible, I wondered, to eat until I ruptured? I had heard such things could happen, but it would take, surely, more foods than bread and cheap chocolate. Meat would have to be involved. The moment I thought this, I craved flesh. I went back to the shop, by this time clutching at my stomach, and bought two fistfuls of heavily spiced salami and preserved sausage, which I devoured while flying squirrels soared from tree to tree in Borneo and a monitor lizard killed a gecko with its festering spit. At some point, I knew, my body would remember that it needed to work. All I had to do was eat enough to remind it, to kick its processing functions back into life.

Late into that second night, after a day spent exactly as I had spent the night before, asprawl on my sofa with the natural world streaming in through my eyeballs and an ever-expanding medicine ball of undigested or semi-digested food at my centre, the dam burst. Midway through another crust of low-quality bread, I felt a great stirring and uncoiling in my bowels and the sudden arrival of scalding liquid at the inner edge of my anus. By the time I got to the bathroom, the process was already beginning. I sat on the toilet and felt it spool and sputter out of me: a great, writhing, frothing, foul-smelling serpent of shit. Wave after wave of contraction undulated through my abdomen until I was twisted on the toilet, reaching out and gripping the sink for support. The stench of what I produced was unholy. This was material that had been trapped inside me for too long, that had passed through the usual cycle of decomposition and entered some rare and extreme stage of reanimation. As it left me, I felt myself emptying, my stomach hollowing, my passages suddenly clear.

I have no idea how long I was on the toilet. An unusual length of time, I know that much. At some point, towards the end of the experience, I realised I was still holding my hunk of bread. In the sudden panic of evacuation, I had bolted into the toilet without putting it down, and then, through the physical ordeal itself, I had gripped it ever tighter in my fist, creating a densely mashed ball. Now that I had emptied myself, I was hungry again, so I took a bite of the bread, imagining that I could feel it replenishing the lost matter in my guts. Still chewing, I stood up and looked down into the toilet bowl. What I'd produced was glorious. My shit was so abundant, so strong, that it had formed a kind of cathedral or castle, a deep-brown edifice that rose out of its rust-coloured moat and tapered to a spire about halfway up the bowl. I thought about my days of detox – all those white walls and green glowing juices, the idea that my body had to be cleansed, that all our bodies had to be cleansed, and that we had to keep from ourselves and each other the aspects of our physiology that were unclean or ugly. I wished, quite suddenly, that I had been able to produce this shit in the dining room and yoga studio, the meditation space and well-swept dorm of the retreat. I wished I had been able to stand beside it, perhaps with faeces still dripping from my backside or running down my legs, and say, even as my fellow detoxifying women were recoiling from the smell, *I have produced something of great beauty and significance.*

In looking at what I had produced, I became aware of what had caused me to keep it to myself. Shame, I thought. Shame of shitting, shame of eating, shame of all the things my body did that were not beautiful. Look, I thought to myself, gazing at my magnificent sculpture of shit, at what shame makes you withhold. Look how ill that withholding can make you.

As if in tribute, and without any particular conscious or intellectual justification, I brought the wadded hunk of bread round to my backside, pressed it into the cleft of my buttocks, and drew it as firmly as I could across my anus to wipe myself. I felt the prickling shards of broken crust cutting into the soft skin, the slick glide of shit and dough. When I reached the peak of my sweep and brought the bread back up to my face for examination, I saw a complex spectrum of browns and creams dotted with the now-unnameable residua of all that I had consumed: green tatters of semi-digested plant-stuff; vivid red spangles of pepper or tomato skin; hard, bone-white flecks of ground-up nuts. I was unexpectedly enraged. I felt as if I were looking directly at my own reality, one that had been taken from me, obscured, denied. I thought of the menagerie of animals I had observed through my television. I thought of the teeming abundance of bacterial life right there in front of me. I thought of all that detoxification and denial, all that panicked purity and pointless struggle to be clean. And then, as a gesture, a statement, I bit into the shit-smeared bread and swallowed it down.

I remember being surprised that I didn't retch. Disgust is muffled by passion. I was, I can see now, looking back, in a heightened state. Was it anger? Idealism? Simple release? It was hard to tell.

Somewhere inside me, though, a condition of my existence had altered, and it was in that adjusted mode of being that I consumed both the mangled bread and the long-festered shit that I'd streaked across it. The texture was thick, slightly gummy. It pressed its way into the crevices between my teeth and had to be worked out with my tongue, at which point I could feel the detail of what I had consumed: the occasional sharp edge or ticklish, papery skin. Such was the power of the stench, I could not dissociate it from the taste, but I remember a surprising sweetness, a top note of honey or treacle that softened the acridity beneath. Once I had taken one mouthful, there was little reason to stop, and so I ate the whole piece of bread, standing there in my tiny bathroom, the miniature castle of faeces still rising up out of the toilet towards me. When I was done, I flushed the toilet, watching as the water first rose dangerously and then, having reached a sufficient weight, sank, pushing everything I had pushed out of myself down the U-bend and away, out of sight, forgotten except for two deep-brown streaks along the bottom of the bowl. I washed my hands, swilled my mouth with water, spat rusty fluid into the sink, and then returned to the lounge, perfectly calm, perfectly balanced. I watched some more television and then, soothed by the sensation of release, I felt the muscles around my eyes begin to loosen, my vision darken, until I slipped, peacefully and with deep relief, into a heavy, dreamless sleep.

How long I had slept when the nausea began I have no idea. Two, three, four hours at most. At some point, half-awake, functioning on auto-pilot, I must have switched off the television, because I came to in heavy darkness, the room silent save for the low rumble of my stomach. My exit from sleep was sudden, jarring. At first, I assumed a sound must have startled me, so I lay on the sofa listening to all the usual noises of the flat: the hum of the fridge, the occasional creak of a wall. Then I realised it had not been a sound at all but pain: a burning, wrenching discomfort that made itself urgently known in my stomach, just a little to the right of my navel, strong enough to make me draw my knees up to my chest and grit my teeth. With a great heave of my abdominal muscles, I felt the contents of my gut launch upwards, striking the back of my throat with acidic aggression. I clamped my hands over my mouth, swung my legs over the sofa, and half-ran, half-stumbled to the bathroom, where I stood over the toilet, gazing down into the depths that so recently had been filled with wonder. There was a brief pause, a suspended moment when I thought it might all have been a false alarm. Then, another whole-body heave that pulled me forward onto my tiptoes and forced me to reach out for the wall to steady myself, followed by a torrent of yellow-brown liquid studded with chunks of half-digested bread, only some of which I was able to direct into the toilet. It was scalding, solvent-like on the soft tissue of my mouth and throat. It hit the edge of the toilet bowl, the water, the floor, even the wall, with a wet round of applause, as if thrilled at its own arrival. The sight and smell of it, the taste and mucoid texture of it across my teeth and tongue, made me bring up more. My stomach turned concave with the effort. My muscles spasmed with tension and pain. So violent was the episode, so complete my body's efforts at purging itself, that I began to fear I would see in my vomit the bloody, fleshy streak of something living and vital. A scrap of my stomach lining, a gobbet of quivering intestine.

Feel it, I said to myself, just as I had in Chad's yoga class. *Feel it, feel it, feel it.*

That night, as I hauled myself in and out of bed for alternating bouts of nausea and rest, my feelings swung in tandem with my physical state. At times, as my body once again clenched and reject-ed everything that was inside it, I felt extraordinarily powerful, awed by the force with which I could purge myself of that which threatened to harm me. Then, almost simultaneously, I would feel insignificant, helpless in the face of my body's behaviour. In between episodes, I lay in bed and drifted in and out of consciousness, rocked by the slow, deep current of fever, until the bed and mattress fell away and I felt myself suspended, held aloft by my own bodily thermals as the heat inside me peaked, broke, peaked again. There was no limit, it seemed, to the extremes of experience my physiology was capable of engendering.

Slowly, exhaustion began to win out over my symptoms, and I lapsed into a terrifying sleep in which all sense of reality was lost and I was at the mercy of whatever my mind and organs produced. I became aware of movement in the bed – a melon-sized mass scuttling beneath the covers, the feel of something sharp and hard brushing against my skin. When I turned back the covers, an enormous, spiny arachnid greeted me. It had the exoskeleton of a crab, the hooked beak of a raptor, a rash of teeming eyes across its face. Exposed, it hunched into a defensive squat, and from its gaping beak sprang a sound like the screech of steam through joints. Then, screaming, it sprang, launching itself with vile speed at my face. I lashed out, struck it, sent it clattering into the wall, only for it to tense, hunch, spring again, hurling itself towards me, its legs scrabbling and scratching, its carnivorous beak wide and searching. I kept hitting it back, harder and harder, until finally I pinned it to the bed, where it squirmed beneath my hand, legs cycling wildly, beak snapping at the air, its screech rising in pitch and volume as I crushed it. Its outer skin was the texture of perished plastic. My thumb went clean through its chest as if I were breaking open a chocolate Easter egg. Inside, it was hollow. I kept punching and tearing until it was in pieces, its limbs disassembled across my bed, and then I sat back, spent and panting, unable to look at the remains.

Gradually, I became aware of a strange sensitivity on my forearm, the rawness of newly healed or exposed skin. Looking down, I saw a ragged, coin-sized hole between my ulna and radius. It didn't bleed, merely hung open, the skin around it the wormy, curling texture and vivid pink of mince. I thought: *It has bitten me.* But then I looked at the splay of skin, its outward bloom. The spider had grown inside me, I realised, then chewed its way out.

I woke with a vicious, whiplash jolt. When I touched it, the skin on my forearm was sensitive, almost painful.

'Harrison,' said Harrison, after two rings.

'It's Maya.'

I was sitting on the sofa, wrapped in two duvets, my mobile propped on the cushion beside me.

'Maya,' he said. 'You must be feeling amazing. Are you feeling amazing?'

'I'm feeling horrendous.'

'Hm.' He sounded casually perplexed, as if his computer had done something unexpected but ultimately irrelevant.

'I can't stop being sick,' I said. 'I have diarrhoea. I can't eat anything. There's no way I can come into work.'

'You know what this probably is? It's probably the detox. Like, this is the detox, right now. I mean, no, this has not happened to anyone else, but at the same time we've never sent anyone else with your . . . background . . . on one of the detox programmes before. I mean, it stands to reason you're going to be way more toxified than anyone else, right? The detox probably started the process, and now your body is finishing it. It's probably actually really good this is happening.'

'So I can stay home?'

A sharp, rhythmic click became audible. Harrison, I guessed, was tapping his pen against his two front teeth. Briefly, I wondered if he was communicating to me via Morse code, if in fact two completely separate and perhaps even contradictory conversations were being carried out at once.

'I'm thinking this is something your body just needs to, like, *do*,' he said. 'So yeah, stay home. We can call it a personal development day.'

'Why don't you just call it a sick day?'

'Because I don't think you're sick, Maya. I think you're developing. And I think that's great. That's what we *want*. If I tell the staff you're sick, they won't know how much you're developing right now.'

'It's going to take more than a day, Harrison. I'm developing from one end or the other every ten minutes.'

Harrison made a noise that was somewhere between sympathy and disgust.

'OK. No need for further detail. Take the rest of the week.'

'OK.'

'Maya.'

He sounded suddenly less flippant. I braced myself for his reprimand, his inevitable warning about making absence a habit.

'Yes?'

'Do you need a doctor? Because we can get you a doctor.'

'No, Harrison. I'm OK.'

'If at any point you're not OK, I want you to tell me, OK?'

'OK.'

I hung up the phone and sank back onto the sofa, closing my eyes and watching the play of lights across the backs of my eyelids. It was as if my brain was sparking: little neon flashes firing in one temple and arcing across to the other. The conversation had infuriated and depressed me. I heard myself saying again, *So I can stay home?* I felt again the fear that had risen inside me in expectation of Harrison's annoyance, heard my voice as I'd modulated it into passivity, apology. Like a child, I thought, a pre-teen skipping school and begging their parents to be left in bed, I was reliant on Harrison's sympathy, his lenience. When had it come to this? When had I begun to need permission to shit, to be sick, to rest? In the early days of having nowhere to live, I had done a lot of asking, sought a lot of permission, at times even pleaded. Then at some point I had given up, stopped asking, started simply living. Now, here I was again, begging the boss-daddy for the all-clear to be unwell.

My rising anger made me sick again. By this point being sick was like breathing, and shitting was just another background bodily function. Every convulsion of my abdomen allowed my rectum to drop its guard, meaning that every mouthful of vomit was accompanied by another spurt of hot, foul liquid from the other end. The only option was to sit on the toilet being sick into a saucepan, feeling myself turned inside out by each fresh wave. In my depressed and weakened state, I wondered: was this rock bottom? After a year without a home, without money, without food, was this really where I was going to find my nadir – in a warm flat with every amenity and a job waiting for me when I was well? Or was this simply the bottoming-out I'd pushed away all that time, the ocean floor of misery I'd always refused to look at for fear of drowning? But why now? Why here?

Temporarily void, I returned to the sofa and un-muted the television, which had shifted its attention from the abundance of the animal kingdom to endless drone footage of our eroding natural realm: a glacier the size of a village melting into the ocean, swathes of forest shaved from the flesh of the land. The voiceover was grave, sonorous. *Go to your kettle*, it said, *set it to boil. By the time it does, another species will be dead.* This was the headlong era of the human. Death, destruction, madness on a planetary scale. Would it matter if I ever got well? In the end, weren't all of our individual ailments little more than atomic elements in the wider terminal malaise?

I thought about the retreat: the yoga, the juices, the desperate detoxification and deforestation of our bodies. All those white surfaces; all that jarring peace. It was mad, I realised now, a lunatic endeavour. All these fragile, fleeting people, purifying and protecting themselves while right outside the window the sickness was total, the world homicidally impure. Everything we had constructed was crumbling. It should have been liberating. There would never again be anything to lose. And yet here we all were, boxing ourselves in, applying ever-tighter restrictions to our lives, desperately seeking calmness, equanimity, purity, some extreme and unattainable ultimate health in the face of all-consuming death. I had known these things before, dimly. All of us know these things. But now, in the heightened reality of dehydration and fever, it was as if the mirror world of illness in relation to which our lives of illusory health are merely a shadow had opened out, revealed itself to me, and I no longer simply knew the truth but *felt* it. Upcoming tropical storms and hurricanes, an unseen tsunami swelling in the outer reaches of the ocean, a rising heat in the atmosphere: I could sense the immanence of these events on my skin. The hairs on the back of my neck prickled with catastrophe. The waters of my body pulled inexorably and tidally towards the apocalypse.

On the television, terrified deer fled the red-hot ferocity of a forest fire. For perhaps the hundredth time, I felt my intestines writhe and spasm. There was nothing left in me to come up or out, so I sat where I was and let it happen: a thin, white-hot spaghetti-strand of bile extending slowly from between my lips and down onto my lap; a last thimbleful of watery shit soaking into the crotch of my jogging bottoms. I lay back, soaked in myself, immersed in my own odours, and laughed. I had figured it out. No-one wanted to smell my shit. No-one wanted to wipe my vomit off their clothes. They would *pay me* to stay away. This was the only condition in which I could be expected neither to work nor to belong.

Feeling beneath me with my fingers, I found my phone and held it above me, pointing down at my face. With the front camera engaged I could see myself in washed-out, over-exposed light: grey-skinned and red-eyed, my face glistening with chilly sweat, my hair matted to my head. I snapped a picture, posted it to Instagram. *Ill!* I wrote in the caption.

Later, I would wonder about that exclamation mark, what it expressed and what it signalled – frustration, or, as I came to believe, triumph, jubilation, joy in the face of everything that ailed me and set me free.

n the unsteady wake of my fever dream, the energy required to
sustain the fantasy that all was well had been depleted. Now I was
left to stare at my life unfiltered. I had a job, but I couldn't be sure
what it was. I had money, but its source was unclear. I performed
tasks without thinking, took money I couldn't trace, came home to
a flat that wasn't mine.

As if to remind me that my sickness wasn't mine either, Harrison
texted me to say he'd gone ahead and booked me a GP appointment. *Better safe than sorry*, he said – he needed me in optimum
condition. I wondered if he'd talked to Ryan and Seth, if certain
health and safety concerns had been raised. I texted him back to
say I was fine. He replied saying in that case my meeting with the
doctor would be swift.

Going out for the first time after my illness felt like slipping back
into old clothes and finding they no longer fit. The daylight seemed
unnaturally bright, the air unexpectedly cold. My legs, after just a few
days in bed or on the sofa, felt awkward, weak. I had to concentrate
on walking, pay close attention to crossing the road. It was as if I'd
become suddenly aware of the ever-present low-level difficulty of life,
the minute-by-minute challenges the body and mind surmount.

When I arrived at the doctor's, it quickly became clear that my
appointment time was notional at best. The waiting area teemed
with life both human and microbial. There must have been at least
ten children, all in various states of health, wiping miserably at their
running noses, or flopping lethargically in the arms of their frayed

and under-slept mothers. Three were crying gently, holding their ears or throats. One was wailing and looked distinctly feverish. Dotted among them were the suffering adults: an elderly man who held himself perfectly still and flinched whenever anyone passed; a young woman encased in scaly eczema. I wondered why Pict hadn't stumped up for private healthcare, given their commitment to expensive wellbeing. Then I realised it was probably the same awkward attempt at balance as that which had resulted in my sub-par flat: just enough help to progress; not so much that it might alienate my audience.

I found a seat towards the centre, squeezed between a middle-aged man with a pronounced tremor and a young mother clutching a red-welted child. Opposite me, a woman of around my age was reading a glossy but well-handled women's magazine she'd evidently plucked from the sad-looking selection on a low table between us. She was, I thought, the calmest presence in the whole waiting area. She was not only reading the magazine, it seemed, but annotating it. Every few seconds she'd pause, tilt her head, then run her pen over a particular paragraph.

Later, I would ask myself what exactly it was about her that seemed so commanding. Perhaps it was the way she appeared in such stark contrast to her surroundings, unfazed by the litany of misery around her. Or perhaps it was her focus – the way that not even a child screaming in discomfort directly to her right seemed in any way to distract her from her task. Or maybe it was the task itself, in which she was so absorbed. She read that magazine like a student, a researcher. Where other people in the room – those that had even bothered to pick up a magazine and were not simply scrolling through pictures on their phones, or trying to placate their children, or staring, slightly dead-eyed, at the wall in front of them – turned the pages with an air of distracted disinterest, she pored over what was in front of her, and the marks she made with her pen were not mere doodles but firm, careful notes. What, I wondered, was she finding of such interest? It was almost as if her absorption was as contagious as whatever airborne viruses were no doubt flying around the waiting room. I wanted to share with her the object of her attention, perhaps even *be* the object of her attention, and at the same time inhabit that attention itself, feel its response to what it saw.

I tried not to stare, made an effort not to angle my head too obviously as I attempted, and failed, to see the front of the magazine in which she was so engrossed. My gaze felt slightly shameful, intrusive. I worried that the heat of my interest might raise the temperature of the air around her, causing her to look up, seeking the source of the atmospheric disturbance.

To break what now felt like an uncomfortable connection, I checked my phone. To my surprise, my virtual world was as filled with illness as my real one. My sickness selfie had proved surprisingly popular. People had posted get-well messages, pulsing hearts, recipes and traditional remedies for managing fevers and nausea. They'd also shared their own experiences of illness, discussing lupus, Lyme, IBS, lactose intolerance, migraines, depression, chronic fatigue, fibromyalgia. When I clicked on the hashtags they used, a whole community of the unwell unfolded before me: *#sosickright-now, #struggling, #lowday.*

At the far end of the waiting area, a door opened and a patient was shown out of the doctor's office by the man who was now my GP. I put my phone away, expecting him to call my name, but instead he simply smiled and nodded at the woman opposite me. When she stood up and began to walk, I saw that it was with some degree of difficulty. The shift from sitting to standing was not, it seemed, an unthinking movement for her. It required her to take it slowly. Once upright, she closed her eyes for a few seconds and steadied herself against the arm of her chair, as if dizzy. As she walked towards the doctor's surgery, she occasionally put her hand out to the wall.

After all that studying and note-taking, all that dedicated underlining of key passages, I'd assumed she would slip the magazine into the little rucksack she had with her. Instead, she'd tossed it casually onto the table with all the others. After she'd disappeared with the doctor, I stared at it, strangely excited. I was desperate to look at it, terrified that someone else would pick it up. But at the same time, as is always the case when you've paid too much attention to a stranger, I imagined I could feel the same level of scrutiny applied to me, as if the other patients in the waiting area were watching to see what I did.

With an air of what I hoped was almost disdain, as if after sitting here for a few minutes I had reached the absolute limit of my tolerance for being denied distraction, I reached down to the coffee table and slid the magazine towards me. It was called *Optimum You*. The cover featured a slim, blonde white woman wearing a pale-pink vest running her hands through her hair while standing in a cornfield. She was attractive, but the magazine was coy. Her nipples and skin had been airbrushed into eerie smoothness. Around her, the headlines of the various articles had been typeset so as to look handwritten. *Fifteen Days to a Whole New Body* was the top feature, followed by *It's Like Waking Up from a Bad Dream: My Journey from Anxious Shut-in to Glowing Extrovert*, and *The Prison Workout: The Latest Craze Taking the Fitness World by Storm*. Inside, I found, were more women in fields, interspersed with women in overly spacious, overly lit homes. There was a lot of decking, several hammocks, an assortment of reclaimed vintage furniture. Between the photos of women were photos of the things the women were eating: platters of quinoa and beans, full-spectrum salads, bowls of brown rice topped with a scattering of seeds.

I leafed through, trying not to look as if I was being too specific in my search. When I got to the *New Body* feature, I found what I was looking for: two closely annotated pages, the notes running down both outer edges of the spread in precise, unusually small handwriting. Even the article's central image was annotated, with sharp lines running out from the face and body of a beaming woman towards further notes and comments. Between the under-linings, the notes, and the annotations attached to the picture, the woman who'd been sitting opposite me had filled every available inch of space the spread allowed. Where there was insufficient room for what she wanted to say, she settled, it seemed, for erasing what had been said already, pressing down hard with her pen so that the ink completely obscured the print beneath.

Beyond the sheer physical force of her writing, what intrigued me about her notes was that they were not, as I had at first assumed, notes to herself, but messages. Sometimes she seemed to be addressing the person who picked up the magazine after her, and sometimes she seemed to be addressing the author of the article, the magazine itself, or the entire industry and ideology behind it. *Ridiculous body image*, she had etched beside the photograph accompanying the text, *almost obscene; maintained through violence*. Drawing a line from the glowing woman's head to the blank space of the layout's gutter, she had written, *bleached/peeled/lifted*. Across the woman's exposed stomach, the words creeping off the woman's skin and onto her vest like a mutating tattoo: *lipo'd/stapled/tucked*. Under the headline: *Idea of the new you begins with the idea that the current you is inadequate. Are you inadequate/faulty/defective?* Several times, she had responded to the article as if fact-checking it, writing simply, *data?* or *source?* or sometimes, when the article addressed an issue of which she clearly had knowledge, *false*, or *discredited*, or *disproved*. Then, under a particularly egregious paragraph that presumed to describe, with a disdain only thinly masked by paying lip service to sympathy, all the ways that the reader of the article almost certainly felt guilty or miserable or lacking in self-worth as a result of their inability to fully commit to the transformation the article took it as read that they longed for, she seemed to step in for the imagined reader, addressed by the article in the second person, and speak directly back to the author, writing, *Are you proud of your part in the misery industrial complex/eroding self-worth in others/in me/profiting from the self-pitying results?*

I closed the magazine and dropped it back onto the coffee table, no longer bothering with my earlier charade of nonchalance. I felt shaken, unsettled. The annotations seemed both to address me and to speak on my behalf. Things I had loosely considered had been stated in firmer form than I would have said them. And yet, at the same time, the very existence of those notes in the magazine's margin seemed to me to be as accusatory as the article itself. On seeing the annotations, I felt a deep relief that they existed, but I also felt strangely shamed. Why had I never written such things in the pages of a magazine? Why had I simply read similar articles in disgust and then moved on? And why did this woman, whoever she was, feel able to add her perspective to the white space around the all-too-familiar perspective of someone else? Who, I asked myself, looked at the void around paragraphs in a glossy magazine and saw in them not blankness or unused space but a canvas, a gap into which she could confidently step?

The moment I thought this, I understood the source of the unease, the discomfort I'd felt on seeing those deeply gouged words filling the spare and unnoticed space on the magazine's page. It stemmed, I thought, from familiarity, and what was familiar to me was not so much the words themselves or the ideas they expressed as the space those words so confidently occupied. If I pictured that page as a city, the paragraphs as buildings, the blank guttering and wide white margins as alleyways and side streets and the shadowed doorways of disused property, then I saw not the unfamiliar scrawl of a woman I'd observed for mere minutes across the hallway of a doctor's office, but a woman I had once myself been. I had lived in those very spaces. The magazine was the world. Her writing was my body.

At this point the doctor's door opened and the woman, moving with more assertion than when she'd entered, stepped out. I found myself standing up, meeting her gaze. As she came closer, I extended my hand. Her eyes narrowed slightly, fading out our surroundings so that she could examine me in isolation. I felt subjected to a critical scan, as if I were undergoing the same cynical appraisal as those dreadful paragraphs in the magazine. I saw her gaze drop to the magazine on the table, noting its new position. And then I saw her smile slightly, nod, and extend her hand in turn. As I grasped it, just I was noticing its eerie heat and slightly urgent dampness, the doctor appeared behind her, calling my name once and then, when I didn't answer, a second time, adding a note of impatience at having to repeat himself. I tilted my head, looked past the woman whose hand was still enclosed in mine.

'It's OK,' I said to the doctor. 'I no longer need the appointment.'

Her name was Zelma, she told me as we left the doctor's office and began to walk down the street, neither of us quite sure where we were heading. She visited the GP often, though left with little relief. She had, over the past few years, developed symptoms, but as yet there was no diagnosis. Without a clear cause, there could be no definitive treatment. The word *psychosomatic* had cropped up a lot, she said disdainfully.

'It's not just me, though,' she said. 'There are forums. There's even a meet-up.'

I sensed she was used to managing the scepticism of others. There was a forthrightness to how she spoke about her illness, almost a sense of challenge, as if she were daring me to undermine or ridicule her. When I asked her what sort of symptoms she experienced, she reeled off a list: vertigo, tinnitus, weakness in her limbs, a sensation like rushing water over her skin, a conviction that things were crawling in her hair and over the backs of her arms, an excessive sensitivity to clothing, strange rashes, shortness of breath, nausea, an inability to get warm, sudden rushes of heat, wild thirst, an aversion to cooked food, black-outs, racing panic, anhedonia. Sometimes she couldn't get out of bed. Sometimes she searched in vain for the stillness required for sleep. Other days she was completely fine, or better than fine – abuzz. But then she'd feel herself slowly deplete, and the cycle would begin again. She used to work, she said, but she'd come to the conclusion that the only tangible advantage to being ill was not having to engage with paid employment. She'd spent a year battling with the Department for Work and Pensions. Finally, they'd recognised her afflictions, awarded her benefits.

'What about you?' she said as we stepped out of the cul-de-sac that housed the doctor's office and joined the flow of life on the high street. 'What's your story?'

I wasn't sure what my story was, and told her so. Then I gave her the edited highlights: job, no job, no home, job, a kind of home.

'What job?' she said.

'Now? Or then?'

'Now.'

'I parse online content for suitability.'

'Meaning?'

'I scroll through thousands of images and censor kiddie porn, bestiality, and graphic violence.'

'Jesus,' she said.

I liked how she acknowledged the obvious shittiness of my job. No empty platitudes or rote positivity, no gossamer-thin assurance that things could always be worse.

'Would you like to get a coffee or something?' I said.

The question was a surprise to me. It came out quickly, almost urgently. I wondered if this was still my illness talking, if whatever it was I'd experienced in the toilet over the past few days was now not only taking over my thoughts and physicality, but my decisions too.

As soon as the words emerged from my mouth, though, I panicked, and filled the brief silence with stammered caveats and equivocations, telling Zelma she was probably busy, or on her way somewhere, or uninterested.

'Sure,' she said, her smile unforced, her voice easy where mine was stumbling. 'There's a place up here.'

We turned onto a narrow, quiet street primarily home to cafes, sandwich shops, and bistros. It was still early; everywhere was quiet. Zelma selected an unassuming Italian place with two little metal tables out front and led us inside, to a narrow, white-tiled establishment with pictures of fifties movie stars on the walls. We both ordered espressos and settled in at a little table towards the back. By this point Zelma was sweating profusely, her skin strangely translucent beneath its sheen of exertion. She poured tap water from a carafe, sipped it, began to breathe more easily.

'Tell me about the magazine,' I said.

She smiled, and I caught that flicker of slyness again. She was pleased with herself, I saw, but unused to expressing it.

'It's just something I do,' she said. 'My little rebellion.'

'Rebellion against what?'

'All that bullshit. All that dead time.'

'Dead time?'

'Waiting rooms, train stations, airports. All these places you're forced to kind of put yourself on pause. All those things that require like this muffled kind of attention or weird passivity.'

'Is it just magazines you do, or . . .'

'Could be anything. I've done cosmetics bottles, billboards.'

'Billboards?'

'Sure. If I'm passing, if it's quiet, if the billboard speaks to me and I want to say something back.'

I nodded, sipped my espresso. After days of nausea and curtailed consumption, it hit my stomach like acid. I winced slightly.

'You OK?' she said.

'Bad stomach,' I said. 'I've had it a few days. That's why I was at the doctor's.'

'You've missed your appointment.'

'Fuck it. Like you said: dead time.'

'Hey,' said Zelma, taking out her phone. 'Mind if I google you?'

'Oh God,' I said. 'I'd really rather you . . .'

But she was already tapping search terms into her phone, shooting me a quick, don't-be-silly look. The sensation was odd, unsettling. After a year in which no-one had been able to find me unless I wanted them to, I was now so visible that I could be summoned with a couple of thumb strokes. It was an achievement, I realised, that some people actually worked for.

'Wow,' said Zelma, scrolling. 'Pretty comprehensive publicity package.'

'They call it my Journey,' I said.

She deployed a pointed look. Half-joking, I asked her if there was a website I could use to get to know her. As if in answer, she laughed.

The conversation shifted, found its own course and rhythm. We talked politics, discussed our hatred of work and the seemingly insurmountable problem of money. Just as we'd established our similarities, though, she looked at her watch – a lurid pink Casio with jarringly Barbie overtones – and said she had to go, but that she'd enjoyed herself, and we should do it again. She tapped my number into her phone and sent me a text that read simply, *Zx*.

'Now you know how to find me,' she said.

From her little rucksack she took out a zippered coin-purse, the contents of which she shook into her palm for scrutiny. As she picked through her change, I noticed there was nothing of any significant denomination, just grimy silver she poked into little piles. I watched her lips move as she counted, remembered again my father and his hopeless five-pound notes.

'I've got this,' I said, laying my fingers briefly over the money in her hand.

She looked awkward, seemed about to object, but then smiled.

'I'll get the next one,' she said.

Then she kissed my cheek and was gone.

From the moment I returned home, the urge to call her was matched in strength only by my fear of what she'd think if I did. I'd lost the habit of connection, I realised. The art and etiquette of reaching out, the social and emotional choreography of emergent friendship, was obscure to me. I wondered if I was still ill. Only that morning, I'd noted the weakness in my muscles as I dressed; the slow, centrifugal spin of my brain as I showered and made breakfast. Was I still feverish? Perhaps the whole afternoon had been a kind of heated delusion. Not the actual meeting, of course – that, I knew, had happened – but the sense of significance, the *thrill* of it.

After a couple of days in which I prevaricated, opened a blank text message, tapped out a greeting, deleted it, Zelma took the matter out of my hands, calling one evening around ten, her voice easy and natural despite the potential oddness of calling a near-stranger at a late hour. She said she was wide awake and wanted to walk somewhere. When I asked her where to, she said anywhere, around, wherever. In the weeks that followed, I would come to understand that when she was well she liked to walk, and liked in particular to wander the city at night. It helped her feel out of time, she said, out of the current.

She lived, I gathered, in Stratford. I rode the night bus to meet her, and instead of arranging a spot to find her she told me to text her my bus route so she could join me. We sat on the top deck and watched late-night East London drift casually by while around us the air was thick with mobile phone conversations, chiming alerts, drunk young men throwing scraps of takeaway food into each other's mouths. Zelma said that what always struck her about these journeys was the number of people who made them for work rather than pleasure. Exhausted construction workers with their backpacks and battered lunch boxes, drinking a can of cheap beer on the way home; red-eyed professionals in their crumpled, fifteen-hour suits. Later, she said, there would be a lull, and then, from as early as three or four, people would again be making their way to their jobs: cleaners, carers, nurses, airport workers – people sleepwalking their way to the graveyard shifts that sustained the city. She'd never been able to decide, she said, whether she preferred working days or nights. She had, for a time, worked nights in a twenty-four-hour shop. Her favourite feeling was walking home in the early morning, watching everyone else stepping out of their houses and beginning their day while she was heading for bed. But then there was a part of her that resented it, that felt as if work had been allowed to intrude into the most private, intimate part of her life. Nights were important, she said; they had to be protected.

It turned out that Zelma wanted to shop as well as walk and ride the bus. She liked, she said, the odd camaraderie of the open-till-late supermarket – its eerie hush and garish, strip-lit glow. She felt a kinship with those who shopped and ate and travelled in what for the rest of the city were interstitial or non-functioning hours. Revellers were excluded from her taxonomy. Drinking until four in the morning, she said, as we wandered the aisles with our shopping baskets suspended from the crooks of our elbows like the handbags of prim older ladies, was not the same as shopping at four in the morning, or walking, or seeing a film, or going to the gym. The party-goers and bar-hoppers liked to think of themselves as rebellious, but really they were as temporally conservative as everyone else – working nine to five, drinking six to twelve, staying out late on a Saturday, sleeping in on a Sunday. Time, she said, was a political issue. It was not possible to be subversive on someone else's clock. Real resistance involved stepping outside of things completely – buying moribund essentials at 3 a.m., jogging through streets choked with drinkers at midnight.

'What about friends?' I said, watching her throw an individual margherita pizza into her shopping basket. 'Doesn't your approach mean everyone has to be on your clock? Otherwise how do you see anyone?'

She shrugged. 'Who cares about people who aren't on my clock? And besides, when you keep odd hours you meet odd people.'

'You like odd people?'

'Exclusively.'

'But I'm not odd,' I said.

She looked at me sideways, smirking. In the shop's harsh glare, her skin was sickly white.

'Oh, but you are,' she said. 'You're very odd indeed.'

'How?' I said, but she ignored me, turning her attention instead to the pressing question of which margarine offered the best value for money.

I was glad her attention was diverted. I didn't want her watching me while I processed what she'd said. I thought about how I felt at work, the way I watched my colleagues' frictionless passage through modern life from a position somewhere on the sidelines. She was right. I *was* odd. Odd in the sense of being extraneous, surplus. Why could I not just say that to myself? And if I knew it, why wasn't I better at hiding it? Why did I wear it so casually, for even the most recent acquaintance to see? But then, I thought, Zelma's observation probably hadn't required any particular powers of detection. After all, here I was, shopping for groceries in the middle of the night with a woman I'd met just once, in the doctor's surgery, who I liked because she wrote in magazines.

She bought us each a Danish pastry, stale from sitting on the shelf all day, and we ate them as we aimlessly walked the streets. We talked about lights – about the growing vogue for bolder colours, especially along the river. Zelma said she liked it to be as dark as possible, with not only the city but the faces and bodies of people around her obscured in the gloom. She reminisced about what seemed to be a lengthy stretch of backpacking when she was younger, saying that in Nepal and many parts of India, each town or village has an allotted two- or three-hour blackout to balance the deficit in the grid. She remembered Kathmandu, she said, on Sunday nights, when all the power went out and shopkeepers lit the winding back alleys with candles and lamps. People's skin took on both a golden glow and an under-lit, horror-film glower, and the city seemed to slip out of reality completely, making itself strange even to people who'd lived there for years. It was how cities at night should be, she thought: eerie, evasive, not quite revealing themselves – filled with people fumbling their way through.

She felt safe at night, she said, when I asked. It was something else she saw as a kind of responsibility – women laying claim to cities after dark. She thought most of what women were told about their safety was a myth. All the wisdom seemed to suggest that it was being out in the evenings that put you at risk, that women were supposed to be careful, drink less, never walk home alone. But for most women, home was the problem. They navigated the city in total safety, came home, locked their front door securely behind them, and were murdered by the men they'd married.

'Maybe that's morbid,' said Zelma, licking sticky icing from her fingers. 'Anyway, tell me more about you.'

We had come to a stop in the plaza outside Stratford station. A few yards away, a group of boys leaned on their bicycles and exhaled skunk smoke while the tinny speaker of a mobile phone spat grainy, distorted grime. It occurred to me that I had not told anyone much about me for a long time. For most of the year before I went on the streets, my daily aim had been to reveal as little about myself as possible. I didn't want people to know how profoundly I was struggling, how difficult I found the very things that they seemed to find so unquestioningly straightforward. I spent a lot of time telling people I was fine, that things were looking up, even though I knew the situation was, by that point, dire. And then of course, on the streets, you're sparing with what you let people know. The people you talk to quickly disappear, taking with them the things you said. Perhaps guardedness was a habit I still held on to, or perhaps it had always been there, and the previous year had simply honed it. Either way, I didn't find myself any more forthcoming now. At work, I stared at my screen, deflected the occasional attempt at conversation. Ryan and Seth, for all their talk of narratives and journeys, weren't really interested in my past or my life beyond what pieces of it could be easily packaged up and posted online in the interests of swelling traffic. I was starting to wonder if there was anything to tell about me at all. The emphasis on my story had exhausted me. Meaning had become not something I experienced but something that was extracted from my life by others. I had nothing to tell Zelma about myself because I had nothing to tell myself about myself.

'I don't know what to tell you,' I said flatly. As I said it, I felt the prickle of tears in my eyes, and blinked quickly to stem the flow.

'Another time, maybe,' Zelma said, and rested her hand briefly on my thigh.

We sat quietly for a few moments, staring out in front of us, watching a low, small aircraft threading its way through thin cloud sickly lit by the spilled light of the city. Aircraft, both seen from below and experienced from the inside, made me lonely, though I couldn't say why. Something to do with distance, the implication of profound departure.

I asked Zelma if she'd always lived in London. She said she'd grown up in Oxford, then moved here when she was eighteen. She said she felt as if she'd always known she would live here, had assumed it somehow, and now that she did she tended to assume she would one day live somewhere else, but she didn't know where.

'I don't want to die in London,' she said, smiling. 'I don't think I even want to be old in London.'

'I don't want to be old, full stop,' I said.

'Oh, I do,' said Zelma. 'Once you're old, all bets are off. You can behave any way you like and people just write you off as eccentric. When you're young, you're supposed to be learning. When you're middle-aged, you're supposed to know better. When you're old, you're allowed to have forgotten.'

I shook my head. 'But at least when you're young people allow you the possibility of change. The reason no-one takes any notice when you're old is because they think that's it, you are as you are.'

'Better that than seeing you as some sort of work in progress that's just crying out for their contribution,' said Zelma, her tone suddenly sharper, a tension in her jaw. I wondered if she was talking about herself, or me, or everyone, the nameless semi-well on whose behalf she annotated exhortations to be better.

The mood had perceptibly altered. I worried that it was my fault, that my unexpected tearful moment had dragged Zelma along with it, into her own private fug.

'Sorry,' I said. 'The mood was light. I brought it down.'

She laughed. 'Oh, I do a perfectly good job of that myself,' she said. 'And anyway, who gives a shit? If we want to sit here and be down then let's sit here and be down. I can't stand these people who panic at the first sign of a complicated emotion.'

'I used to have this housemate,' I said, lifting my voice to shift the tone of the moment. 'Whenever anyone said anything serious, she made a joke. It was pathological. And then she'd obviously worry that the joke was inappropriate, so she'd try and cover that with another joke, until sometimes, if the mood was bad enough, she actually ended up giving a little performance, like, just clowning in front of everyone. She'd look so panicked that everyone would try and laugh, to cover the weirdness of the moment, but it would be really forced, and she'd feel how forced it was and panic more and then work harder to get everyone to laugh. It got so that no-one ever told her anything.'

'Must have been exhausting,' said Zelma.

'Who for? Her, or the people around her?'

'Both.'

I nodded.

'Fighting things off all the time is so draining,' said Zelma. 'But letting them wash over you is depressing.'

'I keep thinking,' I said, 'why can't I just go with things? Why can't I just do this job, do this project, take the money, spend it on things I like? I'd be so much happier if I wasn't *resisting* things all the time, trying to make them how I want them to be. Or . . . No, that's not even right. I don't *know* how I want things to be. I just know that nothing is ever how I want it to be.'

'Of course it isn't,' said Zelma. 'You didn't decide any of it.'

'But other people don't decide their lives either and they're perfectly happy.'

'You don't know that.'

'I know. I just . . . assume it.'

'Things are easier for other people, perhaps,' said Zelma. 'But not necessarily better.' She shrugged. 'That's what I tell myself, anyway.'

The conversation came to an end, but its resonance lingered. Zelma seemed content to remain in a given emotional atmosphere as need dictated, and I found this comforting. We sat still for a few moments, looking ahead, temporarily adrift in our own thoughts, yet at the same time aware of each other, alert to the ways in which our thinking might be similar. At almost exactly the same time, we resurfaced, blinking a little. We had finished our Danish pastries; there was no longer anything to occupy our hands. Although this had been the case for a few minutes, it felt suddenly awkward, as if our excuse for pausing to chat on the street had now disappeared. We both fidgeted, took a breath, smiled, and then laughed.

'Let's walk,' said Zelma.

I knew without asking that she didn't have a particular destination in mind. As she'd said before, she just liked to be out at night, a presence on the streets. It was one of her many pleasures, and one of her innumerable self-imposed responsibilities.

The high street was lined with smoking men – shopkeepers, cafe owners, men sitting at little round metallic tables, bantering in Polish or Russian. Up ahead, a group of five or six boys turned to admire the passing figure of a shapely twenty-something, covering their mouths, mock aghast at the sight. Further up, a homeless man sat with his forehead resting on his knees, his cupped hands held out in front of him, beside a sign that simply said, *God Bless*. Zelma reached in her shopping bag for a packet of biscuits, extracted a handful, and placed them in his hands. He neither moved nor looked up. We walked on.

'When you were homeless,' she said. 'Did you beg?'

'Sometimes,' I said. 'But I preferred to steal or scavenge.'

She nodded reflectively, mulling this over. 'I think I would too,' she said. 'And you know what? I think I'd be good at it.'

'You would,' I said. 'You've got the right kind of face.'

'What's the right kind of face?'

'Somehow endearing and intimidating at the same time. A face that could go either way.'

She laughed – properly, fully.

'I'll take it as a compliment,' she said.

After that my memory of the evening gets hazy. We found one of those rarified East End pubs that are all distressed armchairs and cocktails in Kilner jars. We had gin and tonics with slices of cucumber and I remember being unable to recall the last time I'd done this – got comfortable at a drinking spot and headed back to the bar repeatedly, not thinking or caring about what it all cost. I told myself I was redirecting the money Ryan and Seth had earmarked for furniture. Perhaps out of guilt, I Instagrammed a couple of my drinks and then laughed along while Zelma teased me. I can't remember what we talked about, but I remember that we talked a lot, that there was never a pause, and that it seemed difficult, suddenly, to fit in all the things we wanted to say. We had nowhere else to be, but the threat of leaving seemed ever-present and strangely oppressive, so we raced through the topics we'd tacitly agreed to cover, talking faster and louder, using our hands more and more. I remember that we both said *yes* a lot – not in polite agreement but in a declarative, ultimate way. There was a sense not only of haste but of finality, as if the things we said would be the last things that would need to be said. At some point we moved on, tired of overpriced, fussily prepared drinks. We found an old man's hangout round the corner and switched to whiskey. Zelma had a vocabulary for flavours, but when she used it she always mocked it afterwards, undercutting what she clearly saw as her own pretension, and we got on to talking about the difficulty of expressing enthusiasm or love for something without finding everything you'd said to be a cliché. We had an idea about reclaiming superlatives. Zelma talked about advertising, blurbing, quotes on film posters. She talked about how the language of disgust had grown ever more creative while the language of adoration had grown stale. And then we did that thing where we got self-conscious, where each of us worried that the other one thought we were over-intellectualising, and at the exact same time we each cracked a different joke, undercutting ourselves, and then we joked about that too. The pub emptied out around us. Things were woolly at the edges and people left a trail in the dingy room as they moved. There came a point where neither of us could drink any more, even though we both wanted to drink a lot more, and we talked about how you had to know someone really well before you felt you could be sick in front of them, and how, if we thought back over the friendships we'd had in the past, particularly those eerily powerful teenage 'best' friendships that define your life for a few years but then always end up the victim of geography and circumstance, being sick had frequently played an important role, because there had always been at least one night when one person sat with the other through some drunken or drugged-out episode, rubbing their back and holding some receptacle for them to vomit into, and the things that were said during those nights were always entirely distinct from the things that were said on any other night, when that kind of vulnerability was not on show. We talked about how great it would be to do that again, and then we agreed that it wouldn't be the same, that it wasn't something you could engineer, although we both also agreed that part of the intimacy of those moments came from spending a whole night together and seeing the sun come up just as you straightened out, because there are emotions that only surface at certain hours, and to see them in a person you have to be there with them right through to daybreak. As we were saying this, we were being led out, kindly and gently, by the landlord, and he was asking us if we would be safe getting home, and Zelma was saying that it was other people walking home at night who should be afraid of us, not the other way round, because in that moment we felt not only invincible but dangerous, primed for something. And then we linked arms and walked round the corner to a side alley that stank of distinctly masculine urine and rotting food and pissed together, side by side, squatting with our backs to the wall and our jeans round our knees, laughing as our urine bled into a single steaming stream and disappeared down a crack in the base of the brickwork.

We couldn't work out how to get home. We stared at bus time-tables blankly. I tried to use an app on my phone but I couldn't understand what the map was telling me and ended up just turning on the spot, pointing my phone ahead of me in bafflement at my own location, until Zelma said that if we just walked in any direction we would eventually work out where we were.

The cafes and shops were now shuttered and dark. The city felt unwatched, unsupervised. Some would have said it felt unsafe, but these were London hours to which we were both, though perhaps for different reasons, accustomed. We bought chips wrapped in flat-bread from a Turkish takeaway. Zelma added both mayonnaise and ketchup to hers. Somehow, we had remembered her shopping bags, and in our drunken state we struggled to hold the bags and walk and cram food into our mouths at the same time, ending up with smears of grease and off-brand condiment slicked across our cheeks and lips and clinging to the tips of our fingers. About halfway down the street, at a bus stop from which no useful bus seemed to run, Zelma came to a halt and stared at an advertising poster that had caught her hazy attention. It showed a woman near-bionic in her airbrushed bodily perfection, wearing skimpy workout shorts and a cropped sports top. Her abdominal muscles, rippling and oiled, looked like independent life forms possessed of agency. I imagined them sliding around beneath her tightened skin, subdividing like bacteria and making their own sinister decisions. Her hair was long and wet, her face jewelled with rain or sweat or perhaps water poured over her head from the bottle she held in her right hand. She was standing with her legs apart, her arms down and slightly spread. Her knuckles were taped as if she'd been boxing. Beneath her, in a hyperbolic font of lurid yellow, a narrative of aspirational second-person misery unfolded. *You get up at dawn. You do sprints in the dark until your chest feels like it will explode. You're the first one into the office, the last one out. You can party with the best of them, but not before you've shattered your PB in the gym. You get by on five hours of sleep. Then you get up and do it again.* At the bottom was the logo for a brand of sports drink.

'You read it and think it's a warning,' said Zelma. 'Then you realise it's supposed to be something to aspire to.'

She put her shopping bag on the floor, reached into her purse, and pulled out a Sharpie. Without bothering to look around to see who might be watching, she began, in an unsteady, unfocused scrawl, to annotate the poster the same way she'd marked up the margins of the magazine. She drew bags under the woman's eyes, and on her forehead listed the side effects of sleep deprivation: *loss of memory, loss of focus, poor decision making, a feeling that everything is hopeless and unmanageable.* On her shoulders and limbs, she listed muscular injuries, strains, zones of physical disintegration. Across her stomach, she enumerated the symptoms of hunger: *a gnawing pain, irregular periods, a feeling of nausea when you think about food.* Then she dipped her fingers in her ketchup, bloodied the woman's lips, and adjusted the water bottle so it looked like the woman fed on someone else's haemorrhage. I took a picture but didn't post it to Instagram. It was the first picture in a long time that I'd taken just for myself, because I wanted to mark or remember something rather than communicate it.

Somehow we found a bus stop from which I could get home. Zelma said she would walk a little more, maybe even walk all the way back to where she lived. She hugged me before I got on the bus, said we'd be seeing each other soon. She wasn't asking, I remember, and I didn't bother to agree in the usual polite way. It was a simple statement of fact – something we both knew to be true. On the way home I sat on the top deck with the ventilation windows open and breathed deep, drinking down cold air and diesel fumes and listening to the rising groans of a waking city while across the aisle a woman bearing all her clothes in five tattered shopping bags fashioned a roll-up from a till receipt and then lit it with a conspiratorial wink.

Back at work, I got fast with the photos. I began to feel as if I was no longer even seeing the images as images any more, just as mere data. In a way, this was reassuring. I no longer closed my eyes at night and replayed against the dark screen of my idling consciousness the worst of the day's sights. But my inability to recall specifics concerned me. Whether I had consciously registered them or not, those images had found their way inside me. Now they remained there, semi-dormant and malign. I feared a day when they would all rise to the surface in a single, unbroken stream. I would claw at my eyes, I thought, but it would do no good. All that monstrous humanity would be too deep inside me to be scratched away.

For the time being, though, boredom, not trauma, was my biggest concern. I felt as if my days were no longer my own. Before, I may not have had warmth and shelter, and often not even safety, but my time had been mine to fill, the city mine to wander. Now, I felt as if my pathways across the city in daylight hours were as prescribed as those sad, worn trails in the carpet and linoleum of my flat. Home to station, station to work. Reverse and repeat.

I came to know the faces of my fellow commuters – the saddest, remotest level of human intimacy. There was the floppy-haired thirty-something with his burdensome affectations – a battered waxed jacket, unlaced Dr Marten boots, an enamel cup of black coffee he kept tucked under his arm while he read the *Evening Standard*. There was the fifty-something Chinese man in a trim cagoule who every morning boarded the train eating two pieces of toast with a layer of scrambled egg between them. There was the mid-thirties Nigerian man who spent the duration of every journey messaging not one or even two but four separate women via a dating app. And then there was the school-uniformed mid-teen, pale, ill-at-ease with her own limbs, who frequently got on the train in tears and then, as the journey wore on, did her make-up, texted her friends, and eased her way out of whatever it was at home that caused each day to begin so badly.

Sometimes, I tried to see myself from their point of view. Always, I found I could not. I stole glances at myself in the steamed-up safety glass of the train window, but all I saw was a blurred out-line, as if the streaming city-scape on the other side of the glass was rushing not past me but through me, washing away every last trace of who I was.

The more I vanished, the less things stung. Time lost its fric-tion; the day passed in a glide. The slideshow of debasement felt less vivid, its incandescence muted. Then, on the train home, the vertigo of disappearance would catch up with me again. Some-times I would panic, pinch myself, speak randomly to the person beside me in order to bounce my existence off theirs. But for the most part I grew used to it, and understood it for what it was: a necessary evasion, a retreat.

I saw Zelma regularly, but not routinely. She called whenever she wanted to call, and I became comfortable doing the same. At two or three in the morning, unable to sleep, one of us would try the other, and most of the time we were successful. She liked to come round so we could watch TV together. I wasn't sure she had a TV of her own. Like me, she favoured rolling news and documentaries about the natural world. We'd buy snacks from the off-licence across the road, then curl up together under my duvet and watch humpback whales inexplicably massing off the coast of South Africa, or bus-sized chunks of arctic glacier shearing off into the warming sea.

Sometimes it felt like we were watching the world end, huddled there on my sofa, frightened and filled with doom, untouched and oddly invincible.

I never saw where Zelma lived. Early on, I suggested that I could come to hers, and she simply said that she would come to mine. She might not have meant to put me off the idea, but something in her voice and the speed of her response gave me the impression that she was embarrassed. She never mentioned flatmates or family. I always assumed she lived alone. When I pictured her, at the other end of a text or late-night call, it was in circumstances much the same as my own – a bedsit somewhere, a few simple possessions tucked into whatever space was available.

Sometimes, depending on when she'd come round and what we'd done and how much we'd drunk, Zelma would stay the night. We'd talk in bed until one of us fell asleep. Zelma was a bad sleeper. More than once, I woke her up because her kicking and thrashing made me think she was having a bad dream. She said she didn't really have nightmares, but that sometimes her body seemed to dream for her – cycling through all the physical reactions to an imagined threat while her mind remained still.

'Did you ever keep a dream diary?' she asked me once.

'No,' I said, thinking of that hollow monster in my bed, the ring of chewed-up flesh on my forearm. 'I used not to remember them, then for a while I didn't sleep well enough to have them.'

'I kept one for a long time,' she said. 'But now I don't have anything to put in it.'

'Now you write in magazines instead.'

She seemed to think about this for a moment.

'Yes,' she said. 'Now it's what I'm told to dream that concerns me.'

How she spent her time was a mystery to me. She was not, after all, working. She mentioned groups of one kind or another – loose political organisations, the occasional demonstration – but it was always with a slightly uninvested air, as if she simply went along for the time being, until something better presented itself. I knew that she sometimes volunteered at a local food bank, handing out parcels of provisions to the needy, but there must have been – or so I assumed – substantial stretches of time during which she was unoccupied. Something told me, though, that she found ways to fill her day. I saw Zelma in many different emotional states over the time that I knew her, but I never saw her bored, or at a loss. Quite the opposite: she seemed always to be occupied, sometimes to the point of distraction. Whenever we spoke, and she brought up a subject that had been on her mind or something she had read in the news, it would be clear that she had already thought about it, at length and in detail, and reached conclusions from which she would not be swayed.

One night, while on the television a bowerbird constructed a bejewelled and spectacular nest, I dipped my hand into a crisp packet and found it empty.

'*Nooo*,' I said, widening my eyes and play-acting panic. 'Tell me we're not out of snacks.'

Without saying anything, Zelma rolled off the sofa and slid her hand beneath its base, then kneeled up and explored the cushions, reaching deep into their recesses and coming up with a packet of peanuts.

'Emergency supply,' she said, hopping happily back onto the sofa and ripping at the foil with her teeth.

In the weeks that followed, when I was cleaning the flat or searching for my phone or keys, I came across all manner of secreted foodstuffs: a chocolate bar slid neatly between two books, a tube of Pringles wedged behind the television, little heaps of sweets in the corners of my cupboards. I always left them where I found them, undisturbed. I liked knowing they were there, these cached traces of her presence.

*

'What you have to understand,' said Harrison during my first appraisal, 'is that bodies are like dogs. They want to please, but they have to be trained. I'm thinking that this . . . whatever this recent illness was . . . was just your body learning, maybe even rebelling a little bit. What did the doctor say?'

'I didn't go to the doctor,' I said. 'By the time the appointment came up, I was feeling better.'

'Hmm,' said Harrison, making a little mark on a form he angled away from me.

His solution was to push harder: stiffer targets for my workflow, a more ambitious metric of what he called *image toxicity*. He was at pains to make it a question of personal development, rather than mere productivity. He also proposed an increased programme of detoxing and exercise, a class at least every other day, a food intake diary he could peruse at my next appraisal.

'The trick,' he said, 'is not to back off. You want to push *through*, not shy away.'

And then he smiled, did that half-squint by which he communicated sincerity. 'We can really make something here, Maya,' he said. 'We should be ambitious about what you can be.'

Meanwhile, Ryan and Seth were perceptibly upping the ante too. I was doing well, they said, during a meeting which was definitely not, they said, a meeting, but instead just a *check in*, and which, by virtue of not being a meeting, was conducted not in an office but in a coffee place round the corner from Pict. Like Harrison, though, they felt *well* was merely the jumping-off point for *amazing*.

'This is you week one,' said Seth, showing me an engagement graph with a gentle gradient on his tablet. 'As you can see, there's growth, but no fireworks.'

'But,' said Ryan.

'But,' said Seth, 'this is you sick.'

He swiped sideways on his tablet. The mild incline became a sharp peak.

'Hello,' said Ryan.

The numbers on the x axis meant nothing to me. The peak, however, matched my own experience of posting my ailing selfie: the sudden uptick in interaction and support, the rash of hashtags and emoji.

'Now, we're not going to pretend we understood this immediately,' said Seth. 'But I think we understand it now.'

Ryan nodded. 'If we're honest, we were kind of thrown by it. But in perspective? It makes total sense.'

'This,' said Seth, swiping over the graph and bringing up my sickened visage, 'was real.'

It turned out Ryan and Seth had done some focus-grouping. They'd engaged the services of experts and the results were clear: people were all for achievement, but achievement that came too easily was unrelatable.

'We fucked up,' said Seth. 'I mean, not badly, but I want to be honest here. We were like: sell people the dream.'

'And that was fine,' said Ryan. 'But it turns out people want more than just dreams. They want the shitty little life by comparison to which the dream seems dreamy.'

'When you posted this picture of you unwell,' said Seth, his sudden animation that of a man recounting a scientific breakthrough, 'people *got it* for the first time.'

'How does that feel?' said Ryan. 'Amazing, right?'

I wasn't sure how it felt, but I couldn't honestly say it felt amazing. A moment of honesty now looked like a gesture of strategic brilliance. I'd enjoyed posting the picture, enjoyed the attention that had resulted, but only because I had been, at the time, lonely and miserable, unsure of what I was doing. Now, whatever value there might have been to that moment seemed altered, blurred in the shifting gradients of Ryan and Seth's graphs.

I looked from Ryan's face to Seth's and back again, taking in their smiles, their raised eyebrows, the slight forward tilt of their postures as they leaned into what they imagined was their own discovery, and I knew that what they wanted was the exact same thing that Harrison wanted: more.

Three, sometimes four evenings a week, I started going to the classes Harrison recommended. Wellbeing in the city, it transpired, was a long way from the wellbeing to which I'd subjected myself at BodyTemple. There, the sense of space and light, the long stretches of peace, helped undercut the suspicion that money and time were being prised from people's grip. At the classes I was now enrolled in, there was no such illusion. Yoga took place in a heaving Soho sweat pit so densely packed that our mats touched. The teacher made a grand show of closing all the windows and turning up the heat so we could purge our toxins. Within minutes, the room acquired the dense humidity of an inhospitable jungle region. Afterwards, sticky with perspiration and pulsing with new frequencies of muscular agony, I would drape myself onto a seat on the Tube and will the journey home to be brief. In the morning, when I tried to swing my legs out of bed, my hips and knees would resist me, and I would have to pace the flat to unknot them.

In the mindfulness class, movement was not only not required, but actively discouraged, and with your eyes closed it was easier to convince yourself that you were experiencing something personal. But at some point, however successful the hour of guided meditation had been, you still had to open your eyes and confront a crowded room, dense with expenditure.

I was plagued by inadequacy. In yoga, I tried to hide every wobble and shake, every stumble, every moment of weakness during which I collapsed to my mat and rested with my forehead on the floor. In the silence of the mindfulness class, my self-consciousness was as heightened as my perception of sound and space. I began to feel as if every infinitesimal movement, every readjustment of my limbs or brief scratch at a passing itch was an admission of struggle. Throughout the class I would open one eye a thin crack and appraise the progress of others. When I encountered someone more fidgety than me, someone whose knees audibly creaked when they stretched them, whose awkward posture and repeated sighs marked them out as someone who was struggling, I felt relieved, perhaps even a little smug. When I became aware of someone who simply sat beatifically, breathing with an easy depth, a slight smile playing at the corners of their mouth for the duration of the hour, I felt only cynicism and resentment.

The women who attended these classes were a distinct group: twenty-something, outrageously slim, often tanned, with tattooed feet, wrists, and shoulders. They drank coconut water, snacked on dates, returned from trips to Goa and Thailand with cheap silver jewellery and hennaed hands. Once, they would have been called hippies: vaguely spiritual, alive to the shortcomings of Western life. Between classes, though, their talk was of work. They were employed in PR, in advertising, in media. They organised events, ran ad campaigns, swapped info on clients. It was as if a circle had been squared. Two once-opposed belief systems were no longer in tension. Greed and ambition no longer unbalanced your karma. The rat-race could be a source of peace.

The theme of both classes was to be OK with everything. If you weren't OK with something, you were supposed to let it go. If you couldn't let it go, you were supposed to work on letting it go. Reaching a place in your life where you didn't need anything would allow you to stop fearing anything. I thought again of that phrase, *let go*, with all its degrading associations. But I thought also about the things I now did because I felt I had to, or because I felt I wanted what came with them.

My feelings oscillated, bouncing from one mode or register to another in the space of a few seconds. Sweating, holding a plank position until my arms and abdomen burned, or half-squatting with my arms raised until my thigh muscles felt as if they would physically pull away from my bones, I would experience a sharp pulse of anger. We were making ourselves fitter, all of us, so that we could work more, finding a sense of peace so that our lives would enrage us less. At night, we would do our meditation and then sleep only so as to be able to function the next morning. Contrary to what my instructors advised, it was a feeling I was unwilling to release or soften. If I briefly, without really noticing, went a few hours without entirely hating my job, I saw not progress, but a frightening and unwanted erosion. If I curled up on my sofa and watched television and managed, for the duration of a nature documentary, to stop my stomach from flipping over in fear at the unknowability of my predicament, I saw it not as a well-deserved break from stress, but as a dangerous, perhaps fatal dulling of my instincts. It was, in many ways, a throwback to my previous life, when to remain tense was to remain safe, but it was also a reaction to the mindset I felt was being imposed upon me. The little flame of hatred that I felt flickering into life at odd moments was the only sensation I could be certain my employers were not nurturing within me in order to mould me into the person they'd imagined. Because I knew they would be suspicious of it, I knew it was mine, and so I felt that I had to shield it – even, at times, feed it. When it went out, I thought, it would go out for good. A part of me would go dark forever.

And yet, significant though my desire to protect all my feelings of resistance and scepticism and anger might have been, I found, just as I had found at BodyTemple, that beneath the noise of my determination to resist, another sound, another signal, could clearly be heard. When I sat cross-legged on a mat with my eyes closed, in a room full of breathing companions, concentrating on my breath or the space between my eyes, I *did* feel a sense of oneness, of wholeness; I *did* feel concerns and distractions and irritations fall away. I even felt, at times, a loosening of the boundaries by which I lived: my body and my sense of self; my self and the world through which my body and self moved. And in just the same way, when I was twisted into what should surely have been an unnatural position in a blazingly hot room full of other knotted and straining human forms, I felt I was using my body for the first time not merely as a technology for labour or a vessel for my feelings, but as a lever into experience, into *being*. I began to reach parts of my body I had not previously been able to reach, bend into shapes I had not previously been able to assume. I could feel myself changing, strengthening, taking a form in which, for the first time, I had a kind of faith.

But then, back at my flat, I would shower, lay out my clothes for work the next day, and ask myself again what I was evolving into. A person at peace? Or a person for whom peace had come to supplant freedom? I was plagued by dreams in which parts of my body were no longer my own. I would look down at my arm and find it muscled and tattooed. I would eat a meal and find I had no teeth. Several times, the spider dream recurred – that beaked arachnid once again hatching out of its nest in my flesh. The yoga, it seemed, was not all peace and tranquillity. It stirred something in me that was older and deeper than my own self – something primal and fanged and profoundly at odds with the beaming, coconut-water-drinking culture of the studio in which it took place.

I couldn't reconcile any of these things, couldn't join up the people I felt were being created: this reluctant hippy, this corporate drone, this potential monster. I veered from a sense of peace to a rage so fervent and wild that it manifested less as a feeling and more as an entirely separate entity. I started to feel as if the purpose of the classes became to mediate between these selves, to move them towards some sort of compromise or uneasy balance, but I wasn't always sure I wanted that balance to be achieved. I liked the tension, the push and pull between instinct and decorum. I thought of it in much the same way as I thought of the stretch I felt when I twisted an arm through my legs and tied myself into a bind, or the battling reflexive responses as I sat still in silent meditation and listened to my brain instruct itself to be quiet, then immediately begin chattering, then attempt again to be still: as a symptom of being alive, a sign that my life had regained the complexity it previously lacked.

The more ordered my week became, the more I came to value Zelma's unpredictability, her disregard for socialised time. My calendar was a neat, boxy grid; Zelma was a crazed and wandering line, a scrawl across the boundaries of my regimen.

I started falling asleep with my phone on the pillow beside me, anticipating that deep-of-night contact, thrilling a little at the device's gentle vibration, the increasingly familiar *hey* when I picked up. There was no pattern to her late nights and early mornings, no correlation between how late she'd stayed up and how early she rose. Nor was there any concession to what I might have been doing at any given moment. She called late at night on a weeknight, or so early on a Saturday morning it made my head spin. At first, I wondered if there was some sort of strategy or tactic behind this, if it was a test to gauge the depth and breadth of my commitment. Quickly, though, I realised this wasn't the case at all. Zelma had mastered the art of listening to herself. If there was something she wanted to do, she did it. If there was someone she wanted to call, she called. There was no gap between what she imagined herself doing, or wanted to do, and what she did. As a result, it didn't always occur to her that anyone else might behave differently in relation to themselves. If you wanted to sleep in, she thought, you would sleep in. If you didn't want to answer your phone, then you wouldn't answer your phone. As I came to understand this, I found it liberating. With Zelma, whole strata of etiquette and expectation fell away.

Not working helped, of course. It was something about which Zelma was not only open, but defiant. Her *unproductive body*, as she called it, had liberated her. She was proud, she said, not only of not working, but of what it cost society for her to be unproductive. Her body was its own resistance. It had refused to work long before she had been able to intellectualise the importance of that refusal.

That is not to say, however, that Zelma was content. Her movement through the world, however smooth and assured it seemed to me from the outside, was beset by discomfort. I might have writhed in the confines of a life I felt I'd had no part in shaping for myself, but Zelma had to manage the daily reality of seemingly having no screen or filter with which to block out all the whisperings of the things she hated. A simple walk to the shops involved a barrage of oppressive stimuli to which she felt compelled to respond. Adverts, flyers, packaging in the supermarket, the wild promises of ten-week improvement made by a gym near my house. What I admired about Zelma – the fact that there was nothing in the world to which she felt unable or unwilling to respond, no medium with which she felt unable to enter into dialogue – was also the very thing that had the potential to exhaust her. For Zelma, everything was an open channel. Because everything, in her conception, *could* be responded to, her freedom to make her own case in opposition to the messages by which she was harangued seemed at times more like a responsibility, even a burden.

Slowly, I began to understand the cycle by which Zelma lived. She raged at society's demand for healthy bodies, was grateful for what she saw as her body's autonomous decision to reject that demand, but at a certain point, she would exhaust herself, and the polarities would reverse. Her resistance would become physically and emotionally unsustainable, and then she would rage at her body for holding her back.

Zelma's illness was unpredictable. It struck at odd moments, the severity of any given flare-up ranging along a spectrum from a moment of dizziness to days in bed. At first, she cloaked the worst of her episodes in privacy, calling to tell me she couldn't see me for a few days, or standing suddenly from the table at which we were drinking coffee and saying she had to go home. Later, though, when we'd spent more time together and knew each other more closely, she invited me into the intimate space of her fragility, turning up on my doorstep sweating and shivering and deathly pale, spending a day or two on my sofa groaning with pain while I rubbed her joints and made her soup. As I watched her strength return, I felt strangely powerful, surprised at my capacity to help someone heal.

Once, when she was lying in my bed recovering from a twenty-four-hour burst of sweats and shakes, nibbling weakly at an assortment of seeds and nuts from a packet she'd stowed beneath the pillow, I asked her about the other people in her life, the friends and family I assumed had cared for her before she met me, or continued to care for her at other times, when I was at work or asleep.

'Oh,' she said vaguely, waving the hand that held the dried food before popping more of it into her mouth. 'People come and go.'

'But there must be people you rely on,' I said. 'People you call?'

She pushed herself upright and leaned back against her pillow, eyeing me with an unusual uncertainty.

'Are you getting tired?' she said.

'No,' I said. 'Not at all. I was just asking.'

'People get tired. It's nobody's fault. It happens.'

'Has that happened before?' I said.

'It's just the way it is,' she said. 'What about you? You must have old friends, from before. Or family. Or something.'

'Of course. I just . . . I haven't seen them in a while.'

I looked down at my cheap, geometrically patterned duvet cover, the colours already weakened through several washes.

'I'm starting over, I guess,' I said.

And Zelma just nodded, as if starting over was the most normal imaginable process, as if everyone, all the time, jettisoned whole tracts of their life and then made them anew.

*

I can't remember whether it was through my own enthusiasm or Zelma's encouragement that we began working together on her project of resistance. Perhaps Zelma recognised that the things she wanted to do were more than one person could manage. Perhaps she welcomed the company, especially at night, her favoured time for adjusting street-level billboards and bus-stop posters. What I can remember with complete clarity is how keen I was to spend time with her, to be in her world. Perhaps it was me that persuaded her. Or perhaps, as with many things that came after, it was never clear cut, with events simply unfolding from what felt, at that time, like a merging of thoughts, an inability to tell where one of us ended and the other began. Neither of us even referred to it as a project, and so we couldn't possibly have approached it, then, in any discernibly organised way. It was a series of actions that became a habit, a reflex that took on its own meaning through repetition. It was also a vessel of sorts, a place to put the things we were feeling. This was particularly true in my case. Other people had the internet through which to express themselves, but for me the web was as curtailed a space as any other. Denied the walls on which others posted their thoughts, it seemed only natural that I would find different walls, different surfaces, on which to say the things I couldn't say elsewhere.

For Zelma, it was less about expression and more about reply. She couldn't tune out the exhortations, but neither could she allow them simply to pass through her, unchecked and uninterrogated. She *had* to respond, and yet the responses that were expected of her were proscribed. It wasn't enough, she often said, to discuss these things online. To do so, she felt, was to accept the space she had been allotted. She wanted argument and debate to unfold in the same location it was initiated. When an advert invaded her mental and visual space, she invaded its physical and aesthetic space right back. In our rush to the web, she said, we had ceded ground in the physical world. As a result, ever more overt expressions went unnoticed and unchallenged. What once would have found itself defaced was now, instead, photographed and shared online for critique. But its form, its face, remained unaltered, untarnished, clean.

For Zelma, and for me the more I spent time with her, this creative and unapologetic use of territory that claimed to be at once inviting and off limits was intimately related to our shared love of another space that simultaneously beckoned and threatened: the city at night. It wasn't until that first outing with Zelma, when we'd simply walked and talked, snacking on pastries, then slipped into drunkenness and defaced a bus stop, that I realised how deeply, how painfully, I had missed the feeling that the nocturnal city belonged to me. Sleeping out, finding shelter in disused buildings and empty shopping centres, making those long, solo journeys from one source of food and warmth to another, I had come to experience the city as a place in which I belonged only when it was dark. At first, it had been the nights that terrified me. Later, as I became dirtier, thinner, a little wilder of eye and appearance, it was the days that became hostile. In sunlight, people looked at me with pity. In the dark, there was a touch of fear. Over time, I learned to own that. In the enveloping routine of work, through the commute, the time in the office, the end-of-the-day exhaustion, I had lost my nights entirely. They had become nothing more than an opportunity for sleep or, at best, staring at the television when sleep wouldn't come. When I met Zelma and listened to her talk about the importance of time, of choosing the clocks by which we live, my disconnection with something that had once been mine became clearer to me.

The first few occasions we went out were no different to our phone calls: spontaneous; a response to some instinct or desire we were reluctant to shrug off or tamp down. Sometimes, it was simply a way of breaking the routine of meeting at my flat. Zelma would call, tell me where she was, and I'd meet her without thinking. Or she'd stand up suddenly from the sofa, mid-film or at times mid-sentence, and announce that she was going out, and I was welcome to accompany her. That tended to be Zelma's way: no painfully British discussion, no *What would you like to do next?* Just a statement of what she would be doing, and the option of joining her only if you wished to.

In the beginning, our interventions were casual, spontaneous, sometimes drunken. As had happened on that first night out together, an image or phrase would catch Zelma's eye, prick at her finely balanced boundaries, and she or both of us would respond quickly, thoughtlessly, with whatever tools were at hand and whatever phrases or expressions were in our minds. Initially, our patch was small, curtailed by the fact that both of us preferred walking to any other mode of transport. But we quickly saturated the area around my flat. If anyone had been minded to, they could quite easily have traced our graffiti back to my address simply by marking the defaced posters on a map and then finding in the spread of data an obvious epicentre. No-one did, but we branched out anyway. At the time we told ourselves this was to more effectively cover our tracks, but in retrospect I wonder if the opposite was true: if we wanted more people to see what we were doing, wanted our work to resonate beyond the strictly local.

We began to get a sense of places that afforded us the best opportunity to work. In expansive bookshops with in-house cafes, we'd load up on fashion mags and glossy lifestyle monthlies and then, at a corner table away from the eyes of the staff, mark them up with Sharpies and Post-it notes before slipping them back onto the shelves. Zelma was at home across modes, I noticed. She liked to go against the grain of what she was responding to. Within a few minutes she could shift from footnoting an article with contradictory research to cartoonishly adjusting the bodies of models in a fashion spread. The more vapid and conversational an article, the more tightly knotted and academic her writing became in response; the more pretentious and self-consciously arty a photo spread, the more scatological and crude the drawings with which she augmented it. She was particularly fond of making models appear to shit or piss, or daubing menstrual stains on the crotches of cream trouser-suits.

Confronted with an idyllic image of thirty-something parents in a vivid green urban park, she would add heaps of steaming dog shit, discarded cans, a lecherous drunk.

Statements of physicality always caught her eye: makeup adverts, posters for sports equipment, offers for gym membership framed in the language of wildly pitched promise or needling, hectoring guilt. She had an acute sensitivity to any suggestion she might be, or should be, unhappy with herself.

'Your body's what it's all about,' she said once, sitting beside me in bed late at night, her knees drawn up to her chin and a good deal more than her half of the duvet wrapped tightly around her. 'If you have a body that can't in some way contribute, then forget it.'

'Do you miss work?' I said.

She laughed.

'I don't miss it because I'm still doing it,' she said. 'It's just that I'm doing my work and not someone else's.'

Just as the tension I felt in my classes – between the possibility of a peaceful, becalmed self and its raging, anguished opposite – became something I sought to nurture, so too the tension between my working life and Zelma's increasingly demanding schedule of anti-work became a boundary of conflict I both valued and knew to be unsustainable. I caught the very last train that still got me to the office in time for work, rose at the last possible minute in order to be ready for that train. To buy myself an extra quarter of an hour in bed, I began drinking my breakfast smoothie on my commute. But my attempts at clinging to what rest I could were futile. At work, the pace at which I was expected to operate had been steadily increasing. Most evenings after leaving the office I went to a class of some description, some of which were gruelling to the point that I woke with the memory of them still deep in my musculature. I would get home late, exhausted, in pain, and find myself unable to sleep for the simple reason that I had not had a moment to myself. Sleep, I began to feel, was something that came out of *my* time, and intruded on my ability to do the things I wanted to do, so I came to resent it. Often, Zelma would call or visit. We'd watch documentaries or chat late into the night on the phone, only stopping when, as happened more than once, I fell asleep with the phone in my hand. Then the morning would come round again, and those extra few minutes in bed, while satisfying, achieved nothing. My exhaustion was like coastal erosion – it touched my every edge, shrunk me from every direction. A few minutes snatched here or there were no different to tossing a handful of sand into the sea, hoping it would stave off the waves.

Harrison noticed my mini-slump at work, called me into his office for a one-to-one.

'Numbers are good,' he said. 'Very good. Steady progress, almost daily.'

'I'm really pleased,' I said. One of the consequences of my fatigue was that I seemed to have lost the ability to inject anything I said with any feeling.

'And yet,' said Harrison, 'I find myself concerned.'

'Oh?'

'Because, OK, you're working well. You're doing the job. You're getting things done. But is that everything, Maya? Is that *it*?'

I assumed, with some surprise, that he was talking about the work–life balance. As if sensing my naive misunderstanding, he continued quickly.

'Something I like to say is that doing the job, even doing the job *really well*, is only like sixty per cent of the job,' he said.

He was looking at me as if I was supposed to offer my thoughts on the other forty per cent, but my mind was empty. I had become distracted by the wider implications of my job no longer being the whole of my job, and so had nothing to contribute in terms of what other work, what other input and effort, I might possibly be able to offer.

'Is this about attitude?' I said.

Harrison stared at me flatly. Because of my levelled voice and ground-down affect, the statement had come across with something of a bad attitude itself.

'I mean . . .' I tried to brighten my inflection. I felt as if I was reaching into myself and dredging up silty handfuls of personality, stuff that had resided too long at the bottom of the well. 'Maybe attitude isn't the word. Maybe the word I'm looking for is personality. Or *character*.'

At this last word, Harrison brightened perceptibly. I felt like I was cracking a safe – spinning through combinations, listening for the click of the pins in their barrel.

'Aha,' he said. 'Character. Now *that's* a word.'

I didn't know what to say, so I just nodded.

'Let me put it like this,' said Harrison. 'Can your colleagues, who of course are very focused on their numbers and the images they're processing, *see* what you're doing?'

'Well I suppose they can look at the team numbers and . . .'

'But can they *see* it though? Are they sitting there like, *Wow, Maya's on fire this afternoon?*'

'Not on a minute-by-minute basis, no.'

'What about on a broader basis? What about at the end of the day? What about at the end of a week? What about at the back end of a quarter when we all have a drink and congratulate each other on how totally on fire we've been?'

'I see what you're saying.'

'It's not just about your individual numbers, Maya. It's about everyone's numbers. And beyond that, it's not about numbers at all. Your job, everyone's job, isn't just to do your job, it's to do your job in a way that totally inspires everyone else to do their job. Plus of course, with you, there's like a whole extra layer.'

'The programme.'

'Right. Because with you it's also like: look how inspiring it is that you're even able to do this job in the first place. It's not just your colleagues who are seeing this, it's *everyone*. Do you really want people to scroll through your Instagram and be like, *Well, you know, she has a really grinding, repetitive job now so that's great?*'

'No. Of course.'

'You know how I like to explain this to people?' Harrison leaned forward across his desk, shifting into a slightly warmer, story-telling mode. 'I like to talk about the total person. You know what the total person is, Maya?'

I shook my head.

'The total person is the kind of person that no-one could really describe as being any other kind of person. You know sometimes you hear people talking about someone and they're like, *Oh, that's Ted, he's a numbers guy?* Or, *This is Marsha, she's an amazing PR?* Well with the total person they can't say that, because the total person is an *everything* person. They do everything well. They just bring their total totalness to whatever they do. You know what people call those people?'

I shook my head again.

'Their *name*,' he said grandly. I must have looked baffled because he pressed on enthusiastically. 'You want people to be like, *Oh, that's Maya, she gets great numbers?* Or, *Oh, that's Maya, she's in that pro- gramme where they get you a job?* Of course you don't. You want people to literally just be like, *That's Maya*, and for that simple statement to convey the absolute spectrum and wealth of what you achieve. We need to get the numbers up this week? You're totally Maya about it. You've got some fitness goals you need to meet? You totally Maya the hell out of them. We're all out on a social, building those relation- ships? You are *so* Maya in that situation. So *totally* Maya.'

'I see what you're saying, Harrison.'

'Do you, Maya? Do you really? Because what I'm saying is: how Maya can you *be*? How totally Maya can you *become*?'

I wanted to say, *A lot more Maya than this*, but I didn't. Instead, I went back to my desk and hammered through images at such a rate that it began to feel as if my eyes were sending signals straight to my fingers without any intervention on the part of my brain. I didn't even see them as complete images any more, just impressions: cock-shape, breast-shape, blood-colour. When I was done, I did a little lap of the office, checking in with people. Then I left and went to yoga, where I posted an Instagram picture of my water bottle, my mat, and my little towel with a caption about how much I looked forward to this all day. *My treat*, I said. When the class began, I pushed myself from the beginning, taking every pose as deep as I could, throwing in an extra vinyasa whenever I saw the chance. I was beginning to understand what people meant when they talked about the pain barrier: that there was a place on the other side of discomfort that felt better than mere comfort alone; that you could feel, at times, as if you were beating your heated body into toughened new shapes. Afterwards, I drank my water too quickly and was sick in the toilet to the accompanying sounds of someone else being sick in the toilet adjacent to mine. Then I was starving and shaky. When I stepped out of the studio and made my way towards the Tube, through the huddles of weeknight drinkers spilling out onto the pavements to smoke, the world had the same dimmed and selectively highlighted effect as the images I'd looked at earlier in the day, with only what I needed to see standing out in any clarity. Snack bar, card machine, Tube station, *Way Out*.

I called Zelma that night, still stewing over my talk with Harrison. I told her about his ideas, about the total person. I was sitting up in bed, propped against pillows, the duvet tight around my torso despite the warmth of the night.

'Jesus Christ,' she said when I was done.

'I just . . . I think about it and I'm exhausted,' I said. 'I mean, I'm exhausted anyway, but then I think about how much more I would have to do to get anywhere and it's like the exhaustion magnifies by a thousand.'

'But what *aren't* you doing already? What more can you possibly do?'

'I guess he means the team stuff,' I said. 'The bonding. The camaraderie. I've never really been—'

'Don't start judging yourself,' she said sharply. 'Don't start seeing yourself in the light of those kinds of standards.'

'No but it's true. That's always been the part of work I've struggled with. The unquestioning side. The feeling of joining in. I've always tried to do it at this kind of remove. Maybe what he's saying is—'

'Of course you've done it at a remove. How else are you supposed to do it and still be you?'

'But maybe those days are gone,' I said. 'Maybe I have to accept that. Maybe there just won't *be* those kinds of jobs any more – the ones where you can roll out of bed and stagger in without speaking to anyone and keep your head down and just *do* it, you know? Maybe this is what work is, now.'

She was quiet. I couldn't tell if she was mulling this over or simply giving me the space to talk it through until I drew my own conclusions. Zelma didn't tend to think things over mid-conversation. Her thinking was instinctive, almost physical. She understood her own feelings about things, and took them to be true.

'God,' I said once the silence had hung for a while. 'That's a depressing thought.'

'It's true though, I think.'

'Maybe.'

'Definitely. Simple tasks can be automated. They've already almost got the machine learning to do what you do. It's about what else a human can bring to the table, which is, literally, their humanity.'

It was possible, I realised, to imagine a semi-global future in which the bulk of paid human employment would revolve not around hard skills, but around the messy, blurry business of interpersonal success. A new divide would open up, between the well

136

liked, the easy-to-get-along-with, and the awkward, the rude, the unfriendly. I pictured the encampment on which I'd lived filled not, as it was then, with migrants, unfortunates, hard drinkers, the out-of-luck, but instead the abrasive, the poorly adjusted, the excessively reserved and painfully shy.

'I feel like I don't want to bring anything to the table,' I said.

'Then don't.'

'It's like, I'm grateful, I really am. But—'

'Stop saying that,' she said. 'You've got nothing to be grateful for. A company that is literally on the rich list found it in their hearts to provide the absolute minimum for someone who was destitute – to give you what really should have been your right in the first place. And let's not forget, Maya, that they make you *work* for what they've supposedly given you out of sheer generosity. That's what this total person shit is about. It's not just a case of going into Pict and parsing a few images. It's the wellness regimen, it's your Instagram feed, it's being seen as Pict's little project. They're making you *look good*, Maya. They're getting you ready for the before and after to end all before and afters. When this is done, when you're hugely successful and living exactly the life they envisioned for you, you'd better believe they'll roll you out at speaking events. You'll be their little mascot, their *pet*. They'll dress you up all nice and then stand you in front of a slideshow of how grim your life used to be and say, *We did this.*'

I knew it was true. I pictured myself being paraded around, displayed. In many ways, it was already happening.

'Other people in the office don't do as much of the wellness stuff as I do,' I said.

'Really?'

'I'm on some sort of enhanced programme. Because I've got more to, I don't know, detoxify, or whatever.'

'You always say you enjoy it though. I mean, I've seen you after your yoga class and, OK, maybe you're exhausted, but you seem happy.'

'I am. I kind of love it. I just don't love what it's *for*.'

'You wish you could do it just for the sake of doing it. Just because you enjoy it.'

'I wish I could do *everything* just for the sake of it.'

'So do.'

That was Zelma, summed up in two words. I pictured her at the other end of the line, in whatever room or flat or alternative arrangement she lived in, perhaps sitting on her bed in much the same way as I was sitting on mine, wearing a pointedly baffled expression and shrugging.

'It's not that simple, Zelma.'

'Why?'

'What will I do for money? Where will I live?'

'You managed before.'

'I managed before by being homeless and begging.'

'Did it ever occur to you that you're still homeless and begging? And that as soon as you can't sustain it this way, the most obvious alternative will be to go back to doing it the old way?'

Stunned, I let this statement hang in the air. Several retorts presented themselves to me as possibilities, but each time I moved to utter them they lodged in my throat and then decayed before they could be expressed.

'You're angry,' Zelma said simply. Not, *I'm sorry.* Not, *Don't be angry.* Just, *You're angry.* I wondered how she was able to tell. My silence had been brief – no longer than any of the other pauses in our conversation. Perhaps she'd heard my throat catch a little. Perhaps my breathing had changed. Or maybe, I thought, she knew I was angry because she'd meant for me to be angry.

I knew she wouldn't rush to explain herself, that she'd wait, let the question settle, give me a chance to express myself in return first.

'Frightened,' I said finally. 'It seems like anger because that's easier.'

'So it has occurred to you.'

'It *always* occurs to me. It's all I think about. *Don't fuck this up. Don't end up back on the street.* I feel like if it was just once then OK, maybe I can get past it, but if it happens again, if it *keeps happening . . .*'

'Then you're defective in some way.'

'Maybe. Or just, I don't know, *fucked.* I'm trying so hard, Zelma. I'm giving this everything I've got so I don't fuck up again but everything I've got's not enough.'

Somewhere during the course of the conversation, without knowing exactly when, or what particular realisation had triggered it, I had started to cry.

'I had a dream where a spider hatched out of my arm,' I said. 'It had grown inside me and then it chewed its way out and attacked me and I had to crush it with my fingers.'

Zelma said nothing. I rubbed at the tender patch on my forearm – that tingling, peeled-away reminder of my nightmare. I felt like I had just before my illness came on – before I ran to the toilet to vomit and shit. Only now the feeling wasn't centralised in my stomach. It was under my skin, all over, between my uppermost surface and the layer of muscle and bone below. I felt like I was beginning to rupture, like I'd swelled and needed to split.

'I never told you why I was at the doctor's,' I said.

'No,' she said.

'They sent me on a detox retreat. Yoga and juices. I enjoyed it. I felt energised, like they said I would. But energised in a crazy way. And I felt trapped. And, like, too clean. And separate from the world.'

My sentences were the length of a breath, my breath the duration of a sob. Everything was coming out in spasms.

'I was on the train and it felt so good to be in the world. I wanted to be back in the world. I dug around in the gap between the seats and I ate what I found. Hairs and rubbish and dirt. And then I came back and ate and ate. I couldn't stop. And the whole time I'd been away I couldn't shit. It was all those women around me. All that cleanness. I don't know. I don't know what it was. I just couldn't. And I felt enormous. I was in agony. And I kept eating until finally it all just came out. Like my own body weight in shit. And it felt so amazing that I wiped my arse and ate it. Literally ate my own shit. And then I got sick and I couldn't stop being sick. I had this crazy fever. I just puked and shat for days. And I had that dream. Because I was running a fever, I think. And . . . It was the best time of my life. I'm not kidding. I felt like it was the best thing that ever happened to me. I felt free and changed and like I didn't give a *fuck*. And now—'

'Now you can't change back.'

'No. I mean, I can't in one way, because I remember it and I can't, you know, be the person I was . . . You can't be the person you were before something happened. Even if it was only a small thing. But in another way I *have* changed back. I got well again and I went back to work and I—'

'You hate it. You see it and now you hate it.'

'Do you know what I do on a Saturday morning?'

'Tell me.'

'I shit. I get up in the morning, I have a coffee, and I sit and wait to shit. And I *look forward to it*. I look forward to taking as long as I want to shit. And when I do, I feel like I'm shitting for the whole week. I'm shitting *everything out*. And then I go back to the sofa and I switch on the TV and I *relax*.'

I said this last word with a sort of yowl. My face was marbled with snot and tears.

'It's so fucked up, Zelma. I'm so fucked up.'

'You're not,' she said firmly. 'You're *being* fucked up. It's different.'

I thought about this while smearing my eyes with the heel of my palm and running the back of my wrist across the slickness of my nostrils and lip.

'Maybe,' I said. 'But the end result is the same.'

Neither of us said anything for a while. I could hear her breathing, long and slow, through her nose. I had that particular nausea that comes from swallowing your own snot. I wanted to match my breath to Zelma's, as if through breathing together we might think together; as if by thinking with Zelma I would no longer have to think as myself. But when I tried, my nasal passages clogged and bubbled. I felt shitty: not just in the immediate sense, but in a deeper, more distended sense. My body hurt. My brain couldn't think straight. I was exhausted yet incapable of sleep.

'This is how they get you,' I said. 'They wear you down, until you've got no time and energy for anything except just carrying on.'

'You know what I think?' said Zelma. 'You've got to start small, start symbolic, then grow it until it's huge.'

'Meaning what,' I said.

'Meaning take back certain moments, *enjoy* certain moments. Starting with your body. Starting with how the only shit you can actually savour is at the weekend. I mean, why? Why is that?'

'In the morning I'm rushed. And then I get to work and I'm busy. And I feel like people notice when I'm away from my desk. I feel like either they think to themselves that I'm skiving, or that they just immediately know that I'm shitting.'

'Why shouldn't they know that you're shitting?'

'I don't know.'

'From now on,' she said, 'I want you to prioritise your shitting. In your day, now, starting tomorrow, nothing matters except shitting. Your sole purpose is to shit. I want you to get *professional* at shitting. And when you get good at it, celebrate it.'

I thought about the cathedral of faeces I'd produced after my weekend away: the sense of glorious emptiness that followed it, the way I drank in its stench and knew that it was intimately mine in a way that nothing else, except my guttering flame of rage, could ever be.

'Celebrate it how?'

'Send me a picture,' she said. 'Every day, when you shit, to show me how seriously you're taking it, send me a picture.'

A sense of pressure followed my phone call with Zelma. Shitting *meant* something now. My fear of letting Zelma down meant that my bowels – always excessively attuned to the context in which they were being asked to perform – responded with a case of stage fright. Despite my best efforts on day one, nothing happened.

By day two I had loaded up on fruit and cereal. I had also, following my little chat with Harrison, parsed twenty or thirty per cent more images. I felt as if Harrison and Zelma represented opposing yet in some ways complementary impulses: Harrison exhorting me to increase my intake, Zelma giving me the confidence to digest and discharge. *Start small, start symbolic.* She was asking me to focus on what I was taking in, what was failing to find a way back out. And at the same time, she was proposing a small but significant rebalance: my own image, my own affront to the censored disgrace of who and what we are.

The first time I did it, I felt like I was committing a crime. In the moments before I rose quietly from my desk and slipped out to the toilet, all the usual feelings announced themselves: embarrassment, shame, a little charge of worry at the prospect of having to negotiate some sort of social interaction with colleagues in the cubicle area. As always, when I stood up, I imagined that my co-workers all said to themselves silently, *Maya is going for a shit.* Now, though, there was an added frisson of excitement. I was going not only out of bodily necessity, responding not just to the simplest and basest of stimuli. I was going because I needed release, and because that sense of release was its own act of rebellion.

I didn't encounter anyone on the way, and when I got to the stalls I found them empty. I chose the cubicle farthest from the door and tried to establish myself in comfort. Already, I noticed, even on this second attempt, I was perceptibly less aware of my surroundings, less attuned to the possible arrival of others. I had a mission, a focus; it swelled to fill my attention. When I unbuckled my jeans and pulled down my underwear and sat, waiting, it was with a new feeling of anticipation. Suddenly, strongly, I wished I wasn't shitting in the toilet at all, but on the floor of my office, on my desk, my keyboard, even on the pavement outside Pict's door. I imagined myself in possession of infinite reserves of shit – able to smear and besmirch at will.

This, I realised, was what Zelma had done for me. Even before I took it, the idea of the picture changed everything. I was still playing by the rules of civility. All my unwanted matter – my filth, my effluvia, my toxins – was still being deposited and stored in the right place. To the casual observer, I was a law-abiding citizen. But the moment I took the picture, I knew, that would change. I would be moving an unwanted element from one dimension to another, from the mannered delusion of daily reality to the world of decay and stench that supposed reality masked – the mirror-world I'd glimpsed on the train, in my bathroom as I'd heaved and deliriously evacuated.

At this thought, as if they were the physical doorway into that seething alternate life I'd seen and almost touched, my bowels flew open. It was not quite the joyous, climactic release I'd enjoyed after my weekend away, but it carried its own distinct energy. That particular movement had been both ecstatic and violent; this was angry, resentful, subversive. When I stood up and turned around to look at what I had made, I saw a neat little collection of bullet-shaped turds, light brown in colour, flecked with white nuts from the cereal I'd eaten.

For a moment, I hesitated. I had been about to wipe myself, but the discarded paper, I realised, would obscure what I was trying to photograph. Instead, I reached down into my jeans, pulled out my phone, and took a picture.

There was something about standing there unwiped, even for a few seconds, that felt in its own way as transgressive as the picture I was taking. That feeling of unapologetic uncleanness, of hygiene deliberately delayed, seemed its own kind of tiny, temporary refusal. My thumb hovered over the shutter button on my phone's screen for a second. I noticed that my hand was shaking. Somehow, this seemed even more intimate, even more revealing, than sending a picture of myself naked. I imagined the image I was about to make joining the sewage stream of images I would now go back to my desk to parse, in much the same way as my shit would flow out along London's network of pipes towards whichever local treatment centre was responsible for processing it. I tapped my thumb against the screen of my phone, watched the image I'd taken hop into my photo album, then opened up a text to Zelma and attached what I'd captured. Briefly, I wondered if I should say something, caption the image somehow, but then I realised I had nothing to add. It said exactly what I wanted to say, and exactly what, I hoped, Zelma was waiting to hear.

Then I put my phone back in my pocket, wiped myself, pulled up my trousers, returned to my civil state. As I washed my hands, I felt my phone pulse in my pocket. After I'd dried them, the roar of the hand-drier still continuing behind me, I took out my phone and saw on the screen a single, throbbing heart.

That night, exhausted yet still abuzz, I called Zelma and asked her if she wanted to meet for one of our walks. My little act of rebellion earlier in the day had been intimate, unseen. It carried a particular afterglow, something I felt unable to fully discharge. Now I longed for a public act – something anti-secretive, unabashedly visible.

Zelma readily agreed. We didn't talk about what I'd done earlier in the day, but I knew she understood why I wanted to meet. A couple of times, I felt on the verge of raising it with her, discussing it, but each time the urge arose it vanished again the moment I considered verbalising it. My earlier instinct had been right, I thought: the photograph was the discussion, the shit was everything that needed to be said. Conversation, deconstruction, would only render what we'd done and shared as mundane and desiccated as any other discussion of the day's events.

We met in Stratford, walked in our usual aimless manner. Our route took us through the old shopping centre, which as always was lined with the homeless and drunk. In the central circle, kids practised dance moves to blaring music, hopped on and off benches on their skateboards.

'Did you ever sleep here?' said Zelma.

'Lots of times,' I said.

I remembered weighing in my mind the pros and cons on any given night: getting wet and damp outside if the weather was ugly, or being warm and dry but outnumbered by reeling, desperate men. Sometimes the rain won out, sometimes it didn't. I carried a small, foldable knife with me in those days. During the nights I sheltered in the Centre, I slept with it in my fist, blade extended. Many times, I found a sharp, warning jab into a man's creeping hand was enough to ensure I was left alone.

We bought a flimsy plastic box of honey-soaked baklava and ate it while we walked. I thought of our first night out together – eating sticky pastries and staring out at the glitter of far-off luxury buildings. I was starting to feel like we had our own little pockets of space in the metropolis, our own tracks and trails winding through and below the thoroughfares. It was a sensation both familiar and novel: at once a reminder of the days and nights in which I'd made space for myself in the parks and alleyways and abandoned buildings most people habitually avoided, and a glimpse of a new present in which I selected parts of the city to be my own through simple choice rather than because whole areas and buildings were closed to me. I remembered that someone had once told me, some night or other, beside a small and barely warming fire in the covered and nocturnally abandoned market area at Upton Park, that twilight was the gap between the worlds – a blurring of life and death, good and evil, physical and spirit. It was the kind of talk that passes for profundity among shivering junkies at 3 a.m. with the wind whipping up discarded cardboard and the cast-off ad-pages of free newspapers, and at the time I just nodded in the way I'd become used to then: not quite agreeing, not quite dissenting; risking neither offence nor a continuation of the idea beyond its merits. But now, in the shopping centre, at midnight, walking with a new friend in new clothes through a space and time at once familiar and distant, inhabiting a body that was in so many ways no longer the body that had slept alongside those huddled, bundled figures, the idea returned to me. In relation to life, people talk of twilight as a linear and permanent dimming, an end to what has gone before. But now I saw that this was my twilight: a space between lives and selves, a mid-point of change, a crack between waking moments when all the spirits and ghosts of who you were and might yet be come flitting out of the shadows to dance.

At the end of the walkway we'd taken, just before the strip-lit glare of the shopping centre opened out into the darkness of the East London night, a slender, barely adult model reclined within the frame of a glowing, back-lit advert. She was wrapped in a lilac silk sheet, her manicured toes pointing out one end, the sheet slipping as if by accident from one shoulder to reveal the top of a naked breast. She was immaculately made up in that way men tend to mistake for wearing no makeup at all, her pale skin smoothed to an eerie glow. One hand was spread on the floor to take her weight; the other, perhaps suggestively, was beneath the sheet. From one corner of her mouth, a single, perfectly formed rivulet of chocolate had escaped, and was prevented from dripping onto the sheet only by the tip of her protruding tongue. Beside her, in elegant, cursive font: *Release Yourself.*

It wasn't rage that swelled inside me, it was excitement – a deep and committed thrill. I thought about my own image that day – the neat, almost polite pile of shit at the bottom of a pristine toilet bowl – and imagined it airbrushed to this exact level of hyperreal perfection, the porcelain reflectively gleaming, the water almost oceanically inviting, the shit itself glossed and chocolatey and almost edible.

In front of the billboard, right at the edge of the shopping centre, was an overflowing bin. Ranged around it were the discarded wrappers and objects no doubt picked up by scavenging hands and then cast aside as neither nutritious nor valuable. I walked over to the bin and began ransacking it, not caring that the trash I pulled from its mouth was piling at my feet. I heard Zelma laugh, cottoning on, and then her hands were deep in the bin with mine. We found Burger King wrappers, lidded cardboard cups containing dregs of coffee, melting ice, and souring milk. There were little knotted bags of dog shit, the moulded packaging of children's toys, cigarette ends, drained cans of reeking cider, styrofoam coffins in which were entombed the carcasses of abandoned kebabs. We gathered it all up by the armful, streaking our clothes with ketchup, grease, black coffee, half-dissolved ash, and then arranged it like offerings beneath the advert, heaping it all up until it reached the bottom edge of the frame. We took wrappers sticky with sauce and sugar and glued them on the model's silky sheet. Around her supporting hand, using bits of cast-off gum as Blu Tack, we arranged a scattering of fag-ends. With the melted remains of a half-eaten Dairy Milk, we deepened and widened that smear of chocolate at the corner of her mouth until it darkened her entire chin and ran down her neck. At the end we stepped back and admired her: our model, resplendent amidst her trash. *Release Yourself.*

I snapped a picture on my phone. Zelma jerked her head towards the exit. By the time I got home, the first glow of dawn was burning the skyline and it looked like someone had touched a match to the papery edge of the whole stinking city.

'I just feel like, it's great, but what it's about? What are we *saying*?' said Seth, making a little circle in the air with his espresso cup.

We were talking about my progress, specifically my Instagram feed. It had not escaped my attention that Seth was now saying *we* when discussing the narrative of *Maya's Journey*.

'Or: where's this *going*?' said Ryan.

'You remember before when we talked about the illness pictures?' said Seth.

'Sure,' I said.

'There were going to be more things like that, is my memory of that meeting's outcome.'

'I've been better, though,' I said. 'I mean, I've been busy, and doing well, and—'

'I don't think Seth necessarily means more selfies of you while you're ill, *per se*,' said Ryan. 'I think he means, more pictures and comments that reflect some sort of . . .' He looked at Seth, making vague cloud shapes in the air with his hands.

'That might make people empathise,' said Seth.

'Empathise more,' said Ryan. 'Because obviously we're aware that people empathise already. We're not saying that no-one empathises with you.'

Seth laughed awkwardly.

'Or that you're somehow *difficult* to empathise with,' he said. 'God no. We're not saying that.'

'What we're saying,' said Ryan, 'is actually the opposite of that. We're saying: we ourselves, me and Seth here, find you very easy to empathise with. I mean, we *really* empathise with you.'

'We find you very engaging,' said Seth. 'We're fully engaged right now.'

'What we're saying is can we get more of . . . *this* . . .' – he gesticulated vaguely in the direction of my nonplussed face and folded arms, then moved his hands definitively towards the window – '*out there?*'

That night, at two or three in the morning, as I was watching a pack of walruses clash tusks over their right to a shrinking ice floe, Zelma called.

'No picture today,' she said.

'I forgot,' I said.

'Forgot to take a picture?'

'Forgot to shit.'

I wanted to say that I couldn't remember anything else I'd done that day either. I was fairly sure I'd remembered to drink. At lunch I had eaten something, but its exact nature eluded me.

'Remember our advert?' she said. 'With all the trash piled up?'

'Of course.'

'I've seen it online. Instagram, Twitter. People are walking past it and taking a picture.'

'What people?'

'*People*, Maya. People are stopping to look at it. They're taking pictures of it like it's one of the sights of London.'

I didn't know what I thought about this. But then, I didn't know, at that exact moment, what I thought about anything. I felt trapped in a moving vehicle, the world sliding by on the other side of the glass, one passing event or sensation no different, no more significant, than the next. I wondered if this was fatigue, anhedonia, or simply a mounting nihilism. Maybe they were all related. Experiencing nothing led naturally to feeling nothing. Feeling nothing left you believing in nothing.

'What do you want to do?' I said.

'More,' she said simply. 'More and more.'

I nodded, despite the fact that this would manifest to Zelma as nothing more than silence. I felt there was nothing more to be said. She had, unwittingly, uttered my mantra, the code by which I now seemed to live: *More.*

After our phone conversation, I lay in bed and looked at links to pictures Zelma had sent me: our altered advert, the grimy model atop her mound of trash. On Instagram and Facebook, people had captioned it with onyx hearts and hands of worship. Someone had also seen the advert we'd worked on at the end of our first night out together – the overworked, bleeding woman, annotated with the symptoms of mental and physical decay. There was speculation about a link. Some people liked the idea of these acts sharing a creator. Other people preferred the idea that this phenomenon was less structured, that some mass dissatisfaction with advertising had reached its tipping point.

I didn't want to post my own picture, in case Ryan and Seth would be able to find in it some tell-tale record of my phone's metadata. But neither did I want to suppress what I now understood to be a powerful sense of expression. I had made something in the world that had been seen. I wanted to mark that moment of connection, even if I couldn't quite answer in my own voice.

I reposted a couple of the images on my Instagram, making no comment of my own. That simple act, the pressure of my thumb on the icon of circling arrows, felt charged, almost fraught. I thought about the picture of my shit, the electric moment of its dispatch, the sense of a connection formed through the noise, along which travelled something intimate, something detached from the habitual spectrum of shame and pride. By reposting those images, I was breaking from the programme. Ryan and Seth had never quite spelled out the terms of our intellectual contract but this was, I knew, a deviation. *Maya's Journey* would be altered. A crack in the narrative would emerge through which, if people looked closely, a part of my real self could be seen.

I awoke to no real scandal. The image of our woman amidst her heaps of detritus had been reposted numerous times, but the comments expressed little more than the usual concise support: *Love this!* or *So great!* I wasn't quite sure what I had been expecting. Some flurry of outrage? The immediate lock-down of my Instagram by Ryan and Seth? I had envisioned, at the very least, a concerned talking-to, perhaps even a telling-off.

As I thought about it, though, in bed, scrolling through my feed, I realised I had not really been expecting these things at all, I had been hoping for them. The fizz and faint shudder I'd felt at posting that picture wasn't, as I'd told myself it was at the time, fear. It wasn't even quite excitement. It was relief – a physical reaction to the sense of freedom that accompanied posting something I believed in and was proud of. This, after all, was what other people used their social media for, wasn't it? Surely not everyone felt as forced as I did to curate such a carefully inoffensive feed? My hope for a strong response to the image, I realised, was complicated. I wanted to know that I'd transgressed, wanted the thrill of bad behaviour, but I also wanted to know that the image me and Zelma had created carried some kind of power, and that the platform on which we'd presented it was a meaningful way of expressing that power. Instead, I was disappointed, and in my disappointment I could see clearly, perhaps for the first time, the things I had wished for. It was confirmation I craved. Confirmation that something, *anything* I was doing mattered; that I was not simply overseeing some meaningless, lifeless stream of corporatised lifestyle flotsam, then passing my time at night by daubing a few billboards with what effectively amounted to graffiti – passed by and overlooked by hundreds on their way to work.

I scrolled back through my feed and looked again at our high priestess of trash, resplendent on her fag-strewn bed. The recognition was deep and awful – a slithering lurch in my stomach that harked back to the nausea I'd felt after my detox. I remembered how forcefully I'd turned on the billboard that day, how determined I'd been to undermine it, change it, change *her*. I hadn't really understood it then, but I understood it now. I had started to hate adverts not only through Zelma's encouragement, but because I *was* an advert. My adjustments to that image weren't just a subversive intervention, they were a self-portrait.

I left Instagram and scrolled instead through my own photo album, looking for the picture I'd taken at the end of my first night out with Zelma: the overworked, over-exercised woman, streaked with blood and annotated with the symptoms of breakdown. Without giving myself time to think over what I was doing, I posted it to Instagram. Then I got up, ate, showered, and, for the first time in several days, shat effortlessly and enjoyably before leaving for work.

I waited until I was on the train to send the resulting picture to Zelma. It was more fun that way. Somehow, sending the photo from the bathroom only seemed to reinforce the idea that what I did in there had to remain in that space. Stood on the train, where anyone could have looked over my shoulder and seen for themselves the screen-filling portrait of filth winging its way to Zelma's mobile, I felt the opposite: that nothing I did anywhere could be contained; that everything I held inside me deserved to be expressed.

In the office, I did a full lap of hellos and how-are-yous before I'd even slipped out of my jacket and turned on my terminal. It seemed that people could intuit a change in me. Their smiles were a little wider, their laughs a little louder. I heard someone say, *She's settling in so well.*

I fired up my screen and waited for my dashboard to load. I felt calm and focused, in a state, as Harrison would have said, of flow. I concentrated on my breathing, feeling the swell and rise of the in-breath, the dissolve of the out-breath. I imagined each small task – adjusting my screen, opening up my software – as a yogic sequence. I paid careful attention to my form, my positioning: the exact curvature of my wrist over my mouse, for example, or the angle of my fingers over the keys. Suddenly, there was no such thing as an isolated or insignificant activity. Everything was a whole-body experience. When I typed, I could feel not just my fingers on the keys, not just the tendons of my hands and forearms, but the effect of each keystroke on my spine, my neck, the muscles in my jaw. All at once, an optimum state seemed achievable, as if I could reach a place where I typed and parsed images and said hello to my colleagues at no cost to my physique or mentality whatsoever. I realised this was the goal: an athletics of administrative activity for the olympians of office life.

With each tap on the keyboard, I saw my place in things more clearly. In its own way, it was beautiful. Everyone with their own small function; everyone pushed to perform at the same level because in this world there was no difference between one task and another. Maybe you were a lowly image-processor. Maybe you were a surgeon repairing a heart. What did it matter? Every goal was simply a task not yet completed. There was no real hierarchy, only productivity, flow. All of us were subject to the same demand: as much as possible, as much of the time as possible.

I felt primed, conditioned. I loaded up the first image and was confronted with an arsehole messily agape, a mixture of what looked like blood and faeces dribbling in a dark, wandering line over the bearded skin below. I swiped right for yes, allowing the image through. Next was a picture of two women, one wearing an elbow-length rubber glove and fisting the other. I allowed it through. This image was replaced by another: a dangerously young man, practically a boy, tied by his wrists to a hook in the ceiling, welts and bleeding grooves criss-crossing his naked body, and a man behind him, also naked except for a black rubber mask, thrashing him with a length of wire. I swiped right, approved it. Next up was a woman in leggings and a sports bra doing a headstand in a gleaming conservatory, a small ceramic cup of green tea beside her. I swiped left, disallowing the image. *That image is obscene*, I told myself. *It is pornographic. It should not be allowed.*

After ten or fifteen minutes of this state of reversal, I felt as if I had unlocked some higher level of being. My vision was sharper, my fingers faster, my reflexes seemingly calibrated to bullet-time. I even think I might have laughed, or made some wordless, ambiguous vocalisation, because one or two of my colleagues looked up oddly, raised an eyebrow, and then went back to work. This was the truth of letting go, I thought, the reality of becoming meaningfully sick. All your valves and systems reversed, open to closed, closed to open. The checks on your depravity were lifted.

Because by that point my computer screen felt like a window into the world, I imagined repercussions far beyond my own terminal and office. I pictured a pan-internet unravelling, a frantic scramble for censorship as everything everyone pretended not to look at became public and everything everyone looked at without thinking was censored. Newspaper articles about global trade, distant wars, Anthropocenic decay, would be illustrated with teeming orgies, competitive vomiting, rape-fantasy mock-ups. Online shops would be awash with violence. Under the Nike logo, that gaping arsehole would glow like a rising sun. The Bank of England's homepage would be a tableau of bestiality, dogs and horses copulating freely with men and women. Instagram would be not so much augmented as revealed, the pornography of surfaces, architecture, foodstuffs, replaced with an endless stream of cocks and cunts, strings of drool, cords of leaping semen, a woman squatting over the face of a hungry man and shitting directly into his mouth. People would flood out into the streets, I thought. Parents would rush upstairs to their children's bedrooms and pull them away from their screens. The government would convene an emergency meeting. The UK would call the US. All known metrics of acceptability would be recalibrated.

But none of that happened. Instead, Harrison appeared beside my desk, his face disappointingly compassionate, and said simply, 'A word?'

Harrison led me past his office to a spare meeting room. It was furnished in the blank-canvas fashion to which meeting rooms always aspire: a large glass table, a projector screen for presentations, a jug of water and some plastic cups. The only nod to the self-styled creativity of the tech world were the chairs, which were a vivid, almost shocking orange. I thought again of my life in rooms: the cuboid cells of housing offices and job centres.

'We're just waiting on Ryan and Seth,' Harrison said.

The atmosphere was awkward. Harrison clearly didn't want to say anything he might have to repeat when others arrived, but he didn't appear to have anything else to say either. He looked at his watch and gave an awkward smile. I didn't smile back. My guard was up. I'd slipped back into that old mask of inscrutability. I couldn't decide if I wanted Ryan and Seth to get here quickly, or if I preferred the thought of watching Harrison shift around in his seat checking his watch for another fifteen minutes. I wondered if this was a meeting that had been in their diaries for a while, or if it had been organised in haste, the moment someone had become wise to the slew of inappropriate material that was now finding its way through me to the web. I was a leak in their dam. Something, in the long run, would have to be done about me.

I was not, I realised, as numb as I had been in the past. Before, events had seemed to unfold around me of their own volition. I was implicated, but never quite involved. My emotional register was muted. Things were neither good nor not good, they were simply ripples in the surface of my detachment. Now, I still couldn't be sure what I felt, but this was less to do with a lack of feeling and more to do with my feelings duelling for dominance. Part of me craved confrontation, closure. Part of me was terrified of losing what I had. And yet I knew *losing* was not quite the right word, because I was the one dismantling what had been erected. The thought was oddly thrilling, as was the realisation that I was feeling anything at all. Nothing could be taken from me, I told myself. Everything I had could be expanded or destroyed according to my own whim.

But look, I thought, at what I'd had to do to put myself in this position: jeopardise everything, pin myself between the opposing threats of disaster and moribundity. Was this what I would always have to do in order simply to feel alive?

Ryan and Seth arrived, apologising about travel time.

'Maya,' Seth beamed, extending a hand towards me. 'You look so well.'

'Really well,' said Ryan, shaking my hand after Seth was done. 'Really, really well.'

'We've had her on an enhanced regimen,' said Harrison.

'Oh fantastic,' said Seth. 'Because that's totally what we envisioned for this project too.'

'Well it's been a real opportunity for us,' said Harrison. 'I mean, seeing how Maya develops, asking ourselves how maybe we could implement some of this stuff across the team.'

Ryan nodded. 'That's definitely a conversation we've been having at our end,' he said. 'Like, what are we learning here? What can we take home from this?'

'Because obviously,' said Seth, 'in the run-up there was a real emphasis on what we were putting in.'

'Right,' said Harrison. 'Exactly.'

'But it doesn't have to be this binary opposition,' said Seth. 'I think that's kind of where we're getting to now. What's the *relationship* between in and out?'

Harrison nodded, then turned to me.

'So Maya,' he said. 'We thought it would be good if we all touched base.'

I nodded, but said nothing.

'We think you're doing really well,' he said.

'Really well,' said Ryan.

'And we want you to know that we appreciate this is a hard thing to do,' said Harrison.

'Really hard,' said Seth.

'I mean,' Harrison continued, 'to come from where you came from, to here, now?' He let a controlled breath seep through pursed lips. 'That's already really something. And it can't have been easy. But you've really taken it on, Maya. You've really *given* it some. You know? And we're all . . . We're grateful for that and we admire it. I *personally* admire it very much.'

I had not seen Harrison in this particular mode before. I was unsure quite how I was supposed to react.

'Thank you, Harrison,' I said. 'I appreciate that.'

Clearly Ryan and Seth were uncomfortable too because they had been exchanging glances, then taking it in turns to open their mouths to say something, only to close them again when Harrison struck an emotional tone they couldn't match.

Harrison nodded contemplatively.

'And we'd also like to say,' said Ryan, slightly experimentally, 'that we think you've done great things on the social media side too.'

'Great numbers,' said Seth. 'Really, very impressive.'

In the fist-sized centre of my solar plexus, a globe of burning gas had formed. I had been good at something, I realised, and then I had decided to be bad at it.

'How are you, Maya?' said Harrison, cutting across Ryan and Seth.

I didn't know what to say. I had assumed they would simply tell me how I was.

'I'm . . . *well*, I think?'

Harrison nodded.

'You think?'

'No. I mean, I'm well. I *am* well. I'm . . . I feel like I've started to . . . *adjust*? And I mean physically I'm . . . well. And . . .'

'We push people hard here,' said Harrison.

I nodded.

'We expect a lot of them.'

'Sure.'

'Some would call that exploitative. Or uncaring.'

Ryan and Seth had stopped attempting to interject. If anything, they looked relieved. Harrison, it seemed, was going to handle this in his own way, and any expectation they might awkwardly assist had been momentarily suspended.

'I don't see it that way, though.' Harrison continued. 'I actually see it the opposite way. The way I see it is, what's more caring? What's more empowering? Telling people that actually they can only contribute so much? Or telling people that they can always contribute more, do more, be more?' He held up a hand. 'I know what you're going to say, because I've heard it before. You're going to say that's kind of a grandiose vision for a company that essentially just sifts through pictures all day. But you know, that really is my point. If a sense of worth comes from a sense of expectation communicated through a sense of pressure, why are only those in high-pressure jobs given access to those feelings? Why not make *every* job an opportunity for people to demonstrate just how much they can really do?'

I didn't reply because I didn't, at that moment, have an answer. Instead, I had pieces of answers, ideas that weren't yet formed. I wanted to say something about what all that energy was directed towards, the sense that much was extracted but little replaced, the feeling that Harrison's philosophy, when taken to its natural extreme, risked casting every individual worker into the role of mere power cell, a resource to be used up and discarded. And yet at the same time a part of me believed him. Or at least, I believed that he believed himself, and his belief was oddly infectious. Wasn't it true, actually, that I had developed, that I had changed, that I had, in a way that even just a year ago I would have stubbornly resisted, *grown*?

'What if I told you, Maya, that I believe human potential to be infinite?' Harrison said. 'Would you agree?'

The question brought two things to mind simultaneously: Zelma's apparently bottomless reserves of passion and excitement, and my own profoundly finite ability to give a shit. I thought back to my old job, to being let go – the wide and warming nothingness I'd felt then, the bottoming-out of everything.

'No,' I said. 'I don't think anyone or anything is infinite. I think there are always limits.'

'Your limits, Maya? Or other people's?'

'Both.'

'How so?'

'I feel that there's only so much I can do, that I have the energy to do. And then with things I feel excited about, I feel there's only so much I'm allowed to do. And I feel like I'm always caught between those limitations. I can do things I don't really want to do, knowing that my energy and my ability to do them will run out, like it always runs out. Or I can do what I want and know that there's really only so far anyone will allow me to go before they either pull me back or knock me down.'

Harrison looked saddened by this. He sat back in his chair, steepled his fingers, and seemed to think about what I'd said for an unusually extended period of time. I was finding it hard to get to grips with this sense of Harrison as a man with an inner life, a man who perhaps sat up late, unsleeping, as I did, troubled by abstract ideas. I wondered if he lived alone, if he had a family, if after everyone had left the office he stayed behind and did his cogitating here. I tried to picture him in the cinema, laughing at a low-grade seasonal comedy, or in a club, dancing. But I couldn't. In my imagination, these moments of human release were blocked to him.

Then I thought about Harrison thinking about me. Whatever I thought of him, one thing was clear: his conception of me was more generous than my conception of him. He had considered me more deeply, imagined me more broadly. I felt a tingle of guilt, as if the limitations I'd set around my conception of Harrison might somehow have been translated into the physical world, as if I had actually tangibly denied him something, rather than simply failed to imagine him. But then, with a slight sense of sadness, I realised how stupid this was: my sense of Harrison had no impact on him. He went about his life unhindered. And there, I thought, right there, was the flaw in Harrison's well-meant logic. It was all very well to believe in people, but it ignored the question of how those people had come to be dependent on your belief, how someone could be elevated to such a position that their conception of someone else tangibly affected that person's life and chances.

For the first time since I'd met him, I felt I wanted to discuss this with Harrison, to know his opinion of what I thought. But the moment seemed to have passed, because now he was leaning back in, his consideration either completed or paused, and the look in his eye had changed.

'Is that what's going on here?' he said. 'You're testing your boundaries?'

'I . . . What do you mean?'

'Come on, Maya,' he said.

'Look,' said Ryan, placing his elbows on his knees and his chin on his interlaced fingers. 'Like I said. We really love what you've done on your Instagram. We know you've worked hard at it. We know it's not easy generating that kind of content on a regular basis without some sort of team throwing ideas at you.'

'Which we could look at,' said Seth. 'If you'd like the input.'

'Which we could totally look at,' said Ryan. 'But Maya, these last images . . . We've got to say we're troubled.'

'Not angry,' said Seth. 'Not like, freaking out or anything. Just troubled.'

'*Concerned*, is maybe the best word,' said Ryan.

'The adverts?' I said.

'The *defaced* adverts,' said Ryan.

'They're just . . .' I began.

'Hey,' said Ryan, holding up his hands. 'They're just pictures. I know. I get it. This isn't about the actual pictures, really. It's more about the way those pictures have been received.'

'The whole vibe of those pictures,' said Seth.

'Of which, if I'm totally honest, you're only a small part,' said Ryan. 'Because those pictures are all over the show right now and we're not saying that's down to you.'

'If anything,' said Seth, 'it's the other way round. It's about how it kind of reads if these pictures, which are all over the show in a certain kind of way, come to be something you seem to be endorsing.'

'Maya,' said Harrison. 'It's fine to have your interests. It's great to have your beliefs. You'd be surprised, I think, how many of those beliefs I might share. I don't know, maybe that's something we'll talk about one day. But I think what Ryan and Seth are driving at is the place of your beliefs within the very limited sphere of this project.'

'Or, I mean, really just the expression of those beliefs,' said Ryan. 'Because honestly as far as we're concerned you can believe whatever you like. You can support whatever you like. This is more about amplification and endorsement.'

'Because these adverts,' said Seth, 'come off kind of anti-advert.'

'And that's a problem,' said Ryan. 'For us, for the project, and for Harrison here.'

'As an organisation, Pict is very much on board with advertising,' said Harrison. 'And to be honest with you we're quite keen that advertisers be on board with us.'

'And likewise for this whole experiment we're all a part of,' said Ryan. 'There's very much an advertising angle.'

I nodded. No-one said anything for a while. Ryan did a little smile. The sympathy, or pantomime of sympathy, was starting to smother me. Somewhere at the base of my stomach, in my pelvic region, a hot spring of misery started to bubble. If its heat reached my face, I thought, I would start to cry, and so I focused on keeping it down there where it belonged, in my guts and bowels, where it could roil and simmer but never quite burst forth.

During the silence, Ryan and Seth had opted to look at their note-pads, on which neither of them had written anything. Harrison, however, was studying me intently.

'Can I be honest?' he said.

I nodded. I felt as if anything I said risked breaching my inner dam. Just at that moment, I would have gladly returned to my year-ago state of numbness. Because this – this occluded, stormy weather front of sadness and anger and fear and a kind of infantile shame about which I felt in turn a deeper and wider shame – was too much. I felt as if things had been placed in me that I had never asked for, and which I had never been meant to contain.

'I don't even give a shit about the advertising angle.'

He let that sink in.

'I mean, yeah, whatever. A few sponsors are a bit pissed off. We could always spin it somehow. I mean, to be honest with you, there's probably room to make this whole project a bit more edgy. I think people would welcome it. I think people would actually like to see more of your own spirit coming through in what you do.'

'Well . . .' said Ryan.

Harrison gave him a pointed look and moved on.

'What worries me more is the *feel* of these images.'

He seemed to want me to say something in response to this, but when I offered nothing in the face of his expectant gaze, he pressed on.

'Are you . . . *happy*, Maya?'

'Happy,' I said. It wasn't a question, just a repetition of the word, as if I were feeling it out, turning it over in my mouth, like a boiled sweet developing sharp edges as it dissolves.

'Happy,' he said, as if I needed clarification.

'I don't know,' I said honestly. 'I can't . . . I don't know how to tell.'

He nodded.

'Because these things you're posting,' he said, 'and the images you've processed today. I just get a sense of . . . I don't know. Anger.'

The implication that I might be angry, and that my anger might be something about which I should be concerned or apologetic, made me angry.

'Is it old anger or new anger?' he said.

'I don't know,' I said. 'I don't even know if it's anger.'

The moment I said it, I knew with sudden certainty that it wasn't anger. I suspected that Harrison knew it as well, because his face seemed to register the confirmation of something he'd suspected. The problem was that I didn't want to say what it was, either to the men in this room or to myself. It was hopelessness. Hopelessness in the face of all the hope I'd been offered. Hopelessness in the face of the fact that all the hope I'd been offered, all the possibility that had been charitably extended to me, gave me no new hope whatsoever.

'I've seen what's been happening with your work,' said Harrison. 'We don't check all the images but we do keep an eye on patterns. We know roughly what a person's ratio should be.'

I nodded.

'I'm not angry,' said Harrison. 'You're not in any trouble.'

'Thank you,' I said.

Harrison smiled. I saw that I had, inadvertently, given him what he'd wanted: gratitude. He wanted more, of course, or if not more then a gratitude that was more expansive. But he'd settle for this, for now: this small acknowledgement of what I'd been given.

I experienced a swell of bilious nausea. The outer edges of my vision blurred and swam. I felt as if I had to focus intently on a single, inch-square patch of table in front of me, or everything would spin out into confusion. I worried that I would faint. I disliked myself for what I was doing, for the chances I was throwing away, and which I would, I knew, continue to reject. But it was also a gambler's high: the thrill of unnecessary risk. In that moment, I understood the satisfaction of reckless endeavour. It was liberating, I saw, to brush up against the possibility of throwing everything away. To do so was to make a point about worthlessness. Every time I said, *I could rid myself of everything*, I was reminding myself that I was beholden to nothing.

I understood, too, what was upsetting my supposed benefactors. This wasn't about my work, or my Instagram feed, or whatever uncomfortable email or phone call Ryan and Seth had received this morning from whichever of their corporate partners was currently on edge. This was about the extent to which I was seen to be playing my role. Just as I had come to understand that in the world of Pict it wasn't enough simply to work and go home – that there was, in addition, an expectation of some deeper, human contribution – so too in the context of this programme, this *opportunity*, it would never be enough simply to point to the material gains I had made. They needed me to be not only successful, but happy, evolved, gratefully aglow. It was my job to make them feel good about themselves, and to help them package up that satisfaction for the consumption of others. In my mind, I saw their vision: me, on a podium or stage, perhaps giving a TED talk, gushing about the change in my life they'd occasioned.

'Are we done here?' I said.

They looked at each other.

'I don't think—' Ryan began.

'Sure,' said Harrison, ignoring him. 'We can be done here, if that's what you want.'

I wasn't sure what I or he was referring to – the meeting or the programme as a whole. I wasn't sure Harrison knew either.

I stood up and walked out of the room, still light-headed and seemingly inches off the ground. Outside, in the corridor, I leaned against a wall and breathed. In my mind, I heard the voice of my meditation instructor describing my breath, measuring it in and out. I thought about focus, about thought itself. I thought about fluidity and change. I thought about a lone penguin, its magnetic mechanism gone, tottering away from its colony, out into the icy expanse.

I took out my phone and looked at my Instagram. Then I looked through my own, private, un-posted images. I selected the first depiction of my shit, that neat and ordered heap of faecal bullets, the water browning and toxifying around them. I ticked the picture, hit send, posted it to my feed. Then I walked out of Pict and into the street outside.

I didn't have to wait long for a reaction. By the time I was a few streets away, my feed was already operating at a new, fevered pitch of response. The easiest assumption for people to make, of course, was that the picture was an error. Perhaps I'd been hacked? Perhaps I'd meant to post another image and posted this one instead, and had not yet realised my humiliating mistake. But then, people pointed out in the responses, why had I had a picture of someone's shit on my phone in the first place? Was it *my* shit? Which was worse, walking around with pictures of my own shit on my phone, or walking around with pictures of *someone else's* shit, which, as today had proved, I might at any time accidentally post on the internet for thousands of people to see?

The solution was simple: I posted another photograph of my shit. This time, it was the second one I'd taken. In the caption, I wrote: *Green: express yourself, but not too much!* Then I went to my profile settings and changed the password and registered email address. For a moment, I toyed with the idea of changing the name as well. After all, *Maya's Journey* had never been an idea over which I felt any sense of ownership. I barely even felt any sense of participation. But that, I thought, was the point. This wasn't just about creating a new narrative. It was about taking the narrative that had been created for me, with which I was expected to comply, and reshaping it to my own demands.

Alongside the updates to my feed, a new tier of frantic engagement was emerging: phone calls, texts, emails. I ignored all of them, but ignoring them only heightened the sense of urgency each attempted to convey. Here was Harrison, by text, saying he just wanted to talk, no pressure. Here was Ryan, by email, asking me to take the picture down, then by text asking me to take both pictures down, then by another text asking me if I had changed the login details and, if so, could I please let him know what they were. Then there was an email from Seth, letting me know that they were prepared to be understanding if I just deleted the pictures and handed the login details back, and one from Harrison, striking a saddened tone, asking me to speak to him before I spoke to anyone else. Lastly, there was a text from Zelma, containing only emoji: a flexed bicep, a lightning bolt, two explosions and a beating heart. I tapped the message and called her.

'Hey,' she said, laughing. 'You superstar.'

'I don't know what I'm doing,' I said.

'Great,' she said. 'Perfect.'

'I think I might be completely fucking up my life. Again.'

'Did you like your life?'

'Not really.'

'If someone gave you a meal made of rotten food would you be grateful to them for feeding you?'

'No. Wait. Did they know it was rotten when they gave it to me?'

'Don't overthink this.'

167

'I think I might have under-thought it.'

'How do you feel?'

'I don't know. I'm just wandering around. I don't know what I'm doing.'

'You left work?'

'Walked out.'

'This is incredible.'

'Come and meet me. Or I'll come and meet you. Or something.'

'I wish I could.'

I felt brought up short, momentarily derailed.

'Of course,' I said quickly. 'I mean, no worries.'

I couldn't explain why my momentum, which just minutes ago had bordered on a kind of madness, could be so sharply and disappointingly drained by something as simple as Zelma not being free to meet. Or, worse, not being *willing* to meet. Briefly, I wondered if everything I'd just done had really been for myself, or if in fact it had been in service of the moment I'd pictured myself sharing with Zelma after I'd done it. Then I wondered if it mattered. Finally, I began to ask myself what exactly it *was* that I had done. I imagined going home to my flat, finding the locks changed, my belongings in black bags on the pavement outside. Perhaps I would slide my bank card into the ATM, only for the machine to absorb it. But then, had any of these things – the flat, the money – really been mine to begin with? It made no difference. I would, again, be without the things that were required to make a life.

'No,' said Zelma. 'I mean, I *really* wish I could. It's just . . . It's nothing. Just bullshit, you know? Just bullshit I have to sort out.'

'What is it?'

'Forget it. Don't worry about it. Honestly. Why would I, like, tarnish your moment?'

'Zelma.'

And then she told me, sadly, with none of the defiance to which by that point I'd become accustomed: she'd received a letter from the benefits office. A sanction had been imposed. All her payments had been stopped.

'These things always get sorted out,' I said hopelessly, annoyed at my own inability to say anything useful.

'Yeah,' she said.

'If you need money, just tell me.'

She laughed.

'Says the woman who just kissed goodbye to her income.'

I took the Overground, headed east. I was struck by the emptiness of the trains at this time of day, the way the space in the carriages seemed like another kind of freedom. I tried to remember if I had ever actually sat down on this train or if every journey I'd made had been in the same state: standing, crushed into a corner, a body among bodies. Back at the flat, I ate, stared at the television, watched a Hawaiian hurricane uproot trees and scatter them across a city while my phone hummed with chatter. When I looked up from my phone, or away from the screen of the television, the flat and everything in it seemed distant, as if whatever thin delusion had allowed me to think of it as mine had now dissolved. There was no real surprise associated with this, no attempt to grasp at what was slipping away. Things had turned cold on me before; they would do so again. And besides, this time around the life that was slipping away was not even one I had fully inhabited. It was a set of borrowed clothes, a few pieces of rented furniture, a handful of people who would remark on the absence of my face in their field of view, then return without further comment to their routines.

Several times my phone, perched on the corner of my market crate coffee table, rattled with contact from an unknown number. I ignored it. Later, I thought, the doorbell would ring, and when I ignored that the letterbox would flap. If I ignored that too, at some point someone would turn up with a key. I would be offered a simple choice: pack up and leave quietly, or *be* packed up, then ejected.

I didn't know how I felt about anything. Events and possibilities were simply surfaces off which my emotions slid. It was a feeling I'd felt before; its chilly irony was familiar. After all that friction, all that chafing, all that experience of life as an uncomfortable landscape over which I begrudgingly had to crawl, now there was no purchase at all, just the smooth, breezy glide of freefall.

I had, I realised, no plan. I didn't know if I would dig in and resist, or simply gather my things and flee. Nothing I'd done had been enacted with any forethought. Now, as I sank into the consequences of decisions I'd made according to instinct, it was as if I'd come to the edge of the small world I'd created for myself, or, more accurately, had created for me. I thought again of those walruses on the dissolving ice floe, of red deer pinned behind the surging edge of a wildfire. The thought that it was not only my world that was eroding, but *the* world, was strangely comforting. All I was dealing with was just a more immediate, more individuated form of what everyone was dealing with.

I picked up my phone and swiped it awake. Every possible means of communication was active: missed calls, texts, an over-stuffed inbox. I ignored them all and went instead to my Instagram feed. There, the narrative was changing even as I looked at it. Under the pictures of shit were the predictable responses – hilarity, scorn, confusion. But they were increasingly intermixed with comments and pictures that took an entirely different tone. People – women – had posted hearts and messages of support. They'd even, in a strange twist on the *Spartacus* approach, posted their own pictures of shit. On Twitter and Facebook, to which I was guided through comments on my Instagram, people were messaging Green and Pict directly, sending them image after image of every conceivable type of excrement. To scroll through the posts was to experience a kind of faecal spectrum, from turds so pale as almost to be ivory, all the way through to browns so deep they were practically black. As the posts had gathered momentum, the creativity factor had increased exponentially. At first all the shit was safely contained in toilet bowls, and usually of a relatively firm consistency. Soon, though, people had sourced images of ever-messier diarrhoeic expression: toilets with spattered seats and cisterns, cubicles in which the walls were daubed with smears. Then people had moved away from toilets completely and begun to explore the interface of shit with the bodies that produced it: buttocks, thighs, hands, even faces, all streaked and painted with crap. Finally, the truly creative had moved beyond static images completely and begun sending GIFs and videos: women squatting on pavements, on carpets, on beds, even on each other, snakes of shit uncurling from their arses.

Maya Devereaux, I read in one caption, *has reinvented the dirty protest.*

I picked up the phone to Zelma. She answered after barely a single ring.

'We need a place,' I said to Zelma on the phone.

'What sort of place?' she said.

'For ourselves,' I said. 'But maybe for others too.'

We were both quiet a moment. I realised that in my haste I had made assumptions.

'I mean,' I said awkwardly, 'if you want to.'

'Are you kidding?' she said. 'Of course I want to. All I need to do is pack a bag.'

And that was that. We'd agreed. I was leaving. She was leaving with me. We were starting something, moving towards something, but we didn't know what.

TWO

F inding a building wasn't difficult for Zelma. She had connections. She was vague about their nature, often flippant about
their significance, but they existed. I assumed her contact was
mainly online, impersonal. There were forums, Facebook groups,
private chats. People traded lists of locations, intel on alarm systems,
practical tips for gaining and securing access.

During the couple of days it took Zelma to ask around, I barely left the sofa, killing time by watching what I'd set in motion
unspool across the web. By this point the digital dirty protest was
firmly in the mainstream, dissected across platforms and outlets.
It was radical, people said, emancipatory. It was disgusting, others
countered; a degrading, infantile embarrassment. I didn't particularly care what people thought. I enjoyed the sense of chaos, the
feeling that some laxative and emetic event had triggered the violent
disgorgement of thought.

There was no contact from Ryan, Seth, or Harrison. I assumed
it was because the situation had evolved beyond individual people
talking to each other. Green and Pict would be in a state of legal
lockdown, halfway to firming up their shared stance. They'd go, I
suspected, with whatever afforded them a tolerable sense of balance:
a sensitive end to the PR sewage-spill, a solution that stopped them
looking weak while conveniently obscuring their power.

Just as my presence alone in the flat began to feel unsustainable,
with every street-sound and passing shout and rattle of my letterbox
catapulting me from sleep or sending me jumping for the remote

to silence the TV, Zelma called to tell me there were candidates: an empty office block in Stratford, a disused storage facility on an industrial estate in Leyton, and a vacated Poundland in Ilford. Over the course of a couple of nights, we scouted each of them in turn, weighing the pros and cons. The office block in Stratford turned out to be occupied. The Poundland was empty but impregnable. The storage facility in E10, though, was perfect: a large, ground-floor space with black grilles on the windows, a reinforced shutter at the front, and a small steel door with a broken padlock at the back.

We spent two more nights and the best part of an afternoon on reconnaissance, wandering the rest of the industrial estate, getting a sense of day-to-day life within its boundaries. At one corner, a new complex of flats was going up – four hollow, hulking buildings looming over the main road, a pseudo-Communist banner along the fence promising a *rental revolution*. Further in, there was a bread factory, from which rose the sweetened, yeasty smell of that day's batch. There was also a scaffolding depot, a cash and carry, a unit converted into a Nigerian Pentecostal church and, all the way through on the other side, the borough's dump and recycling centre. Only the more significant enterprises had CCTV. For the others, an assortment of militaristic logos and slogans warned of twenty-four-hour security guards, dog patrols, prosecutions. At night the place felt ghostly and barren. Until the bread factory fired up again around four and the workmen arrived at the building site at six, there was a desolate silence. From midnight to three we sat in a dark and empty yard drinking coffee and eating doughnuts like Hollywood cops on a stakeout, peering through the chain-link fence at the curving road that ran through the centre of the estate. We saw the much-touted security patrol twice – one man only, strolling breezily with his German shepherd, periodically muttering into the crackling static of his radio.

The building we had our eye on was towards the edge, not immediately visible from the road. When we moved our makeshift surveillance spot to the back of our proposed new home, we didn't see the guard at all. Nor did we see anyone else. After a night and a day of watching, we slipped the busted padlock from its chain and pushed open the surprisingly light and hollow door. Inside, the emptiness was thrilling. Dust covered the bare surfaces. The concrete floor and wide steel shutter had their own resonance. The scuffle of our footsteps, the susurration of our breath, seemed suddenly expansive, pregnant.

A single, square, central area dominated, the front of which was half-filled with a row of head-height windows, grimy to the point of opacity. Diluted by the darkened glass, icy security lighting trickled in weakly. Off one edge, away from the windows and furthest from the main steel shutter, was a windowless back room I assumed had been an office, in which we found a functioning electrical socket where we could charge our phones. In the opposite corner, away from the limited light, the floor tilted gently downwards, towards a small drain stained with a spattered rainbow of metallic paint.

I stood in the middle of the main space and breathed deeply through my nostrils, tasting airborne damp, concrete dust, the lingering residue of chemical processes. It was a place, I thought, of vacated industrial activity, once busy, now stripped and ready for life.

I put my arm around Zelma. I felt as if things I'd half-imagined or only partially dared to picture were becoming real, as if things I'd taken to be certain were being edged out.

'I can see it,' I said.

'Me too,' she said. 'I can see it too.'

The next night, I stuffed into a rucksack the few things I thought of as mine: some clothes, some basic documents, my laptop and phone, which of course didn't belong to me but which I felt by that point I'd earned. In the bathroom, I inspected my array of comforting products, the now-totemistic bottles I'd taken from the hotel.

In the end, I left everything, even my toothbrush and toothpaste. Already, without thinking too deeply about it, a sense of personal repulsion was beginning to appeal. I'd cleansed and toned myself in pursuit of a productive ideal. Now I looked forward to undoing it all, rendering myself freshly toxic and unapproachable.

On my way to meet Zelma, I stopped at a cash machine and kept withdrawing until I was refused. I'd expected my account to have been shut down, but I came away with close to two grand from the overdraft. Perhaps it was an oversight on Ryan and Seth's part. Perhaps they still felt this could all be straightened out, shaped into the meaningful outcome they desired. Or maybe they just worried about me turning up dead, and figured that leaving me some funds would at least provide evidence of their humanity.

I met Zelma a short walk away from the industrial unit. Like me, she had a single rucksack and nothing else. Each of us had obtained certain essentials. I'd been in charge of basic provisions, Zelma had taken responsibility for security and tools. Immediately after arriving, we changed the broken padlock on the back door, repositioned it so we could lock ourselves in. Then we sat side by side against the back wall, looking towards the streaked and darkened windows, beyond which the occasional sweeping glow of a passing car or bus was visible.

'I can't promise I know what I'm doing,' I said.

Zelma laughed. 'Let's lean into that,' she said.

Basic practicalities became all-consuming. It was a focus I remembered: the realisation of just how much attention the things we take for granted can consume. Food requires planning; relieving yourself demands a strategy. Somehow, in that grey, undivided space, in which every footstep and shuffling adjustment of posture, every cough, burst of laughter and belch, took on a new and swelling resonance, the effect seemed all the more heightened, to the point where it reminded me of my meditation classes – the amplified gurgle of stilled bodies, the restless thrashing of my mind as I tried to subdue it. When you remove that much from your life and thought, the remaining subject of your attention unpacks itself to fill the void. Suddenly, the emptiness of the space we occupied seemed infinite, the depths of its simplicity both thrilling and dizzying.

We focused down, dealing with each necessity as it arose. That first night, we nourished ourselves on booze and whatever snacks we'd squeezed into our bags, fell asleep still propped against each other, and woke up stiff and starving on the unfriendly floor, urgently needing to pee. A bodily logic dictated our priorities. Our bladders shouted the loudest, so we turned our attention to the toilet.

'We can use the side room,' Zelma said. 'Or go outside. Or . . .'

I didn't hear the rest of her suggestion. I was standing beside the little room that had once been an office, staring at the door. I thought of my furtive trips to the toilet at work, the edge of illness to which I'd pushed myself at BodyTemple. I thought of my crazed unburdening back at my flat, the luxury of my weekend defecations. All my moments of release: hidden away, secret and shameful.

While Zelma watched, I found a screwdriver in her bag and removed the door from its hinges. Then I propped it against the wall and kicked it to pieces. When I was done, I walked over to the small drain set into the floor, squatted over it with shaking thighs, and urinated while Zelma watched. Then Zelma took my place, pissed in solidarity into the little drain while angling her phone downwards through her knees for a snapshot. I knew there were things she wanted to ask, but she could tell I didn't yet have the answers. We were feeling our way, letting our bodies and instincts guide us.

Since neither of us felt any compunction about washing, the next thing we dealt with was food. We had nothing to cook with, no ingredients to prepare, no storage for whatever we might have used or produced. We did, however, have the money I'd been able to extract from my account. That morning we bought greasy, disintegrating bacon sandwiches from one of the three or four food vans that served the workers on the industrial estate, queuing up with the scaffolders and delivery drivers, the reflective-suited recycling crew from the dump. Glances were exchanged, but nothing was said. On the way back, pulling bacon rind from our teeth and glugging Nescafé from styrofoam cups, we agreed to have a takeaway delivered in the evening, until more permanent solutions could be found. Even then, I noticed, we were unwilling to engage with what we would later think of as the outside world. We were only half an hour from the high street. We could have gone to a cafe, the supermarket, a pub. But doing so seemed wrong in a way that was difficult to define. Our project was one of reduction, but also completeness. That room, with its barred-up windows and cold concrete walls, wasn't just a retreat from the world, it was our world in itself, all-encompassing in its denial of everything else.

That night we ordered an excessive Indian takeaway and ate it with our hands, sitting on the dusty floor. I felt oily and slick, lubricated with the grease of the meal. We couldn't finish everything, so we left it in a heap for when our hunger returned. From midnight or one onwards, we roamed the estate, scavenging for discarded food and abandoned materials. Everywhere we went there were stacks of unused wooden pallets, out of which we made a simple raised area to sit on, a table on which to arrange our meals. In a bin at the back of the bread factory, we found refuse sacks full of burger buns, only just beginning to harden. We took a sack each and used the buns to mop up the sauce from our foil tins of cold curry. At some point, Zelma walked casually over to the drain and shat – a thick brown river that splashed the wall and spattered her ankles. She photographed the aftermath in tightly zoomed detail, posted it with no caption. Soon afterwards, I shat on top of her shit, a rite we likened to pricking our fingers and swearing a blood oath.

We fell asleep on our spread-out clothes, Zelma's ankles and calves still pebble-dashed with faeces, my hair caked with the residue of a balti, unintentionally applied when I'd tried to push my fringe out of my eyes while eating. When we woke, the sun was streaming in through the row of windows, the bars throwing a matrix of shadow over the floor, cross-hatching our pile of picked-at food, the hardening remains of our waste on the lip of that already failing drain.

Temporarily rested, empty of shit and no longer hungry, we expanded our agenda outwards from the strictly corporeal. Zelma ramped up my Instagram feed, completing its transformation from corporate puff project to intimate bodily record. There were pictures of us pissing, of encrusted period blood in stiffened knickers, of our mixing faeces on the drain's blocked grille. She snapped the stack of takeaway containers, a streak of drying sauce along my arm. She also posted images of the space we occupied, its bare concrete walls and barred windows, its stained and chilly floor.

It was not enough, though, merely to document the personal. This was something we both agreed on. Our goal was not the easy thrill of a voyeuristic viewership, the dopamine spike of mindless self-promotion.

'Everything's so *clean hands* now,' said Zelma. 'It's like you can kid yourself you did something just because you saw something. And then you can kid yourself you *are* something just because people saw you. We can aspire to more than just being seen.'

At the same time, we were wary of blunt ideological statements, manifestos, bullet-pointed aims. We wanted people to arrive at what we were doing in their own way, by their own means, bringing with them their own thoughts and needs. In a moment of inspiration, Zelma appropriated the slogan from our most successful billboard: *Release Yourself.*

People got it because they were waiting for it. The pictures of toilets and diarrhoea they'd sent to Pict, all of which had been sourced from the web, none of which carried any real sense of risk or exposure, had been too easy. They had spoken of release, implied it, but not quite offered it. Now it was if we had given people permission. In response, our growing number of followers catalogued their own small acts of non-compliance, sending pictures of their mouths and torsos slicked with the residue of messy consumption, unshaven legs and tangled thatches of pubic hair, unkempt armpits, unconcealed acne, chipped and darkening teeth. Meanwhile, the acts of desecration against billboards and adverts continued. Models were adorned with bruises, bags under their eyes, self-injurious wounds. Articles on personal growth were glossed with challenges on points of fact, reworded so that the standard bromides of self-confident positivity became exhortations to rot, swear, spit, and, most pleasingly to me, *let yourself go*. Hashtags began to sprout and proliferate: *#filterthis, #filthyuglyfree*.

People naturally wanted to outdo each other. As soon as enough people offered online solidarity, others wanted to go further. They offered money and supplies, asked us what we needed, what they could meaningfully do. Almost out of nowhere, we became a cause.

Zelma set up an online wishlist, made use of an app that allowed you to buy takeaways and booze for friends. Within a few days we had stockpiles of wine and beer, sleeping bags, blankets, bottled water, chocolate. Almost every evening some confused young man bearing pizza, Chinese, fried chicken, or Turkish mezze would tap tentatively at our back door, peering through the gap and over our shoulders, trying to gauge what we might be doing in a disused industrial facility, late at night. We told them we'd just rented it, were fixing it up for our business. The cartons and leaking paper bags heaped up in the middle of the room. We snacked from the pile whenever we were hungry. Our skin developed an oily patina, our clothes the greasy, meaty funk of fried and heavily spiced foods.

Now that people were sending us donations, there was less need to scavenge from the surrounding area, but we kept up our nocturnal missions anyway. There was something thrilling about claiming what we needed, scraping excess from the world around us. We plundered bins and scrapyards, the car park behind the cash and carry. One night, we carried a mattress between us, one at each end, taking the weight on our heads. When we got it home, into the puddle of light beneath our windows, we saw that it was torn and darkly stained with what might have been tea or food or blood. We lay on it in delight, feeling all its soaked-up life leeching into our bodies through the glistening boundary of our increasingly osmotic skin. Another night we made five separate trips to a pile of wooden offcuts outside a lumber yard, then lit an open fire in the middle of the floor and sat as close to it as possible on our mattress, which began to stink in the heat. Once the place was warm, we became less concerned with clothes, which of course made it easier to shit and piss at will, wherever we slept or sat or lay. I remember vividly the first time I half-woke, at some pre-dawn hour, my bladder stinging after we'd shared a case of cheap beer, and released myself without moving, feeling all that hot urgency and swelling insistence simply drain away. I felt so free that I half-laughed, alone, in the dark, and woke Zelma, sleeping beside me, who stretched out her hand into the warm dampness, laughed with me, then rolled into the moistened space to sleep.

Perhaps recognising that the more people focused on me and what I was doing, the less anyone was likely to focus on them, Ryan, Seth and Harrison went surprisingly quiet, limiting themselves to a couple of non-specific public statements about the heaviness of their hearts.

'It's very sad,' Harrison was quoted as saying. 'But I think we can all honestly say we've learned a lot from this experience, just as we hope Maya has too. It's never easy, this kind of rehabilitative work. There will be obstacles. There will be setbacks. But I think it's really important to convey at this point that we don't in any way regard Maya as a lost cause. She was making tremendous progress, and, although obviously we'd never pressure her, if she ever does want to come back, she knows the door is open.'

'Our vetting procedures,' said Ryan in a carefully prepared statement, 'our safeguarding protocols, the support we offer people in the programme – it's really robust. Of course, when you're dealing with people from this kind of background there will be complications and setbacks, but our primary concern, just as it was when we started this initiative, is Maya's wellbeing. We've reached out to her and she knows she can talk to us whenever she wants to.'

But of course they hadn't reached out, not really, and I wasn't convinced they wanted to. Their distance spoke of fear, but I knew it wasn't me they were afraid of. What was paralysing them now, I suspected, was the very thing that had excited them before: the glow of attention, the serried eyes in whose gaze I bathed.

Intellectualising our choices felt uncomfortable, deadening. The life we began to shape in that empty and unsanitary space was a reaction, as physical and uncontrolled as a rash from a poisonous plant. Elements of our existence had become toxic to us; our bodies were dictating the response. When we talked about what we were doing, as on occasion we felt compelled to, we spoke only in the language of rejection.

'I'm tired of achieving,' I said one night as we lay on our stinking mattress passing a bottle of red wine back and forth. 'I'm tired of saying, this is where I want to get to, then wearing myself down trying to get there.'

'And *explaining*,' Zelma said. 'Explaining myself. Explaining my illness. Explaining the things I do and the things I want.'

'We shouldn't have to explain anything,' I said. 'We shouldn't have to tell some fucking story about ourselves.'

'Fuck stories,' said Zelma.

'Fuck growth.'

'Fuck success.'

'Fuck *health*.'

We were laughing as we listed it all. Fuck work. Fuck progress. Fuck schedules. Fuck obedience. Fuck timidity. Fuck hygiene. Fuck fitting in. Fuck friendliness and easiness and fuck asking permission.

'That's what we should say to people,' Zelma said. 'That's what we should offer.'

I thought about this, and realised as I did so that I had been trying not to think about it. I knew that change was inevitable, understood that in essence our choice was between expansion and failure. But at the same time I worried about progress I couldn't control, feared losing myself in the mess of what I wanted.

'I don't want to change the world,' I said. 'I just want to be rid of it.'

Zelma rolled her head towards me, breathed and blinked a number of times before speaking.

'You mean like die?' she said.

I couldn't tell if it was the wine, the slippage of my diurnal cycle, or just the simple fact of trying to give words to feelings I hadn't yet been able to name, but I felt suddenly tearful, almost hysterical. I could feel myself opening, something long-buried and internally corrosive emerging. I thought of my dream, the arachnid monster hatching from my forearm. I felt again the sensitivity of that little patch of skin, the sensation of air, for the first time, meeting parts of me I'd never previously exposed.

To stop the tears, I closed my eyes. Images unspooled in the blackness – the scenes of catastrophe and devastation in front of which Zelma and I had relaxed, the private snapshots I'd parsed at Pict. I saw a vomit-soaked bed, smokestacks belching carbon, blood

185

pooling beneath the stump of a severed neck. An oil-slicked seabird slipped beneath a heavy, jet-black wave; a screaming woman was dragged by her ankle from a darkened containment facility. Then I remembered us all at the retreat, furiously exfoliating ourselves in the showers, guzzling down plant juice to be pure, desperate to live longer and more cleanly in a filthy, sickened world.

'No,' I said finally. 'I just don't believe that living has to mean anything.'

Zelma rolled over and picked up my mobile from the floor.

'Say it,' she said, passing me the phone.

I angled my wrist, snapped a picture of me and Zelma on the mattress. In the glare of the flash, our faces seemed moon-white, almost translucent, our eyes pinkly aglow. Then I opened up a fresh Instagram post, tapped in the white space of the caption, and wrote: *Come join our disease.*

By the next day, it was already a hashtag: *#cjod*. There were pictures of it written on walls, across the faces of adverts, in a series of hair-thin scratches into the skin of someone's arm.

We needed to screen out the noise, find the people we wanted. Zelma started a WhatsApp group, accessible only after a process of vetting. She pored through social media accounts, weeded out journalistic connections, preying hipsters, people flitting from one emergent trend to the next. She also, although we didn't notice or think about it until later, excluded men.

While we selected our guests, people sought our approval by feeding us, clothing us, making sure we could drink and get high. As our exact location leaked, people abandoned Zelma's wishlist system completely and began sending padded brown envelopes stuffed with dark-web contraband – weed, ecstasy, tabs of acid. Me and Zelma talked briefly about poison, wondering whether any-one would take adequate offence at what we were doing to send us drugged sweets or adulterated intoxicants. We decided we didn't care, that our ethos was to consume whatever we were given, whatever others wanted to redirect, and that we were already poisoning ourselves with spoiled food and mounting shit anyway. What was the difference?

Our chosen women arrived in ones and twos, carrying rucksacks and sleeping bags, boxes of food and hand-me-down essentials. Margot, young and alone, her bobbed hair dyed a bruised mauve, brought a saucepan, a kettle, a set of forks and spoons. Ama, thick-set and heavy-eyed, breezily out of breath from her journey, brought a selection of appropriated bric-a-brac: a shopping bag full of bruised fruit, a dirty blanket, three faded plastic flowers she carefully arranged by the spot she chose as her sleeping area. Sadie and Kim, who arrived together, hand in hand, brought dried goods they'd collected from the nearby food bank, handed out chocolate biscuits by way of saying hello. I'd never met them but I felt I knew them. Margot had left her parents' house to be here, and beneath her shyness and obvious fear I sensed the underlying reassurance of those who've repeatedly but safely eloped: the unconscious knowledge that, if all went sour, she could always go back. Sadie and Kim were older, around my age, and had come from a Lambeth squat where, they complained, the politics and radicalism they'd pined for had been subsumed by the numbing detail of daily life. They were rarely far apart from each other, and liked to sit curled in corners, one resting her head on the lap or shoulder of the other. They had the conflicted openness of the increasingly weary radical: committed to a higher cause, yet experienced enough to know that clinging to each other was their best defence against vanishing into the collective. Ama, meanwhile, was harder to read. She had the wary stare and frowning suspicion of a habitual drifter, but there was none of the wired, rangy energy I'd seen in other hardened wanderers. Instead, she seemed tired, defeated by her nomadism, as if reconciled to her placelessness yet unable to countenance its inevitable endless extension. She sighed whenever she sat down, groaned a little when she stood. Once, she drifted off with her bag sagging open and I saw inside a veritable pharmacy of pills, all in identical little brown plastic prescription bottles, neatly labelled with doses and times.

I regarded the reactions of the new arrivals as a measure of how far me and Zelma had come. By that point, even stepping into our living space took courage. We'd settled quickly into our habits – eating with our hands on that festering mattress, shitting and pissing whenever the urge arose. Our shared stink had become less the urgent and exciting presence it had been initially, and more an ambient, half-noticed comfort to which, like the hum of a road a person has lived beside for years, we were now too accustomed to be disturbed. I watched the women's faces as they arrived, watched Zelma as she watched them in turn, weighing their freshness against our decay, gauging our decay by their response.

Margot was first. I met her at the back door, felt the thinly covered fear in her embrace. When I led her inside, I could see, in her face and eyes, all the luxury and hygiene she had come from. I imagined folded, fluffy towels in her parents' bathroom, scented candles, the smell of wildflowers wafting in from the manicured garden. She was clearly keen to give the impression of ease, but there was no disguising the sudden catch in her throat as she entered, the involuntary leap of her hand to her nostrils.

'Wow,' she kept saying. '*Wow.*'

Zelma regarded her coldly, offered no reassurance or distraction when she spoke.

'Shocked?' she said flatly.

'No,' said Margot, her voice the tactful sing-song of a loyal friend hedging her way around a companion's embarrassing choice of clothes. '*No.* Not at all. Just . . . It's a process of adjustment, I suppose.'

She made an attempt at a carefree smile and walked slowly across the room, taking it in.

'The others aren't here yet?' she said.

'You're the first,' said Zelma.

'Congratulations,' I said. I tried to make it sound bright and upbeat but the words seemed to curdle on contact with the atmosphere. It was awkward for all of us, I realised. Margot was acclimatising to new conditions, me and Zelma were adjusting to a new presence. Each of us had things to get over, resistances we needed to ease.

'I love what you've been doing,' said Margot. 'The adverts, the Instagram. I didn't follow you right at the beginning,' she added, looking at me as if she owed me an apology or an explanation, 'but it was early on. Maybe around the time of the illness selfie? I loved that. Anyway, I've followed you right through all the other stuff. And then you started this up and . . .' She waved vaguely. 'Things were going on. You know. Various things. And the timing just seemed, I don't know, auspicious or whatever.'

Everything she said was directed at me. I looked at Zelma, wanting to credit her input, but Zelma was still peering at Margot. If the lack of recognition upset her, she gave no sign of it. Instead, she pointed at Margot's crisp white canvas sneakers, swept her hand upwards to her shiny, sharp-edged hair.

'You're very well turned out,' she said.

'Oh,' said Margot, self-consciously pushing her hair behind her ear. 'I mean . . .'

She trailed off, awkwardly.

'Just an observation,' said Zelma.

I wanted to interject, but Zelma had a way of sealing the boundaries of a conversation, reducing a debate to its essential participants.

'Did you travel far to get here?' she said.

Margot shrugged. 'An hour or so. Couple of buses.'

'Have you had anything to eat?'

'Just a cereal bar.'

Zelma gestured to the heap of discarded takeaway containers.

'Help yourself,' she said, smiling. '*Mi casa es su casa.*'

Margot looked at the foil-and-plastic detritus, the smeared and encrusted remains.

'Oh,' she said vaguely. 'I'm fine.'

'But we have so much. It needs eating.'

'Maybe later,' said Margot.

'Why not now?' said Zelma. 'Unless of course you don't like what we have on offer? I mean, we could order something fresh, but it seems such a waste.'

'Of course,' said Margot.

An uncomfortable silence unpacked itself from Zelma's gift-wrapped invitation. Again, I found myself wanting to say something, but the void into which my words would arrive seemed airtight, impenetrable.

Margot shrugged and squatted beside the leftovers. She picked around and found some hardened biryani, bits of which she balled between her fingers and popped unenthusiastically into her mouth.

'Mmm,' said Zelma, encouraging her the way one might after forcing some broccoli between the tightly clamped teeth of a resistant child.

'Mmm,' said Margot, managing a smile.

'That's good, right?' said Zelma.

Margot nodded, ate a little more.

'Perhaps you're thirsty?' said Zelma.

Margot shook her head. 'I drank so much water on the way,' she said. 'Honestly.'

'Of course,' said Zelma. 'How rude of us. We haven't even asked if you need the toilet.'

'Well . . .' said Margot.

'Go ahead,' said Zelma, gesturing non-specifically to a patch of floor as yet uncolonised by food waste.

'Oh,' said Margot. 'Right.'

She made no move to do anything, just shifted her gaze between Zelma and the patch of floor.

'You don't have to feel self-conscious,' said Zelma.

'I don't. It's not that.'

'Maybe you'd prefer if we left the room?'

I saw Margot's mouth open briefly, her face take on a momentary brightness, only for it to fall again when she realised she'd revealed herself.

'We're not going to leave the room,' said Zelma, pitching her voice as if she were breaking bad news. 'And you're not going to leave the room either. There's no leaving the room here. Do you understand?'

Margot nodded.

'There are no other rooms,' said Zelma. 'This room is all rooms, and all rooms are this room.'

Margot stood slowly and unbuttoned her jeans. Her underwear was a girlish pink. Through the thin material of her knickers, a neat, shaped strip of pubic hair was visible. I imagined the care and attention that had gone into this, the circumstances in which she had no doubt imagined that her grooming would come to be welcomed, and felt an ache in my chest that it took me a few seconds to recognise as pity. In a smooth motion, so that nothing more could be seen, Margot both peeled down her clothes and squatted, her jeans bound tightly around her knees, her bare backside hovering over the floor. She closed her eyes, breathed, opened her eyes, breathed again. She squatted a long time and nothing happened.

'I'm sorry,' she said, standing back up and rearranging her clothes. 'Maybe I didn't need to go after all.'

'Of course,' said Zelma.

Margot pointed outside, not looking at either of us.

'Can I explore?' she said.

'Absolutely,' said Zelma. 'Familiarise yourself.'

She smiled kindly at Margot, but I couldn't tell if Margot noticed.

Her head was down as she left. Outside, we heard her footsteps crunching over broken glass and shards of shattered plastic. I pictured her adrift in the silence and security lighting, looking for a darkened corner to squat in, probably crying.

'Is that what we're doing now?' I said. 'Humiliating people?'

'It was kinder to do it quickly,' Zelma said. 'She'll see that.'

'This isn't a boot camp, Zelma.'

She frowned at me a little, cocked her head to one side, as if my reaction interested her in a detached way.

'No,' she said. 'But it's not a tourist attraction either.'

That first night, it was just the three of us. Zelma changed her tone, tried to draw Margot out, but the damage was done. Margot was quiet and awkward. She ate a little, drank some wine when the bottle was passed to her, then lapsed into silence whenever me or Zelma paused in our efforts at conversation. Zelma, I could see, was doing her best to conceal her impatience. People's inability or unwillingness to express themselves frustrated her. She would make concessions up to a point, but lost interest if her efforts went unrewarded. I saw it differently. I'd met many Margots during my time on the streets – wayward girls caught between the freedoms they imagined and the comforts they now saw receding. It took time, I knew, to either adjust or retreat, soften into it or rethink and return home. I admired Margot's efforts, and knew too that Zelma had misjudged things at the start. When Zelma ran out of concocted enthusiasm and fell asleep on our mattress, I sat with Margot into the night, telling her stories about encampments I'd lived on, other buildings I'd squatted. Margot seemed to appreciate this. It required little of her beyond listening, allowed her to take her mind off her immediate surroundings and imminent future and imagine another life, another setting, another array of possibilities. Perhaps, also, she caught in what I was telling her the unspoken message I'd intended:

that I had been through worse, seen worse, and was still here, still fine, still alive.

Towards the end of the night, I watched Margot carefully lay out a blanket to sleep on, ball up a jumper for a pillow, then wrap a second blanket securely around her, drawing her knees up to her chest so as to ensure she was completely covered. I remembered my first night in the hotel – as exciting and alien as this night, now, for Margot – and recalled how I'd made that little bed for myself on the floor. There is such comfort, I realised, in shrinking the space around us, leaving the expanse of the outdoors for a small room, blocking out the space of a room by tightening the covers around our shoulders. Margot held herself as she slept, I noticed, as if consoling herself, creating what scant feeling of protection she could. As I watched her sleep, I felt I understood. Her body and the boundaries of her personhood were still fragile; her instinct was to guard them. I remembered my first experience of letting go at BodyTemple, how that had reminded me in turn of the fact that all my fears on the street had revolved around some contravention of my physical autonomy, and I saw, quite suddenly, something that before had been only a vague outline in my mind: that fear arises from the body. Once your body is gone or forgotten there is nothing, really, to be afraid of.

With Sadie and Kim, there was no such hesitation or awkwardness. They arrived the day after Margot, bearing an entirely different kind of energy. The squat in Lambeth, they said, had been a profound disappointment. They, in turn, had been something of an issue for the squat.

'Anally retentive,' said Kim, throwing her backpack into a corner and speaking through awkwardly angled lips as she lit a cigarette. 'The whole lot of them. Give them freedom and all they want is more rules.' She gave me a stern glare. Her eyes bugged slightly when she felt particularly impassioned about something, which, I

193

would come to learn, was most of the time. 'I'm not about that,' she said. 'I'm not about that at *all*.'

'They were really big on interpersonal conduct,' said Sadie, who was fractionally younger than Kim, marginally less intense in her responses, but no less appalled by the authoritarianism of the anti-authoritarian environment they'd just left. 'They kept wanting to have meetings where we all talked about how we talked to each other.'

'What was it they called me, Sades?' said Kim. They were standing side by side now, leaning into each other, Sadie pinching the fag from between Kim's fingers and taking a long, luxurious haul. Kim was a broad, almost heavy white woman, her cheeks and nose slightly rosy with booze. Sadie was smaller, fresher somehow, and although I couldn't place her ethnicity at first, she would tell me later that her mother was Mauritian.

'Abrasive,' said Sadie.

'Abrasive,' said Kim. 'Right.'

She retrieved the cigarette from Sadie, sucked on it until the butt crackled, then flicked the end onto the takeaway pile while casting an appraising eye around the room.

'Don't tell me,' she said, pointing at Margot and grinning. 'You're the quiet one, right?'

Without waiting for an answer, she turned on the spot several times, then let out something between a whoop and a screech.

'Yeah,' she said, nodding vigorously. 'This is what I'm fucking *talking* about.'

Ama was different again. She arrived without ceremony a little after Sadie and Kim, smiling when I opened the door, then walking inside. She seemed neither aghast at the conditions nor thrilled at their implications. Instead, she cleared a patch of floor with her foot, laid out her coat with an air of homely practicality, and rested against the wall with her eyes closed. Later, when she'd recovered from the effort of her day, she told us she'd been riding the buses. She'd over-stayed on her visa, lost her job in an old people's home, then lost her flat and everything in it. Now her money had run out and there was nowhere for her to go. She didn't feel safe on the streets. What money she made from begging, she spent on a bus pass.

'No-one look at you on the bus,' she said in her rich Trinidadian accent. 'If you're asleep, they think maybe you just tired, had a long day. If someone trouble you, you get off, get another bus. And all the time you feel you going somewhere, you know? You going here and there. You have *purpose*.'

At first we couldn't work out how she'd found us. She didn't seem to be tapped into the same networks as everyone else. Later, I found her Facebook page, scrolled through pictures in which Ama wore a variety of colourful, expensive dresses, sipped cocktails, and mugged for the camera. Between the images were a series of inspira-tional quotes: exhortations to stay positive, seek joy; passages from the Bible about God's plan, his love and mercy, his benevolence towards those who believed.

Our first night as a group helped ease the awkward memory of Margot's time with us on her own. Demob happy now that they were away from the commune, Kim and Sadie were awake until dawn, drinking heroically, sustaining a production line of joint-rolling. The more Kim consumed, the more she encouraged everyone else to drink and smoke with her, often with some accompanying game or challenge. Whatever she was doing, she did it in the middle of the room, spinning round to make sure everyone was watching, walking over and nudging anyone she felt was uninvolved, unin-terested, momentarily remote. Margot, I saw, responded to this far better than she had to me and Zelma's efforts at getting her to talk. With us, Margot had clearly felt watched. With Kim around, it was easier to feel swallowed up by Kim's total commitment to what was happening. At some point, Kim complained there was no music, and managed to get everyone to sing and keep rhythmic time by clapping while she danced in the middle of the room, head down, hair over her face, arms extended forward like she was swimming. Soon, Margot was dancing with her, her form and style so different from Kim's – arms in the air, head back, eyes closed – that for a moment it looked as if Kim was a charging bull and Margot a posturing matador. Then Sadie joined them, danced with her arm around Margot's shoulders, and I lost perhaps half an hour of the evening just watching the interplay between them all, the shifting dynamics, the way they seemed to be dancing both alone and with each other. The next thing I knew, Zelma and Ama were dancing too, and sitting aside watching became increasingly awkward, so I joined them, all of us now dancing to nothing because there was no-one to clap and keep time, until Ama started to sing the only line of Elton John's 'Rocket Man' any of us knew, the line about it being a long time, and all of us wrapped our arms around each other's shoulders and formed a ring, laughing, stumbling as one or other of us moved too quickly or too slowly, and then finding a shared speed, a pattern of movement by which we could circle easily and without thought, singing the same line over and over, until finally we grew tired and lay down together on the floor, the room's deep silence broken by our ragged panting and Ama's contagious cackle of delight.

The next morning, we had to negotiate the shift from collective abandon to private, slightly awkward personal ritual. Kim was excited about being the first to piss without being drunk, the first to remove her top and stand with her breasts bared and her hands on her hips, half-daring others to follow. Sadie was as easy in her morning toilet as Kim, but quieter in the way she did things, as if happy not to compete for attention with her partner. Together, she and Kim picked through the takeaway remains and fashioned a kind of breakfast, which they handed round to others as they woke. I thought about their previous experience in the squat, the suggestion they hadn't quite gelled with the group, and wondered if their show of making sure everyone was fed was part of a new ethic or commitment, or simply the kind of thing everyone always does in the early days of a new, shared living arrangement – a dialling up of extrovert energy, a slightly forced display of care.

Margot kept her head down, slipped outside, and came back reclothed. She picked at her food, turning things over in her hands, removing and discarding the more obviously mouldy and degraded parts. Kim joshed her a little, made a gag about her pickiness, and then Margot managed a smile and pushed some food into her mouth with her eyes widened, as if in retort.

From one of her disintegrating bags, Ama withdrew a bright, floral dress carefully wrapped in polythene, slipped it on, gave her hair a pat, and left, her cheap flip-flops slapping against the concrete, her grimy feet and unkempt toenails wildly at odds with her upper half.

And I sat with Zelma, eating and watching, suddenly glad to be close to her, happy that the others seemed some distance away.

Perhaps Zelma had the same feelings and fears – that something we shared had to be protected and nurtured, that nurturing it was its own distinct project. The next night, she suggested we go scavenging together, and in the weeks that followed it became a routine. There was little need for discussion with the others. We knew the area, knew the security guard's routine, and had a knack for coming back with finds that functioned as talking points. And besides, there was no enthusiasm among the others for the kind of engagement with the outside world our missions across the industrial estate necessitated. They all had their reasons, and all of them were fine by me. Margot felt self-conscious, timid. She had a fear of running into people when she was unwashed. She seemed particularly worried about the people who worked on the estate, most of whom were men, most of whom, I tried to explain, were filthy in their own ways – smeared with grease and dust or spattered with spray paint and oil. I tried pointing out to her the unfairness of this divide, the way some kinds of dirt were associated with honest, masculine labour while others were associated with malaise or inertia. She understood this, warmed to it as an idea, but whenever the moment came to leave, she found some excuse to stay.

Kim, on the other hand, balked at the suggestion of work. She was open about her personality, the way what she wanted chafed so reflexively against the demands and expectations of others. 'If you tell me to do something,' she told me, 'then right away I think fuck it.' Sadie, of course, deferred to Kim.

Ama, meanwhile, was alone in leaving our shared space during the day, changing out of her rapidly besmeared clothes, slipping into the dress she kept sealed in plastic, and disappearing sometimes until late at night, when she came home tired but smiling, folded her dress and returned it to its protective packaging, slipped into leggings and a T-shirt, and sat with the rest of us amidst the piled-up food and mounting stench. Kim wondered if she had a man somewhere, if she showered on her way to meet him, kept hidden her lack of a home. I'd known others sustain that illusion for months, sleeping in a shopping centre, then rising at dawn, washing in a public toilet, changing into cheap office clothes and determinedly going about their work while they struggled to pay off a debt or gather enough for a deposit. I wondered if it was more a question of habit, if Ama's nights on the buses had gradually made movement a comfort. I knew only too well how sharply stillness can bring all the absences and obstacles of your life into relief. Sometimes the only option is to keep moving, find some rest in the sensation of passage.

Me and Zelma were different when no-one was around. In the group, there was a certain formality, a sense of something we needed to project – fearlessness, discipline, a particularly pure and distilled commitment to what we were doing. People looked to us for guidance and the effect of this was a strange sort of self-consciousness, as if we had to be at pains to perform our resolve, our independence, our confidence. Out on the industrial estate, in the darkened yards and bare, half-lit car parks, we were different, more playful, closer. The distinction bothered me. I worried that, having dismantled privacy, we now sought it elsewhere. But I valued our time together too much, needed it more than I was comfortable admitting, and so I pushed away my unease and savoured our forays into the nocturnal landscape that was now our home.

Zelma had a gleeful, excited eye for what could be acquired. At the bread factory, we found clear plastic bags, roughly torso-sized, knotted at the top and filled with excess produce – burger buns and flattened brioches, loose white loaves and fractured baguettes. From brimming skips behind some of the units we scavenged old palettes, strips of plastic we used in place of plates when we wanted to prepare a smorgasbord of leftovers. At the dump we found discarded hunks of furniture – armchairs with puffs of white stuffing blooming from their seams, mattresses browned and scarred with mould and spills. The takeaway van and its customers often deposited unsold or half-eaten produce in the bin beside which it parked – sandwiches still in their cardboard boxes, half-full drinks cans, portions of cold and rubbery chips picked at and then discarded. The cash and carry regularly piled in its poorly secured wheelie bins whole cases of past-its-sell-by-date produce which we picked through and boosted with glee, carrying back armfuls of squashed cake, souring milk, dented cans, and crumbling, near-dust biscuits.

Our furtive nocturnal missions for discarded matter aligned us with the urban animal kingdom making a life along the tideline of the city's food-flow – the foxes and rats and freewheeling seagulls drawn to bins and ripped-open refuse sacks, the crows and magpies who gathered at the edge of the dump and plucked up sparkling treasure in their beaks. It also placed us at a kind of productive human nexus. Here, in the industrial units, the production centres and storage facilities, was the throbbing source of all the random, manufactured clutter of contemporary life, a place where signage was cut and coated with decals, where the markings for male and female toilets were made, where a particular brand of hard-wearing and inoffensively patterned industrial carpet was stored in preparation for its journey into banking buildings, insurance companies, the offices of global traders. Probably, I thought, in one or other of these units, workers were either making or packing the gel-filled wrist-rests I'd used with my keyboard at Pict, shaping moulds for plastic desk tidies, filling orders for Post-it notes, mouse mats, and cable ties, while at the cash and carry the same street-food vendors who'd fed me and a few hundred other flagging office workers were probably stocking up on ingredients. Every industry had its sub-industry, every workforce its supplementary support detail, and every highly specialised under-class of production its own systems of waste – the cast-off edgings of mass-produced exit signs, the broken moulds and plastic shavings and heaps of curling sawdust. And then, when the things people bought and used broke, or when they discarded old models in favour of new ones, that which could no longer be used returned here, heaped in the dump's vast skips, interred in its plastic graveyard just yards away from where it may very well have begun its life. This, I thought, was the beating, living heart of the city, the deep truth of its citizens' existence, with which they feared becoming intimate.

We carried whatever we could – working as a pair for larger items, taking a packhorse approach for bin bags and refuse sacks full of useful detritus. The security guard's patrols were easy enough to internalise. He left his little hut roughly on the hour, walked up the curving road and back, and only strayed from the main thoroughfare if some noise or evidence of trespass drew him reluctantly from the safety of his route. Zelma enjoyed trailing him, timing our runs so that we were always slipping into places he'd passed.

The bulk of our time, though, was not spent scavenging at all, but simply talking. Sometimes we walked and chatted, sometimes we found a place to sit and pick at our appropriated food, perhaps on the unlit back step of a shuttered facility, or in the secretive little club-space we stumbled upon between two skips at the dump – a tight circle of three or four stools where, we assumed, the workers took their breaks. Whenever we did, I wondered if we were breaking our own rules, worried we were unable to embody the principles we extolled to others.

'I don't think so,' said Zelma, when I put this to her. 'It's different for us.'

'That's it though,' I said. 'I'm worried that it shouldn't be different for us.'

'We always ask the others. They don't come.'

'Do you really want them to come, though? I mean, when you ask them, are you actually hoping they'll say yes?'

She laughed. 'Not really.'

'Right,' I said. 'So what does that mean?'

'It means we go back further,' she said 'It means that for us this is more complicated.' She waved her hand vaguely. 'The others can come and go. Let's be honest. Kim and Sadie will get pissed off one day and go looking for the next place to hang. Margot will decide she's done what she needed to do, seen another way of life. She'll go back to her parents and then to university. Ama will go out one day and not come back. But we'll have to keep going. We'll have to go on beyond this because there's nothing for us to go back to.'

I wasn't sure what to say. Conflicting feelings arose in me like little storms, gusted, battled, blew each other out. The picture Zelma painted was one I'd tried to paint myself – a vista of bleached negation and cautious hope, a future I halfway believed in.

'I can't imagine anything after this,' I said.

She looked at me in her fascinated, scrutinising way, as coolly intrigued and as wholly caring as ever.

'That's not true,' I said, accustomed by then to Zelma's way of getting you to say more by saying nothing herself – the very habit, of course, that I'd honed through a year of distrustful encounters with uncaring authorities. 'I can, but I don't want to.'

'It'll just come,' Zelma said. 'There'll be a day when we see it, and that will be it.'

I nodded. We fell silent a moment, looking out over our flood-lit, deserted kingdom, our glowing home amidst all that pointless industry.

'I'm not used to needing anyone,' I said. 'I'm not used to anyone needing me.'

'Me neither,' said Zelma.

Just as we found a way to dance together with no external rhythm, so too we quickly found ways to live together with no external schedule. Before, during my time at Pict, I'd entered unwillingly into routine, felt it close around me with the sinister hiss of an airlock. Now it was organic, something we grew and built together. It existed on the borderline between habit and ceremony, eased the transition from the individual to the collective. When we slept, we were alone with our dreams and fears. When we woke, we joined each other in the middle of the space, as if leaving behind the parts of ourselves that were closed to others. Because everyone's sleeping patterns had drifted, because we were eating whenever the urge arose, the relationship between time and action reversed. Coming together was no longer something we did in response to the start of another day; the moment we came together *became* the start of the day, regardless of what time it happened.

Quickly, this cohesive moment came to be ritualised. We waited until we were all awake, then ate whatever was available at the time.

Sometimes we fed each other. Sometimes we painted each other with food. We took to smelling each other in a celebratory way. I would lean over to Margot, or Kim, breathe deeply from the warm pocket of air beneath their underarm or between their thighs, and notice how the texture of what I inhaled was almost malleable, how I could taste it and feel it on my tongue as well as simply smell it, and then I would congratulate them, and they would do the same in turn to me.

As ritual cohered around certain acts, it eroded around others. At first, shitting and pissing in front of each other carried an air of celebration. Someone would announce it, gain the attention of the group, and then shit to a round of applause. We inspected each other's excrement, admired it. I remember very vividly the first time Margot, who I knew had been relieving herself outside when no-one was looking, got drunk enough, or high enough, or simply loose enough, to shit with abandon in the middle of the room, her hands held comically aloft, tears of both laughter and wild release pouring down her face. She seemed so blissful in that moment, so totally gone and unreachable, that I felt moved to embrace her, to tell her how beautiful it was to have done so much undoing at such a young age. And then I found myself crying with her, telling her I envied her, telling her that I wished I'd known what she knew now when I was her age, before bursting out laughing and saying that was the oldest and most parental I had ever sounded to myself, at which point Kim let out her wheezing laugh and said, *Yeah, but if your life had been different, you'd have missed out on all this*, and swept her hand with exaggerated grandeur around the piles of takeaway cartons, the chunks of rotting meat and vegetables, the streaks and puddles of shit, and, as if released, we erupted into hysteria, laughing to that almost frightening point where it becomes uncontrolled and painful, where you feel powerless in the face of what your body is doing, and you can no longer tell the difference between laughing, sobbing, and retching because really you're doing all three at once, and whatever emotion is being released is deeper and more wild than mere happiness or sadness or rage – a feeling eloquently expressed by Margot when she laughed literally to the point of vomiting, and began hiccuping and retching and laughing and spraying a fine mist of sick about the room.

But on the other side of celebration there was another release entirely: the release of no attention at all; the release of not even standing up when you needed to shit or piss, not even interrupting your sentence or pausing in your consumption of food, just relaxing into relief as if it was the most natural thing in the world. This was its own kind of bliss, a state not of release so much as flow – a natural process ecstatically uninterrupted, the cycle of matter through the conduits of our bodies, food in, shit out, unceasingly, with neither ceremony nor concealment. Me and Zelma got there first. In many ways, we were there before the others arrived. Kim never got there. For Kim, everything was performative. When she undressed, when she shat, when she held Sadie in a lingering, drooling kiss, it was always with one eye on her audience. Sadie, in turn, borrowed from Kim's energy, and so didn't need quite the same sense of expression for herself. And Margot got there in much the same way as she'd accessed the ability to shit and undress with people watching: slowly, cautiously, with an air first of embarrassment, then of joy.

Of everyone, it was Ama who fascinated me the most. For the rest of us, our time with each other, in that room that became our world, was a process of total immersion, a renunciation of whatever it was we were leaving behind. For Ama, it was more a question of precarious balance. More than once, I caught her in a shadowed corner, sobbing as she relieved herself, then shaking her head, hardening her gaze, as if, where the rest of us sought ecstasy, she sought stoicism. Each morning, she clothed herself in her Sunday best, hit the city with her flip-flops flapping, each step revealing the grimy, toughened undersides of her feet. For most of us, the less we had contact with the outside world, the less we needed it, but for Ama the world was her anchor. It was only by going out during the day, reminding herself that the world was still there, that she was able to steel herself, little by little, to the life we led at night.

Drunk enough on rum, Ama would reminisce. She told me about her two sisters in Trinidad, showed me their beaming pictures on her phone. She talked about her first impressions of England, years ago: its greyness, its coldness, the sense that in London you could be both reassuringly invisible and brutally, icily alone. Mostly, though, she talked about the care home in which she'd worked: the frail, the bed-bound, the demented, whose existence depended on her daily ministrations.

'Was the same every night,' she told me one evening, slurring her words, squinting through the haze of booze that lay draped across her senses. 'You go round, you take off their pads, you wash their backsides. You lift them into bed and you fluff up the pillows and when no-one's looking you give 'em a little kiss on the forehead, because it's not allowed but they like it. And then all night you clean, get everything ready, and in the morning you do it again, get them up, wash their backsides, get them some clothes. Round and round.'

I didn't say anything, just nodded while she talked, but I remember wondering, almost marvelling, at her journey from there to here, from washing away the embarrassing excretions and leakages of human life, scantily patching up the dignity of the infirm, to living willingly amidst it, letting it all pile up around her, doing nothing to stem the flow or curtail the spread, and not being able to fathom, or muster the courage to ask, how it had possibly all come to this.

Slowly, we left the familiarity of hours and days and entered instead a species of time tracked not on the clock but on the body. Margot's skin broke out. Her face was no longer a smooth, pale, singular surface, but an angry, pustulating colony of what seemed at times to be lifeforms unto themselves – hard, flaming red blisters and straining white spots that always looked as if they might burst or leak at any moment. Kim's hands began to itch. One of Zelma's eyes turned blood red and wouldn't stop weeping. Where the top of my thigh met my buttock, I developed a painful sore, which Sadie lanced using a pin she'd held over a flame.

Around us, the room was undergoing its own process of change and transformation. Our shit and piss pooled on the floor and splashed up the walls. Our discarded food broke down and joined the semi-liquid sludge of our bodily waste. Fungus and spores began to grow in corners. More than one species of mould took root on the walls. Inevitably, flora attracted fauna. Rats made their way in through gaps in the shutter and door, timid at first, then entirely at ease in our presence, scrabbling over our splayed legs and arms as they foraged for edible food. With the rats came fleas, and soon we were all covered in bites, scratching furiously, bringing up little dots and trails of blood on our calves and forearms. I thought again of the documentaries with which me and Zelma had passed the time in my flat – the same documentaries into whose confusing semi-reality I had slipped during my bout of fever. I thought of the serene wingbeats of manta rays disturbing vast clouds of suspended plastic, the cadaver of an albatross with a fistful of bottle caps in its gut. I thought of my dream, the spidery beast to which my body had played host. When I rubbed that spot on my arm, it felt more tender, almost painful. This made sense to me. As ecological divisions fell away, as species and processes intermingled, all other boundaries would eventually follow suit, including whatever membrane or skin separated the things I dreamed of and feared from the things around me I trusted to be real.

I began to imagine that I might disappear. It would be possible, I thought, to be subsumed into the ecosystem we had created, for every imaginable distinction to be erased, until there was no difference at all between myself and the fleas that feasted on me, the rats that dined on my leftovers, the flies that drank from the puddles of effluvia I'd produced. It was a feeling that only intensified when one night Sadie checked on the sore at the top of my thigh and recoiled, before collecting herself and peering closer. She had to take a picture with her phone so I could see: a small cave where my flesh had been, packed tight with writhing maggots.

One night, as we perched on a hip-high stack of empty palettes in the parking area of the cash and carry, snacking on trampled fruit cake and swigging decarbonated Pepsi from leaky plastic bottles retrieved from a bin, I asked Zelma about her illness, which had been on and off my mind since we'd first settled in the empty unit. I worried she would have another flare-up, requiring attention and care our new life made impossible. It was our nearest limit, I felt, the force most likely to be our undoing.

'I don't know any more,' she said. 'In some ways I feel more ill than ever. My stomach hurts. My limbs ache. I have these dizzy spells. It's just that now I don't know if they're because of my illness, or just because of what we've done to ourselves.'

'What if it makes you worse?' I said. 'What if everything we're doing just contributes to what you're feeling, until we can't do it any more? What if we can't do *anything* any more?'

'No,' she said. 'That's just it. I like it. It's not like all the other times I've been ill. Because now I can't tell if it's something that's happening or something I'm doing. If it's something I'm doing, I can stop doing it any time I want. That was always the problem before. This *thing* would come over me, or grow inside me, and there was nothing I could do about it. Now I don't even know *what* this is, but I don't feel helpless any more, and I don't feel alone. Everyone's ill now. There's nothing to be well for. All that energy I spent trying to be well, fighting being ill. That's mine now. It's like you said: we're not changing the world, we're just being rid of it. Well now I'm rid of the world, I can be as ill as I like. Being ill *is* my world.'

I chugged at the Pepsi, felt it puddle uncomfortably in my stomach. It seemed as if nothing inside me was solid. I was a sac of angry liquid, some of which pooled and remained, some of which expelled itself and was gone. I wanted to say, *But what about me?* but I wasn't sure what I meant by it, what I would be asking by demanding that Zelma be well for my sake. The extent to which I was pained by seeing or imagining her unwell, I thought, was a measure of the extent to which I had still not managed to let go.

I reached for Zelma's little finger, clasped it in mine, shook her hand gently. She smiled.

'Nothing to give,' she said, 'nothing to lose.'

I began to realise that decay is not something that arrives, it is something that reveals itself always to have been present. It's everything we live with and try to forget: the mutating cells beneath slackening skin, the blood and viscera beneath a pretty face. In imagining my own gradual putrefaction, I'd fixated on the visible, the tangible, the kind of rot over which I could run my fingers and tongue. As the weeks went on, I came to understand that shit comes in many forms, that there are myriad ways in which we have to clean up after ourselves, and each other.

As we moved through the phase of getting to know each other, through a place of relative comfort, and into a state in which intimacy gave rise to grating irritation, filth and perpetual discharge to a kind of naked emotionality in which anger and joy arose with the swiftness of gastric acid, Kim began to reveal her true depths. The more layers we removed, the less she had around her to hold anything in. Slowly, day by day, what was inside her began to leak.

'I've known a lot of girls like you,' she said to Margot one day, her eyes narrow, a jet of fag smoke fired through tightly pursed lips in Margot's direction. 'Clean little rich kids, wanting to change the world and stay pretty while you're doing it.'

Margot was easily wounded, and that in itself was a problem for her. She was comfortable caring, expressed herself through little kindnesses, but she expected the same consideration from others. When she didn't get it, she weaponised her disappointment. I watched her lip wobble, her eyes well up. She picked at the frayed hem of her jeans and made a show of not looking at Kim.

Kim, of course, didn't soften. It was part of her ethos. She wanted people to push back, not crumple under her pressure.

'You see?' she said, sneering. 'That's the shit that works with your parents, I bet. What are you, too good for this world? I see you, Margot. I see your bullshit. You think you'll get ahead in life by just being pretty and quiet and crying when people upset you. Well that's bullshit, kid. Life's gonna chew you up.'

It was a recurring theme – Margot the wide-eyed innocent, the pampered bourgeois student acting out a gap-year rebellion, getting her hands temporarily dirty before once again washing herself down and returning to a life unthreatened by filth. There was a certain glee, I thought, particularly from Kim, at seeing Margot's designer clothes decay, her self-conscious, asymmetrical bob growing out and turning mud-coloured as enzymes ate the dye. More than once, Kim mockingly asked her if she'd considered slipping into town to get her eyebrows done, or getting a secretive wax in one of the sad, blue-lit beauty parlours along the high street.

I felt uncomfortable in these exchanges. I wanted Margot to bite back, knew that if I interjected I would only be encouraging her to believe she needed my help. But Margot would stay silent, Kim would move on, and the moment in which something might have been done would pass.

In the end, though, it was Zelma, not Margot, who really set Kim off. Maybe she'd grown tired of the bickering, or maybe, quietly, she worried that Kim might have taken her lead from Zelma's own occasionally tough approach to Margot, and wanted to put down some kind of marker. One night, we were all lying around in a loose circle, greasy with takeaway, muddy with booze and weed, when Kim zeroed in on Zelma, who had propped herself against the wall and was gazing into the middle distance with sleepy eyes. Over time, I would come to understand that this was typical of Kim. Because she was all outwards, all the time, the introspection of others made her self-conscious.

'You there,' she said, pointing straight at Zelma. 'You're very quiet. What's the matter with you?'

This, we would learn, was one of Kim's favourite questions. Depending on the emotional climate, it could be warm and joshing, a way of getting you to talk, or it could carry a distinct edge. It spoke to a fundamental imbalance in the way Kim engaged with others: something was always wrong with someone else; nothing was ever wrong with Kim.

'Wrong?' said Zelma. She'd obviously been drifting, only half-paying attention to what was happening around her. Now she was trying to catch up. 'Nothing,' she said offhandedly. 'Nothing's wrong.'

And then, clearly with no thought in her mind other than returning to whatever half-dream or unfinished thought she'd been enjoying, she looked away from Kim, and turned her head back so that she was once again staring into the middle distance of the room.

'Right-o,' said Kim, icily. 'I see.'

'Kim,' said Sadie.

In that one word, that simple utterance of Kim's name, and in the way Sadie placed her hand on Kim's forearm, I could see, despite being drunk and stoned, a whole history, a whole language of warnings, negotiations, fears. I sat up a little, watching Kim, aware that Zelma was once again oblivious to her.

'What?' said Kim to Sadie. 'Don't worry about me, pet. I'm fine. If people want to just blank me like that then that's their problem. I'm not going to sweat it.'

'I don't think she—' said Sadie.

'Uh uh,' said Kim, wagging a finger. 'Don't do that because that's going to piss me off. You know that pisses me off so don't do it.'

'What's going on?' said Zelma, her voice slow, her words slightly slurred. She was looking between Kim and Sadie. Clearly, she had spaced out for the previous exchange, but the new tension in the room must have been unmistakeable to her, even in her disordered state.

I expected Kim to say, *Nothing, forget it.* I would learn that this tended not to be Kim's approach to conflict. Once something had bothered her, trying to forget it only bothered her more. She had little ability to circumnavigate things, or turn away from them. She had to go *through* everything, so that when she was on the other side she could be certain it was behind her.

'I just didn't like the way you blanked me then, that's all,' said Kim. 'Came off a bit up yourself.'

'Blanked you?' said Zelma blinking. 'When did I blank you?'

'Just then. I asked you something—'

'And I answered,' said Zelma slowly. She was squinting a little, bringing her gaze into sharper focus. She'd pushed herself away from the wall and was propped up on one hand.

'Yeah sure, you *answered*,' said Kim. 'And then you blanked me.'

'She's just stoned, love,' said Sadie. 'We're all stoned and drunk and she just—'

'Nah-ah,' said Kim, turning on Sadie. 'I've just told you: don't fucking do that. Don't try and explain things for her. She can explain things for herself.'

'What's happening here?' said Zelma.

'Nothing,' said Sadie.

'Now you're speaking for me as well, is it?' said Kim, straightening further.

'OK,' I said. 'Let's—'

'Let's nothing,' said Kim. 'I was all for leaving it. You heard me say fine. But these two . . .' – she flicked her finger from Zelma to Sadie and back again – '. . . want to turn it into some sort of . . .'

'No-one's turning anything into anything,' said Zelma.

'What's going on between you two, eh?' said Kim.

'Oh my *God*,' said Zelma. 'Paranoid much?'

'Who the *fuck* are you calling paranoid? Huh? Because let me tell you what I'm seeing here, sweetie. OK? I'm seeing you *blank me*, like I'm fucking *nothing*, like you can't even *muster the fucking energy* to speak to me, because I'm not *worth it*, and then I'm seeing *this one*, this one here, pop up like a fucking jack-in-the-box with an excuse. That's what I'm seeing.'

'I'm bored of this,' said Zelma. 'You want to have a little psychodrama? Go ahead, but leave me out of it because I really can't be bothered.'

Now Kim was standing up, and Sadie had stood with her, positioning herself between Kim, whose fists were clenched at her sides, and Zelma, who was still staring up at Kim from the floor.

'Whoa,' I said, also standing.

'Hon,' said Sadie. 'No-one was—'

'Don't tell me what people were and were not doing like I'm fucking blind or stupid, OK?' said Kim. 'Because that is something I will not have. How long have you known me, Sades? In any of the time you've known me, have you ever known me to—'

'This is barely coherent,' said Zelma.

'*Fuck you.*' Kim lunged at Zelma, but was caught by Sadie, and soon after that I stepped in too.

'Hey,' I said. 'Kim.'

I reached out, past Sadie, who was still holding Kim's upper arm but who had begun stroking her hair, and placed my hand on Kim's shoulder. I could feel damp sweat through the fabric of her T-shirt, the knots of her twitching muscles beneath her skin. She was grinding her teeth slightly, I noticed, and her eyes were everywhere, ping-ponging around the room.

'Kim,' I said. 'Kim.'

I could feel her relaxing. Sadie was still running a hand over her forehead and through her hair. I kept my hand on her shoulder.

Behind me I heard Zelma say, 'I was flippant. I didn't mean any-thing by it. I'm sorry.' I didn't look at her but I knew by her voice that the apology bothered her, that she was doing it out of a sense of convenience rather than any acceptance of personal culpability.

Then Kim sat down and burst into a sudden, smoky cackle.

'Fucking hell,' she said. 'Drama, eh?'

She lit a cigarette and smiled to herself, and by the look that Sadie shot me as she sat down beside her, I gathered that we should all move on. I turned and tried to pass a similar look to Zelma. Quickly, so that only I noticed, she rolled her eyes.

We shifted gears swiftly. Kim was laughing again. Zelma either passed out or pretended to pass out. Sadie began talking about something else, steering Kim away from what had troubled her and towards what I sensed were reliable subjects of amusement. It was a fleeting flare-up, I told myself – inevitable when strangers live in close proximity, when people are uncomfortable, when everyone's wrecked and confused and unwell. I'd seen similar incidents count-less times on the streets. Sometimes they turned nasty. Usually they were defused by whoever was to hand. I wasn't unnerved by conflict. I wasn't even particularly concerned about violence. If the need arose, I could defend myself. What bothered me more was the responsibility I'd felt to step in, the pressure that Zelma, having stood her ground, clearly felt to be placatory. Our instinct was to avoid an outburst, sustain some semblance of peace, and it troubled me not because it was new and frightening, but because it was familiar and unwanted. Without meaning to, without even wanting to, we'd established a natural order. Now we were compromising ourselves to protect it.

The next morning, while Kim was distracted looking for something to eat, Sadie nodded in her direction.

'Don't mind her,' she said. 'She's a pussycat really.'

'Sure,' I said.

I knew it wasn't true, and knew that Sadie didn't even believe it as she was saying it. Worse, it was fairly obvious Sadie didn't expect me to believe it either. We were all just paying lip service to the things we were supposed to say. It was a routine, a ritual. I wondered how many times, in how many different settings, in communes and squats and shared houses, after dinners gone bad and episodes in the pub that everyone wanted to forget, Sadie had felt the need to give this little morning-after talk, smoothing over the cracks while Kim wasn't looking.

If Sadie's job was to underplay the incident, Kim's was to over-compensate for it. She was excessively sweet. She spent an hour sitting with Zelma in a corner, her chin resting on her palm, her eyes squinting in sympathy. By the way Zelma gestured towards parts of her body, I could tell that Kim had asked about her illness, and that Zelma was happily telling her. Later, I saw Kim massaging Margot's shoulders, taking some food over to Ama, who'd just returned from another of her excursions. It pained me to see Kim managing herself in this way. I wondered how many days she'd spent effectively undoing herself, how many places she'd lived and worked in had ultimately withdrawn the latitude required for the game to continue. Then I wondered if that was what we would end up doing, what *I* would end up doing, for the peaceful life, the easy order of a space without conflict or rage.

'No-one came here to live a timid life,' I said to Zelma on one of our scavenging runs.

'Yeah,' she said. 'But no-one came here to take shit from a bully either.'

Carefully, almost timidly, we bounced it back and forth. We were learning to disagree with each other. Before, we'd had no occasion for argument. Now, nothing felt hypothetical; the stakes seemed higher. We were talking about how to live, how to sustain what we wanted and believed. There was a sense, for both of us, that mistakes could be costly. The irony bothered me. I'd come here to escape structure, meaning, order. Now I felt pressured to impose it.

'What are we saying?' I said 'Shit yourself, but don't lose your temper?'

As if sensing an ally in my obvious discomfort around Kim's behaviour, Margot began seeking me out, finding moments to sit with me when the others were occupied. At first it bothered me. I squirmed in the skin of all the parts I was expected to play: pacifier to Kim, cheerleader to Margot, mediator, mother, cop. But, slowly, I felt myself softening into what she asked of me. It wasn't the first time I'd played older sister or wise elder to lost young girls. On the street, in a world where the very presence of other women was a comfort, I'd heard all the runaway tales, the accounts of violent, drunken parents, the childhoods in drug dens, the tearful, cowering nights hiding from arguments and fist fights in the next room. Margot's background held none of these familiar stories, but nor was it quite the idyll Zelma and Kim assumed it to be. Suffocation, not rejection, was what she'd fled.

'I was such a bitch,' she said bluntly one night, when Sadie and Kim had passed out and Zelma was having a long and rambling conversation with Ama. 'The more they tried to make everything nice, the more I fucked it up, and the more I fucked everything up for them, the more they worked to make everything nice again.'

I nodded, thinking of the opportunities I'd escaped, the feeding hands I'd reactively bitten, knowing exactly what it was to rail against the good in your life.

'I don't even really understand it,' said Margot. 'I love them. I really do. I know they love me. I just feel like I have to punish them.'

'For what?'

'I don't know. It got kind of ridiculous. They got me into a good school and I did everything I could to get kicked out of it. I smoked weed at break time. I had sex in one of the classrooms. I turned in essays that didn't make any sense. And my parents kept having to go in and kind of debase themselves on my behalf, or negotiate a stay of execution or something. They were really into this idea of *treats*.' She said the word dismissively. 'It was always like, if you do this, or don't do that, you can have this. They loved buying me presents, and anything they bought me I found a way to destroy it. Like, Mum bought me these designer jeans and I just hacked them up, and when I wore them she cried. Whenever we were out in public and they tried to hug me or kiss me or hold my hand or something, I just went ballistic. One time the police came and questioned my dad right on the pavement in front of everyone because I was yelling at him to get away from me and everyone thought he was some dirty old man. He looked so miserable. I remember thinking I'd really done it, I'd really pushed him too far, but there was never any fallout. There was always just this kind of *sadness* whenever I fucked up, and I hated it. I wanted them to say to me, you're a horror, a mistake, we loathe you. I thought it would have made more sense. Like, have the courage to punish me. Then I won't have to punish you.'

Later, Margot asked me what I remembered of my own parents, my life when I was her age, and I found myself recalling again, unexpectedly and painfully, not my early life at all, but my more recent unravelling – my parents' increasingly worried phone calls, their offers of money they didn't have, the look on my father's face that last time I saw him, on his own because my mother couldn't bear it, when I'd told him to put away his cash, give up on trying to help me, because watching them try was killing me, and watching them fail, which I knew by then was inevitable, would be too much.

'They did their best,' I said.

Margot nodded, put her hand on the back of my neck, and for a moment I was lost in a memory: me at ten or twelve, sitting on the back step hugging our mud-caked dog, my ears still ringing from my mother's panicked screams as she'd dragged him from her

pristine sofa, leaving streaks of black earth across the cream upholstery. How I'd marvelled at him, I thought now; how I'd loved his
panting, carefree power. And how frightened I was, even then, by
the fragility of my mother's proud and pretty world.

Margot's chats with me were a refuge from the world she'd accidentally escaped to. Increasingly, they were a haven for me too. With
Margot, I didn't have to discuss logistics and ideology, didn't have
to thrash anything out. I started to understand that everything and
everyone was a refuge from someone or something else. The community we'd made for ourselves was a refuge from the world. My
scavenging missions with Zelma were a refuge from the community
we'd created. My chats with Margot were a refuge from my discussions with Zelma. I kept making homes for myself, I realised,
and kept escaping from them to other homes, from which in time
I again felt moved to flee. I told Margot I worried about myself,
feared I couldn't live with anything, that I needed always the feeling
of flight and that my addiction to release was probably as confining
as anything I felt pressed to escape.

'Some people just have to be in motion, I guess,' she said. 'That's
how I feel. My parents wanted to keep everything still, and I just
wanted to keep everything moving, and every time I found a way to
feel I was moving again they just took it as if I was undoing all the
work they'd put into my stability.'

Another night, over the pained and guttural retching of Sadie
spewing half-digested chow mein onto the already thick and cur-
dled floor, I asked Margot if that was what she was doing here, if
it was really just another way of cutting up the expensive jeans her
mother had bought her.

'Partly,' she said. 'But I also think it's about what I go back to
them with too. I want to go home one day and say, *Look, I've been
away, I've been unwell, I've been in danger, and I'm still here, I'm fine,*

*so you don't have to worry any more because I can handle whatever even
when you're not around.'*

She didn't like Zelma. She was open about it without being
aggressive, honest without suggesting I pick sides. It had begun, I
knew, with her arrival, when Zelma had not only failed to welcome
her but had deliberately debased her, forcing her to squat in front of
us, denying Margot her own time and process of adjustment.

'She's made up her mind about me,' Margot said. 'And so has
Kim. And that's that.'

'Minds can change,' I said.

She shook her head. 'If I try and change their minds, I'm just
buying into the idea that what they think about me matters,' she
said. 'And that's not what we're doing here, is it? What's the point
of all this if we just collectively decide between us that now a whole
new set of standards applies? I thought it was about saying: fuck
standards, fuck expectations. I've been disappointing people my
whole life. I can keep disappointing people until they stop expecting anything of me and then I'll be fine.'

Zelma, of course, denied any animosity.

'She's just young,' she'd say. 'Young and pretty and full of life.
That'll go, and then she'll change.'

'Why does she need to change, though?' I said.

'Everyone needs to change,' said Zelma. 'Everyone *is* changing,
all the time.'

And then she looked off, into a shadowy corner of the room,
from which arose a rodentine scrabble.

'She certainly likes you,' she said, vaguely.

I didn't answer, didn't want to explore any further what that
might have meant beyond the flatly observational.

Kim lived according to a pattern, and as the days became weeks
we began to see it: explosion and apology, friction followed by

balm. She'd blow up, quieten, then cover her edges with softness, making little offerings of food and treats, carving out moments of intimacy with people she feared she might have frightened or upset. Slowly, though, the effort of peace would undo her. Her expression would begin to darken, her eyes to tighten at the corners. Within three or four days she'd be chewing her lip or cheek, staying out of conversations and disagreements in an obvious effort to control her response. Then she'd start drinking more heavily, smoking weed with a more obvious and nervy hunger. We were all, of course, drinking incessantly, consuming whatever we could get our hands on, but Kim would make a display of it, saying, between swigs or drags, *Oh, that's better*, or, *I needed that.* Perhaps because she worried about how this came across, she would make sure everyone else joined her, reframing her own appetites as a kind of joyous collective debauchery, handing out booze like she was playing host, as if everyone was at a party in her honour. But then of course everyone would be wrecked, and Kim would be no less tense than when the whole process had begun, and within another day, two at most, she would ignite again. The more she blew up, the more people tired of her blowing up, and the less patient they became in dealing with her, meaning that Kim in turn only escalated the intensity of her episodes, moving from comparatively manageable anger and provocation, through threats, to actual violence.

Once Kim had picked up on Zelma's attitude to Margot, Margot became a means by which Kim and Zelma could settle into a tacit understanding. She was their shared target, their point of agreement. Zelma could be snide, sometimes cold, but she was rarely openly aggressive, and so with a simple eye-roll or sarcastic comment she could set Kim off and outsource the work of aggression. Kim, in turn, rarely co-operated, rarely agreed to what was directly asked of her. Picking on Margot became a way of doing Zelma's bidding without being seen to compromise or submit.

Because not everyone caught Zelma's cues, Kim's jabs at Margot could seem sudden and unwarranted, especially to Margot. Once, Zelma, unseen by Margot, smirked as Margot idly ran a hand through her hair while she stared out of the window, and Kim said sneeringly, *Enjoying your own reflection are you, princess?*, to which Margot had said that she was simply looking out the window, miles away, *in a world of my own.*

'You're in a world of your own alright,' Kim said.

'I don't know what you mean,' said Margot.

''Course you don't,' said Kim, shaking her head. 'You've got no fucking idea.'

On another occasion, Zelma accused Margot of avoiding the worst of the rotted food, of picking through the pile and selecting only the least mouldy, least congealed bits and pieces for her personal consumption.

'Is that how you're going to live your life?' said Zelma. 'Just pushing all the bad stuff aside and picking out the best bits for yourself? Is that why you're here?'

'I just . . . I just pick out things I like,' said Margot. 'I didn't even really think about it, I just—'

'*I didn't even really think about it,*' said Kim in a nasty, nasal whine. Then she mimed patting her hair into place, pouting slightly. '*I don't even really think about anything. As long as I look pretty and everyone loves me . . .*'

'That's so mean,' said Margot. 'That's not what I'm like at all.'

'Here,' said Zelma, selecting from the heap of discarded takeaway trays a particularly vile-looking piece of half-chewed chicken and throwing it into Margot's lap. 'This is for you.'

Margot ate it while looking directly at Zelma. Almost as soon as she'd finished swallowing the whole thing she was sick. Ignoring the vomit on her lips and clothes, she went over to the heap and found another piece, then ate that too, all while looking coldly at Zelma, who simply smiled and nodded.

Zelma, I knew, welcomed the push-back. She liked it when Margot stood up for herself. Although her methods made me uncomfortable, I still believed that her aims had Margot's benefit at heart. She wanted to toughen her, press her until she pressed back. When she did, Zelma always accepted it, always smiled slightly.

The problem was that Kim didn't see it the same way. Because she'd already decided she hated Margot, she interpreted Margot and Zelma's slightly tense interactions as small battles in which she had to pick a side. Because she fed off conflict, she saw only conflict's occurrence, never its nuanced results.

At the same time, Kim's behaviour had worn away at other people's capacity to put up with her, which of course Margot picked up on in turn. There was a sense that Kim shouted a lot, but ultimately did nothing, meaning the best way to deal with her was to tell her to fuck off, which Margot, after much provocation, finally did.

'What the fuck is your problem?' she said to Kim, after Kim had once again found cause to comment on Margot's hair, her clothes, the way she held herself, or where she had chosen to sit in the room.

'No problem here,' said Kim. 'You're nothing I haven't seen before.'

'Nor are you,' said Margot. 'I've met a thousand people like you. Bitter little bullies, sitting around passing judgement and picking on people.'

'Picking on people?' Kim laughed – a short, vicious bark. 'You're not in the playground now, girly. This is the big girls' world. There's no teacher to go whining to when you think someone's *picking on you.*'

'I'm not whining to anyone,' said Margot. 'I'm telling you: you think you're frightening, or intimidating or something. But really you're just *boring.* I bet you tell yourself that people don't like you because they can't handle you. I've heard you saying it: *Oh, people can't handle me because I'm so honest.* That's bullshit. People can't handle you because you're so predictable, so *deadening.* People aren't upset by you, Kim, they're *bored* of you.'

While Margot spoke, Kim had watched her, her head tilted to one side, an unpleasant smile making one corner of her mouth twitch.

'Well looky,' she said. 'It does have a personality after all.'

This seemed to pierce Margot in a way she hadn't been expecting. I saw her wince, blink back tears, then ball her fists.

'*It*?' she shouted, stepping towards Kim. '*It*? How dare you? How fucking dare you, you nasty bitch. Talking to me like I'm some sort of *thing*.'

And now Kim was laughing – that deep, hoarse cackle that sounded as if something in her chest was breaking up and becoming liquid. With a squeal, Margot swept up fistfuls of whatever was to hand on the floor – gobbets of old food, foil packaging, stringy webs of unnameable goo – and flung them at Kim, who first laughed and then, as Margot drew closer and kept grabbing up whatever she could find and hurling it with ever increasing force at Kim's head, became enraged, stood up, and began throwing whatever she could back at Margot, telling her to cut it out, telling her to get a grip on herself, which only enraged Margot more and caused her to look around for larger hunks of matter she could hurl at Kim and, finding nothing within her immediate grasp, spit straight into Kim's face, at which point Kim crossed what little distance remained between them, back-handed Margot across the cheek and, when Margot dropped to the ground, straddled her and began pulling furiously at her hair while Margot screamed.

'Little *slag*,' Kim was shouting. 'Little *cunt*. You want to fight me, cunt? Huh? You want to fight me, little girl?'

'Get her off me,' Margot was screaming. 'Get her the fuck off me.'

I'd watched all this unfold, unsure when, if at all, to step in. I felt torn, hesitant. The conflict bothered me, but the thought of continually stepping in and massaging away tensions bothered me more. Once I began down that path, I knew, people would look to me to manage every niggling micro-friction. But now Margot was on the floor getting her hair ripped out and no-one seemed sure what to do, and I knew I had to do something before Kim, who by this point seemed to have let the brakes off entirely and was flailing at anyone who came near, including Sadie, genuinely hurt someone.

I stepped behind Kim and tried to grab her upper arms. As I did so, Sadie reached for her hands and began untangling them from Margot's hair. Then Zelma and Ama arrived and together we began trying to prise Kim away while she kicked and thrashed and spasmed. I had to drag her backwards off Margot, down onto the filthy floor, where after a bit of wrestling we managed to turn her onto her front and pin her down, at which point we all lay on her – me on her back, Sadie on her legs, Ama and Zelma spread across her shoulders and upper arms. The feel of her was extraordinary – this bucking, rearing force beneath our weight. She wasn't making words by this point, just guttural barks and howls. I knew that whatever she was expressing now had nothing to do with what had happened; she was beyond it, lost to a purer and more forceful rage. It was as if something unseen was emerging from her, some force or phenomenon that lived in her and had to be driven out. As she screamed into the slick surface of the floor, I could feel her changing, morphing beneath us, becoming less a human body and more a concentrated energy that both pulled everything else towards it and repelled anything it touched. As she changed, I felt us change too, not in ourselves, but in relation to her. To Kim, in this state, we were no longer ourselves. We were a nameless force – a distillation of whatever it was she raged against daily.

'Go for it,' I said into Kim's ear. 'Go on. You want to kill us? Try and kill us.'

She howled and spat, tried to twist and rise up beneath us. At one point she managed to draw up a knee and lever herself onto her back, but we moved with her, still pinning her, refusing to relent while she gnashed and screamed and flailed for a grip on our clothes and bodies.

'Is that all you've got?' I said, my knee now on Kim's chest, my hands on either side of her head, while she tried to turn from side to side. 'Come on. You've got more, I know it.'

She heaved with such force that Sadie was momentarily thrown off her legs, which began to kick wildly. Margot ran over and joined her, so that they could use all their weight on one leg each.

'Yes,' I said. 'Come on. Give it everything. Give us everything. *Feel it.*'

And for a few more minutes she did, until, slowly, the energy began to leave her. Lying on top of her, I could have sworn I felt it departing. First breathless, then quiet, then still, Kim seemed to deflate underneath us. I felt her muscles soften, her body literally shrink. All the parts of her that had been knotted and hard seemed, as quickly as they'd tensed, to dissolve, until we were all just lying on top of her, no-one pushing against anyone else, breathing heavily, while Kim began to cry.

'It's OK,' said Ama softly, running her hand through Kim's hair. 'It's OK. It's over now.'

After the rest of us had cautiously let Kim go, and retreated, panting, to lean against the wall and recover, it was Ama who stayed with her, half-lying on Kim's chest, half-kneeling beside her, wiping the sweat from her forehead and the tears from her eyes, telling her again and again, *It's OK, it's over now. You're fine.*

The next day we woke at different times, dodged the usual preliminary gathering, and sought out little islands of peace and defined space amidst the mess and undifferentiated expanse. The atmosphere was uncertain, not quite awkward but not quite at ease either. It was difficult to tell peace from tension, the reassurance of things passing from the anxiety that they might not have passed at all. Zelma stirred, pissed, rubbed her eyes, then slept again. I ate a little, watched clouds cross the upper quarter of our row of windows, their grey forms merging in places with the grime on the glass. As if daring Kim to comment, Margot paid attention to her face, borrowing my phone so she could study herself in its camera's unflinching gaze, squeezing spots, baring her teeth and running her tongue over their yellowing, food-encrusted surfaces. Kim sat alone, smoking and tracing abstract shapes in the filthy floor with her fingernail. She had a bruise on her left cheekbone, presumably from where her face had been pressed into the concrete, and periodically she touched it and winced. Sometimes, as people passed her, she looked up at them, slightly expectant, then looked quickly down again, as if at pains to perform her lack of hostility. I half-expected her to prostrate herself, or approach the rest of the group with her head turned and her neck bared, like a cowed wolf.

Kim was alone because Sadie was sitting with Ama. They were propped against a wall, side by side, peering at Ama's phone. After a while, Sadie beckoned me over to their side of the room. As I walked over, I passed Kim, who gave me a little smile and a wave, which I returned with what I hoped was warmth.

'Ama's been showing me her Facebook,' said Sadie.

She gestured to Ama, and Ama passed me her phone. I scrolled through similar pictures to the ones I'd seen before: Ama in a wide-brimmed hat and bright-yellow sunglasses, sipping from an over-accessorised cocktail somewhere near a river; a platter of perfectly prepared sushi, garnished with flesh-like slivers of pickled ginger and curls of mandolined cucumber. For a moment I was confused, uncertain as to how I was expected to respond. Then I looked at the dates: last week, a few days ago.

Sadie rubbed Ama's thigh.

'Just tell her, hon,' she said. 'It's not like you've done anything bad.'

Ama shook her head, then looked downwards, idly running her thumb over her palm, the lines of which were blurred with dirt.

'It's stupid,' she said. 'I been doing this all this time but I feel stupid now.'

I didn't say anything, just nodded.

'I put on my one good dress,' said Ama. 'And I find a bathroom somewhere and just get myself together a little bit. And then, you know, no-one pay too much attention. That's what I picked up when I used to sleep on the bus. If you get yourself together a certain way, no-one really trouble you because they think the best. So I get myself all ready, and then I go to a shop and I steal some new clothes. Different places, so they don't catch on. And then I'm looking real nice. And I say to people, *Oh my, oh this is terrible, I been robbed and I need to get home.* You know, crying like. And they say, *Oh my gosh, let me give you something.* And when I've got enough I buy a drink and I say to someone, *Take my picture.* Or sometimes I'm just passing and I say, *Oh, that food is so beautiful! Let me take a picture to remind me to come here.* No-one ever says no.'

'But why?' I said, even though I knew the answer.

'For my sisters,' she said. 'My two sisters back home. Because they're so excited for me. They're so pleased I have this life. It's like they have a little bit of this life too.'

'They don't know anything?' I said. 'Your job, your flat . . .'

Ama shook her head.

'I can't do that to them,' she said. 'I can't take it away from them like that.'

I nodded, knowing exactly what she meant, wanting to say that I'd found my own methods of concealment, ones that didn't allow me, as Ama's approach allowed her, the best of both worlds.

'I get it,' I said. 'I just don't get why you're here if . . . I mean, it would be easier if you were somewhere less . . .'

Ama looked up at me, her face suddenly cold, her eyes hard.

'Because this is what I deserve,' she said. She held up her phone. 'I give them a little bit of what they deserve,' she said, 'what they should have. And then I come back and I give myself what *I* deserve, what *I* should have.'

*

I can't remember who first described what we did for Kim as grounding her, but that was how we came to think of it. Not in the sense of grounding a child who's misbehaved, but in the sense of earthing something electric in order to render it safe. We brought Kim back down, helped her re-establish contact with the ground after she'd risen up into the thermosphere of her anger.

The immediacy with which everyone got on board was striking. From the very first time we improvised our response, everyone, Kim included, seemed to feel it worked. It changed the group dynamic of Kim's anger. Margot, for example, was no longer simply the target of Kim's aggression, she was a contributor to the cure. Sadie, who had always dealt with Kim alone, and who too often assumed the position of both excusing Kim's behaviour to others and protecting Kim from others' resentment, found that she was part of something collective and coherent. Ama, who had often seemed peripheral to the rest of the group, but who possessed experience in handling these kinds of situations to which the rest of us deferred, became central, purposeful, authoritative.

I could never quite be sure what Zelma thought of it, but I noticed she didn't always join in. More than once, I looked up from lying on top of Kim, peering through my thick, greasy hair that now almost always hung in front of my face, and saw Zelma not beside me, as she had been the first time, but off on her own, distant, watching. Once, towards the end of our time in that space, I saw she wasn't watching at all, but turned away, facing the wall, and from the way her hands were held either side of her head, I couldn't tell if she was idly running her fingers through her hair, or briefly covering her ears to drown out the screams.

The mornings that followed one of Kim's episodes changed markedly. Before, there had been the feeling that we were all players in a distinctly awkward and bad faith game. Kim would be at pains to pose no threat; Sadie would work too hard to minimise what had happened; the rest of us would fret about bringing it up. Now, it was as if we'd shared in Kim's anger, woven her hostility into the fabric of our reality. Because everyone helped ease Kim's fury, no-one was a victim of her rage. With no victims, there was no longer truly an aggressor. Apologies became irrelevant, awkwardness a vestigial sensation, half-remembered and redundant.

If anything, mornings after an incident were now among the better mornings we had. We were all struggling physically and mentally by that point, all unwell and weakened in our own ways. It was easy to forget what we were doing, and why, and how important it remained that we keep doing it. We developed strategies for re-enthusing ourselves. I read out supportive messages from Instagram. We took pictures of each other's skin and congratulated each other on how far we'd progressed into dishevelment and decay. Nothing, though, lifted our spirits quite like a night when Kim lost her temper, lashed out, and we grounded her and made her feel protected and felt all that anger dissolve beneath the collective weight of our stinking, sweating bodies. Maybe part of what left her entered us. Maybe something left each of us in turn. Maybe it was just the proximity to each other in the shared intensity of a moment. Whatever it was, all of us emerged faintly changed.

Sadie in particular seemed to bloom before our eyes. It was as if her life had been lived in the close-walled and claustrophobic room of Kim's occurring or imminent anger, and now it was opening out into a house, a garden, fields. She smiled more, spent more time with the other women, away from Kim. Even when she was with Kim it was different. There was an easiness there now, because she knew if anything happened the rest of us would be there to help.

'I feel like . . .' she said to me, Ama, and Margot one night, after Kim had exhausted herself battling the rest of us and fallen into a deep, snoring slumber, 'I feel like I can tell her things. I can say things to her. Before, I was always wondering what would set her off. But now I can say it and if it sets her off it doesn't matter. We'll work through it.'

'What do you say to her?' Margot asked, passing her the bottle of wine from which she'd just taken a hefty swig.

'I tell her what I want,' she said. 'I tell her what I don't like. I ask her sometimes if she's sure about something, and I don't worry she's going to accuse me of calling her thick or implying she doesn't know what's going on.' She leaned her head back against the wall and looked up to the ceiling. 'I love her so much,' she said. 'But it's easier to love her now.'

It was Kim, though, in whom the change was most evident. Now that she felt able to be as angry as she wanted to be, I began to realise how much of her life had been devoted to the careful management of her emotions. When she didn't want to become angry, or when she feared, as Sadie did, what might happen if she lost control, she would smother herself, tamp down whatever was brewing inside her. When she could hold it back no longer, she looked for an outlet, a lightning rod. She'd needle others into provoking her so that she could become justifiably rageful. Her every interaction, I realised, was at the service of her fury – managing it, helping it to find expression, then assuaging its effects on others. Now, if she wanted to become angry, she simply became angry. She didn't need a target, and even if she did pick on someone, that person would inevitably recast themselves as part of her support, and so there was no need for resentment. There was nothing she was either holding back or manipulatively seeking out. She could take people as they were, and they in turn could take her as she was.

For a while, everything Kim-related seemed to work. Without ever discussing it, we came to know our places, our roles. Ama became the signaller. A nod from her, an acknowledgement that one of Kim's outbursts had crossed the threshold between anger and aggression, and we would move in, first surrounding Kim and then, carefully, bringing her down. Each of us had an assigned body part – an arm, a leg, a patch of torso. Sadie always took the head, placing her hands on Kim's cheeks, holding her gaze and speaking to her through the fog of unreason that descended whenever Kim was carried off into the parallel world that formed from her anger. We developed a collection of phrases we repeated to Kim. It grew as we progressed, taking in expressions and affirmations that had provably worked before. We told her it was OK. We told her to let it out. We told her how well she was doing. Sadie would tell her she loved her. Even Kim, I noticed, began to play her part. She still kicked out at whoever was nearest, still thrashed beneath our collective weight and promised she would kill us if she managed to get free, but in other ways she was as willing a participant in what we did as anyone else. Perhaps it was only me that noticed it, but sometimes, particularly when there had been a comparatively large gap between incidents, when Kim was beginning to cycle through the gears of her hostility and we would be looking to Ama for the signal, just before we moved towards her, at the last moment before we had her in our grip, I saw Kim hold her arms slightly out to the sides, as if ready, as if ensuring a part of her was available for us to grasp, even as she screamed at us to leave her alone.

Kim's episodes were like storms: they released all the stored-up static from the air. Afterwards, the room felt fresh and strangely cool. It became a time when we would tell each other things about ourselves, when we would bring to the group the memories and fears that troubled or inspired us in secret. I talked about being homeless. Zelma talked about her illness. Margot talked more openly about her parents.

It was during one of those sessions that Ama told us more about her time as a carer, before she'd lost her job and her home. She was full of amusing stories, most of which revolved around bodily functions and the disinhibited behaviour of the people she cared for. One night, though, after an exhausted Kim had turned the conversation towards death, but then slipped into a slumber before she could really say anything more, Ama had taken up the theme. It was unusual that she spoke at any length. Perhaps it was a trait that spoke of her years doing shift work, but she preferred snatched exchanges to long-form discussion, as if we were all on the job and had to catch up on stolen time when the boss's back was turned. So when she did speak, when she stared slightly into the distance and seemed to settle into what she was about to say, the moment took on a particular significance.

'You know the thing I fear most,' said Ama, not looking at any-one in particular, just gazing ahead and nodding to herself, 'is not death so much as suffering. Or suffering, and not having death come take it away.' She nodded more emphatically. 'That's what you got to be afraid of. When you ready to die, and there's no death coming for you.'

No-one said anything. The room was as silent as I'd known it to be in the time that we were there. Only Kim's deep, peaceful breath-ing and the scrabble of our resident rats were audible.

'I worked this one time in this home,' Ama said. 'Was a new one on me. They just sent me there because they was short. For a favour, like. Extra money. I got there and I could see they was struggling. Laundry was all piled up. People wasn't out of their beds. Was a mess. Anyways, I said to the manager, *What would you like me to do*, and she said, *Go and feed Edith, it's easy, all she eat is yoghurt, you just have to spoon it in.* So I go and find this Edith in her room, with a yoghurt and a spoon, and she's in bed, you know, because she can't never get out of bed. She can't walk, can't lift her arms. She can just barely turn her head. And she's *tiny*. Like she's been shrink-ing. She's got no teeth so her face is all shrivelled up. But her eyes are so big and wide when she look at me. And I say loudly, *Hello Edith, my name is Ama, I'm here to give you your yoghurt.* And she doesn't say anything, she just opens her mouth, and I spoon in the yoghurt. Except when I was done, right, I stood up and was about to leave and I could see she was trying to say something, so I bent down and put my ear to her mouth, because her throat was so dry, and she was so weak, you could hardly hear her, you know? I said, *Are you alright, Edith? Are you trying to say something? Do you want something?* And she said in my ear, *All I want to do is die, and no-one will let me.*'

It was no longer really clear if Ama was talking to us or simply talking to herself. Beside me, I felt Zelma, who was leaning against my shoulder, and who I had thought was asleep because she was so quiet, nod gently.

'Did . . . did you ever see her again?' asked Margot.

Ama nodded. 'I took a night shift there,' she said. 'Maybe a week later. Was just me and one other woman. Was always like that, at nights. Just the two of you, in those big old houses with all those people. I said to the other woman, *You get some sleep for an hour, I'll come and wake you.* Because we always did that, let each other get a little bit of sleep when we could, just to make the night go quicker. And then I went to Edith's room. She was sleeping. There was no difference between her being awake or asleep, really. Just her eyes were open or closed. And I remember how tiny her breaths were, like she didn't even really need any air for that little body. And I sat beside her bed, and I thought about what she said, and I thought: Ama, you got to make this right. This woman is suffering. You are supposed to be easing people's suffering and here you are making it worse by keeping this woman alive. So I got a pillow, and I put it over her face. Just like that. She didn't even move or anything. Just that little breath stopped, and that was it.'

Ama was crying now, her tears glistening in the light of the small fire we'd lit more for illumination than for warmth.

'When I left off shift the next morning,' she said, 'I told them, *Nothing to report.* Just like that. Easy as anything. I never heard nothing about it. Not a phone call, not a little talk with the manager, nothing. Then a week later I got the letter from the Home

Office. And two months after that my job said I had to go and I lost my flat and I knew: it was God's punishment.' She nodded again, then sniffed, cleared her eyes, recovered a little. 'For taking a life,' she said. 'That was my punishment.' She laughed. 'Then I see this place. And I knew God was pointing me here. Because this is hell. This is the hell I deserve. And God is saying, *Get used to it, Ama. Get used to it, because you going to live this way for a* long *time.*'

It's hard to say how long we'd been there when the heatwave hit. Like our skin, the walls, the floor, time had become slippery. Summer had become deeper summer. We were hot, sweating, lethargic. Then the weather turned fierce and we began to boil. We kept waiting for it to break, for a storm to erupt. Rain felt inevitable, but it never came. Instead, it began to feel as if the humidity could increase forever, until it was no longer possible to tell what was welling up from our glands and skin and what was condensing on our surface from the atmosphere around us. Even at night the temperature barely dropped. Our will to move decreased, then our patience followed with it. We were soporific and ratty, lazy and quick to blow.

The heat accelerated what we'd already set in motion. The piles of discarded or not-yet-consumed food began to rot more quickly, stink more pungently. As the liquefying meat and vegetables lost form and bled out into the pools of shit and piss that covered the concrete floor, *smell* was no longer a word that seemed to bear any relevance. The reek was a physical presence in the air, something you could feel on your skin and in your eyes, at the back of your throat and over your tongue as you breathed and spoke.

Flies, already heavily present, now flocked to the space in clouds. At first we swatted at them, killed them if they were drowsy enough. Soon we simply acclimatised to them. Their choral drone became part of the atmosphere; the feel of their legs and wings on our skin, at the entrances to our ears and nostrils, became just another physical sensation amidst a symphony of sensations: itchings and burnings and stinging rashes and sticky pools in swelling, fatty folds. Quickly, the foil and plastic containers that had carried our food, as well as the larger chunks of meat that had fallen aside, writhed with maggots, which carried in turn their own distinct and filthy stench – slightly fishy, slightly earthy. The maggots, of course, saw no distinction between ourselves and our detritus, and it began to seem as if not a day went by without someone discovering about their person some fresh new sore asquirm with life.

Vileness, like beauty, required maintenance. In the late afternoons and evenings, sloppy with what we'd consumed and contracted, we tended to each other's suppurations. Margot would bring her face close to mine and I would squeeze her spots, one by one, enjoying the sudden, subcutaneous explosion, the froth of yellow-white pus over my fingernails. Then I in turn would offer my back or thighs to Kim or Zelma, and one or both of them would dig with filthy fingers into the depths of one of my open sores, which by then were not painful but numb, scraping from the softened, spongy interior of the wound the wriggling activity it had attracted. Sometimes, when no pustules needed bursting, or maggots extracting, we daubed and decorated each other with the liquids we lived with. Menstrual blood was popular. We used it to pattern our cheeks and chests. Other times, we simply made use of the gathering oil-slick on the floor, finger-painting battle-marks onto our faces and arms, or decorating the walls with invented symbols and looping, stylised renderings of our names.

I was attentive to the things that fell away, the meanings and interpretations that fell away with them. First to go were our clothes. They stained and discoloured, then weakened and tore. Finally, they began to rot, and we wore them not as coverings for any particular part of our bodies but simply as adornments, relics of what we were leaving behind. As we shed our garments, we cast off the people who'd been clothed. Margot was no longer middle class. Kim was no longer a tatty anarchist. Any one of us could have been shockingly rich or painfully poor. There was no way to know because there was no longer any way to meaningfully tell us apart.

I began to feel as if we were merging with one another. The process was more than simply emotional. It was biological, systemic. Each of our bodies was a biosphere, slick with bacterial and insect life. We teemed, and what we teemed with brought us closer not only to each other, but to the ecosystem we inhabited, fed off, and nourished. Bacteria bred in the ooze of our waste, our discarded food remains and puddled shit, then travelled onto us and between us, carried not only on the thickened air but by the fleas and lice that hopped and crawled from one body to another. There was no difference, I began to think, between the puddles on the floor and the streaks of filth on my skin and the acne that had erupted on Margot's face. It was all just life, matter, the biome. We were leaking out into the world, and the pooled primordial essence of the world was soaking back into us in turn.

I came to understand that this, truly, was what it meant to go back to nature, that this was nature in its truest form. No forests and campfires, no rolling hills and reassuring rambles. Just rivers of shit and decay, a chamber in which we ate and shat and ate and shat and lived among the carcasses of all the things we didn't want and couldn't fully consume. The processes of the world were known to us. Nature, in all its foul and irresistible force, was not something to be sought and found. It was simply what thrived when you stilled yourself, when you abandoned the futile endeavour of holding it back.

It became difficult to mark with any confidence the point at which one thing ended and another began. Bits of clothing had rotted and adhered to parts of my flesh that were oozing, creating an amalgam of fabric and skin. The sludge on the floor was neither food nor excreta but both. We ate from it, then shat, pissed, and puked back into it. Because it was alive, and, thanks to our fights and dances and moments of abandon, now coated not just the floor but the walls, so that the whole space seemed to swill and flow and feel unstable, I no longer thought of the room as a room at all but as a living system in which everything was simply matter – breathing, rotting, shedding its form.

The more we festered, the more we binged. As attention on us grew, the gifts and donations we received both swelled in volume and soared in value. At first, we had subsisted on takeaways. Now people were sending us caviar, truffles, Swiss chocolate, Bollinger. It became a kind of game among the people who supported us. How much money could you toss into the pit of our consumption? People saw it as a privilege to have us gorge on the products to which they affixed value. They didn't want to see pictures of us neatly arranged around a table, toasting our benefactors' generosity with wine in thin-stemmed glasses. They wanted to see us smearing our faces with foie gras, sloshing Courvoisier down our fronts like it was cheap cider from the local off-licence. They wanted, I sensed, to watch us kill ourselves quickly and freely using all the things with which they were killing themselves slowly and expensively.

The more we wasted, the more people sent us to waste. The more we discarded, the more appealing we became to the life we supported, and the less we regarded the maggots and flies and cockroaches and rats with whom we lived as vermin. They ate our food, our waste. They lived among us and on us. They were part of the ecosystem we created and inhabited. Over time, some of the rats even became semi-tame, tentatively taking scraps of meat and squares of chocolate from our fingers, moving confidently among us as we lay on the floor. When we slept, they walked over our skin as they explored, sometimes waking us, sometimes not. Zelma in particular was fond of them. She'd sit perfectly still with offerings in each hand, smiling and giggling as the rats nibbled at whatever lay on her palms. She made attempts to name them, as if in doing so she might disrupt the established order of human and animal. But it was difficult to tell them apart, with only the injured or freakishly large seeming truly distinct.

At some point, the rats moved from nibbling at unwanted food to eating away the plastic wrapping that contained our assortment of drugs. Hash seemed to be the most popular, perhaps because its form was inviting to their teeth. This made the rats lazy and slow, even less scared than usual of our presence. Sometimes they would sleep out in the open, curled up in corners in little knots of fur and tails. Soon, though, they found the acid and speed, and became by turns distressed and aggressive, either charging from one side of the room to the other in flight from some imagined emergency, or hurling themselves without warning at unsuspecting, equally drugged women. Margot was bitten on the face as she lay on the floor, rearing up suddenly with a rat clamped firmly to her chin, screaming as Kim gripped the rat's body and tried to prise it loose. Three times, Zelma was bitten on the finger as she fed them, and in the end she had to dash a particularly determined attacker against the wall, killing it before it gnawed clean through her digit. After that, we went from comfortable cohabitation to paranoid anxiety. Margot became afraid to fall asleep, so terrified was she that rats would chew at her ears and nose while she was unconscious. Finally, Kim began killing them. They were easy to catch by that point, either so tamed by Zelma's feeding that they no longer considered running away, or so deranged by substances that all fear of the larger beasts with whom they lived had evaporated. When Kim lunged for them, they reared up rather than fleeing, and she would gather them confidently in her hands and snap their necks.

'Little fuckers,' she'd say as she casually twisted their heads with the motion of someone wringing out a flannel. 'Nasty, vicious little fuckers.'

She dropped the bodies on the floor with all the other detritus, and the menagerie of creatures with whom they lived feasted on their carcasses as naturally and swiftly as they fell upon food and faeces. Live rats nibbled on the dead. Flies laid eggs in their bodies. Maggots hatched in their wounds. We grew attached to this process, watching with fascination as discernible recent life became increasingly shapeless death. After a while, Kim began killing one a day and laying it out in the centre of the room as a kind of offering, a gift to the life-system that sustained and eroded us. We watched as they stiffened, began to stink, then writhed with maggots and beetles and puddled into viscous liquid, leaving behind ragged skeletons bejewelled with dwindling hunks of fur. It was as if we were always both feeding and warding off something larger – some swelling, thickening, shared intelligence that needed death in order to survive.

One night, in a particularly heightened state, when we'd narrowly avoided another fight with Kim and found in the aftermath not the usual lull but a fevered need for the very confrontation we'd just denied ourselves, we asked Kim to show us how to kill them, and we all chose a rat at random and dispatched it with detached fascination. Mine writhed and bit while I held it in my fist, kicking its little legs and twisting its head around to bite the inside of my thumb before I finally took a deep breath, squeezed its face in my left hand, and turned its body one way and its head the other until I felt the distinctive crunch of murder. I was so excited that I called out, laughed wildly, and Kim and Sadie and all the others applauded, then gathered round to admire my handiwork. Then Kim took the body of the rat and fashioned from it a pendant using the strip of plastic binding that had once held closed a delivery box. This seemed to excite everyone further. Each in turn, they selected another rat, killed it, and attached its body to mine with a strange and uncomfortable reverence. Then, laughing, they kneeled at my feet and pretended to worship their new goddess, bowing their heads and flattening their hands against the floor while I stood awkwardly over them, feeling the dangling weight of all those little corpses around my neck.

I didn't remove the rats. Somehow, untying their tails and tossing their bodies into the sludge that coated the floor would have felt disrespectful. Instead, I lived with them, felt them lapse into rigor mortis, desiccate, and begin to dissolve. The rats marked me out. I was adorned in ways the others were not. I had upon me the reek not only of putrefaction but of death itself, as if I was death's bearer. When I rolled in my sleep, their tiny bones crunched like biscuits under my weight, and I felt possessed of power over life and destruction, protected by all my dangling, decaying talismans.

Ama was our link to an increasingly distant reality, bringing news of the outside world. People were *crazified*, she said, walking round in as few clothes as possible, talking to perfect strangers at bus stops about the weather, fretting about what the temperature might portend, as if this was a summer that warned of summers to come. At Tube stations and shopping malls, teams of people in matching T-shirts handed out bottles of water from buckets of melting ice. Once, she brought back an *Evening Standard*, showed us a picture of Yorkshire moorland ferociously ablaze.

One late afternoon, when the light was golden and the heat had pushed us all to the point of near-madness, Kim blew up just as Ama tapped on the back door to be let in. Kim had been tense and edgy all day, chewing the inside of her cheek and kicking angrily at trash she could just as easily have stepped over or around. I realised she'd been waiting for Ama, timing her explosion for when the person charged with defusing it was available. As I opened the door for Ama, Sadie said something I didn't catch, and Kim ran at her. Ama was surprisingly fast, slipping past me, interposing herself between the two of them as Sadie hurled insults and threats in Kim's direction. We went through the routine, taking Kim down, covering her with our bodies, calming her. When Kim quietened, and we all rolled off her onto the slimy floor, gasping for breath in the painful closeness of the room's stale air, I saw that Ama's dress, the one she so carefully preserved in plastic, was streaked with food and shit. She lifted its edge hopelessly, ran her hand over one of the stains, hoping perhaps to clear it, but succeeding only in deepening the damage.

'Oh Ama,' said Margot, rushing over. 'Maybe we can . . .'

But then Kim saw what had happened, and burst into throaty laughter. Ama seemed about to respond, angrily, but before she could say anything Kim had stood up, crossed over to her, and thrown herself on top of Ama, laughing, running her hands all over Ama's dress, over her face and into her hair, her fingers tangling in the curls.

'Gimme a hug, babe,' Kim was saying, still laughing. 'Come on. Give Aunty Kim a big old hug.'

Beneath her, I heard Ama laughing too, squealing as if being tickled, writhing around on the floor until her dress was slick and heavy.

'No!' she said between peals of laughter. 'No, Kim!'

And then we all joined the messy embrace, piling on top of her and Kim, bringing all the filth and slime and stink we had about us, all of us laughing until we could barely breathe.

After that, Ama's excursions ended. There was no other Ama now. The part of her she sent back to her unsuspecting family, her sun-soaked day-self, was dead.

It was no longer just the six of us, or not always, anyway. Others came, stayed a while, left. It wasn't how I'd imagined it. Zelma, I knew, had hoped for more: exponential growth, a grand swelling of our ranks. There was certainly plenty of enthusiasm. The more people sent us, the more we documented our consumption of what they donated, the more people wanted to join us. But when they arrived they recoiled. The environment was impenetrable, toxic.

Our small core group, whatever our internal differences, was too close-knit. Fresh arrivals struggled to locate themselves in what we shared. As people turned up and disappeared, our faith that anyone might stay was diminished. We became lazier about welcoming people, remembering their names, helping them find their place among us. The result was a kind of self-fulfilling prophecy. Our failure to hold onto newcomers was proof of our power to repel.

We became aware of a species of visitor Zelma called tourists. They stood in the yard outside, often in little groups of three or four, took pictures on their mobile phones. Two or three times, someone tried to break in through the back, only to be frightened off by Kim. Online, journalists tried to masquerade as joiners, but were exposed by Zelma's searching.

Slowly, a certain kind of man began to get wind of our alluring reek – awkward forty-somethings with a toilet-related kink. Their messages cleaved to a basic script – how much they admired what we were doing, how hard it was to meet women like us – then asked if we could send them our stained and reeking clothes, or offered to come round and lie on the floor while we took it in turns to shit on their faces. We hadn't discussed, as a group, what to do about men. I'd assumed there would be strong feelings, but as it turned out no-one really cared. I saw the word *militant* used in some of the coverage and it made me laugh. Male commenters wanted to believe we'd enacted some stringent misandrist policy. The truth was that we could have gone out and found men any time we wanted, but none of us felt moved to. We simply didn't care about men enough to miss them.

Perhaps it was easier to forget about men because sex was always available, if you wanted it. Kim and Sadie were our only couple, but in the spirit of shamelessness on which the community was founded, they only occasionally slipped outside and found a disused yard or shed in which to fuck. This was partly Zelma's doing. She'd told them, much as she'd told Margot, that what hidden space there might be around us was not to be used in order to seek out privacy. Mostly, though, it was a perfectly natural response to the way we had all begun to live – with every urge and desire unapologetically and unceremoniously met. When Kim and Sadie wanted to screw, they simply did so, and when anyone else wanted to join them, they did so too. It began with Ama. Somehow, from the tangle of bodies that followed Kim's grounding, Ama, Sadie and Kim had wound up kissing and writhing together. Slowly, it became just another thing that could happen, an outburst of energy hardly much different from Kim's episodes of rage and our by that point reflexive response. All of us at some stage or another wound up between them, and the way our sweating, stinking, greasy bodies slid against each other became just another facet of our celebration of everything those bodies produced. We knew the odour of each other by then, we knew the sight and texture and characteristic reek of each other's shit, why not know the taste of each other too? It was a way, I came to feel, of drinking each other in, another means by which we dissolved the barriers between one body and another.

Maybe me and Zelma needed the feeling of intermediaries, of a liminal zone, in order to be with each other. There had never been that dimension to our relationship. We'd shared a bed, fallen asleep with our arms round each other on the sofa, but we'd never explored further. For some reason, friendships are always described in a language of impoverishment by comparison to relationships in which people fuck. I never saw it that way. There was no less of a charge between us than there would have been if we were physically attracted to each other; it was simply that the charge led in another direction. On the occasions we were both involved with Sadie and Kim at the same time, I was aware of Zelma, open to her, happy that she was there, but I still couldn't imagine us doing anything similar alone, in less heightened circumstances. When we saw each other afterwards, during our scavenging runs to the dump and the bread factory, we didn't talk about it. I wouldn't go so far as to say that nothing had changed – there was a sense, if nothing else, that we'd tested another boundary, pushed outwards into a space that seemed always available, if not essential – it was simply that the change felt less significant than all the other changes in which we were now so deeply immersed. We'd drunk and inhaled from each other's bodies, what did it matter if our bodies touched? That was what sex revealed to us: that there was no greater intimacy than the absorption and exchange we'd already nurtured; that our room was a single body now: semi-fluid, many-faced.

As the visitors and gawkers and harassers multiplied, we became aware of ourselves as an event in the wider world, which we increasingly imagined as having no hold or influence over us. Ama was no longer going out during the day, and so we didn't have her reports and observations to tie us to the tangible fabric of the city outside. The world of the room was the whole of the world, by that point, and so it was jarring when the world we'd determinedly abandoned seemed unwilling to allow us to cast it off so easily. Indeed, it was our very rejection of society that seemed to first rouse society's interest, then stir its sense of indignation. A story circulated that suggested we were funding the community by selling drugs. Another, picking up on some of the contact we'd had from interested men, suggested it wasn't drugs we were selling, but ourselves. At one point it was even suggested, through a particularly convoluted link with missing donor organs, that we were consuming human meat, that hearts and livers discarded from transplant surgeries when the patient died on the table somehow found their way to us, and that we not only ate them but also, prior to eating them, performed what the article vaguely described as *rituals* with them.

Through it all, Harrison left the occasional message, including one where he said he'd been thinking about it a great deal and that he felt like he *got it*. After that it became clear he had other, more pressing priorities. An unnamed worker at Pict, probably see-ing an opportunity in the fact that they'd once said hello across a crowded office to someone who was now in their own small way a news story, had gone to the papers with a detailed description of their working life – the images, the wellbeing programme, the constant pressure to parse – and then gone on to relay the side effects of a daily reality built entirely around horror, describing in detail the night terrors, the visual hallucinations, the exhaustion, and the progressive feeling of being unable to detect any kindness or humanity in one's fellow man due to the fact that every human you met while parsing pictures for a living seemed only to be a hollow vessel filled to the brim with pornography and images of torture, which had led to the worker in question being found unfit for work for three months while he or she underwent a period of rehabilitation thankfully not arranged by Pict. Almost overnight, Green's position became easier to defend: they had given me a place to live, money, a work placement, access to wellbeing programmes, a chance at rehabilitation. Pict had subjected me to traumatic imagery, used me as just another cheaply paid drone responsible for the dirty work of internet upkeep. Who knew what effect that might have had on me?

As the media speculation around me deepened, attitudes to the community became more confused. What you thought about what we were doing in that repurposed industrial space depend-ed on why you thought I was encouraging people to do it. Was I some sort of activist? An agitator? Was I dangerous? Or was I in fact a victim – a troubled, vulnerable woman deserving of sympathy? Everyone, it seemed, had their own position. I knew this because they made me aware of it – online, and in the street outside. Every day, I scrolled through supportive messages on Instagram, took delivery of more donated food, opened at least one hand-posted death threat, or saw off some scurrying, wild-eyed man from the window.

Zelma sustained her commitment to ignoring what was said about us, always refusing to affirm or rebut the theories and interpretations we attracted. At the same time, perhaps because she no longer had her largely fictional Facebook as an outlet, Ama began to turn her self-taught photographic skills to our Instagram, elevating it from mere record or archive to a more fully realised extension of what we were trying to express. She favoured partial, often horrifically close-up portraits. You could rarely see her subject's face, but a patch of acne, a blister, a lice-infested parting of hair, would be documented in the kind of forensic detail that blurred the boundary between the expansive and the microscopic. Often, it was impossible to tell whether you were looking at a dried-up riverbed or the cracked-earth textures of filth on skin. Equally, it wasn't always possible to discern what body part the image depicted: a folded elbow looked faintly pornographic, a smooth expanse of belly flesh could have been any skin, at a variety of possible distances. Frequently, she mimicked what by then could almost have been described as traditional Instagram arrangements – a book, a scuffed second-hand table, the outer edge of a half-drunk latte – but replaced the expected elements with details from our life in the building: a mouldering foil take-out tin crawling with flies, a filthy hand picking at the greasy crumbs that remained. On the rare occasions she prompted us to take selfies, she offered guidance on lighting, framing, angle. There is one of me from that time, still probably available somewhere, in which I am lit from below, my face in monstrous shadow, my eyes blackened pools in the eerie light, my cheeks and forehead slick with grease, my half-open mouth ringed with spots and sores. I'm not wearing a top, just my necklace of rats, and my torso is smeared with a perfect, streaked hand-print of what might be either food or shit. To the right of the image, a face can be glimpsed – Kim's, if I recall correctly – the features lost in a streak of motion, leaning in and firing a web of stringy, sticky phlegm in the direction of my face. The response to that one was through the roof. For a while, it was everywhere. More than once, I saw women in the street outside with it printed on their T-shirts.

Only Margot remained ignorant of the evolving online atmosphere. She'd disposed of her phone on her way over to us. It was a statement of commitment, but also a means of avoiding temptation. She knew her parents, she said. Their voicemails and texts would become increasingly distressed. When direct appeals went unanswered, her mother would begin a campaign of daily updates designed to awaken in Margot a sense of loss or regret. She'd text her to say they'd just done her laundry for her, or filled the fridge with her favourite foods. For some reason, Margot found this leveraging of the quotidian more difficult to withstand than outright begging or shouted demands. It wasn't so much that it spoke to her sense of responsibility or belonging, she told me, or even that it evoked in her a yearning for home. Instead, she said, these promises of comfort from her parents communicated directly with her laziness, her desire to take the path of least resistance. At some point, wherever she was, however long she'd been away, however fraught and furious her parents may have become, her mother would simply remind her that she could return to a life of comfort and ease, and Margot would buckle, and then as soon as she was back home, in her freshly made bed, with one or both of her parents treating her like an invalid and bringing her food and drink where she lay, she'd hate herself, and then hate herself for hating herself, and then resent her parents all over again, even more furiously than before, for continually putting her in comfort's way.

Zelma and Kim, of course, tended to talk about Margot as if she'd seen something cool on Instagram and decided to give it a try. But in Margot's obvious consideration of the challenges she would likely face if she came to live with us, and the hooks and lines most likely to weaken her resolve, I saw a degree of preparation not always acknowledged by the others. Margot, I thought, was not wandering into our little world blind. She knew it would be difficult. She recognised her own tendencies towards weakness. She had taken steps to insulate herself, and I respected that. Indeed, we all respected it, even Kim and Zelma. Everyone appreciated what Margot was resisting, saw in it some avatar for what each of us were individually rejecting, and so no-one wanted to enable her failure by passing her a phone.

Or at least, that's what we told ourselves. That was how we framed it, justified it, when each of us, individually, opted to tell Margot nothing about her parents.

The first I knew of it was a newspaper article about what people were now calling our commune, for which Margot's parents, whose names were Lottie and Tim, had provided a brief quote. *We know where she is,* they'd said, keeping things simple and direct. *We're in discussions with all the right people about how we can bring her back.*

That was it. The rest of the piece was more interested in the salacious detail of what we were doing. There were screenshots of our Instagram – anonymous bodies, or parts of bodies, in various states of degradation. The reporter had encouraged two or three unnamed sources to comment, and in doing so had given credence to certain misguided rumours about our practices and aims. We were a sex cult, one person had said, or, according to another source, a death cult. The pastor of the Pentecostal church, which operated from a building similar to ours a little way down the industrial estate's central road, gave a statement about sin and the devil's work. A charity claiming to advocate on behalf of homeless and undocumented women raised concerns about what they called *vulnerable adults,* and said that they'd made efforts to contact us so they could check on the wellbeing of our guests. In fact, we had received no such contact, leading me to conclude that there was already a move afoot to portray us as secretive, exclusive, unreasonable. Throughout the piece, a central paradox went unaddressed: we were supposedly uncompromising in our commitment to a clandestine, almost certainly illegal existence, and yet for reasons the article was apparently unwilling to explore, we maintained a very public presence.

The co-operation and significance of Margot's parents seemed, at that stage, minimal. They had responded to a degree of journalistic pressure, I assumed. Their statement was terse to the point of being dismissive, hardly the tub-thumping rhetoric of an aggrieved middle-class family on the warpath. And of course, I thought, their aim was to bring her back. That was understandable. Their daughter, who they almost certainly still regarded as their little girl, had run away from home, not for the first time, and joined what everyone seemed to agree was a cult devoted to, if not death exactly, then at least a kind of nihilistic hedonism. Only the word *discussions* gave me pause. Who were *all the right people*, and what were these discussions that were apparently taking place?

Of course, my solidarity was with Margot. By the time the piece arrived, I was all too aware of her history with her parents. I knew she had her reasons for ceasing contact with them, and I believed in those reasons. I knew too that, however Lottie and Tim might wish to present themselves, their love for Margot was stifling, and she'd spent the bulk of her teenage years chafing against it in all the same ways I'd chafed against the things that were expected of me. If Margot's commitment was to a clean break, to time away from a home life that had clearly become oppressive if not outright suffocating, then I felt I had to respect that. Why make her daily emotional life any more complicated, I thought, any more conflicted, by allowing her parents back into the space she'd so recently cleared?

A week later, however, another article appeared, this time in a tabloid, and this time devoted entirely to Lottie and Tim, who had, the headline claimed, struck an exclusive deal with the piece's author to tell *their story*. Beneath the headline, a half-page colour picture presented a careful cliché of parental concern: Lottie and Tim, seated side by side on a teal chaise longue over which was draped an expensive Indian fabric, their knees touching, their hands tightly intertwined, their faces pinched and pale and etched with a record of sleepless concern. *Come Home*, read the headline. Halfway down the article was a picture of Margot's room – the awkward infantilism of which struck me as either forced or staged. She had a single bed, not a double. The duvet and pillow set was boldly, cartoonishly colourful. In front of the heaped pillows, three cuddly toys were arranged like an hallucination of a two-parent family: a large brown bear on one side, one eye and one ear missing; an even larger cartoon character on the other side, wide-eyed and neon pink, with oversized, alien features and a drugged-out grin. In the middle was a small, cuddly, yellow duckling. There were no posters. The only nod to a life outside of childhood was the dressing table, which was littered with all the accoutrements of adolescent beauty management: hair straighteners, makeup, the kind of over-perfumed body spray I remembered clogging the air of girls' toilets and changing rooms at school.

Lottie and Tim spoke openly of what they called Margot's difficulties. They described similar events as Margot – dead-of-night elopements, outbursts of rage and tears, sudden surges of destructive fever that left torn and vandalised clothing, broken furniture, and even a smashed window in their wake. Now, though, filtered through the saccharine prose of the columnist, these phenomena were no longer symptoms of Margot's distress, but a record of Tim and Lottie's labour. They loved her so much, they said, but it had been so very difficult. They had lived in a perpetual state of anxiety. They had tried everything to make her feel loved, but she had consistently rejected them. If she was reading, they said, they wanted her to know they weren't angry, just worried. Even if she didn't want to come back, couldn't she at least call them or write to them, to let them know she was safe?

And then, at the end of the article, the paragraph I'd feared. Margot, said Tim and Lottie, was vulnerable. She'd had mental health interventions in the past. She was both impetuous and trusting. She could easily be exploited, and indeed had been in the past. They'd given a full statement to the police, and were doing everything they could to make sure that whatever Margot had joined was not allowed to continue.

That night I sat with Margot on one of our stinking mattresses and half-listened while she talked about how she was changing, how she was seeing things anew. A couple of times, I opened my mouth to say something about what I'd read, but then silenced myself, entirely unsure how I was supposed to bring the subject up, or how Margot would respond if I did. I was finding it hard to think straight. When I tried to piece things together logically, it felt as if everything I pictured in my mind was in motion, so that a complete image could never be achieved. If I focused too hard, I'd feel dizzy and weak and have to lie down. Perhaps this was why I didn't say anything. Or perhaps it was the opposite – I'd overthought the situation, brought too much of my own instinct to bear.

'Do you still see your parents?' she asked me, after we'd sat quietly for a few moments and each dealt with whatever head rush or white-out or wave of sickness was at that moment afflicting us. That was how things were for all of us by then. It was as if we'd lost whatever part of our consciousness blinds us to the world's spin, and so sometimes we just had to hold on as the ground rushed away from us.

'No,' I said. 'Not for a long time.'

Up until then, I'd always been able to close the conversation down. A symptom of my progressive physical weakness, however, was a mounting inability to control what I expressed. My defences had thinned and frayed. Whatever wanted to emerge simply arose, pressed at the back of my throat, then showed itself.

'They didn't want me to be poor,' I said. 'That was their one big wish. That I wouldn't have to struggle.'

'So they stopped seeing you?' said Margot.

I shook my head.

'I stopped seeing them. It was too hard. They kept trying to give me money when they didn't really have any themselves. They didn't know what else to do. And I didn't know either. They asked me. They kept asking me, *What can we do?* And I didn't know. And because I didn't know, I didn't want to be asked, so I just . . . I mean, once I'd slept rough a few times I just thought, I can't let them . . . And then I thought, I'll wait. I'll wait until this is all sorted, until I've figured out how to be better, and then I'll surprise them.'

I couldn't quite say what I'd felt. It wasn't just that I'd been uncomfortable seeing them, I'd *feared* seeing them, feared them seeing me. I wondered why I was unable to say this and then, through the haze of my wondering, a space cleared, and I saw my answer. I'd been ashamed to be seen; now I was ashamed of my shame.

'But then, when you were working. You know. *Maya's Journey.*'

'I thought, Give it a few more weeks. Give it a few more months. I could be even better. I could surprise them even more.'

Margot nodded.

'They must be worried,' she said. 'They must have been so worried all this time.'

I leaned back against the wall, my stomach roiling, my fingers shaking from the strange adrenaline of disclosure, remembering again my mother's flushed and tearful face as she dragged our dog from the settee.

'Yeah,' I said. 'But if they saw me now, it would finish them.'

'Of course you shouldn't tell her,' said Zelma, as we walked towards the dump in search of salvage. 'Why the fuck would you tell her?'

'Because she might want to know?'

'She doesn't want to know. She's said that. She's said it to everyone. She doesn't want to hear from them. She doesn't want anything to do with them.'

'You think she means that?'

Zelma turned to me irritably. 'Is that what we're doing now?' she said. 'Assuming we know better than someone else what they want, what they *mean*? If she wants to speak to her parents, she'll borrow a phone and get in touch with them. There's nothing stopping her.'

'Maybe she thinks they don't care. Maybe she's doing that thing where you storm off and then get upset that no-one comes after you.'

'Or maybe she *just doesn't care*. And maybe that's a good thing. Maybe you shouldn't try and fuck with that or undermine it.'

I couldn't work out why Zelma was angry, or why I was becoming angry in response to her anger. We'd stopped walking and were now standing to one side of the central road. Zelma had turned away from me and was running her fingers over the chain-link fencing that separated the pavement from yet another darkened yard piled high with scrap iron – the skeletal remains of structures been and gone, all a beautiful shade of reddened brown.

'I'm fine with her not caring,' I said. 'I admire it. I just want to be sure she genuinely doesn't care and isn't just pretending not to care because now, instead of caring what her parents think, she cares about what *we* think and she thinks we want her not to care what her parents think.'

Zelma laughed slightly unpleasantly and turned back to me.

'Or *maybe*,' she said, 'you don't actually care whether she cares, you just care about the extent to which you're able to be caring yourself.'

'What the fuck does that mean?'

'It means that by trying to think for her, you offer her a level of protection you don't offer anyone else here and which you arguably shouldn't offer anyone at all because we're here to *strip that shit back*.'

'Strip what back? The extent to which the people who come here care about what they've left behind, or the extent to which we care about the people who come here?'

'What's the difference?'

'There's a *massive fucking difference*, Zelma.'

She pointed at me.

'Let me put it to you this way,' she said. 'By carrying on with your concern act, you're just buying into another bullshit expectation that you ought to be shrugging off, and at the same time you're patronising the very person you claim to be looking out for. She can decide for herself how she feels. That's the whole point. That's why we're all here.'

'She can't decide how she feels about something if we don't fucking tell her there's anything to feel anything about.'

'What is this? Is this your own, like, *mother complex* or something? You want to be Margot's mother instead of her actual mother?'

'Oh fuck you, Zelma. Don't make this about me when this is so obviously about you.'

'How is this about me?'

'You've resented Margot since the day she arrived. I've never seen you be that mean to anyone else. You think she's a spoiled little middle-class brat and for some reason I'm not going to even prod at, you seem to be actively hostile to the fact she has a relationship to her parents.'

'Whereas *you*, for some reason I'm not going to prod at either, seem to feel it's incredibly fucking important she *maintains* a relationship with her parents.'

'I think it's important she *decides*. That's what I think is important. Jesus Christ, how have you managed to turn this into some kind of psychodrama? *We have information, Zelma.* We know things she doesn't. And you want to talk about what's maybe the point of what we're doing here or its ideological foundation or whatever? We're all supposed to be *exposed* to each other. We're supposed to be in a place of *no shame*. How the fuck is anyone supposed to get to that place if we control all the information and keep secrets from people?'

'We're hardly controlling all the information, Maya. I mean, holy shit, way to be totally melodramatic about this. We're simply *respecting* the stated wishes of one of our group who's *told us*, time and time again, that they don't want any contact with their parents. It's not fucking complicated.'

I sat down heavily on the pavement and leaned my back against the chain-link fence. I felt as if my body couldn't physically cope with having to win an argument and exist at the same time. My vision had narrowed to a tight disc with a blurred circumference. My heart was working too hard. This was my new reality: my molecular structure had loosened to the point where I was only partially physically present. Everything I encountered either subsumed me or broke me apart.

'I don't know why we're arguing about this,' I said. 'I don't even know if we *are* arguing about this or if we're arguing about something else, or . . .'

Not for the first time, I was unable to formulate either my thoughts or my expression of my thoughts. In the slackened and slipping structure of myself, I could no longer easily distinguish between who I was, or *what* I was, and what I thought and felt. Everything was just matter in furious motion – as if the facade of stability had eroded, exposing the humming, entropic blur beneath.

It occurred to me that we were arguing as much about what we weren't saying as what we were. After my conversation with Margot, I'd wanted to tell Zelma about my parents, the way I'd removed myself from their lives simply because I felt what I'd become was too painful for them. Even as I'd been telling Margot, my mind had been on telling Zelma. Everything I said, everything I thought and felt, I wanted to tell to Zelma. But now the moment was wrong, and saying what I wanted to say would feel like some sort of admission, a yielding to Zelma's painful logic.

Zelma sat down next to me, her breathlessness in rhythm with mine. Under the sodium flare of the security lights, her skin glistened with sweat. She was, I reminded myself, as full of things unsaid as I was. She didn't know why I was conflicted; I didn't know why she was so furious and determined. We could guess, but not quite be sure. That was the problem with telling yourself you were leaving the past behind. It lingered, clung. By the time you needed to talk about it, you realised it wasn't the past you'd abandoned at all, just the language you'd once attached to it. It wasn't that the past no longer existed, it was simply that it could no longer be named.

'I don't know either,' she said. 'I'm sorry.'

'I'm sorry too,' I said, leaning against her shoulder and catching my breath. 'I'm not . . . I don't know who I'm supposed to be.'

Zelma nodded.

'I never asked for responsibility,' I said. 'I never said I wanted to make these kinds of decisions for people.'

'I know,' said Zelma.

We sat a while, taking each other's weight, Zelma's head on my shoulder and my cheek pressing down on her cranium so I could feel the slickness of her hair on my skin and almost taste the depth of her unwashed stink when I breathed. A little way up the road, a fox crossed casually from one yard to another, bearing in its mouth a pink flap of processed meat. In the beams of the street lights, dazzled moths flitted, danced, burned.

'I feel like I have to worry about people,' I said. 'Because I know what I'll become if I don't.'

'And I feel like I can't,' said Zelma. 'Because I know what I'll lose if I do.'

People were still passing through, arriving hesitantly, slipping away without announcement. Most nights now, in the strained, weak light that made it through our windows, I saw the pale glow of frightened, unfamiliar faces. Sometimes I tried to talk to them, sit with them, but I was losing the ability to give anything of myself to anyone new. I'd begun to feel as I had when I was homeless – that I met people beside fires, in the warm and sheltered spots of the city, told them things about myself, then found them gone.

Barb was the exception. She was one of the last to arrive, but by the time we met her she already felt familiar. She'd been an early donor. Some of the food we'd eaten, the blankets we'd slept on, had been from her. She sent us cheerful, slightly zany messages of solidarity via WhatsApp. We gathered she was older, perhaps quite a bit older, by the way she texted – a strange mix of fully punctuated, grammatically precise sentences and strings of not-always-apposite emoji that made Zelma smile. Barb was that kind of woman: someone whose personality attached itself to everything she touched. She was with us in spirit, she always said. We assumed she lived in another country. Then, with no warning, she sent a message: *I have been thinking I should come. Can I?* Zelma responded with an enthusiastic string of party hats and lightning bolts.

I worried about her when she arrived – this ageing little woman in a patchwork shirt, baggy jeans and furry shoes. She came up to about my chest and was slightly stooped. Her face was round and soft and all of her expressions were ranged along a spectrum of smiles – nervous smile, kindly smile, frosty smile. Her grey hair was cropped so short it stood up, which added to her slightly fuzzy aura. Her eyes, though, were like tiny black stones, and when she turned them towards you, even when they hovered above that implacable smile, you felt them touch you. When I held out my hand to greet her, she stepped smoothly past it and wrapped her arms around me.

'I've just come along to help out,' she said, as if she were simply calling in on a sick or bereaved neighbour.

I looked over her shoulder, catching the eye of Zelma, who was stood behind her, awaiting her own hug. I widened my eyes a little, raised my hand from Barb's back, palm upwards. Zelma just shrugged and grinned, and when Barb was done with me enfolded her in an embrace of her own.

'You must be Zelma,' said Barb, before Zelma had introduced herself. 'What a *delight*.'

Besides her ancient backpack, she had with her two hessian bags-for-life which she'd stuffed with cakes, breads and spreads, all of which seemed to be home-made.

'Just a few little bits,' she said, setting down her bags and rolling up the sleeves of her shirt.

Then she turned to the rest of the group, taking in the room, the unholy stink, the filthy, besmeared women and the heaps of trash and faeces that dotted the space. The broad smile tightened a little. She blinked rapidly.

'Well,' she said, addressing the baffled group before her. 'Who is everyone, then?'

Barb was, by her own description, a potterer. Rarely still, but never in any hurry, she moved breezily from task to task. When she ran out of jobs, she simply invented new ones.

'I like to keep busy,' she said as she unearthed from a heap of debris a set of pots and pans we'd been sent. 'Why haven't you been using these?'

'People send us so much food,' I said. 'Takeaways, whatever. We've never really felt the need to—'

'Oh, but you have to think of the potential,' said Barb. She gestured around the space. 'Look at all this packaging and plastic. If people sent raw ingredients we could—'

'If she even mentions a cooking rota,' said Kim dryly, addressing no-one in particular, 'I'll brain her.' Then she looked up at Barb and smiled sweetly. 'Just kidding, hon,' she said. 'Don't take me serious.'

'Don't worry,' said Barb, her black eyes firm and her smile as wide as ever. 'I won't.'

She had it in her head that we could be entirely self-sufficient, that we could live off the things the industrial estate both produced and disposed of.

'I've picked around in bins half my life,' she said happily. 'Nothing new in that. It's all this *added* food I'm not sure about.'

She didn't drink, we quickly established, or smoke. In the mornings she performed some sort of yogic ritual outside, raising her hands above her head to welcome the sun and then cycling through a series of aggressive, rasping breaths with her eyes closed.

'I don't get it,' I whispered to Zelma while through the open back door we watched Barb do her stretches in the small patch of yard outside. 'I feel like . . . Why is she here?'

'I don't know,' Zelma whispered back. 'But I hope she stays.'

She was impervious to aggression. Kim tried her best to rattle her, especially in the first few days, but Barb was unassailable.

'I get you,' said Kim. 'You're the earth-mother type – all garlic muesli and clothes made out of straw.'

Barb laughed. 'Guilty as charged, I guess.'

'Met a lot of your sort,' said Kim. 'The places I've lived, there's always one or two. Hippies or whatever. Never had much time for it myself, all that happy-clappy crap.'

'No?' said Barb.

'Not how the world works, is it?'

'Whose world?' said Barb.

'*The* world?' Kim made a globe shape with her hands and rolled her eyes. 'The world we live in? Fuck me, get a load of this one.'

'So you know how the world is,' said Barb.

It was unclear if this was a question, but Kim interpreted it as one.

'I know how the fucking world is, yeah. I've lived in the world. The real world. Not like you airy-fucking-fairy types, tie-dyeing some hemp while everything goes to shit.'

'No,' said Barb. 'Just part of the shit instead. Much better.'

'Oi,' said Kim, leaning forward and fixing Barb with one of her glares.

But Barb just raised her eyebrows, as if inviting her to continue, as if genuinely interested in the insult or threat that was to follow, and Kim tailed off, the thread of her indignation suddenly lost. I would come to think of this as Barb's patented brand of resistance: interested, open, and absolutely immovable.

Barb had lived many lives, worldly and otherworldly, physical and spiritual. Her biography constituted several existences on its own, but she remembered lives before this one too, impressions of experiences been and gone. She sensed a particular kinship with stags and foxes, suggesting she had taken these animals' forms before assuming her present body. She was a woman now, but tattered traces of what she thought of as male memories tickled the edges of her deeper consciousness. She thought she might have been lordly, even regal once, and at another time nomadic, desert-dwelling.

In this life she'd shape-shifted too. She married at twenty, had two children, devoted herself to their care. Then she came home a day early after a weekend away with her mother and found her husband screwing a mutual friend upstairs while the kids played in the garden.

'I wasn't angry exactly,' she said to me brightly, sitting cross-legged on the floor and eating one of seven enormous pizzas that had just arrived by delivery bike. 'I was effervescent. Like one of those tablets you drop in a glass of water. I just stood there in the bedroom door and *fizzed*. And then I was someone new.'

She left him on the spot, calmly packing her bags in front of him while he babbled about the children. That was when she realised she had to leave the children too.

'Do you still see them?' I said.

'Oh *yes*,' she said cheerfully. 'All the *time*. I mean, I didn't at first. They hated me, if I'm honest. And I don't really blame them. But you know, they're very smart girls. They got my emotional aspect, not their father's. Now I think they still hate me but we've managed to have quite a good relationship anyway.' She laughed, and for a moment I thought she was being flippant, but then I recognised it for what it was: modesty. They had a workable relationship, I guessed, because Barb, in her practical way, had made sure that they did. Now she laughed about it in place of congratulating herself.

After that had come what Barb called the flitting years, during which she dipped into whatever took her fancy.

'I travelled,' she said, slightly dreamily. 'India, of course. Sri Lanka, Bangladesh, Morocco, California. I was a Hare Krishna for a while.' She hooted with laughter. 'Madness. Wasn't me at all. Then I was a Buddhist. More me but I couldn't get on with the bowing. And my guru at that time was a *lech*.'

She'd ended up in a commune devoted to some sort of experimental group psychology. She talked about encounter sessions and something called *the work*. The outlook had become increasingly ecological, the emphasis shifting over time from personal change to changing the world. A splinter group had formed, five or six like-minded individuals with a taste for direct action. Barb was arrested after she chained herself to a freight train full of industrial waste. After that, she'd retrained as a lawyer, developed a specialism in land rights cases, lived the regular life for a while. Five or six years, though, turned out to be her limit.

'I always say about myself,' she said, pushing a final bit of pizza crust into her mouth and licking her fingers when she was done, 'I'm a reptile. I have to shed my skin to grow. Other people can just sort of . . .' – she frowned, as if trying to visualise a profoundly alien concept – '*expand*. Or the opposite – settle, contract. I have to step clean out of myself.'

I thought about this.

'I feel like that's what I've always wanted to do,' I said, 'but I never quite worked out how. Until recently, maybe.'

'That's because you're different,' said Barb confidently. 'You don't want a new skin. You want no skin at all.'

*

Everybody liked Barb, even Kim. Zelma, I knew, was particularly fond of her. Barb brought a lightness to things that everyone welcomed. Where the rest of us could sometimes become weighed down, not only gloomy but perhaps a little enamoured with gloom itself, Barb was able to float lightly over events and phenomena, never ignoring anything, never making anyone feel as if what they held to be significant was in any way trivial, but not quite caught up in things either. When me and Zelma had first arrived here, we'd always said that we didn't want to get too wrapped up in what things meant, what our actions or refusals were for or what we were hoping to achieve. I wasn't sure how successfully we'd cleaved to that original idea, but Barb seemed in her own way to embody it. She enjoyed not knowing what might happen, or where things might lead. That, to her, was life, and Barb loved life.

That's not to say, though, that Barb didn't have ideas. She wasn't strident about them, didn't wield them with obvious force, but she made them known, and something about the clarity and ease with which she presented them was unsettling. Beside Barb's, our own thoughts seemed suddenly formless, disembodied. It took me a while to understand why this was: it was because, up until Barb arrived, we'd never really had to give them shape. We'd lived with these vague outlines of conceptions, and everyone, more out of convenience than anything else, had seemed comfortable with that. Under Barb's sharp gaze, however, things had a way of becoming uncertain. Maybe it was in part a symptom of my bodily and psychological decay, but at moments, with Barb more than anyone else, I would lose the thread of myself, my location amidst the ideas and objects around me, and then I would look up, trying to remember what I'd been about to say, or what seemingly benign question Barb had asked that had even led to me needing to say anything, and I would see her smiling as always, waiting patiently for me to

261

order my thoughts, but watching me as I did so, interested, but not quite invested.

It started with the outdoor space at the back of our building. We'd done nothing with it, of course, except pile up excess trash and scavenged items for which we hadn't found a use. For a while, we'd been cautious, worried about drawing attention to the fact that the building was occupied, but over time we left that concern behind. We knew other people were aware of our presence. In many ways, we wanted people to know we were there. Whatever we were doing, it had to exist in opposition to something, some insubstantially defined oppression, and so we needed it to be visible.

Despite that, we didn't tend to spend any time outside. Me and Zelma went out looking for food and junk we could scavenge, but we only did that at night. Because we tended to spend much of the night awake and drinking, a good portion of each day was lost to sleep. Even in the late afternoons, when the sun was fierce and all of us were battling the symptoms of being confined in the semi-darkness of that room, I noticed that we still tended to cling to the insular, womb-like familiarity of that space. It was only when I stepped out with Margot, looking for a place we could talk, that it struck me why this might be. We simply made less sense in sunlight. In the darkness, indoors, we could revel in what we were, what we were becoming. Outside, in full-spectrum illumination, we could see each other in uncomfortable detail – our rotting clothes and pinkened eyes, our bleeding gums and off-white pallor. The less we saw ourselves, the better we could imagine ourselves. As soon as we saw each other too clearly, it was as if there was no longer anything to imagine, and that frightened us.

Barb, of course, had been there a far shorter time than the rest of us. The outside, she said, was her natural habitat. She didn't do well with being cooped up. It was one thing being filthy, she said, but she didn't see why she had to be miserable.

Even that statement troubled me. Exactly why, I couldn't say. Something to do with the way she looked at me when she said it, as if I was miserable, as if I was making myself miserable. For a second, I felt angry at her. She had no idea, I thought, how miserable I'd been before, how miserable the injunction not to be miserable had made me. It was all very well for her, with her sing-song voice and her easy way with people and her obvious comfort with being in the world. But even as I thought this, Barb was already off, pottering around the small courtyard, abeam with enthusiasm and possibility.

'Look at these,' she said, delighted, hefting a breeze block from a small stack. 'We could make an oven!'

As quickly as she'd picked them up, she put the breeze blocks back down and moved on to a loose pile of broken pallets and warped wooden boards.

'You know what I'm going to do?' she said, looking back at me. 'I'm going to knock together a little growing area. There's so much potential here, Maya.'

I smiled and nodded, pained by what was being suggested, yet uncertain of the pain's cause. It was so obvious that Barb meant well, that the things she was suggesting would in fact be positive, that there *was* room for improvement. But the moment I heard that word – *improvement* – I felt it stick in my psyche like a splinter. That was it, I thought. That was the problem. We had not, surely, spent all this time allowing ourselves to beautifully decay, only to have someone come along and improve us again?

'We're not a project,' I said, more sharply than I'd intended.

'This is a project, though, no?' said Barb, gesturing inside.

I shook my head. 'No, it's . . . It's the opposite of a project. It's not about making anything or producing anything. It's not about becoming anything. It's not about self-improvement or self-help. It's the opposite of all of that. It's an anti-project.'

Barb tilted her head to one side.

'So then this' – she gestured around the little courtyard, which I could already see was becoming in her mind her own personal project space – 'can be the anti-project to the anti-project.'

I didn't know what to say. I felt as if rules were being broken, but I also knew that there weren't any rules, and that I didn't want to make or enforce any.

Barb nodded her head inside and gave me a sly smile. 'And anyway,' she said, 'we're not short on fertiliser.'

I burst out laughing, surprising myself.

'No,' I said. 'That's true.'

Barb reached out and fingered my necklace of stiff, gaping-mouthed rat corpses. Then she moved her hand upwards and rested it on my hair, which by that point had become a carapace over my head and neck, a brittle shell of hardened sweat and encrusted food. There was no hesitation in her touch, I noticed, no repulsion.

'Everything has to go somewhere,' she said.

That was Barb. We hadn't argued. There had been almost no detectable conflict. But somehow positions had been taken, my own stance had been made to feel shaky, and I had emerged from the exchange subtly altered. Such was Barb's distinct power: benign, almost silent, but oddly irresistible, and always apparently on course, regardless of where in relation to it you stood.

I may not have been sure about Barb's plans for the outside space, but I wasn't certain about my opposition to them either. I had to remind myself not to guide things but simply to watch them, to set life in motion and see where it went. The online arguments, Barb's scrutiny – it was as if, after a period of letting go, I was tightening up again, allowing myself to be pressed into shapes that made me uncomfortable, simply because there was so much pressure for everything to take some kind of form. I was beginning to understand that resistance can do that – become as hidebound and oppressive as whatever it was you felt you needed to reject in the first place. Constrained by the stories others tell about us, we start to tell stories of our own. But then even those begin to harden, become suffocating, and have to be shrugged off in turn.

Me and Zelma started collecting things for Barb on our scavenging runs – more palettes and pieces of wood, empty drums of cooking oil, a sheet of metal we found at the dump. As Barb's designs took shape, we started filling refuse sacks with loose soil and ferrying it back to her little garden. One night, we ventured off the industrial estate completely and appropriated plants from the neighbouring suburban streets. We had no idea about horticulture, so we stuck to what we recognised: some tomato plants lifted from their grow-bags, some woody stems we identified as herbs purely by their smell, anything that looked colourful or classically floral. Barb, of course, knew what everything was, where to put it, and how to make it happy. Within a short space of time, she'd put together quite the little garden – a rough semicircle of cans and beds that from a distance had an ironically Instagram aesthetic of artfully repurposed junk and stage-managed beauty. Up close, though, the beds and pots reeked. From inside the industrial space in which we lived, Barb had scooped up fermenting, liquidising food waste and semi-solid human effluent and used it to fertilise the soil. The plants, particularly the flowers, seemed to be thriving. If we ever managed to grow anything edible, I thought, the whole process would come full circle.

We framed these modified goals for our nocturnal excursions as a way of helping Barb, but the truth, which neither of us quite wished to confront, was that there was no longer anything we needed to scavenge. We'd expected donations to tail off as people grew bored and distracted. The currency of the internet, Zelma always said, was novelty. In fact, the opposite happened. The more we received, the more we photographed our gifts and posted the images online with messages of thanks, the more people seemed moved to give.

We were inundated with food. Delivery vans from local supermarkets arrived, laden with crates of booze, fine chocolates, cooked meats, exotic fruits. We opened our back door to find piles of pizzas, boxes of wine, even things that seemed to have come from people's homes and gardens – a fresh chicken, still feathered; potatoes covered in mud; a slab of dripping honeycomb. They were no longer merely donations, we realised. They were offerings, sacrifices.

What once had felt necessary, then abundant, now began to feel obscene. In part, we revelled in that obscenity. We took pictures of ourselves awash with food, not just eating it but rolling in it, lying on it, burying ourselves in it. When people found this offensive, we simply absorbed and digested their disgust in much the same way as we re-absorbed the shit we produced from our bodies. Zelma, in particular, enjoyed this aspect of what we did. It harked back to her adjustments of adverts, her violent hatred of consumerism. *This isn't our life*, she wrote in the caption of a particularly excessive and indulgent image – Kim lying on her back while from above eight bottles of champagne were emptied over her face – *it's yours.* The post attracted a particularly high level of outrage. What was this, people wanted to know. Was this protest? Or just debauchery? Were we anti-consumerist, as many seemed to feel we should be, or in fact hyper-consumerist, an idea which some people found as offensive as the idea that we were some sort of plague cult.

Images of food being 'wasted' seemed to set people off almost more reliably than photos of our bodies smeared with shit and grime. To Zelma, this was easy entertainment. She made little films of expensive victuals going down our filthy drain, of Belgian chocolate melting on the concrete floor in that fierce, debilitating heat, of perishable goods growing green fur, then gaping brown holes, before turning eventually to soup in rapid time-lapse videos she made with her phone. *Think of the starving children in Africa*, people would write. *Yes!* Zelma would reply. *The starving children of Africa require me to eat so that they may not starve!*

And yet, surrounded by crazed abundance as we were, me and Zelma craved the feeling of finding more, the opportunity to be back once again within our own world, away from the shared existence we'd now created. No matter what we did, it seemed, no matter what we created, there would always be something to escape, the promise of some further space into which we could flee.

Perhaps this was the thinking behind Barb's garden, or perhaps, as she always claimed, the garden was as unburdened with purpose as the interior space to which it increasingly seemed to stand in opposition. Either way, it was surprisingly popular. Where at first the garden was Barb's eccentric little side-project, it quickly became unifying. First me and Zelma added plants and containers to our scavenging runs. Then, when the pots were arranged and filled with soil and the tangible development of Barb's plan could be seen, the other women started drifting out from the gloomy room on sunny afternoons and either contentedly planting and pruning little shrubs Barb had no doubt found at the grassy, disused edge of the industrial estate, or listening while she explained to them the finer points of makeshift horticulture.

At one point, after an hour or more spent stewing about our supposed ideological position and the pressure I felt to solidify something I'd always hoped could remain fluid, I found Margot and Kim at work together with Barb, stacking breeze blocks in a ring while Barb stepped back to admire the shape.

'Barb's showing us how to make an oven,' said Margot, excitedly.

'All sorts we'll be able to do in here,' said Kim. 'Baked spuds. Bread, maybe.'

'So now you get along,' I said. I'd meant it as a tease, a way of laughing gently about something I hoped was now behind us, but it came out sounding bitter, cynical. They both looked at me in surprise.

'I'm sorry,' I said.

'You know what?' said Kim. 'If you're feeling shitty about things, go back in there, don't bring it out here where we're enjoying ourselves.'

'That's right,' I said. 'That's what you want, isn't it? Just another place where all the fucking shit and horror isn't allowed.'

I turned and walked back into the building, into that shadowed, humid, reeking space, where I sat on my own with the filth of the floor seeping up through my clothes and sulked.

Later, Barb came and found me, took me outside to sit on the edge of the half-finished oven and talk. At first, as always, I resented that calmly smiling face, that almost showy implacability. Barb was so smug, I thought, so ostentatiously enlightened, so *healthy*. But then, as became the routine with Barb, I started talking, not to her exactly, but around her, encouraged by that hard-eyed stare and soft, beaming face.

'I know I sounded like a child,' I said. 'I just . . . This is what I've been trying to express, you know? Why is *this* . . .' – I gestured to the flowers and shrubs – '. . . more unifying than that, in there?' I pointed vaguely, almost dismissively, back to the building. 'Why does everyone get so fucking excited about pretty things? Why do Margot and Kim, who hate each other's guts, and who in there would probably be *wrestling* each other, suddenly find a way to get along just because there are a few fucking flowers to bond over?'

It was all my old feelings coming back – the feeling of being shut out, of not knowing the language by which other people became close to each other.

'Did you want what you're doing to be unifying?' said Barb.

'Of *course* I did,' I said.

'Because the impression I got was that you wanted it to be a place where everyone was free to be whatever they wanted to be,' said Barb.

'Right,' I said.

'But that's not necessarily unifying,' said Barb. 'Those are two different things.'

I nodded. I felt suddenly stupid, ashamed, as if, once again,

I'd fundamentally misunderstood something that was obvious to everyone else.

'Maybe you hoped,' said Barb, 'that once everyone was free, they'd miraculously turn out to be the same.'

'No,' I said. 'I don't think so. I don't want everyone to be the same. I just . . . I feel like before, there was no choice. There was us and the world, you know? And people were here because they renounced all that shit, all that comfort and luxury and attractiveness and wellbeing. And now it's like there's that, but there's also this, and it's a choice, and people are choosing all the same bullshit they chose before.'

Barb nodded.

'But there was always a choice,' she said. 'The world didn't go anywhere just because you decided to withdraw from it.'

'That's true,' I said. 'But I'd hoped we'd forget about it.'

'Sometimes we want to hang on to people,' said Barb. 'And we do that by taking away their choices.'

With a little stab at my centre, I wondered if she was talking about Margot, if she knew, as I assumed everyone else knew, about Margot's parents. It struck me that maybe everyone hadn't reached the same unspoken conclusion. Perhaps, instead, everyone was looking to me to lead, and wondering in private why I wasn't doing anything.

I shook my head, then patted Barb's leg.

'You've seen it all before, haven't you Barb?'

She laughed. 'I wouldn't say all. But a lot, yes.'

'And it always ends the same way, doesn't it?'

'Not always,' she said. She broke into a broad, slightly wicked grin, entirely different from her usual smile. 'Things can go to shit in a surprisingly broad variety of ways.'

'So I'm beginning to see,' I said.

She put her hand on top of mine, let it rest there a moment. She felt very still, as if I could feel beneath her the sturdy foundations of her breeze-block oven, and beneath them the earth, which seemed to hold Barb that little bit tighter than it held me. I looked at the differences in the dirt our hands had accumulated – Barb's pattern of dried earth and deep-green plant-blood, my sticky webbing of liquefied food and bodily discharge.

'The only thing I'd say,' said Barb, 'is don't let your beliefs make you lonely.'

The grin was gone, the little smile was back, but this time it was sad, and there was a flicker at the corner of her eye, a tiny flaw in that steely gaze.

From the blazing sunlight of the yard I looked across to the open back door of our repurposed space, the darkness and filth it both led to and contained, and saw what my alienation had produced: a statement of inaccessibility, repugnance, rejection; a world that was as alienating to others as the wider world was to me. It wasn't a place at all, I realised. It was a manifestation, a feeling given form.

Does the world change when we change? Is the world we see after a shift in our understanding a different world? Or was there never a world to begin with, only our sense of it, our perception?

Sometimes, looking back, I try to isolate a moment of change, a day or a night on either side of which things were demonstrably different. I never succeed. Partly, I think, it's because it's simply not possible. Outside of sudden, violent events, change is ongoing; we measure it only by holding what we've become against the memory of what we once were. But it's also because, in that space, at that particular time, we were so enmeshed in change, so completely caught up in it, that singular, momentary factors became lost and blurred. Day and night slipped their boundaries. Our bodies ached, contorted, then were numbed with narcotics and went slack. Our fingernails became sharp, then broken. In regular life, the life we'd left, we would have managed these processes, checked them, turned things back to how they were and how we liked them. There, in that concrete room, we surrendered ourselves to time and all its effects. The heat was unrelenting, pooling us in sweat and thickening the stink in which we lived. The floor was a shifting, flowing pattern of living ooze, its colour and texture seemingly different by the minute as people splashed through puddles of semi-liquid matter, or opened their bladders and bowels and added to what was already there. The walls began to seem as if they were growing their own skin – a slick, occasionally encrusted living surface that crawled upwards from the sludge of the floor. If you swept your hand through it, or fell against it, a black cloud of flies would erupt from the stickiness and circle wildly and angrily before landing elsewhere. If you remained still, the flies simply landed on you as if you were just another surface, drinking from your skin and laying their eggs in your wounds. We were part of the cycle, and the cycle was endless. No wonder that no single moment stands out.

Some of it began with Sadie. In the early days of our helping Kim, there had been a new shine to Sadie, an expansiveness that previously had been shrunken down by worry and exhaustion. Slowly, though, something shifted. After a period of talking about the future, she began, once again, to talk about the past.

'Funny thing about shit getting better,' she said to me and Ama one night. 'You look back on how it was before it was better and suddenly you're angry that it had to get better.'

Ama was changing too. Where before, grounding Kim had been both a last resort and a gesture of care, now it was a threat.

'Don't make me take you down,' she'd say to Kim whenever Kim shouted. 'Come on now, none of us want that.'

Strangely, though, it began to feel as if everyone *did* want that, including Kim. After a period of erupting less, I began to notice that she was challenging Ama more and more.

'Do it,' she'd say. 'Come on. I'm not fucking scared of you. I'm not scared of any of you. *Do it.*'

She was telling the truth; she wasn't scared. But to me, watching Kim as she set the stage for another confrontation, it seemed as if it was more than that. She needed those confrontations now. They were part of the pattern of her life here, a fixed and immovable point against which she measured herself.

Slowly, it all began to feel more choreographed. Kim would start shouting about something. Ama would warn her that she was heading for a grounding. Kim would push harder, pressing Ama for the signal. Sadie would defend Ama, take her side, and this would enrage Kim further, until, despite the fact that we all had any number of choices, there seemed to be no other choice, and we'd take her down. Afterwards, the conversations got shorter, the space we'd previously enjoyed seemingly smaller. I brought it up with Zelma, who brought it up with Ama. Ama in turn tried not to take Kim to the ground when there was no need. But then it seemed as if everything was reversed. The very thing with which Ama had threatened Kim had become the thing Kim wanted, and now she resented Ama withholding it.

'Come on!' Kim screamed one night, looking around the room, baffled by the lack of response from her exhausted, unmoving audience. '*Come on!* What are you doing? Look at me. Aren't you going to *do* anything, you fucking cowards? Is this *it?*'

It was awful to watch – Kim no longer upsetting anyone but instead seemingly begging people to become upset, standing alone in a corner of the room and raging to an increasingly unbothered audience. I'd thought she would enjoy the development, but instead I saw that something, some contact, some acknowledgement, had been taken from her, and she found herself in empty, desolate space, unsure of her place and direction.

The outcome should have been obvious, but nothing was really obvious to us then, because none of us were quite seeing things as they were. Kim simply escalated her rages until she achieved the punishment she wanted. Because Ama effectively had the power to make the grounding happen, it was Ama towards whom Kim directed the full force of her hostility.

'You know what?' she said one night. 'You should enjoy this arrangement while you can, you fucking immigrant bitch. Because when this is all over, the rest of us will be getting on with our lives and you'll be in a fucking detention centre, and *you'll* be the one getting pinned down by guards.'

'You shut up,' said Ama.

'They'll keep you there for years,' said Kim. 'That's what they do. And then finally they'll throw you on a plane back to your shithole of a country and you'll never be able to come back.'

'No,' said Ama.

'Yes,' said Kim. 'Yes, you fucking stupid cunt. So come on. Enjoy it. Enjoy taking me down while you can.'

'No,' said Ama, looking at Kim. 'I won't do it because you're asking for it. Because you want it. I won't give you what you want.'

And then Kim was on top of Ama, pinning her to the floor and trying to choke her, and we were all on top of Kim, giving her, as Ama had put it, what she wanted.

This time, as we one by one released Kim, rolled off onto the floor, and lay wincing in the heat, shattered from what was by that point an effort few of us were able to muster, Sadie held on longer, her hands either side of Kim's face, and just before she stood up I saw her lift Kim's head perhaps an inch off the ground and then push it sharply downwards, so that Kim's cranium struck the concrete with a jarring crack.

Across the room, through the combined haze of my blurred vision and the possibly hallucinatory steam that seemed to rise, shimmering, from our overheated bodies and the evaporating mush on the floor, I saw Barb staring straight at me, her face unusually stern, her gaze like a knife through the pliable matter of what I'd become.

*

Just as it was hard to isolate the pivot-points of change in the space, the group, the ideas we lived by, so too it was impossible to pinpoint the moment at which our personal physical decay felt no longer liberating, but terminal. Alone among ourselves, sealed off from the demands and challenges of regular life, we were self-contained, impenetrable, strong. When we rubbed up against the forces and conditions of the outside world, we were fragile, weakened, ill-equipped to protect and sustain what we'd created.

One night, around the back of the cash and carry, half-drunk and fogged with what was by then a perpetual, lingering high infused with a deepening, deteriorating malaise, me and Zelma came across two discarded cases of smashed biscuits. Breaking open the boxes and fondling the packets, we felt not the firm, discernible discs of matter we expected, but a shifting rubble of uneven crumb. We tore one open and took it in turns to pour the chunky near-powder into our mouths, the dust of sugar and oats and dark, half-melted chocolate clinging to our lips and chins. By then we'd developed a junkie's need for sucrose. I was beginning to feel as if I could live on it, as if it recharged me with each fresh dose. We were in a slightly manic phase of what was rapidly becoming a boom-and-bust cycle of lifted spirits and murky, nauseous incapability. The days and nights had reduced themselves, as if boiled too long, to a treacly essence. We psyched ourselves up for a task, completed it in our wayward, struggling manner, and then collapsed, spent and shaking, back into the foetid pools of our own excretion.

'We'll take one each,' Zelma said. She was laughing, although at what I had no idea. Somehow, the pointlessness of her amusement seemed amusing, and soon I was laughing too, and then we were both laughing together, taking it in turns to bring each other to a stop by saying something like, *right, OK, seriously now*, only to pause in mock seriousness for a few seconds and then double over helplessly with another fit of the giggles. I felt short of breath, strangely panicked by my own delirium. It seemed suddenly necessary, even essential, that I gather myself, pick up the box, carry it back to the others, and then rest. I remember saying, *This is serious*, and I sounded so serious saying it that it set us both off again, each of us mimicking the other's gravity, until it felt as if we were in a feedback loop of emotional response: hysterical, then frightened, then grasping for sobriety, then undone by our efforts and once again helpless with mirth.

Momentarily pulling herself together, Zelma placed her feet either side of her box and squatted slightly, her hands gripping the corners. She succeeded in turning it, the cardboard making a rasping bark against the concrete, then lifting one edge, her upper arms, shoulders and thighs shaking with the effort. Then she dropped it again and began laughing. The combination of laughter and exertion seemed to exhaust her and she paused for a moment, one hand on the top of the box while she leaned downwards, catching her breath.

'Jesus Christ,' I said sternly. 'It's a box. Pick up the box, Zelma.'

'Why don't *you* pick up *your* box,' she said, mock-outraged.

I remembered that moment of strength I'd felt at the market, carrying my purchases in that wooden packing crate – the way it had reminded me of weaker moments; the way I'd felt myself being rebuilt from the inside out, only to then feel it all drain away by the time I was halfway home. I felt sure that strength was still there – unused, unneeded, latent. But when I gripped opposing corners of the box and pulled, I felt as if the box were pulling me, as if my arms and legs no longer contained anything but their own simple and useless matter. There was no stored energy, no added magic to my body. It existed, had notional form, but everything it encountered seemed to cast its solidity into doubt.

'I think my hand is like, passing through the box,' I said.

I was frightened, shocked by my own inability. But Zelma was laughing again.

'You're just high,' she said. 'You're so wrecked you've gone numb. Look.'

And she pulled again at her box, shifted it maybe an inch towards her feet before doubling over so far that she ended up lying on top of it, balanced on her stomach, her hair falling down over her face and trailing on the ground, her feet comically upended and pedalling uselessly in the air.

'Someone's going to hear,' I said. 'We've got to . . . We've got to take these boxes and . . .'

It was hard to speak. I wasn't even sure what we had to do. The task seemed both urgent and meaningless. We didn't *have* to do anything, I thought. We didn't even need the food. But of course, that was what scared me. I had to be able to find things for myself, exist for myself. Barb had been right about self-sufficiency. Without achieving it, I would make myself dependent. I would sit and wait and hope for the generosity of others. I would be back in the programme, trapped by handouts, only this time the programme would be my own, an extension of the world I'd created, the projection in which I now lived.

I was starting to panic. The less urgent the task seemed, the more I felt I had to fight against my perception of its unimportance. I remembered my time in the programme – feeling I had to keep the little flame of rage and resistance alight inside me so I knew I was alive. If I relaxed too far, softened into what was occurring, it would consume me completely.

'We've got to feed ourselves,' I said hopelessly. 'We can't just rely on . . .'

In my hands, the box developed its own unearthly gravity, and began to suck me downwards, into its orbit, until I collapsed on the ground beside Zelma, lying on my back looking upwards, my heart racing like I'd just charged up ten flights of stairs. I could feel the soles of my feet perspiring into my shoes, my eyelids sweating onto my retinas, my fingernails loose and spongy in their beds. Beside me, I could hear Zelma taking huge swills of breath, trying to drink in the air, and I imagined that the heartbeat I heard and felt in my

276

ears like jackboots kicking at a hollow door was not my heartbeat, but hers, echoing out around the stillness of the industrial estate, ricocheting off the prefabricated aluminium panels of the buildings and alerting everyone within a five-mile radius to our presence.

I held my chest, rubbed at my eyes. I was terrified of no longer needing to do anything. In place of the feeling of connection to which I'd become accustomed, I felt only a vast and oil-dark emptiness, a great void that unfolded from my chest and swallowed everything within reach or sight. It struck me that this was death – not arriving, not imminent, but approaching, signalling me as it drew closer. Today I couldn't lift a case of biscuits. Soon I would be unable to lift myself. Everything would become less important. Nothing would hold any meaning. I would become ever more still, ever less able to care, ever more in need of rescue. If no-one rescued me, I would die.

I rolled on my side towards Zelma. I wanted to tell her what I'd seen, what had touched me, but she was already turned towards me, her knees drawn up, her arms locked around them, shaking with a laughter that was not so much emotional as muscular, tears running in rivulets down her cheeks and leaving pale streaks of washed-clean skin through the landscape of grime.

I wanted to laugh with her but I worried that if I did I would forget what I had just felt. I reached out and grabbed her shoulder, tried to hold her still while I told her: *It's coming. We're vanishing.*

'We've done it,' she said finally, breathing deeply and running a palm roughly across the tear-tracks on her cheeks.

She turned to look at me, no longer laughing but moved, wide-eyed with whatever had become clear to her. She reached out and touched my cheek.

'Maya,' she said. 'We've done it. We've finally done it.'

'Done what?' I said, those two words taking the entirety of my available breath, my heart about to punch its way clean through my ribcage and hop out onto the ground between us, throbbing and blackened and trailing a tangle of veins in its wake.

'We've become useless,' she said, smiling. 'The world won't want us. No-one will want us. We're free.'

We tried one more excursion. After the incident with the boxes, I felt ever more aware of our limitations, conscious that they were no longer simply spatial or structural but now also physical. Our bodies had lost the ability or willingness to do what we asked of them. In a way, it was what we'd wanted. We were of no use to society and so, to an extent, we were free of it. The problem was that now we struggled to be free of ourselves. If our bodies not only failed to do someone else's bidding, but *our* bidding too, what would become of our urges, our desires, our instincts? Without the scavenging runs, I feared we would feel too contained, too boundaried, that we would end up fashioning for ourselves not so much an exit as an ingress, a one-way route into ever more constrained circumstances.

When it happened, the end was not only swift, but crushingly predictable: a man, stepping from a peripheral shadow into a puddle of security lighting, blocking our path.

'There you are,' he said angrily. 'There you fucking are.'

We stepped back, started to turn, but he grabbed Zelma by the arm and tugged her towards him. He was squat and muscular, his face half-hidden beneath a Nike baseball cap. I could see from the way Zelma winced that his grip was strong. She tried to pull her arm away from him, opened her mouth to shout, but then clearly thought better of it, perhaps worried that by doing so she would only attract more unwanted attention. The security guard, after all, was not there for our benefit, and besides, the man may have had friends.

'Get off her,' I said.

'Dirty bitches,' he said. 'Dirty filthy fucking bitches.'

I stepped forward and pushed against his chest. It was an immovable, rigid surface. The weak force in my arms rebounded back into my increasingly frail body, forcing me backwards as if magnetically repelled.

'Off to nick more stuff?' he said. 'More stuff for whatever it is you're doing in there? You fucking slags. We're getting in trouble, you know. People are coming round accusing us of stealing shit from where we work. All because of you. All because you want to live like pigs. But I'm telling you: I see you. I don't know what you're about but I see you. And if any more stuff goes missing, I'll come down there and kick the door in and make you wish you'd never been born.'

Zelma wrenched her arm free.

'You'll never come near us,' she said. 'You'd shit yourself before you were even five feet away.'

'Try me,' he said, stepping closer again.

'Don't fuck with us,' said Zelma.

'Or what? What will you do? Call security? Call the police? Seriously. Who are you going to call, you stupid cow? No-one's going to help you.'

'If you come in there,' said Zelma, her teeth bared, her fists clenched, 'we'll bite you, and then you'll catch everything we've got.'

Now the man paused.

'What have you got?' he said.

'Everything,' Zelma said. 'We've got fucking everything and if you come near us we'll give it all to you.'

'You stink,' the man said, wrinkling his nose. He looked down at his hand, and then rubbed it suddenly and with laughable terror down the side of his jeans. 'Jesus Christ,' he said. 'You're fucking covered in . . . What is this? Is this shit?'

'You don't want to know what that is,' said Zelma, and then she spat directly into his face. In the eerie, unnatural luminescence of the security lighting, I could see that her spit was dark brown and stickily thick. When the man, shouting incoherently, moved to wipe it away, it strung itself between his fingers and his face like a web.

279

'Cunts,' he said, retching slightly. 'Fucking . . .'

And then he turned and walked away, still rubbing furiously at his face, then at his jeans, trying to rid himself of whatever he'd just unwillingly acquired.

Zelma turned to me. She was smiling, but I could see that she was shaking too.

'Arsehole,' she said simply.

'We'd better go back,' I said.

She nodded, and in that nod and the downwards turn of her gaze, I could see there was a sadness, and I knew she was thinking exactly what I was. We could no longer fight anyone off. Our only hope was to repulse them.

So now we were trapped, sealed inside whatever it was we'd hallucinated into being. With dirt as our only defence, there was no choice but to stay filthy. Was this what freedom looked like?

The whole time we'd been there, we'd insulated our belief from the processes of decay we'd nurtured. Our clothes rotted, our skin erupted and peeled, we lived knee-deep in all the things we'd been socialised to contain, but somehow our faith was immune. Even when I'd stared into the shadows of that space from the warmth of the sunlit courtyard and recognised there the depths and outline of my own projected fears – a vision I'd kept from the women I lived with, even Zelma – it still didn't occur to me to leave it behind or change it in any way. We were all committed to the same thing: seeing this through to its ultimate conclusion, discovering how far the processes we'd stopped controlling could really go. As soon as we felt we couldn't leave, however, the last remaining boundary – that between what we lived and what we believed – broke down, and all the rot and death and putrefaction with which we'd surrounded ourselves rushed inwards, eating away at our convictions as if they were just more vegetal matter.

Zelma became ill. It was as if our trips together into the wider world of the estate had sustained her. Without them, she unravelled. I'd long worried about a flare-up but, perhaps through simple superstition, I'd largely kept my fears to myself, as if by mentioning it I might usher it into existence. I'd asked myself if we would even be able to tell she was relapsing, or if, in the symptomatic fog we all by that point inhabited, the sharp outlines of Zelma's older, deeper ailments would be blurred. When it came, though, there was no denying what was happening. Zelma was no longer simply weak, or vague, or nauseous. She burned with fever, sobbed with bodily pain, coughed up quivering slugs of blood. I helped her to fresh bottled water from our supplies, held a dampened rag to her forehead until she cooled. More than once I whispered to her that we could go, leave, give up on all this, but she always refused. She would not have her illness, she said, be the reason for everything falling apart.

The sense of confinement and disintegration, of freedom both curtailed and soured, was heightened by the queasy work of keeping a secret. No-one had said anything to Margot about her parents. The more we kept her in the dark, the more the secret grew and festered, until finally it became unmanageable.

Lottie and Tim graduated from print to television. The clip circulated widely on social media, where it sent our most outraged critics into new paroxysms of fury. Suddenly, thanks to Lottie and Tim, we were no longer just degrading ourselves and others, or offending the genuinely unclean through our privileged appropriation of squalor, we were preying on, and quite possibly abusing, teenage girls.

Me and Zelma watched the clip on Zelma's phone, sharing a pair of headphones so Margot couldn't overhear. Sadie and Kim had not said anything but I felt certain they'd watched it, partly because the clip was everywhere, impossible to avoid, and partly because Kim had, in the past few hours, been particularly unpleasant to Margot.

Lottie and Tim had been guests on a breakfast TV show. They had, me and Zelma both remarked, undergone a bit of pampering since the photo shoot for the newspaper. Lottie's hair was shorter, sleekly bobbed and freshly highlighted. Tim had changed his glasses to a pair with slightly more robust black frames, giving him what he clearly thought of as a more authoritative appearance. Both of them were focused and well prepared, emotional but eerily controlled. Every time they looked briefly into each other's eyes and gave a little wince of support, every time they squeezed each other's hands or removed their glasses to wipe at a tear, I couldn't help imagining the stage direction, the dramatic beats inserted into the script.

'We're not saying we're perfect parents,' said Lottie.

'Or that Margot is a perfect daughter,' said Tim.

'Because she isn't,' said Lottie. 'And we're not.'

'The point is she's *our* daughter,' said Tim. 'And we love her and we miss her.'

'We don't know who else is in that . . . that *place*,' said Lottie.

'But whoever they are,' said Tim, taking a moment to pause, then breathe with pointed depth, 'they're *somebody's*.'

'And some of them,' said Lottie, 'are very young.'

'Maybe even younger than Margot,' said Tim.

'And just remind our viewers,' said the interviewer, 'how old is Margot?'

'She's eighteen,' said Lottie. 'So very much still a teenage girl.'

'And, I mean, I know this is hard to talk about,' said the interviewer, 'but am I right in saying that Margot's a particularly *vulnerable* teenage girl?'

'That's right,' said Lottie.

'She's . . . she's had a lot of issues,' said Tim. 'A lot of difficulties.'

'It hasn't been easy for her,' said Lottie. 'Or us.'

'But the point is,' said Tim, 'from what we've learned about these . . . *movements*. This is absolutely how they operate.'

Lottie nodded vigorously, then widened her eyes for emphasis. 'Targeting people,' she said. 'The weak. Radicalising them.'

'The first thing they do,' said Tim, 'right away, is they drive a wedge between the person and their family.'

'They tell them,' said Lottie, choking back tears, '*Your family don't love you.*'

'*They don't* understand *you*,' said Tim.

'And then they say,' said Lottie, '*We understand you. We love you.*'

'*We accept you for who you are*,' said Tim.

'*With us*,' said Lottie, opening her arms sarcastically, '*you can be yourself. You can be whoever you want to be.*'

'Except,' said Tim, 'teenage girls don't *know* who they want to be.'

'They don't know what they want,' said Lottie. 'They can't know, at that age.'

'That's what parents are for,' said Tim. 'That's why people need families as they grow. To guide them, to show them how to be.'

'That's why we wanted to come on the show,' said Lottie. 'To say to people, to parents: your daughters, your children, are looking at this stuff right now, online.'

'And suddenly it's not just, I don't know, sign this petition,' said Tim, 'or come along to this protest. Or boycott that shop or whatever.'

'It's come and live with us,' said Lottie. 'It's give up on society for good. Forever.'

'Really radical,' said Tim. 'Really dangerous.'

'And once they're there,' said Lottie, starting to cry properly now, 'who's taking care of them?'

'Margot has dietary requirements,' said Tim. 'She takes medication. She needs help with things. Who's doing all that?'

'Who's taking care of our girl?' said Lottie, now off-script and fully anguished. 'Who's making sure she's OK?'

And at this, while Tim wrapped an arm round his wife's shoulders in such a way that he seemed to be simultaneously supporting her and preventing her from getting away, the interviewer, who by this point had also teared up, and was trying to both stem the tears and maintain her mascara by laying her index finger along the lower lid of her eye like a breakwater, leaned forward and patted Lottie on the knee.

'You are,' she said. 'You're taking care of her. Even though you can't be with her, you're doing everything you can to make sure she's alright. And I know every parent out there watching will admire that.'

In the video-clip's wake, people's feelings about us calcified. Before, we'd been complicated, now we were simply problematic. The feeling was one of diminishment, of cresting a swelling wave, then descending its trailing edge into the watery trough behind. Donations began to slow, then dried up completely. The few other women who'd held on at the periphery, coming and going, toughing out the lack of meaningful connection, now let go. There were no new arrivals, fewer messages of solidarity. Fearful of what the world outside our room now threatened, we bolted the back door. As we shrank into the gloom, everything that had grown began to shrivel.

I'd imagined that without the comfort of anywhere else to go, the rough edges of who we were, the stifling sense of being constrained by what we'd brought about, would cause us to rub against each other uncomfortably. The truth, though, was that once we were sealed in, a new softness took hold. Perhaps we knew the end was close. Perhaps we were simply too ill and too weak for conflict. Either way, our nights took on a quietness they'd previously lacked. We spoke less, lapsed more often into collective silence. We were not fearful or preoccupied. If anything we were resigned, accepting.

Sometimes, in the early hours, Barb told us stories while we lay still and listened, drifting in and out of sleep. She liked mythology, tales of magic. I remember that she told us, in her light and breezy voice, of Tlazōlteōtl – the Aztec goddess of filth, adultery, purification, and sexually transmitted disease, who fed on the shit of others and whose mouth was smeared with holy excrement –

and Palden Lhamo, Tibetan protectress, who rode on a horse sad-dled with the flayed skin of her son and carried in her hand a bag of the world's diseases. We found comfort in these stories, release in the conjuring of a world beyond the one we inhabited, beyond even the one we'd left and could no longer access. There is always another world, these stories seemed to say, another reality behind the visible, the remembered, or even the imagined.

I felt gnawed at by what I knew. Too much had been forced upon me. I hadn't asked Margot to come and live with us and bring with her all the things she was supposedly trying to leave behind. I hadn't asked to know about her parents, or tell her about mine. Most of all, I hadn't asked for any kind of moral authority, to be placed in a position where decisions had to be made, where some sort of stance had to be both conceptualised and defended. I didn't want to defend myself at all. Even the very thought of it disgusted me. But whatever I did now, some level of justification would be required.

'Fucking *ideas*,' I raged one night, my voice caroming off the wall beside me and raising a black cloud of bluebottles from its film of filth. 'Why must there always be *ideas*?'

'But didn't you want . . .' said Zelma, her voice thin, her breath damp against my thigh, where she'd rested her head.

'I didn't want anything!' I shouted. 'I *don't* want anything! I want *nothing*. I want to know, just *once*, what it feels like, what it *means*, when everything just falls away. Why can't I have that? Why is noth-ing too much to ask for?'

Zelma looked up from my leg and nodded. Across her face, a shadow of sadness moved at speed, as if thrown by a racing sun.

'No-one gets to make no decisions,' she said flatly. 'No-one gets to be nothing.'

And then she clenched, gasped, and rolled away to be breath-lessly sick.

*

As I turned what Zelma had said over in my mind, I realised that she was wrong. One of us *did* get to make no decisions: Margot. Here I was, I thought, managing all her shit, when really, if she'd bothered to engage in any way with the world around her, she'd have known what was going on, and would have had no choice but to manage it. Instead, I'd afforded her the very luxury I'd wanted for myself: the luxury of doing nothing, attending to nothing, accepting nothing.

On days when I felt this, I came close to telling Margot what was happening. On other days, though, when I was able to achieve a degree of clarity and cut through the brain-fog that was now a fixture of my perception, I was able to understand that telling Margot about her parents was just another means of absolving myself. If I told Margot, I would no longer have to decide anything. I would no longer even have to think about it. I might dress up my decision as radical, but deep down I would know that it was selfish, perhaps even oppressive.

I began to feel awkward around Margot. Given that I was already, by that point, experiencing the space we inhabited as a pulsing, living thing, the knowledge I'd kept to myself and failed to share became just another throbbing life-form in the feculent air. When I sat with her, I could feel it between us, hovering, circling, breathing its foul breath into my face. Maybe Margot sensed it too, as she seemed keener than ever to be near me. Or maybe my fear that she'd sensed it simply expressed itself in an unconscious attempt to overcompensate, and Margot responded to that instead. Either way, it became a kind of feedback loop of emotional stimulus – all of it, I came to think, fake.

Determined to break the cycle, I decided to tell her. As it turned out, I didn't have to.

*

They arrived in what to us was the early morning. Sadie saw them first. I woke to her urgently waking Kim, who then woke everyone else by immediately beginning to rage. We gathered at the windows. Margot was the last to stir. By the time she joined us, everyone was looking at her anyway.

Outside our front shutters, across the open space that separated our building from the road, was a row of perhaps ten or twelve people, with another loose row behind that. Front and centre, flanked by photographers, were Margot's parents, each of them holding a placard bearing a picture of Margot, across which was written, *Come Home*. Behind them was a motley group of mostly women. Some were clearly there to support Lottie and Tim, but others seemed to have their own muddled agenda. *Respect Yourselves*, said one placard. *Shame*, said another.

'Oh,' said Margot. 'Oh God.'

'Looky look,' said Kim. 'Mummy and Daddy, come to get their baby.'

'Alright, Kim,' said Sadie gently.

'Don't alright me, Sades. OK? Because—'

'How do you know they're my parents?' said Margot.

She wasn't looking out the window any more, she was looking at Kim. Her face was still puffy with sleep. It was difficult to tell if her frown was due to confusion or the simple discomfort of having woken too early. We were operating on three hours' sleep at best. On top of the nausea, the discombobulation, the dizzying weakness that was by then our daily physical reality, the wooziness of interrupted unconsciousness was almost too much to take. I sat down against the wall beneath the windows, leaned my head back and rubbed my eyes. Zelma, who was the weakest and illest of all of us, had already slid to the floor, sweating and wincing.

'You what?' said Kim.

'How do you know they're my parents?' said Margot.

'Well they're holding fucking pictures of you that say *Come Home*,' said Kim, 'so it's not like I exactly need to run a DNA test.'

Then, from the room's darker edge, towards the back door, came Barb's soft voice, followed by her pottering form as she tiptoed to the window and looked out.

'They've been on the telly, Margot, hon,' she said. 'They've been all over the place.'

Margot looked from Barb to Kim.

'And you knew about it?' she said. Then she looked at me.

'I knew too,' I said, before she could ask me or draw it out of me any other way. 'Everyone knew. I'm sorry, Margot.'

'So everyone was just . . .' Margot's lip was going. She was entering, I could see, her habitual wounded pattern.

'Everyone knew you didn't want to hear from them,' said Zelma from the floor. She'd rested her head on her forearm, her cheek in the ooze. Her voice was thin and wavering, like that of a singer straining for high notes beyond their range. 'People were just trying to respect that. Trying to protect you.'

'It was stupid,' I said quickly. 'It was the wrong decision.'

'Fucking right it was the wrong decision,' said Kim. She pointed at Margot, her forefinger quivering, as if even holding aloft a digit meant dipping into a dried-up reservoir of resolve. 'We should have sent her packing. Then we wouldn't have them—'

'If it wasn't them, it would be someone else,' I said. 'It doesn't matter who it is. People were always going to come.'

'Whatever,' said Kim, still looking at Margot. 'Who cares. It's your shit out there so go deal with it.'

'No,' said Margot.

'What?' said Kim. 'What do you mean, *no*?'

'I mean no,' said Margot. 'It's not my shit. It's their shit. And I don't want to deal with it. And I won't deal with it just because you want me to. Because you don't want to deal with it. Because you don't want to deal with anything.'

'Listen sweetie,' said Kim. 'I've dealt with more shit than you can imagine, so don't come around here—'

'You've dealt with absolutely fuck all,' said Margot. 'We've dealt with *you*. This whole time. We've managed your anger for you and helped you through it and tolerated your little outbursts and tantrums, and now someone else has something going on you don't want any part of it because that's how you are. You go on and on about parents, Kim. Mummy and Daddy this, Mummy and Daddy that. But you never seem to get how people have to parent you, every single day. Because you're a child, a fucking *child*.'

'*I'm* a child?' said Kim. 'Am I hearing this right? *You*, a child yourself, with your parents stood outside, are gonna stand there and say to *me*—'

'Shut up, Kim,' said Sadie. She'd sat down too, by this point, heavily and wearily, and was now running a hand through Zelma's hair and over her back. 'For fuck's sake. Just shut up for five minutes.'

A heavy, humming silence began to squeeze the air in the room. Somewhere, something was dripping, perhaps gunk or condensation from the wall. As I had in other moments of silence and stillness, in the meditation room at BodyTemple, and here when me and Zelma had first arrived and every tiny sound had reverberated around the concrete space and bounced off the steel of the shutter, I became aware of a rising chorus of bodily noise, rasping breath and creaking joints, the churn of multiple rebellious stomachs.

Kim was staring at Sadie. Emotions and moods seemed to chase each other across her features. For a second her eyes pinched and twitched with rage, before filling with sudden tears she swiftly blinked away.

'Sades . . .' she said.

'Don't,' said Sadie, not looking up. 'Just don't.'

Kim nodded, sniffed, then sat down beside Sadie and rested her head on her shoulder. Then Margot and Barb sat down too, so we were all in a line.

'Hooboy,' said Barb.

Outside, it seemed as if the shouts of the assembled demonstrators had become louder. Maybe they could hear the commotion inside and this had emboldened them. Maybe they were simply warming up, settling into the day's purpose and tone. I pulled myself upright and peered again through a corner of the windows. There were more of them now, I saw. Through the smears of grime both industrial and human that caked the glass, I could see new protesters, new banners. *Degradation ≠ Liberation*, read one. *Consumption = Complicity*, said another. Someone was shouting that we were reducing women to pornography, to filth. Someone else was shouting that we were killing women and calling it emancipation. Yet another person was shouting about children, teenage girls, saying we had *more in there*. I wanted to say to them: *I don't even know what we're doing. There is no scheme. There's nothing we want or hope for.* I felt as if everything was pressing in, as if my mind was as sludgy and toxic as the slurry that covered the floor, the walls, our skin. There was no difference any more, I realised, between what we were taking in and what we were expelling, between what we were and what we might aspire to be, between what we consumed and expelled and what we'd become. It was all shit. We were shit. Our world was shit. Everything was a single, flowing, un-dammed, undifferentiated river of filth, and within that river we were formless and liquid and horribly free, and all anyone wanted to do was fashion new moulds into which we should pour the cooling and hardening putrescence of who we were, so they could force what was formless into a form they could comfortably condemn.

I closed my eyes. Against the darkness of my unlit vision, I could still see the outlines of the protesters, their faceless profiles edged in neon blues and flickering reds. Now, though, their signs carried not words but pictures – images I either remembered or thought I remembered from my time filtering photographs at Pict. Women with animals, men with children, bodies without limbs or heads, the obliterated mush of a caved-in face – everything that was out there in the world, everything that had been enacted, recorded, absorbed by my reluctant consciousness, coming back at me redoubled and alive.

And amidst all those images and forms, an absence. I'd looked for faces I recognised, hoped for a flash of familiarity, and found nothing. Was this what I'd been doing all along? Sending out my twisted, distorted signal, hoping for a moment of connection? If so, I'd failed. Margot's parents had come for her; mine had not.

When I turned and opened my eyes, I saw pale and wide-eyed faces angled towards me, waiting.

I stayed quiet for what seemed a long time, long enough for the women on the floor to blink and shuffle and rearrange themselves in the shifting atmosphere. Then I said, 'Stop looking at me.'

When no-one said anything, I said it again. 'Stop looking at me. All of you.'

'We're just . . .' Sadie began.

'I can't tell you what to do,' I said. 'I can't tell any of you what you're supposed to do. So stop looking at me like I know.'

Zelma had managed to raise her head from the vile floor, a fresh, glistening patch of deep-brown filth imprinted on her cheek like a wax seal. Margot was looking at me with an expression of fear. Kim was glowering, on the verge of speaking but clearly chastened by Sadie telling her to be quiet. I felt as if I was thinking clearly for the first time in weeks. A fog had lifted. The world won't let you leave it, I realised. You'll push it away for as long as you can, and then it will turn up at your door, demanding you let it in.

After the clamour of the last few minutes, the stillness seemed to hum in the space around us. Outside, I could hear the babble of the assembled crowd coalescing into a rhythmic chant, but I couldn't make out the words. I was beginning to understand that silence was not an option, that if we didn't respond in some meaningful way the space we had made for ourselves would close. I pictured the crowd outside growing by the day, swelling until it spilled out onto the road that ran through the estate, spreading out to encircle our small and undefended building. No-one was going to allow us our chaos. If we remained undefined, we would be dissolved.

At the side of the room, piled against the wall, was a heap of trash we'd been using to feed our occasional fires – broken-down pallets and bales of flattened boxes. I walked over and selected a blank sheet of serviceable cardboard, then carried it back to the middle of the room. Squatting down, I dipped my finger into the primordial ooze. The liquid was slick and stringy, webbed with phlegm and faeces and the juice of rotting meat. On my forefinger, I gathered a red-brown blob, then used it to write on the cardboard. The others watched me, then, saying nothing, began to find bits of discarded board themselves.

Only Ama didn't move. She was still sitting under the window, her head tilted back against the wall, squinting a little so as to direct her gaze downwards in our direction.

'You know I can't go out there,' she said.

We all stopped, put down what we were doing.

'Ama,' said Sadie.

'You all can get arrested, get in the papers, get in a fight or whatever. I can't.'

'Of course you can't,' said Barb. 'You can't risk it.'

'I'd like to,' said Ama. 'I'd like to be there with you. But they'll put me away, and I can't be having that.'

Sadie went over to Ama, knelt down in front of her.

'We won't let them,' she said. 'Honestly, Ama. We'll keep you safe. Won't we, Maya?'

I wanted to say that we would, wanted that ability to be real. But I also knew that wanting it, and promising it, wouldn't make it so.

'No,' I said. 'We won't be able to. I'm sorry, Ama.'

'So what are we going to . . .' Sadie sounded distressed. 'We can't just . . .'

'Let her go, for fuck's sake,' said Kim.

'*Fuck off, Kim.*' Sadie turned quickly. For a moment I thought she was going to run at Kim, take her down a final time. But she simply stared at her, ran her wrist along her streaming nose, then again across her eyes. 'Just fuck off,' she said.

All of us looked at Kim, waiting for her to erupt. Instead, she seemed to slacken, her shoulders dropping forward, her arms loose at her sides.

'Fuck it,' she said. 'I haven't got it in me.'

I looked at Ama. She was wearing what we used to call her day dress – the bright, richly patterned garment that had once allowed her to make her way in the world. Only now it was unrecognisable, thick with shit and spilled food, torn at one side and heavy with all the matter that was encrusted on it. Her hair was wild, her eyes bloodshot. At some point her flip-flops had fallen apart; the soles of her feet were not only blackened, but in places bloody. If she went out like that, I thought, she wouldn't even get halfway down the high street. I thought about what Barb had said, about taking people's choices away. I couldn't tell any more who I'd helped to be free, and who I'd simply trapped in my private idea of freedom.

Through the heatwave, bottled water had been one of the most common donations to our cause. We had whole cases of it dotted around the room, all of it warmed by the atmosphere, plasticky and cloying on the tongue. I grabbed a couple of bottles and gestured for Ama to stand in the middle of the room. Carefully, we helped her out of her dress and, using our hands and bits of rag, washed her. She stood quietly, very still, closing her eyes as all the layered encrustations of filth across her face first melted, then drained away, over her shoulders and chest and down her legs to the floor, where the water carved out a patch of bare concrete beneath the pooled effluvia and trash in which we'd lived for so long. We took the same approach we'd taken when grounding Kim: portioning her out, taking a body part each. Sadie worked on Ama's legs; Barb did what she could with her hair, not even attempting to wash it but instead slicking it down

293

with grease. Then we ransacked the space for any clothing we could find that seemed halfway presentable, and Barb fetched from her garden the bright-orange bloom from one of her stolen flowers. She placed it in Ama's hair, behind her ear, and smiled.

'Trust me,' she said. 'That's all anyone will notice.'

She was right. Somehow the freshness of the flower, its radiance, drew the eye from everything else. When Ama slipped on her sunglasses, she was barely recognisable.

'Go out the back,' I said. 'When everyone's looking at us.'

We took it in turns to hug her. I was struggling, I realised, with the concept of saying goodbye. After so long in which everything was a cycle, a process, in which things decayed and grew, fell apart and reformed, it seemed impossible that anything should be final. In the end I said simply, *Be safe*, and stepped back to let others take their turn. Sadie hugged her for a long time, whispered something I couldn't catch that made Ama smile. I heard Ama say, *You know it*, but caught nothing further.

When Kim's turn came we all looked at her, uncertain. She hugged Ama so hard I heard her spine crackle – a vertebrae or two realigning themselves under the pressure.

'I hate you,' said Kim, squeezing tighter. 'I fucking hate you, you bitch. OK? Now fuck off and don't come back.'

As she said it, she held on to her, and Ama held onto Kim, nodding.

We left her standing in the horror of that room, still in the middle of the little washed-clean patch of ground we'd made with the water, halfway back to her daytime self, halfway released from the hell she'd come here to find.

I led the others outside through the small back door. As we rounded the corner, moving towards the front, we fell into a single line with Margot in the middle, as if we were protecting or shepherding her. When we reached the front of the building, we saw the crowd that had gathered. There were thirty or forty of them now, all with their own placards and banners representing their own agendas. When they saw us, they began shouting and jeering. Margot's parents, front and centre, called her name. I turned to look at her, but she was ignoring them. Her face was stern but calm. The sun was high and fierce, throwing hard shadows against the side of the building and laying bare the processes to which we'd surrendered ourselves. Our eyes were crimson and rimmed with goo, our faces streaked with dried-on filth. Our clothes were stiffened and tattered. Through the torn material, patches of rotting, oozing skin could be seen. From the plastic band around my neck hung the skeletal, patchily furred remains of my talismanic rats, stiff and hollow-eyed and riddled with fresh life. Perhaps I was imagining it, but in the sweltering heat it seemed as if each of us was accompanied and clothed by a shimmering aura, a haze of living vapour that distorted the air around us, as if our foul stench had become manifest, or as if we ourselves were beginning to dissolve into mirage-like insubstantiality. There was no difference now, I thought, between who we were and what we gave off. We were foul-smelling air, a toxic cloud in loose and disintegrating human form. I saw the protesters take a step back, repelled by our presence. If we walked towards them, I realised, they would flee.

But we didn't walk towards them. Instead, we lined up with the steel shutter behind us, evenly spaced, facing forwards, saying nothing. We stared out at the people who'd gathered – the feminists and Christians and anti-capitalists, the misogynists and puritans, the worried parents and concerned citizens. They weren't here to confront us, I thought; they were here to confront the idea of us, the idea of our ideas.

'Margot,' said Margot's mother, sobbing. 'Oh my God, Margot. What have you done?'

I'd wondered if someone, perhaps Margot's father, would step forward, try to grab her, but no-one moved. They couldn't come near us, I realised. We'd become untouchable.

'What you're doing is disgusting,' shouted a woman wearing a T-shirt that said, *We Are All Beautiful*. 'You should be ashamed of yourselves.'

'Shame,' someone else shouted, taking up the theme. 'Shame on you.'

Margot's mother was still sobbing. Tim was holding her, his own eyes reddened. He looked utterly lost.

I had my cardboard sign in front of me. Slowly, I turned it around. On it, in the red-brown ink of our expelled and unwanted matter, I'd written: *Living in Anything Other Than Your Own Shit = Complicity*.

One by one, the other women turned their signs round too. I couldn't see all of them, but Zelma's, beside me, read, *Trying to Be Well Only Made Me Sicker*. Margot's read simply, *Nobody's Child*.

For a few moments we all stood there in silence, face to face, slogan to slogan. Then, behind the assembled protesters, in the gateway to our empty front yard, I saw a man in work clothes and a hi-vis jacket. I recognised him from the other night, when he had confronted me and Zelma near the dump and, effectively, put an end to our scavenging runs.

'Zelma,' I said.

'I see him,' she said.

The man turned to the road behind him, called back to people we couldn't see.

'Hey,' he said. 'You gotta see this. They're out.'

I couldn't hear what was said in reply, but it made him laugh. Other men appeared, dressed similarly. For all their amusement, their pointing and gesturing, they seemed reluctant to come any closer. After a minute or two, they left, leaving the man we recognised once again standing alone.

'Oi,' he called, cupping his hands around his mouth to make the sound carry. In front of us, Margot's parents and the people with placards turned to look at him.

'Oi,' he said again. 'We got you a present, you fucking slags.'

From the road behind him, the deep rumble of a heavy engine could be heard, followed by the pulsing alarm of a vehicle reversing. The man stepped aside and a truck became visible, backing its way into the courtyard where we'd gathered. Uncertain what was happening, the small crowd that had turned out to protest parted, allowing the truck to pass. From the passenger window of the truck's cabin, a face emerged, bearded and grinning.

'We felt sorry for you,' he said. 'Having to scrabble about. So we got a collection together.'

Other men had again joined the first man at the gate. They were all laughing. I could feel the other women looking at me, asking what we should do. I refused to look back at them, refused to guide them in any way. Whatever we did, I thought, we would each have to make our own choices.

In front of us, the truck again emitted a loud, rhythmic beep, and its back section began to tip upwards, until it reached roughly a forty-five-degree angle. With its heavy wheels and rumbling engine, it had already felt enormous and threatening. Now it towered above us, inhuman and vast. Finally, its rear end swung open, and with a heaving, liquid rush that was momentarily deafening, it disgorged itself onto the ground in front of our feet.

It was hard to tell the exact contents. Clearly, the men of the industrial estate had made use of multiple sources. Most obviously, they'd gathered the contents of various bins. In the heap that amassed in front of us, I could see endless food wrappers, polystyrene cartons, loaves of bread bearing bright-green mould, heaps of rotting fruit and veg. I suspected, though, that they'd also emptied out some of the portable toilets that dotted the estate. I saw wads of soaking, shit-smeared paper, a couple of tampons, a used condom, incongruously knotted, as if the milky fluid contained in its rounded tip had to be kept separate from all the other waste. As the lorry finished emptying, liquid followed the solids, spreading quickly out across the concrete and lapping hungrily at our feet. Behind the truck, the protesters scrambled backwards towards the fence. As everything came to a standstill, the heated reek of what the men had unloaded became a tangible presence. Decomposing vegetal matter, the cider-ish acridity of early fermentation, and beneath it the distinctly masculine tang of days-old piss and the heavy defecation of junk-food diets. I wondered, briefly, if they'd stopped at emptying the toilets, or if there might have been a more ritualistic aspect, the men climbing the sides of the truck and gathering in a precarious circle to relieve themselves into the amassed detritus and sewage of their working world.

The men were laughing hysterically. As the truck pulled away, a gloved hand emerged from the driver's side, middle finger raised. To the side of it, the man me and Zelma recognised grabbed his balls in his fist and pumped his crotch in our direction. For a moment, I considered attacking him, imagined the whole group of us falling on him, biting and scratching his face, pulling at his skin until it was coming away in flaps.

I still wasn't looking at the rest of the women. Instead, I kept looking at the man, holding his gaze. Slowly, I put down my sign. Then I walked forwards, into the heap the truck had left, until I was ankle-deep in the garbage, and flipped my middle finger at the man. Then I lay down, and baptised myself in the filth.

Beneath me, I felt a cornucopia of textures: crumpling cartons, bursting fruit, squishing cushions of paper towel and toilet tissue. I stretched out my hands and feet, a snow-angel in the sewage, and felt between my fingers the brief solidity and sudden liquidity of barely-there matter. I spread my hands and gathered as much as I could, then threw what I'd gathered over myself, over my face and chest and hair. I felt plasticky leaves touch my skin and slide off, or fall against my cheeks and adhere. Then I felt other bodies beside mine, a writhing mass. I couldn't open my eyes until I'd cleared them of gunk, but when I did I saw Zelma, chest down beside me, momentarily well again, her face raised and laughing and filled with delight. Beside her was Margot, on her back, kicking her legs in the air. On my other side was Kim, on her knees and roaring, scooping up great handfuls of what had been dumped in front of us and throwing it over herself. Then we were all throwing it at each other, pushing each other over, running our hands through each other's tangled, knotted hair, embracing each other and laughing.

I knew everyone was still watching us, but now I could neither hear them nor see them. All I could see was the stuff we were bathing in, and all I could hear was our own joy at our total immersion. In the soup of filth and offal in which we swam, a slickness came over our skin that erased the boundaries between one body part and another, one person and another, one form of matter and its supposed antithesis. Whatever my fingertips touched – my skin or someone else's, my hair, my clothes, the tarmac beneath us, the discarded junk amidst that slurry of rot – it all felt the same: slick and slimy and impossible to fully grasp or know, as if now that everything was equally coated, everything was tangibly the same. Greased with what I thought of as the primordial fluid of my birth, I felt wild and near to death, hysterical and weakened and free.

That, I would later come to know, would be the image of us that endured, by which we came to be known by people who never knew us: not the picture of us with our signs, although that existed, not the many images we had captured of ourselves and posted to our Instagram, but a single photograph of a small group of tattily clothed women, splashing like children in the aftermath of some kind of spillage. In the photo, the pool of effluent looks smaller than I remember it – a puddle of water dotted with trash, rather than the ocean I felt it to be in my heart. But we are exactly as I recall: a single, many-limbed goddess, possessed of the power to repel and change, summoning forth filth and abundance, degradation and joy.

That night, although no-one said it, we knew it was all over, and so we lost ourselves to the space and each other as if there was nothing else to come. There were no tensions any more because there were no differences. We could barely even recognise each other, let alone differentiate. With our hair slicked down with offal, our faces glistening with translucent slime, our clothes rotted and tattered and revealing bodies in equal and complementary states of decay, we appeared to each other simply as shining, semi-fluid forms in the darkness. We reached for anything we could consume – food old and new, detritus from the floor, our own squelching shit – and washed it down with all the booze we could manage. By that point people were sending us drugs we could no longer confidently identify, and the effects blurred into each other as seamlessly as everything else. We were neither up nor down, tripping nor speedily sharpened, rushing nor comfortably numbed. Everything seemed to be at once pin-sharp and bleeding out at its edges. Eventually, we screamed and bellowed and roared to such a point that it seemed as if our voices detached themselves from our bodies and merged in the air as a single, unified noise. If we kept on, I knew, our skin itself would leave us, rotting from our bones and pooling at our ankles, until there was nothing at all to tell one of us from the other, or any of us from anyone else. Even in the haze, I understood what I had achieved. I'd stripped everything back, rendered myself down to nothing but the shit I contained. I had transcended even wildness and animality, become bacterial, amoebic, viral. I was infinite and self-dividing, no longer near to death but death itself, airborne and particulate. The skin of the world had been peeled away, and what was beneath, I knew, was the true face of God: pulsing and writhing and ugly with life.

At some point, I remember us all going outside, into Barb's garden, unafraid now of disturbance or discovery, and first watching, then helping, as Barb, with a fury so alien that it seemed for a time as if she was possessed, tore everything to pieces, kicking at breeze blocks, ripping flowers up by the roots, and scattering around and over herself the soil and sewage in which they'd grown, until finally she was stood among the ruins, her stony eyes wide and flashing with glee, her blackened hands raised skyward, her face split by a mighty smile as she roared that she'd done it, finally, after all these years: taken the maker and doer inside her, the mender, the healer, the helper, and throttled her to death.

'I'm a destroyer,' she said, her voice high and wild. 'I'm a destroyer and I'm *glorious.*'

And then I remember holding everyone, each in turn, and feeling myself bleed into them, porous and spongiform and shorn of all solidity. I knew Zelma by touch. When we disappeared into each other, I wept.

I awoke face down on the concrete floor, one cheek in the warm and mucilaginous ooze, my mouth and nostrils tilted airwards in an effort not to drown. There was no clamour, I remember. No breaking down of doors or threatening stand-off. Just black rubber boots in front of my face, the papery legs of what looked like a hazmat suit and, when I rolled and looked up, a row of eyes, hovering over surgical masks.

'Jesus Christ,' someone said.

And then someone was kneeling beside me, placing a blue latex-gloved hand on my shoulder, their eyes wide and straining for warmth, speaking to me in a woman's voice, muffled through the mask.

'Maya,' she said. 'It is Maya, isn't it?'

I said nothing. I couldn't, I realised, say anything. My throat felt glued shut, my lips sticky and unwilling to take the shapes I requested.

'My name is Felicia,' said the voice. 'I'm a social worker. These people with me are police officers. We also have doctors here, and people from environmental health. We're not here to hurt you, OK? We're here because we're worried about you. We're here to try and help.'

It was the word *help* that did it. I had been helped before; I would not be helped again. Before I knew what I was doing, I'd grabbed a fistful of Felicia's boiler suit and was pulling her down into the shit with me. She was very calm, I remember, unfazed by my aggression. She simply leaned back, held my wrist in her gloved fingers while police officers pinned my upper arms. Her lack of distress shattered me. I had felt so strong, so infinite. Now I saw that I was frail, that other bodies could outdo me and master me with ease. For so long I had felt frightening. Now I was simply pitiable.

I tried to shout something coherent. It seemed important to me that I explain myself, if only to show that I *could* explain myself. But now there was a gloved hand on the side of my face, impeding the movement of my jaw, and all I could manage was a sound – hoarse and guttural, too easily mistaken for distress when what I meant to convey was fury.

'OK,' said Felicia gently. 'It's alright, Maya. It's OK.'

My shout had been enough to wake Zelma, who had fallen asleep a few feet away from me. She jolted into consciousness, clearly confused, and took a moment to register what was happening. Then she shouted, reached for me, and made to stand, but three more police officers quickly restrained her too.

'Get off her,' she shouted. 'Get the fuck off her. You don't have any legal basis to—'

'This one's a legal expert,' joked one of the officers. Some of the other cops laughed. Felicia didn't. Later, I would remember that Zelma had said *Get off her* rather than *Get off me*, that her concern was for my safety and freedom, not hers.

It took five officers to restrain Kim once she realised what was happening. It felt strange, almost unreal, seeing the process of grounding her enacted by others, for such different reasons. They knelt on her thighs and upper arms. One straddled her back. She thrashed like she always did, spitting and snarling and spewing out threats. I saw two of them punch her hard in the ribs. Then they pepper-sprayed her and, while she was retching, hauled her out by her feet as she clawed hopelessly at the slippery floor.

One by one, each in turn, they dragged us out into the sunlight.

THREE

Another room. Another laminate tabletop against which my fingers tapped out the slow drip of time. On the wall, another airbrushed flower on cheap, mass-produced canvas. No glass, of course. Nothing that could be shattered and used as a weapon.

I wondered where all these interview rooms and places of confinement, these holding areas and places of routine processing, found their matching furniture – their uncomfortable plastic chairs, their tables that bolted at either end, the kind of artwork for which numbing moribundity is an aspiration. Then it struck me that at some point in their life, all of these things had probably passed through an industrial estate much like the one on which I'd so recently lived; that probably, somewhere, there was a room just like the one we'd called our own, concrete-floored and steel-shuttered, stacked to the ceiling with the trappings of bureaucratic torture.

There were three people in front of me this time, not two. One of them was Felicia, who had removed her mask and overalls and was now wearing a stylish tweed jacket with the sleeves turned back to reveal a vivid, candy-striped lining that reminded me of exposed gums and teeth. The other two were psychiatrists, Doctor Somebody and Doctor Somebody Else. I hadn't listened when they introduced themselves. As always, I'd said nothing back either.

The room was located not in a police station, but in a hospital. I had the feeling I was being processed quickly. This was partly, I knew, because no-one wanted to touch me unless suitable protective clothing was available. Even now, Felicia and the two doctors had positioned their chairs a good foot from their side of the table. All of their mouths were open, their noses slightly pinched, so as to prevent any possibility of breathing through their nostrils. There were no reflective surfaces in the room, so I couldn't see myself, but I'd caught glimpses in the blacked-out windows of the police van, and had a good view now of my appearance effectively mapped across the expressions of those three faces. The chair I sat on was already stained and damp. On the tabletop in front of me, under my wrist and fingers, a deep-brown streak had formed. I liked to think they wouldn't even be able to clean what I'd touched, that after the interview they'd carry all the furniture outside and burn it.

'So,' said Felicia. 'Maya.'

She waited for me to engage. When I didn't, she made a note. As I tapped the table, approximately once every two seconds, she looked up from her pad, then put her head down and made a note of that too.

'Do you like to be called Maya?' she said. 'Or something else?'

Her voice was quiet and sweet, as if she was interacting with a frightened child. Whenever she finished a sentence, she smiled.

'You're not much of a talker, no? That's fine. But I should say, Maya, that the more involved in this you are, the better the outcome is likely to be.'

'We're not here to talk at you,' said Doctor Somebody. 'I'm sure you've had enough of that.'

'We're here to listen,' said Doctor Somebody Else. 'And hopefully help.'

Everyone nodded and smiled. I gazed at them flatly. I had let my heavy, dirt-caked hair fall in front of my face, so that I peered at them as if through a veil.

'So the reason you're here,' said Felicia, 'as you probably know, is because we've received some concerns about you. OK? And because, when we received those concerns, you were not on your own property, that allowed us to come and see you and, because we felt it was the only option, remove you from that place to what we call a place of safety, which is here, at the hospital.'

She was, I realised, slightly nervous, and yet she didn't give the impression of being new to her job or unsure of what she was doing. I began to understand that I was something of a story, that Felicia had landed the person everyone was talking about, and now felt talked about herself.

'I want to say right off,' said Felicia, 'for the benefit of my colleagues here who did not attend with me this morning, that I was deeply concerned by what I saw.'

For the first time, I broke my blank expression and smiled at Felicia. Not my smile, but hers, copied and thrown back at her. Friendly concern. Pity.

'One of the things we look at, Maya, when we're thinking about how we need to help someone, is whether they're able to take care of themselves. Because sometimes, when people aren't able to take care of themselves, which is nothing to be ashamed of, just something that can happen when people are unwell, we have to ask ourselves if maybe we need to take care of them for a bit until they feel better. Do you understand?'

I was still smiling at her, still tapping the table.

'The other thing we have to think about,' she went on, 'is other people. Everyone, obviously, has the right to make choices, but everyone at the same time has the right to be safe from people who might harm them. One of the things that struck me, Maya, when I came to see you, was that not only were you perhaps not taking care of yourself, you were maybe not taking care of other people who needed you to take care of them. One of the people living there with you was quite young, and I think it's fair to say quite vulnerable. At least one other was really very vulnerable indeed. Those are people we have a responsibility towards. They are people who need looking after in quite a complicated way. I think perhaps, if I'm honest, that looking after them was a bit more than you were able to manage.'

Margot, I thought. And maybe Kim. I knew there was history there, knew I didn't know the whole story.

'I'm not saying you meant anyone any harm, Maya,' said Felicia. 'I'm saying that maybe the situation got away from you, became complicated, and then it was hard for you to stay on top of things.'

I looked around the room, at the bare walls, the grey industrial carpet. I wanted to say that things hadn't got away from me; I had got away from things.

'One of the reasons for me attending with the police,' said Felicia, 'is to give my opinion on whether the situation is a criminal matter, or something a bit different. Now I know there's the issue of the trespassing, the criminal damage and what have you, but I don't think to be totally honest with you anyone is going to be pursuing that. So if that's why you're staying quiet, I just want you to know that it's unnecessary. OK?'

'This isn't an interview, in that sense,' said Doctor Somebody Else. 'You're not under caution.'

'It's more just an opportunity for us to get a sense of things,' said Doctor Somebody.

'Maya,' said Doctor Somebody Else. 'Do you hear voices?'

My tapping by this point was very slow, perhaps every four or five seconds. My breathing had slowed with it. I felt as if there were stretches in which I didn't even need to inhale, where I had breathed everything out and was able to remain empty and still. I pictured my pulse on a screen, shifting from a series of sharp peaks to a gentle, rolling landscape, then to a static flatline.

'Or see things?' said Doctor Somebody.

'Maybe,' said Felicia, 'things come into your mind, either sounds or things you see, and they frighten you. It's perfectly understandable.'

'What about the washing?' said Doctor Somebody. 'Is it because you physically can't? Because it's painful in some way? Or is it a lack of motivation?'

'Or perhaps,' said Doctor Somebody Else, 'you feel as if you have to hold on to everything, not let anything go, even your urine and faeces.'

'What about thoughts of harming yourself?' said Doctor Somebody. 'Or thoughts of harming others?'

'We all get angry sometimes,' said Felicia.

'Or sometimes we feel hopeless,' said Doctor Somebody. 'As if life is not worth living.'

'As if everything,' said Felicia, 'is a struggle.'

I wanted to tell them that my life was less of a struggle than theirs. That everything *was* a struggle, but that I had found a way to struggle no longer. I wanted to say to them: *You're struggling away, and I am not struggling at all. Look! It is barely even necessary for me to breathe.*

The three of them looked at each other. Felicia shook her head slightly. Doctor Somebody held his hands palm up.

'OK, Maya,' said Felicia. 'We're not going to pressure you. I don't think there's anything to be gained by that. If you don't want to talk, that's OK. There will be other opportunities.'

She leaned forward, moved her face to try and find my eyes through the veil of encrusted hair.

'Maya,' she said quietly. 'We're going to admit you to hospital, OK? We feel that you're unwell and need treatment. We don't feel that you're able to consent to treatment properly, and we feel you would be at risk of self-neglect if we were to release you now. So you'll come and stay here in hospital for a little while. Not forever, just a little while, and we'll see if we can find a way to help you get well.'

I didn't move. I had stopped tapping. Everything, I felt, had stopped completely. There was only stillness and silence. The windows were too thick to hear anything through, but outside I imagined the birds, frozen and songless in the trees, all winds and breezes halted, a line of motionless cars along the road, peopled by mannequin drivers. Felicia looked at me for so long that I began to wonder if she too had ceased to move. Then she looked away, down at the table, and stood up. The two doctors stood with her and said they'd be seeing me soon.

At the door, Felicia stopped, turned.

'Is there anyone you want me to call?' she said. 'Any next of kin? Anyone who might want to—'

'No,' I said, my voice ragged, almost a whisper. 'No-one to call. No next of kin.'

She nodded, left. Behind me, the door through which I'd arrived opened, and two nurses wearing blue uniforms and latex gloves appeared. One of them put her hand on my arm.

'Time to go now,' she said.

'Come on,' said the other one. 'We'll show you where you're going to be staying.'

'Then you can have a good old shower,' said the first one. 'Won't that be nice?'

I took hold of her hand, where it rested gently on my upper arm, and held it a moment while she smiled at me. I smiled back. Again that smile of pity, that smile that said, *I'm sorry you don't understand.* We stayed like that for a second, smiling at each other, me patting the top of her warm, gloved hand, and then I took hold of her index finger and snapped it like a twig in my fist.

I held on to it while she screamed and kicked, while the other nurse got her arm round my neck, while more nurses, male this time, appeared behind them and grabbed at me. Beneath the latex glove and the flesh it sheathed, I could feel that I had cleaved the bone completely. Her finger hung loose and useless in its fragile, meaningless bag of skin.

I heard someone shout, 'Jesus Christ, those are rats. She's got rats all over her.' And then suddenly they had all sprung back, unwilling to touch me. One helped the injured, sobbing nurse outside while the others remained, staring at me.

'I'm not touching any fucking rats,' I heard one of them say.

I drew myself up to my full height, held up my hand with its palm facing towards them. I felt as if the remains of the rats, which by that point were only just recognisable as the animals they'd once been, were glowing, heating up, taking on a new kind of life. When I walked slowly towards the nurses, they backed away, uncertain what to do. I understood that I was too repellent to touch, too proximate to death to control. I moved towards the door. Nobody challenged or even reached for me. Everyone was silent now. In a moment I was out in the hallway, and at the end of the hallway I could see a door beyond which, I imagined, lay the outside world. I visualised myself walking that hallway, nurses and orderlies and clipboard-carrying psychiatrists falling back as I passed, lining the walls while I calmly walked between them. I imagined myself turning the handle of that door, stepping out into a foyer, on the other side of which would be another door. Then I imagined myself through that door and out in the world, under the heat of the furious sun, the entire city staying out of my way as I walked, unchallenged, to freedom.

I made it roughly halfway down the hallway, and then a male nurse, who had arrived through the door in a rush, blocked my way.

'What's the problem?' he called over my head, as if I wasn't there.

'She's covered in dead rats,' someone behind me shouted.

He looked calmly, pityingly down at me.

'Rats don't bother me,' he said.

And then he reached out, grabbed one of my rats, and pulled it sharply away. It broke in his hand, its body the texture of rotted cardboard. As it disintegrated, it loosed a cloud of grey-brown dust. Its tail, still strong, remained plaited to the plastic band of my neck-lace, trailing a swatch of torn torso at its end. As he tugged on the others, one by one, I tried to hit him, but he held my upper arm in his fist. I had so little left, I realised, and the moment all the rats were gone, I had nothing: no talismans of protection, no spells of repulsion to ward off harm.

Now that the rats were safely dealt with, the other nurses felt able not only to approach me, but to grab me, attach themselves to me as they had before. I felt as if they had perfected special grips and holds. They found places on my arms that not only made it difficult for me to struggle, but which caused a particular kind of weakening pain that extended downwards to my hands. They had a professional insight into the workings of my body, knew every nerve ending, every point of weakness within a joint. To them, I was nothing more than a complex lock: they pressed here, twisted there, and I yielded.

Nurses, I understood, were kind to you until you hurt one of them, and then they stopped being nurses and turned into cops. There was no gentle coaxing now, no words of reassurance. When they laid their hands on me, it was to remind me where I was, who made the decisions, and what might be the consequences of transgression. They lifted me clean up off the ground by my legs and arms, then tipped me forward so that my face was lower than my feet, skimming the recently mopped floor as they carried me along the hall, away from that door and the world I'd imagined beyond it. I tried to kick and squirm, but without the anchorage of the ground it was too difficult. I was exhausted, but terrified that they would see my exhaustion, and so I used what energy I had left to twist pathetically and scream for all I was worth.

We turned a corner, then another, and then we crashed through a set of swinging doors into a shower room. There were no cubicles, not even a curtain or tray to demarcate the space. The floor – blue-green and spangled with fine, glittering grit for optimum traction – simply sloped downwards in one corner, towards a drain not unlike the one we'd filled in our room at the industrial estate, over which hung a silver hose and a stainless steel shower head that looked, in this overly clean and sanitised space, like an implement of either surgery or torture.

They put me face down on the floor and sat on my arms and legs. I was calling them anything I could think of, threatening them, spitting. In the chaos, I must have bitten my tongue or cheek because the strings of saliva I launched across the floor were marbled with scarlet swirls. I couldn't feel any pain, couldn't locate the wound when I licked the flesh of my cheek. I wondered if the blood was coming from somewhere deeper, if I was corroding or dissolving inside.

'Just cut them off,' I heard someone saying. 'None of it's salvage-able, for God's sake.'

I felt thin, cold metal running up the backs of my legs, and real-ised they were cutting away my clothes with scissors. As it was sliced open, the material gave off an entirely new odour. It was the reek of time, the history of everything my tattered garments had touched and absorbed. As my trousers fell away, I felt the awful cleanness of that hospital air hit my skin. I experienced it as a kind of pain – the sensitised tingle I'd always felt in that one isolated patch of skin on my forearm. I was nothing but exposed nerves, now, I thought. With my shell gone, every encounter would be agony.

They worked up my spine and cut away what was left of my shirt. I began to feel cold, and realised that it was the first time in an unknown number of weeks or perhaps even months that I had not felt swaddled in heat and heavy air. It was like turning back the duvet on a winter's morning. I was being roused from a place of comfort, a place of rest. I didn't want to enter the world, didn't want the timelessness of sleep to end or the unforgiving schedule of the day to begin. I found myself remembering my working life – commutes in the rain, hot coffee from a cardboard cup on freez-ing days, clouds of steam billowing from my mouth as I breathed. I remembered clean sheets on Friday nights, the luxury of lie-ins on weekend mornings. I remembered sitting in the flat that Ryan and Seth had found for me, before I met Zelma, holding a cooling mug of coffee and staring at the television, alone, with all of time unfolding out in front of me, and no idea how to fill it or live within it.

They didn't stop at my shirt. Someone had my hair in their gloved fist and they were hacking away at it with the scissors. I started to scream again and they told me to shut up. I could feel that they were cutting right to the root, leaving me nothing. Again, that sudden touch of cold air, the feeling of awful exposure. On the floor in front of me, hunks of stiffened hair appeared, piling up as if in preparation for a sacrificial offering. Then I heard a deep, angry buzzing, and felt the blades of a clipper moving from the nape of my neck, up the back of my skull, and over my scalp in a single, remorseless sweep. Then again, and again, roughly, painfully, until my scalp seemed able to detect the touch of every molecule in the air, and it felt as if the world had laid its icy touch directly against my brain. When they picked me back up off the floor by my limbs I saw, retreating away from me, a halo of hair and stubble, the outline of who I'd been, ready to be swept away.

Then I was lying over that drain, the shower beating down on my skin while one of the female nurses worked on me with a rough sponge and antibacterial disinfectant. I became aware of sores I hadn't previously noticed, patches on my back and thighs, in the cleft of my buttocks, in my groin. On contact, they caught alight with pain. A chemical fog filled my lungs, pushed there by the steam of the shower. I felt the nurse's hand reaching deep into every fold, to my anus, then round to my vagina, while another nurse's fingers found their way into my ears, my nostrils, the corners of my eyes, even into the holes in my body that had once been filled with maggots, whose dead white bodies I saw disappearing down the drain beneath me.

I don't know how long I was in that shower, stripped and probed and cleansed, but it felt like a lifetime, or several lifetimes, and the pain was such that it forced me to flee, so that I was no longer in the hospital at all but back in my hotel room, the evening after I'd been picked up at the encampment, in that glistening pod of a shower, lathering myself with everything I could get my hands on in anticipation of that freshly made bed and the sleep that was surely to come. I could smell that shampoo again – seaweed and eucalyptus – feel the cool sting of it in my sinuses and throat. Whenever my body, back in the hospital, pained me, when the sponge went over a wound or a nurse's finger located yet another place that hurt, I found that I could simply leave, move away, and be wherever I wanted to be, even places I had never been before. In the room we'd called home, I stood hidden from view in a shadowed corner while men in protective clothing hosed our history from the walls. On the empty upper deck of a juddering night bus, across the aisle, I watched Ama rest her head against the window as the city slid by, Barb's bright-orange flower still fresh in her hair. Beside a campfire on some half-abandoned estate, I looked out across a ring of drinkers perched on crates, and saw Kim and Sadie, roaring with throaty laughter. In the back of a speeding people carrier, with her parents stonily silent in the front, I watched Margot pick determinedly at the hems of her new clothes.

And in a darkened park, beneath a benevolent, sheltering tree, I curled up with Zelma, under a clear night's sky, and slept.

My room contained a single bed, a small table and chair, and a chest of drawers, empty because I had arrived with no salvageable possessions. I was given a tracksuit, pale grey and formless through over-washing, along with a white T-shirt and fresh underwear. That first night I failed to sleep. The boundaries of the bed seemed to be everywhere; however I positioned myself, a part of me seemed to be escaping over an edge. My blanket was thin and rough, prickly against the rawness of my skin. I felt peeled and in pain. Outside my room, through the small square window in my door, the hallway light was always lit. I heard squeaking, sneakered footsteps, voices rising, passing, fading away. Sometimes there were screams. At one point someone was removed from their room, shouting and struggling, and taken to a place where I could no longer hear them. At regular intervals, unmeasurable because I had no clock, a face appeared at my little window, looked in, caught my eye, and left.

In the morning, two nurses encouraged me to get up, and when I did they found I'd shat the bed. I couldn't remember if this was deliberate. My body was accustomed to doing what it wanted; it no longer needed to notify me of its urges and actions. The nurses made me strip the sheets myself, brought me a bucket and sponge so I could wipe down the plastic-wrapped mattress. Then they led me to the shower and talked through each motion in turn: *Now wash your hair, Now wash your backside, Now scrub your nails.* When I got out, they handed me a toothbrush. When I spat scarlet froth into the sink, a kind of panic came over me, and I reached down and scooped up the foam so I could swallow it. Immediately, a hand closed round my wrist, and a voice said firmly: *Spit.*

That morning would be repeated ninety-three times. By the end I could do it entirely in silence, watched but never prompted. I no longer needed the bucket for my bed. When I spat, I saw only a milk-white cloud, in which I left no visible trace.

Establishing a ritual of hygiene was part of my care plan, which was filled out on a seven-page pro-forma and placed in a soft cardboard binder on the table in my room. Over unending evenings alone, I could study it, and learn by heart who I was. *Maya has a history of severe self-neglect. She requires support and supervision in all aspects of her daily care. She should be encouraged to wash daily, change her clothes, use the toilet as appropriate. Maya has a history of both faecal hoarding and destructive behaviour towards her environment using urine, faeces, and blood. At appropriate times, Maya should be encouraged to eat. She has a history of deliberately inducing illness through either non-consumption of food or the consumption of food that is spoiled or rotten. Maya should not be allowed to pick up her food with her hands. If Maya becomes non-compliant with her care plan, she should be gently but firmly reminded of the plan's agreed goals. If she continues to be non-compliant, or if she becomes physically aggressive towards herself or others, the restraint protocols outlined in her risk assessment should be initiated.*

Routine was a system, a machine that would make me well. Where before I had noted the ease with which routine arose, here I felt its implacability, its remorselessness and determination. It was a schedule designed to stifle possibility, because an excess of possibility had made me ill. At night, the lights in my room snapped off and told me it was time to sleep. In the morning they flared and told me it was time to wake. After I woke I showered. After I showered I ate. Then I washed down a rainbow of pills and went to my first class or session. My body was irrelevant, my desires redundant and discouraged. To each external stimulus only a single, pre-approved response was acceptable.

It was easy to follow the routine because it was difficult to picture anything else. Repetition erased any sense of an alternative; medication short-circuited my ability to imagine. Life seemed flattened, detuned, as if the strings of my being had been unwound and left slack. The world held no reverberation; nothing echoed or sang. I woke, I washed, I ate, I listened, I slept.

My inability to picture a world beyond the hospital was compounded by the impossibility of connecting with it. My phone and laptop had vanished. Even if I'd sought permission to use the communal phone in the corridor, I didn't actually know anyone's number, because all I had ever done with numbers was store them unthinkingly in my phone. Often, I would imagine my mobile, locked away in an evidence bag somewhere, or lying unnoticed on the floor of that industrial space, filling with messages of concern and support.

Like Pict, Meadow Ward, as it was called, seemed determined to counter its assault on my sanity by insisting I prioritise my wellbeing.

I could attend all the same classes I'd frequented during my time in the programme. In the mindfulness class we were encouraged to let go of our feelings, allow them to arise and dissolve. In yoga we were encouraged to be in the moment, to let a growing intimacy with our own body replace any obsessive relationship we might have formed with our thoughts. In some ways, it should have been easy given my medication regimen, but it wasn't. Being calm was simple enough, but when I sat cross-legged and closed my eyes, I was unable to find myself. Looking inwards, I saw only silence and darkness, a black expanse that was neither me nor anything else. Touching that emptiness, I would feel immediately as if I was falling; my body would lurch and my eyes snap open in a manner similar to the jolt I would sometimes experience when I was unbalanced on the threshold of sleep.

Unable to find myself in the scorched-earth landscape of my medicated state, I began to experience a heightened, uncomfortable sense of my own periphery. It was almost as if, with so much numbness on the inside, my shrinking self sought to defend its existence by ratcheting up my sensitivity on the outside. I began to feel as I had when the nurses were washing me, when my every orifice had been probed by gloved, uncaring hands. My skin, not only washed but regularly disinfected, felt cold and exposed, recoiling from both touch and the possibility of touch, from the breeze of a swinging door, the droplets of water from a shower, the fingers of a nurse as she re-dressed my sores. My shaved scalp felt peeled away, my pulsing brain open to the air and the elements. And all the while, in therapy, in my one-to-one appointments, at my review meetings and tribunal, there were the questions. How was I feeling. How was I doing. What did I think about this. What did I think about that. They'd poke the pulsing, fragile membranes of my mind and watch as they tensed and twitched.

In this gap between my core and my periphery, between an excess of emptiness and an excess of presence and attention, new forms of pain began to grow. At night, when the lights went off and I knew that no-one would look in my little window for another hour, I would pull my blanket over my head and push the corner of my pillow into my mouth to muffle the sobs. At first, because there were no tangible feelings I could access or observe, I couldn't understand the tears. Later, I began to understand that I was mourning the loss of myself. I still knew enough to know what I should be feeling, and its absence became a unique and distressing torture. They'd taken my rage, I thought. They'd taken my grief. They'd taken my resistance. They'd hollowed me out like a halved melon and told me it was healing.

It began to occur to me that my imperatives were twofold and in tension. To get out, I had to perform perfectly the person I was supposed to be. To take anything of myself with me when I left, I had to remember who I was through the performance. Drugs and the flatland of routine had dulled my short-term memory. Of yesterday's class or meal, I had no recollection. The older things, though, the moments from further back, were more vivid for having nothing in front of them. I remembered, for example, the knife I'd carried when I lived on the streets, the scattered moments I'd been forced to hold it up between me and an advancing attacker, the times I'd jabbed it into the arm or leg of someone slipping under the flap of tarpaulin that covered my lean-to at the encampment. I remembered biting down on a man's arm, tasting his blood. I remembered my first night in the hotel, sleeping on the floor because I was so unused to the bed, eating my breakfast in my room because I was still tense for the moment when I would be discovered and asked to leave. I remembered meeting Zelma, the parts of myself that felt suddenly visible and seen through the simple act of her writing in the white space of a glossy magazine article. I remembered that first night we'd got drunk, thrown up together, defaced that advert, and the unconstrained joy I'd been able to touch, to hold onto, as I rode the night bus home alone, the top-deck windows open, the smells and sounds of the city in spring streaming in. I remembered the ecstasy of my shit when I came home from BodyTemple, the wild delirium of my fever. I remembered sitting with Zelma when she was ill, running my hand over her sweaty hair while she whimpered. I remembered the photos I'd sent her, the thrill of sharing my most private act, the pulsing emoji by which she showed me I'd been seen. And then I remembered the space we'd claimed for ourselves, those first few nights when it was just the two of us, and the nights that followed when it was all of us: the mounting stink, the feeling of glorious decay and release, the sense, every day, every moment, that we were making a living world, and that the living world we'd made was making us back in turn.

These were the moments I'd known and defended myself, shaped most purposefully the life I wanted to live. Now they would be my co-ordinates, the stars by which I steered myself back.

I said little to my fellow patients. With so much of myself stripped back, I had to police my boundaries, control how close I allowed anyone to get. The effort to hold on to myself made me flinch at the prospect of giving anything away.

I continued attending my classes, partly to stave off the madness of stagnant time, partly so as to be seen to be compliant. But in the spaces between organised activities, I avoided the communal areas – the television, the games room, the deathly lounge and inadequate, fenced-in smoking area – and spent my time in my room, sitting in silence. If I placed a pillow on the floor in just the right spot and faced the wall at precisely the right distance, it was possible to create a visual field that contained nothing but the wall itself, an expanse of cream plaster that if I stared at it long enough, with the daylight through my tiny window dimming and my eyes locked in half-focus so that details disappeared and the world smoothed itself out into a series of large surfaces and the shadows they held or cast, it no longer appeared as a wall but as a kind of blindness or void. I could sit for hours, I found, in this place I could never be reached and from which I could never be forcibly removed, casting into that emptiness whatever I felt, summoning from it whatever I needed to imagine.

I stopped swallowing the drugs. The performance required for my release, I thought, had to remain a performance. Medicated, it risked becoming real. Making sure the tablets missed my throat wasn't difficult. Medication time was busy, fraught. Incidents were not uncommon. It was the moment many patients resisted, became frustrated, tried to raise with the nurses all the issues that had been ignored. You could feel, then, the fragility of the system most keenly, the way it depended so totally on compliance. I suspected the nurses felt it too. They were always fractionally on edge whenever too many of the patients were together in one place. They didn't watch you for long. They looked for the gestures they expected – paper cup of tablets knocked back, paper cup of water to follow, a grimace as you choked it all down – and then turned their attention to whoever was next. The pills could go under the tongue, the water over it, leaving the little capsules behind, to be transferred to my palm at the first opportunity, then flushed down the toilet when the chance arose.

The fog took several days to clear, but when it did, when I woke one morning and saw my room in sharp focus, and felt inside myself so many of the familiar pieces of who I remembered myself to be, tangible and heavy and there to be picked up and weighed in my hand, I began unexpectedly to cry. I can't honestly say that I felt well – the drugs, it turned out, had been concealing from me a whole landscape of physical pain and heaving nausea – but I *felt*, and in feeling it seemed as if I knew myself once again – as if, etched in pain, the contours of my being became visible. When I sat down at the wall and disconnected my gaze from its subject, blurring out the edges of my vision and entering, as if pushing my head through a curtain, that blank expanse, I confirmed what I had suspected before: that the world I'd glimpsed there was not a medicated projection; that it was all the more accessible now nothing was interposed between what I encountered and what I felt.

Now a new challenge presented itself. Somehow, I had to remember who I'd been before I stopped taking the drugs, and pretend to be that person still. I began to think of my face as a mask, fixed and immobile and only cursorily human, behind which I could find a way to live. The less of myself I demonstrated, the better the doctors told me I was doing. Calmer, they said, cleaner, more in control.

I made up things to say in therapy. If I'd told them the truth – that I had experienced my own essence through the matter I excreted, that I had touched the truth of the world through an intimate relationship with decay, and that everything now had the shimmering visual quality of a mirage, as if what I saw of daily life was not the original image at all but a reflection on gently shifting water that distorted and refracted depending on conditions – I would never have been allowed to leave. Instead, I simply repositioned my moment of epiphany. This, now, I said, was my moment of insight, here in the hospital. I saw how low I'd been, how I'd struggled to cope with the after-effects of my homelessness, how I hadn't been ready to re-enter society, and how, when I had, I'd been subjected to all the trauma society contained. Like all good lies, it had its roots in truth, but wildly misrepresented what grew from that truth. I would never be ready to re-enter society because I no longer believed in society at all. I would never progress towards anything, because I had come to believe that progress is simply a story we tell ourselves to distract us from decay. There was no journey because there was no destination. I had reduced myself to nothing, and so could not be further reduced. This was what separated me from the other patients. All of them, by being in the ward, had been denied something, had something taken from them. I had already pushed deep into discomfort and indignity's lowest limits. Nothing was being taken from me because there was nothing to take. I had given the last of myself away, and so nothing remained for me to lose.

The more people engaged with the story I sold them, the more I began to see that everything was a story. Out on the ward, in meetings with my doctors, in therapy sessions, over breakfast, I watched people swallow what I said because it fitted with the stories they already knew. Back in my room, on my cushion, with nothing to which I could narrate myself besides the blank white wall whose every microscopic detail of texture and shade I now knew intimately, I began to understand that I had done the same, that I had saved myself from one story by telling myself another. The moments I had thought of as my co-ordinates – nights in the city with Zelma, feverish visions, Damascene moments of crippling illness – were not co-ordinates at all. They added up to nothing, led to nothing. The more I looked, breathing deeply, projecting onto that bare wall the scenes from my past that I thought explained me or held some truth of who I was, the more that watery pool and the thin reflection of reality on its surface began to churn, breaking the connections between the things I remembered, until all sense of order dissolved and I was left only with the empty truth of what I had always wanted to be: a person with no history, no future, no purpose. A person of no stories and many. A person who, when contained by the way they were seen, could simply change, disperse, and re-form.

For those who asked, as everyone asked, what lay at the end of all this, what could be expected after all this labouring to be well, the ward had a ready answer: work. On the walls in the public areas, where patients whose care plan permitted it could meet with family, friends, charity workers who would help them when they were back on the outside, there hung a series of pictures of ex-patients, all treated with Instagram filters and captioned like they'd just popped up in your feed. Someone had a job stacking shelves in Tesco and felt like a whole new person. Someone was training to work on a building site and saw light in their future for the first time. Someone had just passed their probationary period at an Amazon warehouse and was no longer claiming benefits. There were no pictures, I noted, of the people I'd known when I was on the streets: the man whose reflection instructed him to kill; the woman who said she was wanted by the FBI because she knew the truth about pasteurised milk; the man on the night bus who kept up a constant conversation with God. Returning to society, it seemed, was one thing; being a productive member of that society was entirely another.

A meeting was scheduled with a woman who would be my discharge and onward-planning co-ordinator. Now that I was a full-time patient here, no-one did the two sides of a barrier-like desk routine any more. It was all comfy chairs and cups of tea. I no longer did the silent routine either. I was all hopeful smiles and humble gratitude, tracing the shapes of my person-mask.

My co-ordinator's name was Janice. She was in her sixties, wore Indian smocks, and had a tattoo of a crab on the inside of her forearm.

'So,' said Janice, having made me a cup of tea using a travel kettle she kept on her desk. 'You're to be leaving us, Maya.'

'I think so,' I said.

She smiled at me. 'And how does that feel?'

I knew better than to say, *fantastic*. Instead I said, 'Scary, but really positive. I feel like I can do it.'

'That's great, Maya. I think you can do it too. But I also think that maybe it's helpful to have a bit of a hand, at least at first.'

'I'm open to whatever's on offer,' I said.

This was the new me – always conscious of who and what I needed to be, always able to be it when necessary.

'I have to say you've done really well here, Maya,' said Janice. 'I feel like you've really committed to getting better.'

'I want to be better,' I said.

'And I think you are,' said Janice. 'Or at least, I think you will be, and I think you're a lot closer than when you first came in.'

I nodded, remembering that vision of myself who had first been admitted to the ward: carapaced in filth, wild-haired and talon-nailed, bedecked with the corpses of rats. She seemed ancient to me now, that woman, and I worried that the longer I had to enact her antithesis, the further away she would get. My mask would grow its own skin. The basic outline of my being would be lost.

'I don't know if you agree,' said Janice, 'but I feel like one of the things that's really helped has been structure. You've been so good with your classes, Maya. You've really taken your timetable seriously. I hear from the nurses that you've even continued some of the things that you do in class on your own, that you meditate in your room, for example. That's wonderful.'

'It's important to do things properly,' I said.

'It is,' she said, beaming, as if I'd just given her extraordinarily good news. 'And I think we can continue that, after you leave here. We can make sure you have access to the same things. The yoga, the mindfulness, the therapy. That can all continue.'

'Great,' I said.

'Because continuity is so important, isn't it, Maya? It's really how we find our way in life. We need consistency, certainty, stability.'

'Absolutely.'

'But we also need meaning, purpose, a place in the world. Is that fair to say?'

'Of course.'

'So we're really keen to get you engaged with some kind of employment programme. Nothing too demanding at first, but with the goal of building up, getting you back to where you were before.'

'Wonderful.'

'We're very lucky here,' she went on. 'As I'm sure you know, it's such a struggle to support people at the moment, what with cuts to services, no-one being properly funded, and so on.'

'I can imagine.'

'That's why we're so proud of our employment programme. Because we really thought outside the box with it. Instead of saying, *How can we take care of these people*, we flipped it around. We said, *How can we demonstrate to companies the unique contribution our patients might be able to make?* Do you see?'

I nodded.

'We went out there and we said, *Look, you need the workers, our patients need the work. Let's help each other out here.*'

She raised her splayed fingers in front of her and then interlaced them into an X shape.

'It's a much more enlightened perspective,' she said. 'It's not about charity. It's about saying that you, Maya, are a resource. People should be thrilled at the opportunity to draw on that resource. Isn't that better?'

'So much better,' I said.

'Anyway, long story short, in the past year I think it's fair to say we've got it down to something of a fine art. Look outside, at some of our previous patients. Look at our success stories. People are leaving here, going into work, and *staying* in work. And you know what they're not doing? They're *not coming back here.*' She patted her thigh to emphasise these last words.

'You must be so proud,' I said.

'Oh, we are,' said Janice. 'But mostly we're just thrilled to bits for our patients. No more feeling like you've been tossed on the scrapheap. No more feeling like you're defective, or that society doesn't want you. You leave here, you get straight on with it, and you *keep* on with it.'

I could feel my mask slipping, cracking open, revealing what was beneath. I knew that if I erred now, then decisions about my release could be quickly and dispassionately reviewed. I managed to swallow and say nothing. Beneath me, I felt the awful wheel of daily existence, of modern urban time, of early starts and repetitive commutes, begin, once again, to turn.

'So what we do is we make you a little profile,' Janice was saying. 'Tell your story a bit, get a CV together. And you know what, Maya? One of our corporate partners jumped on your profile in *minutes*.'

I was just making face-shapes now. I couldn't even tell if they were the right ones. I felt it was important to respond, that if Janice found my affect too flat she'd become concerned. *Tug at the corners of your mouth*, I told myself, *and that will make a smile.*

'And it turns out,' said Janice, clapping her hands together, '*that you already know him*. Isn't that just absolutely fantastic?'

She leaned over and rested her hand on my knee.

'You can go *back*, Maya,' she said. 'Do you know how few people get that chance? A second chance? A chance to *try again*? What an opportunity, Maya. A *unicorn* of an opportunity!'

They found me a dingy box room in a pay-by-night hostel, set up my benefits, and ejected me worldwards with two second-hand sweaters, a pair of jeans, and a plastic bag full of cheap underwear. I had to present at the hospital once a month. When I did, they would review me, assess my current levels of self-neglect. If I became unclean or unkempt, I would be readmitted. If I failed to show up, I would be readmitted. If I failed to engage with my work placement, I would be readmitted. I was not especially concerned. I could see everything for what it was: that wavering reflection on the surface of a dark lake. I could dip my fingers into what seemed real, swirl up the world's filmy, floating projection, and watch it all fracture into meaningless colour. When I removed my hand, nothing of reality would cling to my fingers. I was cleansed of the world. I no longer needed to be filthy to prevent it from touching me.

The room came with an aluminium-framed single bed, a small wardrobe, a little folding table at which I could eat. In the centre of the ceiling was a single lightbulb. Outside my door was a meter into which I could insert a prepaid key. Down the hallway was a mouldering kitchen and a bathroom that reeked of misdirected masculine piss. At night, on the floors above and below me, I heard the rumble of parties and arguments, the arrival of police, the screamed pleas of the evicted and detained. Under my door, like visitors from the spirit world, crept the vapours of exhaled weed and cheap, plasticky crack. On my first night, a man invited me to his room to drink, then demanded I watch while he sliced his arms. None of it fazed me. A person who has given themselves to death cannot be harmed.

At night, just as I had on my return from BodyTemple, I feasted on armfuls of junk, then shat deliriously in that reeking toilet. This was what rehabilitation looked like.

I set up a pillow on the floor, facing the wall, and nightly lost myself to the blankness. Outside my window, sirens dopplered off into the night, and the weak, hopeless glow of the street lights made a milky screen of my paper-thin curtains. Everything was just a passing simulacrum of experience. Sound was the idea of sound, light the merest notion of light. When I slept, I dreamed only of things I'd already tasted and seen: distinctive stains on familiar walls, the crunch in my mouth of bread and crisps, the sensation of melting chocolate on my tongue. I understood that there was no dream-world or otherness to enter, only the endless recycling and reordering of quotidian experience. Everything I could become, I had become. There was nothing to imagine and so nothing my sleeping mind could conjure.

When the room felt small, on the nights I struggled to summon from that bare wall the empty expanse in which I knew I could live, I stayed out. I'd missed the feeling of sleeping outside, of curling up at the feet of banks and churches. Sometimes I went to places I knew, ran into faces I recognised attached to people who failed to recognise me back. I felt cocooned in anonymity, in the city's ungrasping lack of memory. For a while I started carrying a knife again, seeking out the places from my past in which I'd been threatened or attacked.

I longed to be fucked with, but I must have projected an aura of risk, because no-one came close. In the mornings I watched the sun come up over all that towering glass, felt a little warmth drain from each day as autumn advanced.

I still didn't have a phone, or any numbers to put into one. I continued to imagine mine somewhere, its memory full to bursting with messages from Zelma, whose presence seemed so strong to me now that I was back out and walking the city without her. I stole a marker from a stationery shop, wrote messages in the margins of adverts only she would understand, then returned to see if my scrawls had been answered. I wanted her to know I was here, that she was real to me in my solitude. I found no sign, no trace. Of all the things I'd endured, that was the most unfathomable. Her imprint on the city had seemed so deep, so permanent. I felt stunned by her absence, unable to conceive of the possibility that she was no longer leaving her mark.

On the first floor of a local library, at a row of computers marbled with fingerprints, the keyboard clogged with biscuit crumbs and flakes of rolling tobacco, I scoured the web in much the same way as I'd scoured the city. All of our accounts were gone – the Instagram, the Facebook. Zelma's personal account was gone too. Three times I tried to log into my emails, but each time I was told that my password was wrong, that a text had been sent to my phone to help me retrieve it. I still remembered Zelma's email address, though – could picture it with sharp-edged clarity at the top of messages I could recount by heart. I set up a new account and sent her a message, then sat forlornly for an hour refreshing my empty inbox. I felt like a deep-sea exploration vessel, pinging the unexplored ocean with my sonar, my signal dissipating into the depths, unheard.

*

Harrison came and found me personally. No trip to the office this time, no pointed wait in that corporate holding space. He turned up at my door with a new phone, a bag of expensive clothes that were a size too big on account of the weight I'd lost, and a bunch of flowers he said were from everyone in the office.

'Maya,' he said, looking me up and down, taking in my tufty hair, my skinny body and pallid skin. 'Jesus Christ.'

He insisted on lunch. The thought of an expensive restaurant made my skin crawl. We haggled and settled on a pizza chain. Harrison was on a detox so watched me eat while he sipped a spring water garnished with cucumber. He didn't know what to say; I didn't know what he wanted to hear. For a while we just nodded awkwardly.

'So how great is this?' he said, hopelessly.

'It's wonderful, Harrison,' I said. 'It's like all my dreams have come true.'

I didn't feel the need for my psych-ward rictus with Harrison. He'd taken me back out of guilt. He wouldn't be calling the ward to complain any time soon.

'We've partnered with the hospital for a while now,' he said. 'We've had some really great successes, actually.'

'I've seen the pictures,' I said. 'They're very heartwarming.'

He nodded, but looked like I'd slapped him.

'We wrapped up the programme with Ryan and Seth,' he said. 'In case you were wondering.'

'I wasn't. But good to know.'

'I followed you,' he said. 'Followed the whole thing. Ryan and Seth were on the warpath, as you can imagine. I was able to negotiate on your behalf.'

'Thank you,' I said.

'Maybe you're wondering why I bothered.'

'Maybe.'

He took a swill of his cucumber water, winced a little as the bubbles sparked at the back of his nose.

'I know you think I'm . . .' He waved a hand in the air. 'Detached,' he said finally.

'Because you are,' I said.

'OK,' he said. 'I am. But there was a time of my life when I wasn't.'

I looked at him. I wasn't sure where he was going, so wasn't sure what to say.

'If anything, for a while, when I was younger, I wasn't detached enough,' he said. 'Things affected me. I didn't know what to do with that.'

I nodded.

'Long story short is that I find what I do now comforting,' he said. 'Routine, numbers. That kind of thing.'

'Fine,' I said. 'There's no need to—'

'I know what it is to lose your anchor in things,' he said. 'That's why I wanted to partner with the hospital. It's why I was keen on the whole programme thing but I can see now that it was the wrong approach.'

'So now you go straight to the source,' I said. 'Get them fresh.'

'Something like that.'

His cucumber water was all gone. He tilted the glass and stared down its barrel.

'I want you to know that I'm sorry,' he said. 'For how things went. For how we fucked it up.'

I dropped my slice of pizza onto my plate and sat back.

'I'm not going to be a teachable moment for you, Harrison,' I said.

'No,' he said quickly. 'No. I get that. But I want . . . Is there some other way we can—'

'Well now thanks to you I have to come into work or go back to the hospital,' I said.

He looked pained.

'I'm not saying this is a perfect solution,' he said.

'What do you want, Harrison?' I said. 'What do you want from me?'

'I'm trying to help,' he said. 'That's it. It's not complicated.'

'Well I don't want to be helped,' I said. 'So it is complicated.'

He sighed.

'This isn't how I saw this going,' he said.

'Tell me honestly,' I said. 'The wellness stuff, the pictures on my Instagram. You imagined a before and after, didn't you? You thought: We'll transform this sorry person, and people will—'

'Obviously we hoped for change. The Instagram stuff was just—'

'The proof.'

'The *record*. For you as much as anyone else. Maya, all we ever offered you was the best we had to offer. The things other people had. The things other people wanted.'

'What about what I wanted?'

'You know,' he said, leaning forward on his elbows, his water glass now carefully set to one side, as if even the slightest obstacle had to be cleared from his path in order for him to move forward, 'I saw a picture of you, Maya. Not the one that was everywhere. Another one. You were holding up a sign. It said that living in anything other than your own shit is complicity.'

'Great,' I said. 'So what.'

'I thought about that phrase for a long time. I *obsessed* over that phrase.'

'Good for you.'

'I'm trying to own my shit, Maya.'

'No you're not, you're trying to get me to take it away for you.'

He raised his hand, pointed his finger in my face.

'I can call the hospital,' he said. 'I can call the fucking hospital right now and say, I've seen Maya. She's skinny as shit. She's not talking sense. She's not engaging with the work programme we've set up. I can have you recalled.'

Recalled, I thought. Like a fatally defective product, a helpful gizmo with the potential to combust.

334

'You'd do that?' I said. 'After all your talk about helping me. All your talk about doing good. You'd have me sent back to a *psych ward* because I don't want your help?'

'Because you're biting the hand that feeds you. Because you're not making a sensible decision about—'

'I don't *have* to make sensible decisions, Harrison. No-one *has* to make sensible decisions. That's what freedom is.'

'Is that what this is about? *Freedom?*'

He spat the word out like it was something unexpected he'd imbibed with his cucumber water, some floating, foreign object crossing his tongue.

'Life is compromise,' he said.

'And how are you compromising, Harrison? Name one compromise you have to make.'

'I'm offering to compromise now.'

'OK, tell me the compromise.'

'You're a tough negotiator, you know that? If this is how you negotiate when someone's offering you an opportunity, I'd love to see what kind of bargain you drive when they're trying to fuck you over.'

'Fuck opportunity,' I said.

'Alright,' he held up his hands, palms outwards, in a gesture of surrender. 'Let me counter-offer.'

I spread my arms, as if to ask him what he was waiting for.

'Obviously you can't come back to your old job,' he said. 'I already ran that past the hospital and they said it's too traumatic. They feel it might have been a . . . a contributing factor, or something. But anyway. We have to find another job. And it just so happens we're down a member on our social media team. And I *know* you're good at social media, Maya. Yes, you went somewhat off the rails and started posting pictures of shit, but I don't think you're going to do that again. Anyway. This job. It doesn't need to be full time, and you don't need to come into the office to do it.'

I thought about this.

'So like a couple of days a week?' I said.

He waved his hand vaguely.

'Whatever, frankly. Log into the fucking thing, do a few things I can feed back to the hospital, and then do what you like the rest of the time.'

'How much will you pay me?'

'Way more than we should. Enough that you can get out of that hell-hole of a hostel.'

I said nothing, imagining myself logging into Twitter or Facebook and fielding inane requests from faceless members of the public. Then I imagined myself on the other days, doing nothing, roaming, all my time my own.

'And when I want to leave?' I said.

'No-one will stop you.'

I looked at him a long time. He didn't look at me back. He picked up his glass, swilled the ice, sipped the few drops of water that had appeared as it melted. Then he put the glass down and tugged at the edge of the tablecloth, straightening it, pulling everything into ordered alignment.

'Thank you, Harrison,' I said.

He nodded, still not looking up.

'It's fine,' he said. 'There's no need to thank me.'

'But the answer's no.'

'What?'

'No. The answer is no.'

He shook his head.

'Jesus Christ.'

'If you really want to help me,' I said. 'If you really want to do something good, you'll let me go.'

*

336

I began to see this most recent phase of my life as a process of slow shrinking, of reduction. I'd had a city to myself and then moved to a flat. From the flat I'd moved to a room I shared with others. Now I'd moved to a room that couldn't be shared. I was beginning to understand that nothing I strived for would be rewarded, that everything I wanted would arrive only if what I already had was offered in return. The more inward space I needed for myself, the more time and attention I wanted to devote to the task of simply existing, the more I would have to resign myself to living in a tiny box room, the walls close enough to touch, with barely enough belongings to fill a backpack. The more outward space I allowed myself to accept – not just a room but several rooms, a flat, or even a house – the more my time and interior expansion would have to be curtailed.

Maybe, I thought, this was what I had been working towards. I had endured extraordinary discomfort so that the pains of a comfortable life no longer seemed so unbearable. Or maybe it had all been in the service of no longer *needing* the comfortable life, so that I could walk away from it all and find myself, again and again, in the city's vacant and neglected spaces. Or maybe all I had really been engaged in was the process of exhausting myself, wearing myself down more completely than any work programme could ever manage, so that finally I was too tired and weakened to resist, and I was able to slip frictionlessly into the motions of daily life with none of the pain that accompanied resistance. It seemed a hopeless place to have reached: all that work on becoming, and now I didn't know what I wanted to be.

In contrast to physical space, time was endless and expansive, a vista of unfilled hours and days. I was comfortable with this. We only fill our existence because we're so frightened of its uncaring, implacable emptiness. I'd been intimate with life's passage, seen it at work on skin, on the carcasses of animals, on food. I didn't have to delude myself any more. I could sit in a coffee shop, in a park, and simply observe life's ceaseless vanishing: clouds lightening and darkening the sky, the blur of pedestrians on a busy crossing, a gust of wind stealing scraps of trash from a bin.

People had ceased to repulse me. I'd seen every conceivable function of the human body, every secretion and excretion, every pus-dripping wound and seeping, festering sore. I knew every human smell – breath and farts and spicy sweat. I even knew the feel of everything – the slickness of clammy skin, the mucoid webbing of snot and sick. When I found myself on a crowded bus, when I stood in line for free food at a soup kitchen and inhaled the earthy, rain-soaked reek of human bodies habituated to the elements, I felt no aversion. Instead, I felt as if I knew everyone intimately, and could see, as I looked at them, not just what they were, but what they would become in time, the carcass that lived a millimetre below their flesh. The more I pictured the disintegration of their skin, the more I could picture that skin fusing with mine, until we were all just a single, rotting being. Sometimes, at the strangest moments, as I squeezed into a lift or onto an escalator, as I huddled under a bus stop with twelve other people trying to escape the rain, I would feel this understanding press so forcefully against the inside of my chest and throat that I would begin to cry. This, I understood, is what lies on the other side of disgust, not opposed to it, but arising precisely at the point of its exhaustion: love.

Harrison had given me a new phone. Within days I came to see it as a curse. Before, I had only really confronted Zelma's lack of contact when I went to the library to check my email. Now my connection to that particular void was constant. I sat on my bed, late into the night, thumbing the screen to refresh it. I slept with the phone beside my pillow, and the first thing I did upon opening my eyes was to reach for it. I remembered how Zelma had always called at the most unpredictable hours – late at night or so early in the morning that waking takes on a hallucinatory, vertiginous unease. I remembered how I had always been reluctant to sleep, resistant to the possibility of missing even a single message.

Now I fell asleep to the sound of silence, my own blood in my ears, my stomach digesting its food, the tidal sigh of my breath, and woke to all the same variations of nothingness. Sometimes my head chattered to the point where I couldn't sleep at all, and so I would rise and sit cross-legged facing the wall, waiting for the noise of my consciousness to clear. These were thoughts with neither a vector nor a destination. They were the things I would have said to Zelma that now I couldn't say at all.

One night, lying on my uncomfortable bed, the glow of my phone spilling eerie white light over the ceiling and walls, I stumbled across a version of myself. I'd been clicking around, as I always did, trying to think of new ways to find people I'd known. I'd typed in Margot's name and read a couple of news articles by her parents. Then I'd found myself on Tumblr, scrolling through a series of posts about something called Transcendental Degradation. It was a form of retreat, it seemed, based around ideas of embracing decay. Women were encouraged to fester and unravel. At the end of the process, they ritually washed, then emerged reborn. It was run by Margot, and in the part of the website that contained her biography, she talked about her period of *study* with her *mentor*, a woman called Maya who I only half-recognised. Maya, it seemed, had emerged from the homeless community. She was an outsider figure, a radical. Disillusioned with the grind of contemporary life, she had begun to explore ideas of renunciation. Appalled at the social obsession with beauty, she'd embraced ugliness. Her first attempt at a community based around the shared values of degradation, putrefaction and freedom had changed Margot's life. Margot offered her thanks, she said, and tried to embody Maya's spirit in everything she did. The Transcendental Degradation movement was dedicated to Maya, and each retreat began with a prayer of gratitude for her existence and work.

I was tempted, of course, to write to Margot, to tell her simply that I had seen what she was doing, that I was thrilled for her, and proud.

It would, I knew, have meant a great deal to her. Indeed, I suspected that the Tumblr was there not only to attract newcomers, but also in the hope I might find it. I also knew, though, that much as Margot might have wanted to hear from me, it was better for both of us, and for the women who attended her retreats, that she didn't. I liked the idea of myself as an idea. It was my purer, mythical form.

During the day, I ate and drank in cheap cafes when I could afford to, queued at street kitchens and day centres when I was broke. At night, I walked the city, sat in parks and empty spaces, cleared-away markets and deserted playgrounds, watching life come and go. It struck me that this was what it meant to be saintly, hallowed, free: to live in rags, hand to mouth, while somewhere distant the deathless thought of you brings light to the minds of others.

Harrison kept texting. Someone seemed to have told him that consistency without pressure was key. He texted to remind me he was there, the offer was still open, would always be open, but there was no expectation. He texted to ask how I was. Sometimes he told me how he was, which was always basically the same. I never answered. Then one day he sent a message that just said, *Need to see you. Urgent. Please.* I thought about it for an hour and then replied. Maybe Ryan and Seth were back on the scene, I thought. Or maybe the hospital were chasing him for an update. I suggested lunch but he said no, somewhere quiet, so I waited for him in a park around the corner from Pict.

He arrived looking strangely awkward. His mouth was downturned, his shoulders slumped. He greeted me with a pat on the shoulder. We sat on a bench, staring at the grass in front of us, on which strutted a brazen, beady-eyed crow.

'Beautiful here,' said Harrison.

I nodded. Then neither of us said anything for a while.

'So,' said Harrison finally. 'I have some news.'

'The hospital?' I said.

'No,' he said. 'Not the hospital.'

I didn't know what to say so I asked him if he was OK.

'I'm fine,' he smiled. 'Honestly fine.'

'Then . . .'

'I don't believe in very much,' said Harrison, 'but I believe in transparency. I think we should all be able to know the same things. I don't believe in knowing things and not letting other people know them too.'

I thought about Margot, my own discomfort with knowing and not sharing. It was the first time I'd ever had any sense of Harrison's thoughts and dilemmas overlapping with mine.

'I was so sad you didn't take up my offer,' he said. 'I really . . . I thought it would have been good. I believed in it.'

'I know.'

'Arrogant, maybe.'

'Maybe.'

'So anyway, after you said no I started to think, What can I do for her? What can I offer? What can I do to show her that I'm sincere and I want to help?'

'I *know* you want to help, Harrison. That's never been the problem. The problem is that I—'

'You don't want to be helped. I know. But still. I wanted to do something. A gesture. Something meaningful. I knew you wouldn't accept most of the things I was able to offer. A flat, maybe. Money. I don't know. It was good for me, really. I had to think about what might actually be of value to you.'

'Alright, Harrison. I give in. I'm curious. You don't need such a long preamble.'

'As I said,' said Harrison, completely ignoring me, 'I followed what you got up to after you left. So I knew about your friend, Zelma.'

I didn't say anything. Slowly, like honey leaving the lip of a suspended spoon, sound drained out of the world around me. Birds flew, people passed, a wind stirred the grass at my feet, all in gathering silence, as if moving aside for Harrison's voice.

'I know you did it all together,' he said. 'I know she didn't go to the hospital with you. I know you lost your phone and all your contacts because you told me. I thought: This is something I can do. This is one simple thing.'

'You found her,' I said. I could feel my breath catching in my throat, my heart hammering in my body, as if my skin was no longer thick enough to secure it, as if it wanted to be free of me entirely.

'I put some people on it,' he said. 'The kind of access we have, the kind of search power. It's not difficult.'

I became aware of what he wasn't quite saying. There was a delicate membrane in the air around me, I thought. If I moved, or even spoke, I would break it.

'She was put in a hostel,' he said. 'Beyond that it's not really clear what help was offered.'

I could see the membrane now, if I squinted. It was made up of tiny, glistening filaments, mapped to the outlines of my form. I took a deep breath, held the air in the pit of my stomach, and watched the whole structure swell, vibrate, threaten to tear, then settle.

'Her benefits were all fucked up,' said Harrison, and then his voice caught, and he looked downward suddenly enough that the crow on the grass in front of us hopped back.

I felt myself shaking my head. I had never before been so profoundly conscious of the past tense, of what it means to no longer speak of something or someone as continuous.

'The police put her door in,' said Harrison after a swallow and a shake of his shoulders. 'I guess someone must have complained.'

I put my hand over my mouth, and as I did so I saw the silver filigree around me shatter into dust and disperse, and when it did so an old and familiar feeling returned – a feeling of extraordinary physical sensitivity, as if my skin could no longer endure the air's touch, as if there was no layer between my nerves and the world whose pain and danger they spoke of.

Harrison put his hand on my leg.

'I'm so sorry,' he said.

I just shook my head, kept shaking it.

'She'd starved,' he said, half-swallowing the words. 'She'd starved herself to death.'

Again and again, Harrison asked me if I would be OK, but I couldn't answer, because I didn't know. Allowing him to see me weep felt like a privilege I wasn't prepared to extend, so I simply stared ahead, imagining I could see in the air around me the last drifting strands of the fragile web that had been my life. I ended up saying something like, *Just go*, which I could see upset him, and then waiting until he was out of sight before allowing myself, morsel by morsel, to be pecked apart by grief. Then I returned to my little room, my bare walls, my single bed, and pictured Zelma, on an identical bed, between similar walls, alone and unwell, emaciated and slipping away. I thought about the fact that she would have become unwell while I was in the hospital, that while all those nurses and psychiatrists and social workers were foisting their determination to care on me, Zelma went unaided and ignored. Protection was finite, I thought. The world was prepared to offer only so much. I'd taken what was rightfully hers.

I remembered Zelma's previous episodes of illness, the days and nights I'd held a cooling flannel to her brow while she sweated and moaned and gritted her teeth in pain. I wondered if I'd misjudged the severity of her symptoms, or if she had somehow kept from me the depth and breadth of her pathology. But then I also thought about the long stretches between flare-ups, the ease with which she'd taken to the life we made in our repurposed concrete space on the industrial estate, the *feeling* of Zelma in full flow, scribbling in magazines and editing adverts, and the way I'd wondered, at those moments, just how she'd managed to successfully claim benefits, to evade the world of work when so many others, equally or more

343

seriously unwell, had been forced into jobs they were physically incapable of doing.

Even as I thought that, though, I thought also of the things she hadn't shared with me. I'd never seen where she lived. I knew nothing of the other people in her life. I remembered the way she'd talked about her physical decay during our time with the other women, the way skin-level discomfort had happily masked or occluded deeper instances of pain. I wondered if perhaps this was not a new process for her, if indeed she had layered one illness over another, less manageable condition at least once before. Perhaps, I thought, the benefits office had seen it the same way: her physical ailments as both symptom and distraction, evidence of the darker malaise beneath.

At least one person in our group, Felicia had said, was *really very vulnerable indeed*. I'd assumed it was Kim. Now I saw that in all likelihood it was Zelma: the person I thought I knew best, the person who'd helped me find in myself the person I was struggling to be.

Zelma's suffering seemed untraceable. I had known her, but the exact texture of her pain remained distant to me, blurred by the person she was. I wondered if her joy, her energy, like her illness, had been a distraction, another layer of skin on the body of her discomfort. I'd sensed this, I thought, surely. I knew there were shadows beneath her surface. I told myself that I'd searched for them as far as she'd let me, but I knew this wasn't quite true. I'd searched for them just deeply enough to keep the person she was to me, the person I needed and wanted her to be, safely in sight. I needed her joy, her passion, her energy. I'd been too frightened to lose that part of her to whatever I found if I probed. Because I loved her, I'd been unable to know her.

I remembered Zelma's night walks, her supermarket trips at antisocial hours, the claim she staked on the city. Then I imagined Zelma in her last days, tracing those same familiar routes at the same odd hours, stripped of her liberated purpose, reduced to mere wandering. I saw her: skinny and staggering at bus stops, begging for change outside a supermarket, wild-eyed, periodically raving, frightening the people she approached. I saw her making her way home, shivering in a downpour, sitting on her damp and filthy bed under a bare bulb in her uncaring room, counting out coins in her palm and weighing the decision between something to eat and something to drink. Wherever my phone was, I thought, it would have been filled with her final, progressively desperate texts. I pictured her holding onto the phone long after her credit ran out, on the off-chance it would chime with a message. Then I pictured her giving up, succumbing to hunger, and selling the phone in exchange for a meal. Maybe that was when she stopped bothering to beg, when it all began to seem pointless. Or perhaps she was too weak, too ill, too far gone. Confined to her room, she'd have searched for hidden and forgotten snacks, the little caches of treats I used to find around my flat. At some point she would have stopped finding anything. At some point after that she would have stopped getting out of bed. Someone might have knocked on the door, but she wouldn't have answered. She'd have fought for a few days, maybe even weeks, and then stopped battling, let go. I knew this Zelma, I thought, this final Zelma, because I'd known so many other Zelmas. On the streets, on encampments, in squats and night shelters, in soup kitchens and hostels, under railway bridges and curled at the feet of cashpoints. A whole city of Zelmas, all alike and alone.

I remembered Zelma when we'd all lived together – shit-smeared and beaming, free from the things that pained her. Or so I'd thought. I remembered her utter determination, her fearlessness, the speed with which she moved beyond aversion and abjection, into a place of freedom. I'd always felt that she was leading me, and that the others too looked to her when they were struggling. Of all of us, she seemed the least tethered to what we were leaving behind. While the likes of Margot moved there slowly, Zelma had soared, and seeing her soar had made it easier for all of us to follow. Now I had to wonder what that had felt like once she was forcibly returned to the life she'd left, alone, unable to un-become what by that point she was. Maybe I'd failed her, refused to conscience the extent to which I was needed, or failed to accept that in the end I was irrelevant, a mere moment, never a concluding destination. Maybe, I thought, I'd helped to cut the cord that bound her to the world, then disappeared from her life, leaving her to drift, groundless and placeless, until she burned up in the atmosphere on re-entry.

This, I thought, is how a radical life ends: at dazzling and unfathomable altitude, incinerated by its own friction and the pitiless heat it inspires.

I didn't eat for a couple of days, then snapped out of it and binged. For a moment, I felt as if Zelma was taking me with her, dragging me into that destructive orbit. I felt terrified by how easy that seemed: to just stop, lie down, cease to function. When I ate, I felt as if I was returning from the brink of something – a feeling not entirely dissimilar to the marathon of consumption that had followed my weekend at BodyTemple. Grief, it turns out, is as purgative as starvation, vomiting, rage. It keeps going until you're hollow. As I lay on my bed pushing brioche into my mouth and washing it down with Polish beer, I saw that this was how it would have to be. I had to keep my strength up, or my mourning would eat me alive.

I began to think of my grief as a totalising activity. I had to devote myself to it, shape myself according to its needs and schedules. For a while, in that room, there was no world, no time, and I had no body. I felt as I'd felt in the asylum, as I'd sat in front of that bare white wall and experienced the sensation of all my peripheries and outlines dissolving into nothingness, only now what I was staring at wasn't a wall, it was the unscalable expanse of my loss. The more I stared at it, the more I offered myself to it, the more I began to see that what I was looking at wasn't even Zelma's death, but death itself, that beast at the edge of the skyline, looming over the buildings, burning the borders of the forests, chewing away the ice floes on which starving birds stood huddled.

At night, I swung between an awful, empty wakefulness and a frightful, over-stuffed sleep. Some of what I saw was familiar – old dreams and phantoms strengthened by despair. I saw again the scrabbling, screeching arachnid that had eaten its way out of my body. Now, though, it was trapped in a small, darkened, empty cave that I knew to be the inside of my skull. It scratched at the walls with its sharpened legs, tore at layers of pink and shivering membrane with its beak, trying and failing to find a way out. On the floor was a crimson cesspool: the ravaged remains of my mind, processed into soup by the whirr of the monster's limbs. Then I was back on the industrial estate, lying on the slippery, stinking concrete floor, which now bore an eerie familiarity to the blitzed mush of my brainpan. My forearm was ragged and torn. Newly hatched beasts hunched over the bodies of the women I lived with. Street light slipped through the windows and turned the surface of our pooled excrescence mirror-like and vertiginous. I felt the room spin and reverse. I understood that we were not the reflected subject on the surface of that pool, but the reflection, and that the slightest disturbance of its skein would scatter all trace of our forms. As I thought this, a rat ran across the floor and skidded through the primordial ooze, and I felt myself whipped into a formless, swirling cloud. Then all around me was black, and I saw a towering female form wearing my loose and ill-fitting skin, peeling away the sagging mask of my face. Reaching down to steady myself, I found no floor beneath my fingers, just the fluid that filled the room, deeper now, and calmingly warm. In the distance, I heard laughter, the sound of coursing liquid. And then, finally, I was beside Zelma, outside the bar in which we'd first got drunk together, both of us backed up against a wall and urinating with our jeans around our thighs, hysterical and drunk and filling the world with our piss and delirious joy.

I woke in a soaking bed, and knew that she was with me.

I started leaving my room again, walking the city. I remembered what Zelma had believed about time, about the necessity of claiming it for yourself or finding space within it you could call your own. I began to remember that I loved the city at all hours, in the gathering dark and warming pre-dawn, in the noisy crowds of a Friday evening and the dead silence of a Sunday sunrise. I could feel the world on my skin. I was no longer separate from it because it was impossible to be separate from it. It was impossible for anything to be separate from anything else. There was no difference, I thought, between an oil-soaked seabird struggling in the surf, and a man on a packed Tube, sweating inside his suit. All of us were living in the great pool of our own collective shit. Every day, we waded through it, swam in it, were pulled under and then hauled ourselves momentarily out, only to slip back, recede, struggle again for purchase.

After a number of nights of leaving my room, I stopped returning. I could be found there, I thought, contained again. When I was admitted before, the hope of seeing Zelma had sustained me. Now I didn't know what would keep me going, and so I didn't know what I would do if I was taken back. I took my rucksack, some clothes. I don't remember sleeping; I recall only walking, night and day, until my feet began to throb with pain, until every footstep was a fresh wound. I was that woman now, I thought – limping, muttering, her skin greyed by smog and her fingers blackened and cut from scavenging.

I went to all the places I thought of as ours, but found them gone. Our amended adverts had been replaced by other adverts; the old man's pub in which we'd first got drunk had been stripped and aggressively refurbished. Streets had rearranged themselves in my memory, so that when I arrived I found I was not where I'd expected to be, but somewhere else, some strange and silent avenue to which I attached no recollection. The only place that still remained as I remembered it was the supermarket in which we'd shopped on our first night together, where I bought a Danish pastry at 2 a.m., only to sit where we'd sat that night and find myself unable to eat.

I don't recall how many nights I'd been outside when it started to rain. I remember only the downpour, the bulging weight of the droplets and their percussive strike against my skin. I had no raincoat. My clothes became too heavy to bear. I started to walk towards shelter but felt, quite suddenly, as if I couldn't go on, and so I stopped, and then kneeled, and then finally lay down, ignorant of everyone around me, and placed my cheek against the pavement, cold ground and coursing runoff stinging my skin, cigarette butts and random trash adhering to my forehead, and saw in the off-white orbs of hardened chewing gum and the deep-space expanse of the black macadam a galaxy light-years deep, through which, stripped of gravity, I floated, leaving behind my body and the earth to which my body was bound, until, weighed on all sides by a mighty pressure that robbed me of the ability to breathe, I felt the heat-death of existence itself, the burn-out of every once-fierce sun.

And then Zelma was in front of me, looking down, enshrouded in the same haze I'd seen rising from all of us as we walked outside that last day and confronted the protesters, the refracting shimmer of evaporating fears around which the hammering rain diverted and bent, and I closed my eyes to see her better, and heard in my ear her voice, its tone the same as when she'd turned to me at the start of our time at the estate, saying, *Do you want to die. No*, I heard myself saying, *I don't want to die.* And then I heard her one last time, so close I could feel her breath against the opening of my ear, her whisper fierce and hotly ragged, saying, *I am not your tragedy.*

I had no place to return to, so I kept on. My shoes fell apart. The pain in my feet remained, but now I wanted it, needed it. *Feel it*, I told myself. *Feel it.* Things began to blur at the edges. I felt the warp of the city as it reshaped itself to absorb me, the distortions of my body as it swelled to absorb the world. I began to see, again, played out across the screen of my mind, Zelma's last days. I saw her on street corners, outside supermarkets, wide-eyed and ecstatic, lost not to weakness but to wildness. I thought of her as beyond words by that point, raving in an imagined language, past meaning's edge, inhabiting the spaces between what could be said and what could only be screamed, until finally there was nowhere to go but out, through, beyond.

On the top deck of a night bus, where I finally came to rest, across the aisle from a woman breaking open cigarette butts and packaging up their desiccated contents in a fresh Rizla, I imagined not just Zelma's final days and hours, but her final seconds, rising from her own fragile body on its bed, turning briefly to examine the room she was leaving and, finding nothing to carry that might weigh her down, nothing to collect and nothing to leave behind, releasing herself, back into the world we all shared, into the smell of sweat on the seat I now occupied, the traffic fumes I breathed, the layer of dusty smog on my ever-disintegrating skin. I reached down with my hand, into the crevice at the back of the seat, dragged my fingers through the shrapnel of fallen crisps, chunks of nameless dough and strands of dead hair, and just as I had on the train, all that time ago, I swept what I found into my mouth, felt it tangle around my tongue and wedge itself in the gaps between my gums, and this time I knew I would not be ill, knew that I would simply absorb it, just as I had absorbed so much else.

And then, just I had on the train back from BodyTemple, exhausted by what I'd done, I slept, and in my slumber I was clothed in whispers, warmed by a chorus that had shaped from my name a prayer. When I woke, the bus was nowhere I recognised, and so I slept again, until things became familiar.

I n the mornings, at the centre, when we have no guests and the building is quiet, Margot likes to tap on my door and bring me tea. Then we go downstairs, to the lounge that looks out over misted fields, and tell each other stories in the stillness. At some point, Barb will join us. We talk of the women who have been and gone, the guests who are to come, our plans for the people who need us. Mostly, though, we go over the things we remember. We like to narrate ourselves, tell each other what we already know, as if to remind ourselves who we are. Margot talks often of her arrival at the industrial estate, her nervousness, the gradual loosening of her feelings and body. Barb talks of her garden, which she has replicated here, on a patch of disused ground beneath a solitary tree. I recall the message I wrote to Margot, after my night on the bus, the speed with which Margot replied. *I was waiting*, she always says, laughing. *We both were.* Sometimes we look at the picture on the wall, which Margot pulled from Ama's Facebook: Ama in faded jeans and hooded sweatshirt, Sadie and Kim either side, all of them squeezed together and beaming, their cheeks touching. These are our anchors, our fixed points. We come back to them between vanishings.

Soon, another group of women will arrive. We'll take their phones, exchange their clothes for boiler suits of a bony white. We'll show them to the showers and encourage them to wash. Then we'll lead them to a plastic-lined room, and lock all the doors until it's time to leave.

Every moment that they're there, I am with them. I hold their hands and hair as they vomit, embrace them as they pour forth shit. I tell them: what we have is never really with us; what we shed is never really gone. There is nothing to lose and nothing to fear.

I lead them all the way out, past all sense of themselves. And then I bring them back, wash them, and let them go.